"Into the wood

She'd left Eudes, her family, and home without a fight, accepting marriage to a stranger. Now the odds were slim they would survive the bloody battle, but she wasn't going to give up without trying.

A quick glance over her shoulder showed only a few guards remained alive. Loyalty kept them together; courage kept them fighting. Brigands and soldiers were sprawled on the ground around the caravan. Frowning, Marina pushed a dead man's arm away and scooped up his sword. The heavy piece wobbled in her untrained grip.

She shrugged off the sensation and stabbed at one of the brigands. Her attack caught him by surprise and she lunged again, this time striking him in his groin. His cry of outrage drew other brigands to her and Stav. They turned as a single unit and leered.

Marina held the tip of the bloody blade out like a protective talisman. "Stay away. I'm not afraid to use this."

A bald man batted other men out of his way and stepped to the forefront. His icy gaze studied them for a moment, then he ordered, "Kill them both."

Praise for Darcy Carson

Darcy Carson has won Second Place in Heart of the West and in Valley of the Sun Romance Writers contests.

He Walks in Dreams

by

Darcy Carson

The Dragons Return Series

He Walks in Dreams

Cover Art by *Abigail Owen*

The Wild Rose Press, Inc.
PO Box 708
Adams Basin, NY 14410-0708
Visit us at www.thewildrosepress.com

Publishing History
First Fantasy Rose Edition, 2019
Print ISBN 978-1-5092-2605-4
Digital ISBN 978-1-5092-2606-1

The Dragons Return Series
Published in the United States of America

Dedication

To my wonderful critique group—
Marcella Burnard, DeeAnna Galbraith,
Carrie King, Lisa Wanttaja.
You're the best, Ladies!

Chapter One

"Dragonfire! Save the princess."

Princess Marina Hersher recognized the gravelly voice of her captain of the guard. She sat up straighter in her plush travel wagon. The royal caravan was under attack. Who would dare? Brigands? The Demic lords? In Eudes, she'd heard rumors of the land-poor lords massing for an assault. Which unsuspecting kingdom would bear the brunt of their savagery?

Her driver's whip snapped over the backs of the horses. The wagon lurched forward, then came to an abrupt stop. Marina and her maid, Stav, jostled against padded cushions and then were tossed on the floor.

"A dragon!" Stav squeaked, crushing Marina's velvet gown in her hands. "Mighty Kubala, great god of the sea, protect us."

Marina embraced her companion. "Fret not, Stav. We're surrounded by my father's best guards. They will keep us safe."

"But a dragon, Your Highness. No one can win against such a fierce beast."

"Don't be silly. Captain Lacroix said dragonfire. It could just be a fireball of some sort. Dragons do not exist."

Stav's brown eyes widened. "They lived once. All know that. Who can say they have not returned?"

Marina patted Stav's hand. "There is no such thing.

1

Dragons are myths, stories meant to scare small children."

An explosion outside rocked the ground, followed by a tree crashing. Horses whinnied in fear. Above the din, Captain Lacroix shouted orders.

Marina's curiosity got the better of her. She peeked out the window. The last supply wagon had overturned, and the panicked horses galloped free.

Looking at the sky, she tracked the glowing path of another fireball. Her assumption proved accurate. No dragon. The fireball struck the ground with a thud, rocking her wagon.

Stav moaned. "It is a dragon. I know. I smell the brimstone from its belch. We're going to die."

"No, we are not!" Marina responded, even as armed men in jerkins and tunics the color of the forest slipped through the trees and halted in front of the first wagon.

The royal caravan had no means of escape—the thick woods prevented them from turning around.

The fireballs had been a ruse to create panic and chaos, but thankfully, the Eudes soldiers had more courage. Though grossly outnumbered, they drew their swords and circled her conveyance.

"Your Highness, what are we going to do?" cried Stav.

"Hush," Marina snapped, knowing a show of bravery was needed. "Once they learn who we are, they will allow us to pass. Remember, you are masquerading as me! Act the part."

The wagon rocked side to side, and boot heels knocked against the wood. Canvas separated as a sword slit the material.

A heavily muscled arm reached inside, and fingers curled over Stav's arm. "I got her," said a rough male voice.

Stav screamed as if a dragon had finally captured her.

A pock-marked face popped through the opening. The brigand gave them a grisly and gap-toothed grin.

Marina struck him with her fists. His hold on Stav wouldn't break. Failing to free her maid, she changed tactics and tried to pry his thick fingers loose.

Eyes wide with fear, Stav emitted a steady whimper.

Taking a deep breath, Marina demanded, "Unhand the princess this instant."

To her chagrin, the man laughed. "Quit your yammering," he said. "I'll be back for you as well."

Outside, swords clanged and rough voices bellowed to one another to seize their prize. Men shrieked in pain. The coppery scent of blood and gore polluted the air.

The brigand pulled a hysterical Stav from the wagon toward the slit in the canvas.

Suddenly remembering the small, bejeweled dagger tucked into her gown, Marina wrenched out her weapon and plunged the knife into the man's arm.

A loud curse colored the air as the man released his hold on Stav. With a growl, he swung his arm at Marina. She ducked and stabbed him repeatedly in his arm. Unable to hold on, the brigand tumbled off the side of the wagon.

Marina drew Stav to the opposite side of the wagon, sliced an opening in the canvas, and urged her to jump. Hesitating, the maid shook her head until

Marina grabbed Stav's hand and they leapt together. All around them men fought, shouted, and died.

Their feet had barely touched the ground when Marina urged, "Run."

Fear brightened in Stav's eye. "Where?"

"Into the woods. We'll hide there."

She'd left Eudes, her family, and home without a fight, accepting marriage to a stranger. Now the odds were slim they would survive the bloody battle, but she wasn't going to give up without trying.

A quick glance over her shoulder showed only a few guards remained alive. Loyalty kept them together; courage kept them fighting. Brigands and soldiers were sprawled on the ground around the caravan. Frowning, Marina pushed a dead man's arm away and scooped up his sword. The heavy piece wobbled in her untrained grip.

She shrugged off the sensation and stabbed at one of the brigands. Her attack caught him by surprise and she lunged again, this time striking him in his groin. His cry of outrage drew other brigands to her and Stav. They turned as a single unit and leered.

Marina held the tip of the bloody blade out like a protective talisman. "Stay away. I'm not afraid to use this."

A bald man batted other men out of his way and stepped to the forefront. His icy gaze studied them for a moment, then he ordered, "Kill them both."

****

For several days, Narud had peered out of the honeycomb of his lair. Every day he rejoiced that fate had led him to this secret place halfway up Brenalin's highest mountain.

For more than a thousand years, the dragons of the planet Feldsvelt had been absent from the blue skies. He'd plucked that information from his human side, Duran, the high prince of Brenalin. Also from Duran, he had learned that humans had destroyed all of the dragons for their treasure.

Narud knew so little about being a dragon, yet so much. He hoped his dragon senses would grow as he aged so he could survive longer than his dead predecessor, a crimson dragon and the last protector of the Ruby Throne.

Though why *he* should protect the throne still puzzled him. Yet he could not shake the strong urge to do something.

Sunning on a rock in the cool mountain air, Narud surveyed his domain. The land of Brenalin was bordered with lakes full of silver-scaled fish and gurgling rivers. Towering trees swayed in the wind. Misty valleys filled with gray fog. When the sun rose, the land transformed into shades of browns, blues, and greens splashed with red and purple.

An hour before dusk, his sense of smell caught the metallic odor of blood. He raised his head and flicked out his tongue. Faint iron particles drifted across his taste buds. His lips smacked, savoring the taste.

In the deep recesses of his brain, his human half urged for him to investigate.

"I will do no such thing," Narud mindspoke to the nagging voice. *"I am full and have no desire to upset my digestion."*

"You will, or I'll not leave you in peace," his human-self warned.

"All right, but only because I am curious myself.

Who knows. There might be treasure."

With a downward sweep of powerful wings, Narud thrust his massive weight off his cliff perch. Cold air rushed over him. Flapping his wide, leathery wings, he followed both the blood scent and the ley-lines his kind could see patterning the earth below.

Turning in an easterly direction, he saw the smoke, the death, the destruction, and the bravery. A young girl with delicate features and gold-bright hair wielded a sword against a group of men circling her like a pack of wolves. The sword was far too large and heavy for her slight build. Her brave stance created an illusion as she swung her sword in a wobbly circle. She fought to protect another woman bedecked in royal finery huddled on the ground.

"My princess, my intended bride," his human-self whispered in mindspeech. *"Save her."*

At first Narud rejected the command, then decided to obey, not because Duran demanded it, but because he admired the human female. He spit out dragonfire at the rear of the attackers.

Men cried out when their skin, hair, and clothing ignited. Screaming, they dropped to the ground and rolled.

The brigands who remained standing fought all the harder. They butchered the last soldier, then turned their bloody swords on the women as well.

Howling with anger, Narud tucked his wings close to his sides and swooped low. He sensed their rising terror and savored the dragonfear flowing through their veins. Fireballs hurled from his mouth, but he made sure to avoid the golden-haired woman when she fell to her knees.

Horses panicked. Whinnying in terror, they fled into the thick forest. Wood splintered, and the wagons they pulled fell apart.

Narud landed, claws extended, ripping and smashing the attackers beneath him.

He spewed a narrow beam of flames, and the fleeing brigands disintegrated into ash. Those he did not kill fled into the safety of the forest. He let them go. They would spread the word of his appearance and put fear into the minds and hearts of the humans.

Looking around him, the human side of his heart sank into despair. He had arrived too late. The princess and her servant were dead. Narud roared in fury, his long tail flipping back and forth, beating the ground as he fought against the urge to destroy everything within his sight.

The princess lay upon the ground covered in blood, her dark hair spread out like a cushion for her head. Though she appeared asleep, Narud knew she was dead.

He touched her lifeless body with a long claw. "*Wake,*" he commanded through mindspeech. "*You cannot die.*"

Then Narud shook his great head. Why should he care if all that he held important was gone? Why did he remember foolish jealousy? A broken trust? Not his memories, he realized suddenly. He shifted his great bulk. Why care about his human half's problems? The sentiment had no place within a dragon.

He sniffed the air. Beneath the scent of blood and gore he focused on something far more pleasurable—treasure. Gold. Silver. Rubies. Gemstones of all kinds. A vast, wonderful treasure was stored in the last wagon.

Then he heard a moan. Soft. Pitiful. Someone

lived. He whipped his huge wedge-shaped head around. The sound came from the brave servant, her golden hair, sprinkled with dirt.

He lumbered over and sniffed the air above her body. Her pulse was weak. A deep gash ran along her scalp. His great tongue flicked out and tasted warm blood.

She lived!

His gaze went from the girl to the princess and back again.

"Such bravery should not go unrewarded," his human side whispered. *"Take her to the cave."*

"Impossible," Narud replied. *"My treasure is there. I share it with no one."*

"You twist my words," his human half said. *"This woman cares not for your precious hoard. I will care for her. She deserves to be nurtured back to good health."*

Narud did not want to cooperate, but the glint of her hair proved a strong lure. *"Fair enough,"* he replied. *"I might find use for a servant with golden hair."*

With exquisite precision, he closed his claws around her broken body. Flapping his wings three times, he lifted his burden into the air.

He'd carry the girl to his lair and return for the treasure.

Every second counted. He could feel his human side demanding freedom.

Balancing just above the cave floor, he laid the serving girl down, then flew back toward the caravan.

Sapphires. Emeralds. Rubies. The spoils belonged to him.

****

The dragon had barely returned to the rocky outcropping when a red mist formed and the change came upon him. The dragon's roar of protest echoed in Duran Abbas's head as he uncurled from the mist.

Weak from the transformation, a red shimmer tinted his vision. Standing on wobbly legs, he brushed the fine granite from his clothing.

He stared down at the woman. She lay pale and still as death; not even an eyelash fluttered. He checked her wrist and found a faint pulse. Relief washed through him. She'd survived the journey.

He gazed at the woman, astounded at her endurance. "Don't die," he murmured. "With your help, I'll try my best to cheat the gods."

Duran retrieved plush blankets and furs from the dragon's growing stockpile of treasure. Laying the serving girl on the thick hides and blankets, he stripped off her gown. Underneath she wore the fine linen reserved for nobility. Passed down from the princess, he assumed, feeling a dart of regret for the dark-haired woman left behind.

Urgency filled him. He built a fire to boil water, feeling thankful for his basic soldier's training. As soon as the water became heated, he washed the dirt and blood from her body—a finely proportioned body which smelled faintly of roses.

She moaned under his gentle touch.

"I know it hurts," he spoke softly. "I must clean your wounds to prevent festering."

Her moist hair glinted in the firelight and tightened into tiny coils of gold. No wonder Narud had agreed to save her. The creature had a fondness for anything bright and shiny.

He tended to the deep, nasty cut. His patient gasped and twisted within the covers, perhaps caught in a nightmare, fighting an invisible enemy.

Duran crouched beside her and gently laid a soothing hand on her forehead. "Hush," he whispered. "You're safe now."

Her eyelids fluttered open. Fear sprang into her eyes. "Stay away from me!"

Her fist lashed out, and pain rocked his jaw. He stepped back. "I mean you no harm. Save your strength. I found you injured and brought you here to heal."

Hazel eyes, once glassy and unfocused, cleared. "Forgive me, good sir. I wasn't thinking. I'm Ma…My name is Stav. Where am I, and who are you?"

She would never believe his true identity, so he said, "Names don't matter. Just call me friend."

Golden brows pulled together. "I feel dizzy, and my head hurts."

Being aware was a good sign. He smiled. "That's expected. You survived a severe blow, but you're quite safe now."

"The others?" she asked, endeavoring to sit up, but he lightly held her down.

"All dead, I'm afraid."

A sob escaped her throat. "No, please, not everyone."

"Lie still," he gently ordered, then noticed the moisture beaded on her forehead—a sure sign of the onset of fever. "Sleep now. All will be well. I'll stand guard until you recover, then we'll talk again."

"It's my fault," she mumbled, delirium becoming evident. "Ambushed. A trap. Swear. Send word to my father. He needs to know what happened, that I am alive."

"Stav, enough talk," he replied, remembering her name. Gazing at her, he wondered if the brave servant would live through the night. He hoped she survived. He was so tired of being alone. "Here, drink," he gruffly ordered.

Her trembling hands reached for the cup. "Thank you. You've been very kind."

"My pleasure. I wish I could have done more."

Delicate brows arched. "I—I think I owe you my life."

Her words were muted, a combination of severe injuries, exhaustion, and the mountain lavender he added to the water.

"You need sleep," he said. "Rest. There's nothing we can do until you recover."

With a nod, she closed her eyes and fell asleep. He walked to the mouth of the cave. Stars twinkled in the dark sky. An owl hooted off in the distance. Boulders wore white snow like a mantle of thick fur. Since his escape from the sorceress, the mountain had become his home. How he had arrived at this cave, which felt so natural, was a mystery he would solve at a later date. For now, he assumed the dragon part of him was better suited for survival.

Dragon during the day, man at night. His existence had turned into a nightmare. He never imagined he would endure betrayal. Never thought it could happen to him. Not to Duran Abbas, the high prince of Brenalin and the heir to the Ruby Throne.

Yet now, through sorcery, he was neither man nor beast.

His thoughts turned to Calandra Genoy, a traitorous sorceress and his foster sister since childhood. She'd arrived at the castle in his youth. When he began his warrior training, she chose to dedicate herself to the mystical arts. His father and Einer, the castle wizard, disapproved, but eventually they had relented to her pleading. In the evenings, Duran and Calandra had sought each other out. They'd sit before the fire after a long day of training, he with his blade and she with her potions. Duran showed his bruises and Calandra, her fingers glowing with magic, would use her new sorcery to heal or demonstrate a spell.

Calandra had been upset when she learned of his pending marriage. She had begged him to wed her instead. Taking pity on her, he tried to ease her heartbreak with kind words.

A shudder swept through him, remembering when Calandra's magic slammed into him, throwing him off balance.

His head filled with her curse:

Deny me as your mate,
Deny me the power of the Ruby Throne,
Deny not your fate,
Deny not your inner self.

A wind had risen in Calandra's workroom the likes of which he'd never felt. He'd stumbled backward and crumpled onto the rotting rushes.

A burst of bright yellow flames had blinded him. A roar of agony ripped from him as pressure squeezed him so tightly rational thought became impossible.

With that single, ill-conceived spell, Calandra had destroyed his life.

A cool mountain breeze caressed his cheek. Duran shivered from the chill and the bleak prospect of his future.

Trained as a warrior, he instinctively waged war with his sword and fists. However, raised to use reason, he knew logic would get him further. He had to find a way to break the evil magic before he could plan revenge.

The serving woman tossed in her sleep. Duran shook himself out of his reverie. Her presence caused problems, and he wasn't sure what steps to take. A sense of loneliness filled him, and a ragged sigh escaped his lips.

"You can't stay here, and I can't take you to Brenalin or Eudes," he whispered. "What am I going to do with you, my brave little servant?"

Chapter Two

Marina awoke on her back, nestled within a cocoon of soft furs. Groggy, she blinked into the hot coals of a fire, then realized she stared into red, glowing eyes. She blinked again.

A huge dragon lay sprawled on layers of pearls and rubies.

She shook her head. Impossible. Unreal. She had to be hallucinating.

The creature watched her. Intelligence gleamed in its crimson eyes, and ensnared between its claws was a dead ewe.

The dragon yawned, revealing yellow rows of razor-like teeth.

"Kubala, protect me," she whispered, calling on the ancient sea god of Eudes.

Fear screamed inside her, urging her to do something. Anything. She tried to move, but went instantly still when sharp twinges of pain radiated all over her body. Her hands trembled. She tried to tell herself this wasn't real. She was dreaming.

"What is dreaming?"

Words formed like pictures in Marina's mind. Was this sorcery? Magic? Dragons didn't exist. They couldn't speak. Surely, it was a vision brought on by the blow to her head.

She'd dreamed of a man with strong, warm hands.

Where was he? She ran her fingers through her tangled hair. Blurry details failed to help her memory.

A prism of light danced off the vertical slits of the dragon's eyes. Warily she watched the giant creature rise up and plod toward her. The dragon lowered its sinewy neck. Warm breath burst from his wide, flat nostrils. She clinched her fists and fought her fear and discovered another emotion.

Amazement.

"What is dreaming?"

The question repeated inside her head. The compelling urge to answer could not be denied.

"Something not real," she said. "A fantasy, usually while one sleeps."

"So you think yourself asleep," the dragon replied. *"Interesting."*

This wasn't real. She must be delirious. "I don't believe in dragons. You're a figment of my imagination."

"Is it light out? Do dreams occur during the day?"

She tilted her head toward the apparition. The creature wasn't genuine, but still she answered. "Sometimes, but generally at night."

"I see. Perhaps dreaming is another reality."

"There cannot be two realities. Dragons aren't real."

"How are we having this conversation? Don't answer. We've spoken enough. Sleep. Heal yourself."

At his words, her eyelids grew heavy. Marina yawned, then oblivion enfolded her.

An unknowable time later, a sound awoke her. Frowning, she pushed herself into a sitting position. The cavern spun, and her muscles quivered.

She'd had another dream, stranger than the first. She'd awoken and spoken with a giant crimson dragon.

A man drew near. She swallowed hard, feeling a rush of something undefinable. Big and muscular with hair that reflected a touch of red in the firelight, he dressed in a bulky fleece coat to protect himself from the cold mountain air. His thick hose were tucked into black leather boots. He was taller than the men of her country. Handsomer, too.

Feeling uncomfortable with her thoughts, she looked away. A dart of surprise stabbed at her. Her fingers touched the powdery dirt of the cold ground. She found herself in the vast cavern of her dreams. Stars sparkled in an ink-black sky beyond the mouth of the cave. Her gaze noted a bucket, a load of wood, cooking pots, and a large, ornate chest. She frowned at the familiarity. The chest came from her caravan.

"Where am I?" she demanded.

The man turned. "In my home," he answered, then sat next to the fire. Using a stick, he shoved red-hot coals together, coals the same color as the eyes of the dragon in her odd dream. The fire popped, sending embers twirling toward the ceiling.

"You live in a cave? Where are my traveling companions?"

"You remember nothing of our talks?"

She shook her head, quelling feelings of panic. She had to remain calm, though instincts screamed that something terrible had happened. "No, I don't," she replied past her dry throat. "We spoke?"

"Several times. You were badly wounded and burning up with fever. For a while, I thought you would not survive."

He paused as though giving her time to process the information. "Unfortunately, the princess and others never had a chance."

Numbness engulfed Marina. A lie. She didn't want to believe him. "You know about her, then?"

"The trident pattern of goldwork in her gown proclaimed her the Eudian princess," he said in a quiet voice. "I knew you were her servant by the clothes you wore."

Marina blinked back tears and drew a fur up to her chin. Only then did she realize she was naked. Never had she been near a man, without clothing. Shoving aside her embarrassment, she focused on what he had said. This man had recognized the royal emblem of Eudes, a clear implication that he possessed some knowledge of the world outside this cave.

She must correct his false conclusion, then decided it was in her best interest to keep her identity hidden.

He stood and moved past the fire to a ledge along the wall. Why did he live here? Was he a shepherd? A hermit? An outlaw?

Her mouth went dry. Would an outlaw waste his time tending an injured servant? She doubted it.

He walked to her side and handed her a bundle. "Here are your clothes. I mended and cleaned them as best I could."

"Thank you for your kindness."

A void of sorrow formed inside Marina. Her father's decision to send her to this new land had proven disastrous. She had lost her traveling companions, people she had known all her life. And for what?

The man sat cross-legged from her. "What do

you remember?"

Slipping into her clothes under the blankets, she studied her benefactor. His eyes reflected the fire. A red light danced in the center of his pupils.

"Very little," she said. "I do remember our attackers seemed intent on killing us."

"Would you recognize them if you saw them again?"

Marina stared into the fire, watching the hypnotic dance of the flames. "I don't know. Some, I think." Her weary mind envisioned the ambush while searching for clues.

Captain Lacroix had been among the first to fall, and the other guards were never given a chance to announce their identity. The assault against them had been deliberate, murder the objective.

"Everything happened so fast. There was shouting, blood, and fire, but most is a blur. How long have I been sick?"

"Nearly two weeks."

His unexpected answer stunned Marina. "So long. Have you sent word to anyone?"

He gestured with his hands. "Who would I tell? It's a long way down the mountain—a dangerous trek over rugged crags and across a steep and narrow valley, then through Demit Woods. A long way to go for a servant, albeit a royal servant."

Accustomed to the openness of the great ocean, the thought of anyone traveling alone near Brenalin's enormous dark forest made her shiver. "How did you get me here?"

He used his boot to bank the fire, and when he spoke, his pupils took an oddly vertical form. "I did what anyone would do."

An unsatisfactory response if she'd ever heard one. She was tempted to demand more, but watching him across the fire, uncertainty kept her silent.

****

Narud waited impatiently for his guest to awake. Watching the human female had become an unexpected pleasure, but his patience had reached its limits. She slept more than necessary, thanks to the drugged water and broth his human half fed her while her body mended.

She'd spoken with his human side at great length the prior evening. Now, his turn had arrived and he planned to do so.

His long, narrow tongue skimmed along the arm she'd tossed out from under the furs—tasting her warmth, seeking her essence. At last, she stirred on the sleeping pallet.

"Wake up, my brave beauty. I promised we would talk again."

"Go away!" With her eyes closed, she lashed out with her arm. She frowned when she encountered empty air.

"You've rested long enough. I have little patience for the mundane, and the day grows short."

"Mighty Kubala, save me," she whispered, sitting up, her eyes wide.

Narud's blood sizzled. *"Why surprised?"*

"Because I'm dreaming again. I see a dragon." She spared a glance at the bones between his claws. "From the looks of it, he's very hungry."

Narud shoved aside the carcass of a pig. *"Be grateful my appetite is satisfied at the moment. You have naught to fear."*

"But you're not real. You're an illusion, and you're red. Everyone knows dragons are green."

"Little you know. Before the Great Dying, dragons came in many colors and sizes. You think I'm not real? Fascinating."

"I'll prove it." She jabbed an accusing finger into his soft underside.

A dart of surprise spiraled through his veins. How did she know the exact spot where his scales were less thick and hard?

She poked him a second, then a third time.

He stretched his neck so high, his head brushed against the cave's ceiling. The female human only reached the middle of his chest. How could she be so brave, yet so ignorant of his power?

"Cease!" He dipped his head and carefully flicked a sharp claw down her face.

Fury glared back at him. "Ouch!"

"Did you enjoy that?" he asked, amazed at the softness of her flesh.

"It hurt."

"Then don't poke me again. I find it irritating. Dragons don't take well to being prodded."

"I could say the same." She glanced around the cave. "Where is the man who tended me? I wish to speak with him."

Narud inflated his nostrils and sucked in a great breath. The female human brought the fragrance of roses into the cave. *"Do you believe in me now? Maybe he is the dream?"*

"Impossible."

"Are you so sure? Who you are talking to now?

Me. You see me during the day. You see him at night. Think about it. Dreams occur mostly at night. Which of us do you think is real?"

"This is a trick. Dragons lie."

"For someone who doesn't believe in the existence of my kind, you have many misconceptions. Dragon tales fill human scrolls, yet know precious little about us? Myths and legends. Full of fallacies."

"You dare lecture me?"

Her incredulity amused him. He watched her settle onto her sleeping pallet, then said, *"You are in need of a lecture. Don't you want to be enlightened?"*

She stared at him, hard. "That means you really are a dragon."

Sensing no fear, he felt compelled to ask, *"Does that frighten you?"*

"I'm not afraid of you."

"Excellent. Then you won't mind doing me a favor. The deed must be accomplished before another day is over."

"Why? What can I do?"

He had to gain her cooperation. Instinct demanded it. *"I require a certain treasure."*

"Why?"

Narud decided a bit of truth was necessary. *"A fraction of my power comes from gemstones. The more riches I acquire, the higher my rank within the realm of dragons. That is, if and when the realm ever exists again. Your kind exterminated the dragons during the Great Dying. You owe me."*

He paused, watched her lower her gaze, then continued, *"Deep in the mountain are caves too small for me to enter. Within one of these caves, the previous dragon secreted his spoils. About three hundred feet on the left, you'll find a chest filled with a collection of gemstones and other valuables. I need you to fetch it to me. I'll even lend you a smidgen of my power."*

"And if I refuse?"

"I could eat you."

"You wouldn't dare!"

He flicked his tongue over her arm. Intimidation went a long way in achieving one's desires. *"Wouldn't I?"*

"Leave her alone," said the human sharing his mind. Both knew permission had to be granted for another individual to hear their private conservation, and neither were willing to let the female hear. *"I'm stronger. I will not let you do the opposite of what I want. This woman is under my protection. She fought bravely to save the princess. Even a dragon should be glad to call her friend."*

The words reminded Narud of the reprimand he gave the woman. *"Dare you lecture me?"* he demanded. *"You will not be strong forever. By summer I will be in control. Dragons are superior beings who seek knowledge, treasure, and beauty. I have an obligation to teach the woman. She and this place will be mine long after you are gone."*

"Not without a fight."

Fear tweaked Narud's scales, but he pushed it aside. Weakness had no place in his new life.

"We shall see," he replied. *"We are bound by a sorceress's riddle. You would be wise to find a way to break the spell, not waste time with this female."* He paused, in thought, then continued, *"Unless you have figured out the answer to the spell."*

"I will."

Narud flicked his tongue at the woman and saw her tremble. Let his human half worry. The diversion would give him the time he needed to become the stronger of the two.

"Well then, human," he mindspoke. *"Until you do, don't bother me. I have things to do that do not concern you."*

****

The giant red dragon frightened Marina, but how could she be scared of something so reminiscent of her huge white tabby, Sinner. The cat habitually rolled on his back and demanded she rub his tummy. Thankfully, her pet had not been on the wagon, but was scheduled to follow with the furniture.

She rubbed the tender spot on her check. The place where the dragon's talon had touched still throbbed. She stared at the dragon, enthralled. He was alive. Real. Wait until she told her sisters, Olla and Woola, about him.

The girls were identical twins, but totally different in personalities. Olla was the dominant twin and would attempt any feat, always eager for adventure. Woola was quieter, less inclined to jump into danger. Yet Marina knew they would be giddy at the prospect of meeting a real, live dragon.

Dare she fetch the treasure? Would the dragon be beholden? Maybe the creature would help her in return, become her ally?

She waited for him to say more.

He didn't.

He cocked his head one way, then another.

Weariness fell away, as though she had never been

injured or sick. Dragons were not known for their generosity. Had he really shared a portion of his great strength with her?

Surprisingly, noise came and went in the huge cavern. Wind rustled, sometimes keening, other times a whisper.

Stranger still, it reminded her of waves of home lapping at the shore, or pounding against it—always the same, yet ever different.

She stood and tested her muscles. They responded with weak quivers. The dragon sat on his bed of pearls and rubies, ignoring her. She took another step, then halted and peered into the shadows.

Common sense told her she needed a light, or it would be impossible finding anything. She noticed a small lamp on the ledge and lit it with a stick from the fire.

Left, the dragon had said.

She wondered if the creature sent her on a fool's mission. Maybe no treasure existed. Maybe the monster thought she'd become hopelessly lost within the maze of caverns, an easy way to eliminate an unwelcome guest.

Marina would deceive him. She'd survived an ambush and beaten a fever. Nothing could defeat her—not even a dragon. She would find his treasure and obligate him to her.

Brimming with determination, Marina held out her arm until she found chilly stone and then picked her way along the wall the same as she'd done a thousand times while climbing on the rocks near the great ocean.

The chamber opened up. Dust tickled her nose. She sneezed. The air reeked of the musk of rusting iron, decomposing wood, and moldy dry rot. Her hand went automatically to block the stench. Nothing living had stepped here for many a year. At least, nothing human.

A domed chest merchants used to store and transport their wares sat in the middle of the cave. It appeared ready to crumble at the slightest touch. The treasure chest?

She set her lamp on the ground and kneeled down. As she lifted the lid, inches of thick dust fell off the top. She coughed again and sneezed again.

Strings of pearl, chains of gold, blood-red rubies, green emeralds, dark-blue sapphires, and sea-blue aquamarines glistened in the dim light. Never in her wildest dreams had she seen such treasure as this, and her father's treasure room contained many wonderful riches.

Marina didn't bother dragging the chest. It would fall apart or break her back the instant she attempted to move it. Lifting the hem of her skirt, she started scooping up jewels by the handful.

She left the lamp where she set it, aware she had to go only a hundred or so feet before reaching the large cavern. She set her first load beside the bed of pearls and rubies.

After several trips, she paused to sniff the air. A prickle raised the hairs on her arms and neck. Licking her finger to see if it was the wind, her entire finger tingled. Most odd, she thought, then began walking again, careful not to drop a single bauble.

The dragon was gone! His timing seemed ill chosen while she worked so hard to bring him what he claimed to most want.

By sheer force of will, she trudged back to the

smaller cavern. Her fingers brushed the bottom of the chest and she smiled when she found it empty. With aching arms and sore back, she returned to main cavern, the weight in her apron feeling as though she carried a pregnant whale.

A man crouched before a low burning fire, stirring a pot containing the savory aroma of boiled rabbit and wild onions. Her mouth watered, and her stomach rumbled in delight. She hadn't eaten the entire day, and now night fell. Stars twinkled in the dark sky. She had taken a full day to fetch and carry the dragon's treasure.

The memory of the mysterious man's tender ministrations heated her body.

She stumbled forward.

Hearing pebbles scatter, he turned. "Where have you been?"

She sputtered at the sound of anger in his voice. "There's no need to be upset."

He tossed a log on the fire. "Isn't there? You've been ill. I feared you had wandered off. I searched for tracks in the snow."

Her burden of gemstones and gold dragged at her arms, and she let the treasure tumble onto the others. "As you can see, I'm on the mend!"

He frowned at the pile she'd collected with suspicion. "You're doing Narud's bidding. It's unwise to give in to him."

"Narud? The dragon?" she asked, pleased to finally learn the creature's name.

The man turned away and frowned. "That's what he's chosen to call himself."

A warmth filled her. "You know about him?"

He bent forward, his expression suddenly full of

disgust. "Oh, yes, I know him, though by the gods, I wish I didn't. Once I…"

A mystery existed in his unspoken words, something inexplicable, even tragic. "What?" she asked softly.

"Nothing. My problems don't concern you. Don't aid him again, or the creature will drain you."

While what the man said made sense, she wasn't ready to acquiesce without reason. "We worked together. He gave me strength."

"What he bestows, he can just as easily take away. What then, huh? You would be more drained than before. Do not trust him. That dragon's machinations are like twisted knots in a silken cord." His tone sounded firm, then he softened it, saying, "Sit. Take food."

He handed her a plate full of steaming meat when she stepped forward. It smelled lightly of sweet berries. He didn't eat but watched her gobble down the meal.

"This is much appreciated," she murmured between mouthfuls, wiping her lips with the back of her hand between bites. "And delicious. As I improve, so does my appetite. I'm sorry to be such a bother."

His broad chest rose and fell as he chuckled low. "You please me greatly, except for your pact with that bothersome beast."

"He's not so bad. Really. When I first saw him, I thought I was dreaming. Dragons aren't supposed to exist. He suggested you were the dream…not him."

She slid a glance at the mystery man as he heaped a second portion on her plate. His gaze settled on the fortune. The dim light left much to her imagination about his features. If only she could study him in the light of day.

"What do you believe?" he asked, glancing back at her.

The dragon real? The man not. Marina refused to consider the matter. "Stuff my opinion. That's not the issue. What's important is you and Narud are on opposing sides."

Wariness surfaced in his eyes. "You have no idea how dangerous he is."

The lack of a clear answer stoked her curiosity. "What did he do to make you dislike him so?" she asked softly.

"Not him."

His deliberate evasiveness and confusing answers only made Marina curious. "Who then? Is that why you stay hidden in these mountains?"

"Enough questions. It's a waste of time and energy. Meanwhile, know this…we are not alone on the mountain. Other men are here."

Fear, then hope leapt to life in Marina. She smiled. Thank Kubala! Her father hunted for her. Rescue was near.

But what if she was wrong? Her smile died. What if the attack had been spawned by Demic lords eager to destroy the alliance her marriage would establish between Eudes and Brenalin?

"Who are they?" she asked, keeping a wary eye on the man. "Travelers? Merchants?"

He shrugged a broad shoulder. "I wish I knew. I came across their tracks yesterday while setting my traps. They advance in a grid pattern, like a hunting pack, which means trouble."

Marina sat back, her arms wrapped around her

legs. "Could you be wrong?"

A look of sorrow passed over his shadowed features. "Few dare venture into these mountains during the last of wintertime. Tonight, I saw the glow of their campfires. Real travelers would be gone." He gave her a hard stare. "Whoever is out there is searching for something…or someone."

Chapter Three

Duran watched Stav sit up straighter. Light from the fire gleamed in her hazel eyes. He found it impossible not to admire the creamy beauty of her skin. Heat radiated from her body stronger than the fire, and her womanly scent flavored the night air with the hint of roses. The floral bouquet would forevermore remind him of her.

"I want to see their camp," she announced with more authority than he expected from a servant. "We can identify them by their clothing or uniforms."

"They aren't wearing uniforms, if that's what you think. Why do you want to see them?" He was amazed at her obstinacy. Most women would be a bundle of nerves, fearful and wanting to flee. But not Stav. "I don't need to seek any more trouble, and strangers are nothing but trouble."

"Take me, please."

"What's so important about them?" Resentment climbed in him at her pleas.

She leaned forward. "We're out in the wilderness. Being vigilant is only prudent. If this were my mountain, I would want to know who traveled here."

The rightness of her words niggled at the back his mind. "A brief glimpse won't hurt," he conceded, shoving himself to his feet. "I'll go. Not you."

"What if they're the men who attacked the royal

caravan?"

"Look, Stav, I credited you with a good head on your shoulders. Don't prove me wrong. Unless, you wish to die."

Her eyes stared straight at him, flashing. "No."

"Then heed my warning. I would hate to see you forfeit your life." He doggedly ignored the look of determination on her delicate face. He wanted to tell her he feared for her welfare but didn't say the words.

"I must see them," she pleaded. "I have to be sure."

He turned his head away to stare at the vastness beyond the cave. If the travelers were just that—travelers, Stav could leave with them. He would be rid of her and glad of it.

"Liar!" Narud's voice intruded upon his thoughts. *"You enjoy her company far too much."*

"Leave me alone. I merely worry about her safety."

"Then protect her," his foe was quick to say. *"Do not let any harm befall her."*

"That's easier said than done."

Duran's innards twisted with a sharp pain. He used to love tramping through the Dragon's Teeth mountain with the cold, and always believed a bond existed between him and it. The feeling of being close to the sky, to feel the wind against his skin seemed exhilarating.

Being on the mountain had always helped him think clearly. Common sense warned him Stav would leave someday. And someday would have to be soon—before she discovered his secret.

Duran grimaced. Narud had one thing right. His dragon side grew stronger every day. The conversation they just held proved that.

The dragon half of himself harbored desires that Duran sensed, and he suspected Narud intended to keep the serving woman at his side.

Someday Duran would be powerless against the dragon's wishes. This offered him an opportunity to deliver her out of Narud's keeping. She could continue on with her life, even while he could not.

It made perfect sense, and then another thought materialized. Winter held the mountains in its icy grip. Men wouldn't be here unless they had good reason. They hunted for someone. Who? Himself? Narud? Or Stav?

Duran glanced out the cave's entrance again. An intense full moon rose in the east and peeked out from the veil of thickening clouds, reminding him how quickly time passed. The moon had already traveled halfway through its nightly journey.

Flurries of downy snow began muting the moon's brightness and dusted the ground in a veil of white.

He knew Stav waited for an answer, but he couldn't find the right words. Until now…

"Fair enough; this is my mountain. It is my responsibility. I'll investigate alone."

"I must come, too," she answered, undaunted.

He swallowed hard. "I forbid it."

Her eyes narrowed in defiance. "You cannot stop me. If you leave me behind, I'll follow."

Dragon's teeth! What a stubborn servant. He'd never met such a strong-willed woman in his life. All he had to do was imagine her dead at the caravan, and his insides turned to mush.

He brushed back his hair. "Think about your well-being. You are still recovering from your wounds and fever. You'll only slow me down. Besides, you're not trained for stealth."

"I'll be careful."

How long he stood still, he knew not. Seconds. Minutes. He could only stare at her. "No," he said, his tone deeper when his ire grew. "This weather is unpredictable. It could turn into a full-blown snowstorm within moments. You wouldn't be able to make out your own nose."

Stav frowned. "If those men are the same brigands, I have the right to see them for myself."

"I won't be long. I can travel faster alone." He laid down the law and stomped toward the opening. "I'll relay everything I see upon my return. I promise."

Crusted snow cracked beneath the new with his every step. Flakes grew bigger, thicker, until visibility became nearly impossible. Only white lay before him. He walked slowly in the wet snow and felt his feet getting wet. In these conditions, he faced the danger of frostbite. Duran knew he'd made the right decision forcing Stav to stay behind.

He headed for where he'd first seen the tracks—a hollow at the base of the mountain's cleft. It was an unsafe place for people to camp, but it prevented them from seeing him approach.

Silent snow fell, muting his steps. The snow became deeper, the terrain more difficult to traverse. The smell of smoke filtered through the trees until he heard the crackle of burning wood. Campfires glowed in front of him. The same big, rawboned men he'd seen earlier were huddled around the fires. Some stood before tents. Others paced. The raspy sound of metal on whetting stone sliced the air as men bent over their blades, sharpening their weapons.

Who were they? Calandra's henchmen? He had asked himself over and over what possessed her to betray him. She had to have a reason. He couldn't believe he'd been so wrong about her character? He'd loved her like a sister, and yet her disloyalty had caused havoc in his life.

Braying laughter erupted from the motley group.

"If I wasn't afraid of the sorceress," said a gruff voice over the laughter, "I wouldn't set a foot in this forsaken icy land. Why couldn't she use her magic to find this servant if she's that important?"

"Hush, you fool," snapped a bald-headed man. "The sorceress has eyes and ears everywhere."

Duran's hand went for his sword. Gone. Dragon's teeth! He'd forgotten to wear it when he had visited Calandra on that fateful day. He couldn't remember the number of times he'd regretted his negligence. All he carried was his short knife, practically useless as a weapon.

"Now there's a rare sight," came a low, churlish voice. "I go for a leak and find company acalling."

A cloud of ice crystals formed when Duran's breath froze. He swore and turned slowly, instinctively crouching into a fighting position as he pulled his weapon.

He blinked and swallowed bile. A squat man stared at Stav stumbling in the snow.

She raised her arms. "Stay back. Stay away from me."

"Why would I do that," the short man answered, "when I think you're the one who has me and all me pals up here in the first place."

A rise of protectiveness slammed Duran in the gut. He looked at Stav, hazel eyes gleaming round and wide, her slender form bundled in his fur gloves and woolen blankets. The sight of her terror increased his worry. She'd suffered enough—seen her friends and companions murdered, nearly died herself, and encountered a dragon.

She had every right to fear. These were Calandra's men. The sorceress must have used magic to locate the princess's servant. Magic and men. She wanted no witness left alive to speak of her misdeeds.

Duran's gaze flew from Stav to the brigand. He lifted his arm, took aim, and threw his short knife with all his might. The blade whistled through the icy air and planted itself in the man's eye. With a grunt of pain and surprise, he crumbled, face first into the snow.

Duran stepped out of hiding. "You little fool!" he hissed through clenched teeth. "What madness compelled you to pursue me?"

"Oh, good sir, thank the gods," Stav gushed with gratitude, then stepped toward him. "Thank you, thank you."

It felt natural to pull her close and hold her. When he did, the subtle fragrance of roses tickled his nose. "Be quiet! Don't say another word."

She disregarded him. "I was never more frightened, but I had to find out for myself," she babbled. "I couldn't have lived with myself if I didn't."

Her heart pounded against his chest. She could have been hurt. Killed. He would never have forgiven himself if anything happened to her.

"Let's get away from here," he said, sparing time

to retrieve his knife and kick snow over the brigand's body, "and hope they don't find him any time soon."

Luckily, the heavily falling snow covered their tracks. They reached their cave, and Stav moaned. Violent shudders shook her slender body. Desperation etched deep furrows on her face. It became more than he could bear. With a tenderness that surprised him, he gathered her into his arms and let her sob.

"Stav, don't think about that man," he tried to soothe. "Listen to me. It's all right. You're safe, honest. Nothing will harm you. I'll protect you."

She lifted her chin with visible determination. "I recognized a voice from the campsite. It was the leader of the men who attacked us. I can still hear him ordering my death. Dear Kubala, he mustn't find me."

"They won't. He won't." He realized he meant it. "This cavern is invisible from the outside. The dragon protects his home with magic. No one can see inside or is allowed within unless Narud wishes them so."

She broke his hold slowly, drawing away. He would have sworn she wanted to stay next to him. She curled into a ball on her sleeping pallet, then began rocking as though the horror of what she experienced rolled over her.

Her reaction surprised him for he had come to expect endless strength from Stav. Duran settled down beside her—not touching, but close enough to offer comfort if the need arose. The effects of battle on the unprepared mind affected everyone differently. Some soldiers puffed up with false bravado. Others wept and shook. Stav suffered from the latter. His sense of duty bound them together as tightly as he and Narud. She was an innocent. He owed her his protection.

Straightening, Stav wrapped her arms around him in a tight hug. "You were right. I shouldn't have searched for them."

Duran brushed his fingers through her thick, golden hair, feeling warmth grow within him. "Hush," he whispered. "I was wrong. You were right. We needed to know who they were. Ignoring their existence would have been foolish and dangerous."

"You've done so much for me. I do appreciate your efforts. I should be dead. I swear," she vowed, looking up at him, "your kindness will be rewarded. Take me to Eudes. Please. I must return to my homeland."

"I was thinking of Brenalin."

"I have to get home," she insisted without a pause. "My father will be worried."

"I forbid it!" Narud shouted in mindspeech to Duran. *"She cannot leave."*

Duran fought to hide his surprise at the dragon's intrusion. *"No need to shout,"* he countered. *"You simply have no say in the matter."*

"She is mine!"

"You do not own her."

Duran felt the sharp sting of claws as Narud attempted to free himself. A red haze glazed his vision, and heat surged inside him. He fought back with a will of his own. This was his time to exist.

"I do not wish to own her," Narud said, relinquishing the struggle for dominance. *"If she stays, I would treasure her, surround her with gifts of immense value."*

Shaking his head, Duran saw Stav watching him curiously, but his thoughts dwelled on Narud. His worst fear had materialized—the dragon had surfaced during his time, and he wanted Stav.

He understood her desire to go home. It matched a similar sensation burning within his own heart. Home. He thought about his father, hoped the elder Abbas wasn't overly worried about his absence. The thought of Calandra living among those he loved set his temper to a slow burn. Duran knew his habit of taking off unannounced worked against him. His father would have no idea of Calandra's curse, or of the evil existing within her.

"We have no other option," he finally countered to Stav. "Brenalin is closer. The princess's caravan would have been discovered by now. Since your body was missing, I'm sure the Eudes king sent word to your father of the chance you survived."

"You don't understand." Stav's voice rose.

An unexpected pang of sympathy swept through him at the fright in her eyes. "Understand what? Tell me."

A frown pulled her lovely mouth down as she stared at him. "I'm sorry. You'll have to trust me for now. Please. Someday, I promise, I will explain the whole story to you. Some secrets are important to keep."

Secrets. Stav had secrets. It saddened him to think she didn't trust him. Secrets led to lies, a dangerous combination. Then again, he had secrets of his own.

Duran exhaled hard. "All right, then, let me convince Narud we need to go to Brenalin. Without his aid, I fear both cities will be out of our reach."

"Fair enough. How does one convince a dragon to do their bidding?"

Duran scowled. "How, indeed?"

****

Being a dragon had advantages—the ability to fly, exceptional vision, a better sense of smell, sharp claws and teeth. Narud was more powerful than puny humans could ever be, and his powers escalated daily. He couldn't be happier. What other talents would he ultimately gain?

He adjusted his position on the bed of gemstones, restless with anticipation.

The tenacity that kept his human side clinging to life would eventually weaken. The man would never figure out the riddle trapping him.

That thought left Narud's mood congenial. He might even grant the sorceress a favor or two for giving him life.

"No!" came an intense disavowal from his human side. *"Calandra was trusted—my friend—and she turned against me and Brenalin. There is nowhere she can hide. She will be hunted down and punished for her crime. Magic will not keep her safe."*

Sighing, Narud cocked his head. *"Oh, human, do you sincerely believe that your silly notion will make it fact? Can't your tiny wits sense how my strength grows daily even while yours dwindles? Her spell will never be broken. Your craving for vengeance blinds you, and our guest keeps you from concentrating on matters in your best interest."*

"What do you mean?" his human side asked.

Narud preened, delighted to have thought of something the human hadn't. *"You plan to take Stav down the mountain."*

"What if I do, you conceited fool?"

He refused to argue. *"Humility is not a strong*

dragon attribute."

"I know what is—arrogance."

Narud growled, his scales rising like ruffled feathers. *"Careful, human. Do not criticize me."*

"Afraid I might be right?"

The conversation rapidly irritated Narud. He was the superior being. *"How far will you travel before the change overtakes you? A league? Two perhaps? Whatever distance you cover during the night is a waste of energy. I will pick up the woman at dawn and fly her back here in minutes. You cannot win against me. Give up now. Save yourself the frustration. A dragon is the superior creature, far more deserving of life and the pleasures it provides than a puny human."*

"Your ego outstrips your logic, dragon."

"How so?"

"You think I will tell you? I promise to find a way to beat you and break the spell."

A wispy breath of smoke spewed from his nostrils when Narud snorted. *"I tire of this exchange. Begone! Leave me in peace. I wish to speak with Stav without your interference."*

"Do not frighten her. I'm warning you."

Laughter rumbled in Narud's throat. Disdain supported a far more effective reply. The human's presence receded, and the day became his to enjoy as he chose.

His dragon senses concentrated on the female. What secret did she keep from Duran and him? He nudged her with a talon, a less enjoyable experience than tasting her skin with his tongue, but more practical.

"Wake up, sleepy head," he urged softly. *"We have*

much to discuss."

She rolled over, knuckling sleep from her eyes. "What do you want?"

"It's time I teach you about dragons."

Sitting up, a surly expression appeared on her smooth face. "You assume I wish to learn."

He glared at her suspiciously. *"Why would you not?"*

"I will listen on one condition."

Her words ignited reservations. Humans were deceitful. *"You would impose conditions upon me?"*

"Yes."

He laid a claw on her leg. *"Very well. Name your request."*

With both hands, she deftly lifted his claw off her arm. "Just this. I can't stay here. I have a family, people who miss me, people who will worry. You must help the man and me reach Brenalin. You must. Say you will."

Ugly outrage coiled within him, wrapping around his chest until squeezing his breath away. *"I will not aid him. Never him. He will die eventually anyway."*

Stav's eyes went wide. "Where is your compassion?"

"Compassion belongs to fools."

She climbed out of the sleeping furs and pointed at him. "I don't understand. You won't help, but you let him live in your cave. He told me the entrance is invisible to people unless you allow them to see it. How can he? It doesn't make any sense."

"We tolerate each other. That is all you need to know."

She stepped back. "What about me? I need his help

to reach civilization, and he claims we must have your cooperation. Did I not bring you your treasure? Does not one favor deserve another?"

What a clever human female. *"Friends do not tally favors. Are we to keep columns with one for you, one for me? What if I asked you to retrieve more baubles? Will you refuse because I have a few additional favors on my side?"*

Stav waved toward the great maw. "You have given me shelter in your cave. I owe you much and am beholden to both you and the man. I couldn't refuse either of you."

Exactly the words he hoped to hear. Except for the bit about Duran. *"I would have your pledge on that."*

"I give my word as a pri...servant."

It pleased him immensely that the woman did not blink before agreeing to his stipulation. *"Accepted. Remember, in true friendship, the scales of balance are always uneven."* He watched carefully for any sign of protest and saw none. *"Given your blunt reminder of my debt, I promise not to interfere in your journey's progress."*

"What do you mean by 'interfere'?"

"A slip of the tongue."

Smiling at him, Stav nodded, and her shiny gold hair glistened in the dying coals of the fire. He could never share gold. Or her. It would be good for her to listen to his tales of glory, to have her bask in his magnificence, to have her appreciate him once he was completely in command. He would go along with her silly plan, but remain alert for an opportunity to keep her with him without breaking his word.

"Make yourself comfortable, my brave beauty. It is

time for you to learn about the glorious history of stupendous and spectacular dragons."

"Why tell me?" She sat.

Narud flicked out his tongue. He couldn't deny the delight he felt at the opportunity to relay the legend. *"Well, for a start, I'm bored,"* he said, the hint of mockery in his tone. *"I have nothing else to do at the moment. Now listen…Dragons came from the stars, born of water, air, and fire. We sensed a force on this world and sought it out. It was the gemstones. They called us here. They contained magical powers far beyond their intrinsic value, and we agreed to protect their secret unless they gave us permission to share it with others. Dragons formed a magnificent society where we gained ranking according to our treasure. The more one had, the stronger they were. Each dragon paid tribute to a dragon leader who governed our behavior and conduct."*

Narud waited for Stav to acknowledge his revelation. She arched a brow like a golden finch's wing, and he bowed his great wedge-shaped head in approval.

"After eons of living together with humans, it was innate in your ancestors' nature to lust for our treasure and the secret of our gemstones. Humans thought if they got rid of us, they would gain the powers. How wrong they were. They were ignorant. Foolish. When dragons disappeared, the gemstones fell silent. Because of human zeal, the secrets they coveted enough to kill for were lost."

"Are you saying no dragons escaped back to the stars? That can't have…You're here. How…" Stav's words trailed off.

A twinge of gratitude at her empathy made his great chest swell. *"Death has a finality which leaves no explanations. If I believed some survived and knew where they went, I would join them. Only the Guardians of Secrets know for sure, and they are probably dust, too."*

"How do you know all this? Who are these Guardians?"

Narud lifted his snout, catching scents of sun, trees, and snow in the air. *"The Guardians were the keepers of dragon history. They were unique among my kind—tiny dragons no bigger than insects. Most humans never even recognized them as dragons. Now, enough of them. I am the ruby dragon. The presence of every previous red dragon lives within me. Their spirits exist in this cave where they resided for thousands of years."*

The quizzical look on Stav's face was easy to read. Plus, he'd heard her tiny snort of disbelief. Desire to gain her confidence grew within him.

"Twice you've implied gemstones speak to you," she said. "How can rocks…even precious jewels talk?"

"I do not expect you to grasp such a premise immediately. All you need know is that they do. How is unimportant. Although I can tell you a secret, a real one, if you like."

"A secret?"

He silently reprimanded himself for wanting to tell Stav a thing but couldn't stop himself. *"What you see before you now was not born of fire, but from a sorceress's creation. It was she who turned me into what you see—a red dragon. The most prized of all gemstones, the ruby, is my chosen jewel, and they give me glimpses into what was."*

"Are you talking about the gift of prophecy?"

"Heavens no," he answered with a hushed laugh. *"I'm talking about rubies. They are the most precious of all gemstones. Naturally, I'm slightly prejudiced. They protect against misfortune and signify fire and emotion. And more, but that is not for your ears to hear."*

When he finished, Narud looked up to find the day had slipped away from him. Dusk fell beyond the cave. His human side fidgeted, defiant and eager. He resisted the urge to give up his time with Stav. A dragon didn't make requests. He took what he wanted.

****

Marina had sat spellbound, listening to the dragon and succumbing to his immense appeal as he told the history of dragons. She knew she shouldn't trust him, knew she shouldn't believe him.

Something about him made him compelling. His tale of magical gemstones, guardians of secrets, and an enlightened time beat any bard's she'd ever heard.

Not once did she interrupt or ask for details. Narud might have interpreted her curiosity as desire for his precious rubies. He certainly was touchy enough about his treasure. Later would be more appropriate.

She didn't feel scared for her life any more. His actions proved that, except why did he stare at her? She arched a brow. She doubted she would be his next meal. At least she hoped that was the case. He ate with a ravenous appetite all the time.

"Who says I'm hungry, little girl?"

She jumped, shocked. "Can you read my thoughts?"

"You really don't know much about dragons, do

45

you? Normally, we only eat once a month."

"You ate a pig last week, and a sheep the week before."

Narud stretched his long neck, his scaly head scraping the ceiling and sending a shower of pebbles to the ground. *"I didn't know you were counting. Amazing. Well, if you insist, I'll eat you!"*

The dragon's mocking tone crashed Marina's hopes. She caught Narud watching her. What if he wouldn't keep his promise? Would she ever return home?

"I want you to stay with me." His red eyes sought hers. *"Here in this cave."*

"If you don't mind," she said, heading for the entrance. "I need to go outside for a breath of fresh air."

A setting sun danced on faraway treetops, casting them in a fiery glow. The wind stirred the air. Marina had never seen this much snow. It seldom fell along the great ocean's coast and never in such vast amounts.

She wanted to return to Eudes, to her family, and the open expanse of ocean, beach, and sky. The ocean provided all manner of food they required, and ships conveyed goods from around the known world to fill in the vacancies. The memory brought forth the vision of dolphins breaching as they escorted vessels into the harbor. There, while her life might seem restricted, held much joy and a bit of fun once in a while.

"Aren't you cold out there?"

She spun around at the deep and familiar voice. Duran's chest heaved as if from hard exercise. Her heart swelled at the sight of him. Why did an air of desperation surround him? He was built large, and everything about him seemed larger than ordinary.

Certainly, he could handle any problem that surfaced.

"I didn't know you were inside," she said. "I assumed you were checking your traps or spying on those men."

"Why did you bargain with Narud?" he asked, his voice neutral. "I was going to!"

She craned her neck to see past him into the cave. "But—"

"Who are you to argue with me?" he interrupted with such cold authority she edged back.

"I could demand a similar thing from you," she said when she realized her actions. "You have no right to chastise me?"

The flash of reddish color through his sea-blue eyes had to be anger. Why be upset? She had done nothing wrong. Rather, he should be pleased. Grateful. Thank her. Especially if he was dying, as Narud implied. The dragon's reference had slipped her attention until this moment. He certainly looked fit for a man in failing health.

The man waved his arm with a flourish. "I know this dragon's tricks better than you. You were at his mercy. I would have gained his agreement without agreeing to any conditions."

A flutter raced through Marina's body, and she stiffened. "It's not like I was trying to help us." She marched up behind him to grab his shoulder and force him to whirl around to face her. She was Princess Marina Hersher, middle daughter of the King of Eudes. She had her dignity. "If you're afraid I obligated you, let me ease your fears. I only pledged myself." She spotted the empty bed of rubies and pearls. "Where's Narud?"

"Dragons are magical creatures. Maybe he whisked himself into another place."

Her heart hammered in her chest. "He would have bid me good-bye."

The man winced. "Forget about him. He's an unpleasant, arrogant beast who thinks he's all-knowing. I don't want to talk about him. I was wrong to snap at you." He offered a smile as way of an apology. "You want to go home, an understandable ambition. You were right to take action. Forgive me. You are not like most women. Another would have done nothing. In my mind, lack of activity is worse."

"My thanks." She was surprised how her mood brightened. She'd never fallen for a man's praise, but this time she beamed with pride. "Mind you, good sir, Narud is my friend. You would do well to become his friend, too."

The man's face reddened. "I spend enough time with him. You think you know him, but you don't. Never trust a dragon."

Chapter Four

"Why shouldn't I trust Narud? He's honored me with his confidence."

Duran felt pinpricks of guilt jab his conscience. "But you do not know Narud's."

"Do not try swaying me. I know my own mind." Stav anchored her hands on her shapely hips. "Today he shared the history of dragons and gemstones with me. I wager he hasn't done that for you."

He felt his anger fade at seeing the defensive expression appear on Stav's face. "I credited you with more sense than to believe those old legends. Narud is not what he seems."

"You don't believe he suggested I follow you to the brigands?" she implored, as if seeking a reason for his distrust. "It was my own idea."

"Which turned out badly," he couldn't help saying. "If I hadn't saved you, that man would have carted you back to the others."

"You have my gratitude, good sir." She cleared her throat, the warbly sound drowning out the breeze thrusting snow into the cave. "I take full responsibility for what happened."

As you should, he thought.

It occurred to him that Stav played only a small fragment of his problem. She was unaware of the gravity of his circumstances. She hadn't been betrayed, nor was she desperate to resolve his predicament. Her life had not been destroyed.

Only his.

Duran was reluctant to admit how Stav's presence grated on his sense of fairness, especially when her intent had been to help. Her presence eased his temper. Being an innocent after all, she didn't deserve the blunt force of his anger.

Calandra did!

He knelt down and took Stav's hands in his own. Her soft, smooth skin glided against his and launched quivers up his arm. "Listen, Stav, I can't explain everything at the moment. You asked me to trust you. Well now, I ask the same. Be careful around Narud. His objectives are not mine."

"What are yours?" Her thumbs glided over the tops of his hands. "Living in a cave for the rest of your life?"

A groan welled up from deep inside him. Her eyes were so clear and bright he suspected she saw right through him. "I know it's a lot to ask, but please, please trust me."

"I would be happy to cooperate if I knew who I was dealing with." She licked her lips. "Tell me your name?"

Duran felt his throat tighten when the wetness glistened on her mouth. He tore his gaze away, only to fix his attention on a flutter in the slight hollow at the base of her neck. His gaze returned to her face, and he saw her eyebrows rise and her nostrils flare, all signs of how strongly she battled within herself, the same as he.

Smiling, he said, "You can call me Duran."

"Oh, like my…I—I mean like the princess's betrothed."

"It's a common enough name in Brenalin," he said, mildly puzzled by her reaction, but also pleased to have told her.

A quirk lifted the corner of her lush mouth. "That it is. Meanwhile, do you have any extra hides and a sharp knife, good Duran?"

"What for?"

"Stop fretting. I have an idea, and it's a surprise. You want to get off this mountain, don't you?"

"Yes," he said, unease ruffling his belly.

Her smile widened. "Good. Oh, and I'll need some strong, supple tree branches about an inch in diameter. Can you fetch me some?"

On a whim, he decided to go along with her. "I suppose, and you can use the hides over there. Don't worry if I'm gone a while. I have other supplies to gather for the journey."

A half-lie. He wanted to check on the brigands' camp, to see if Calandra's henchmen found their compatriot's body.

Or if they had moved off during the day.

Narud had been furious they'd dare draw closer to his treasure. Duran did some fast-talking to convince him annihilation wasn't the way. It gave away their location, and the sorceress would only send additional men.

Giving Stav a nod, Duran hurried outside. At this elevation, the temperature dropped below freezing every night. He tugged on gloves and tightened his heavy fleece coat to keep out the worst of the bitter cold.

He wanted a better look at the brigands' leader. Duran wanted to mark the man's face in his memory.

One day, he intended to kill him. For Stav's sake, he told himself. Her fear brought out a protective feeling in him. She would never feel safe until the man died.

Duran found the brigands by the red tongues of their campfires licking the cold mountain air. The sweetness of wood smoke filled the air and combined with the odors of leather, sweat, and cooking meat. Little had changed from the previous night. He wondered briefly if their lack of guards stemmed from arrogance or stupidity.

Duran listened carefully and then heard the leader's distinctive voice. The man sat before a low burning fire with a half dozen others. He wore heavy outer garments that added bulk to his girth, but clearly the man was far larger than any of his cohorts. A long, narrow face with wide-set eyes that constantly scanned the surroundings reminded Duran of an ex-soldier or mercenary. His neck was heavily veined, and his bald head went hatless. The tips of his ears and nose glistened bright red in the cold.

"How does our mistress know this is where we'll find who she seeks?" asked a man through chattering teeth.

The leader sloshed down his tankard, swallowed, and wiped his hand over his mouth. "By magic, of course."

Wrapped in a woolen blanket, the other brigand stood and poured the dregs of his tankard into the fire. Hissing smoke raced into the air. "I smelled sulfur-stink the other day. Does that mean the dragon is close? Him, I fear running into again."

"We've been looking for over a full moon and ain't seen hide nor hair of dragon or servant," said a third.

"We all saw him carry her away for his afternoon meal. Sure as I'm standing in this icebox, she's probably long dead."

Duran went very still.

Another man stood and poured his drink onto the fire. "What would a sorceress want with a serving girl anyway?" He looked at the bald-headed leader.

Exactly his question, Duran thought. He bit his lip, wondering if the man would pass on replying. Calandra was vindictive, but to send mercenaries after a mere servant. What made Stav so important? It seemed extreme. Even for Calandra.

"I know not why she wants the girl dead," snarled the bald-headed leader. "Don't care. I've been ordered to do a job, that's all."

The fine hairs at the back of Duran's neck rose and though covered in his thick fleece coat, a chill raced up his spine and over his scalp at the words.

Glowering, the leader looked around the campsite. "Where's Aug? Has anyone seen him?"

A man sharpening his blade stopped. "Seen him last nightfall when he left to take a leak. You followed him, didn't you, Fahid?"

"I did not have the pleasure of seeing him."

The lilt of a lyrical accent surprised Duran, and he narrowed his gaze for a closer look. Heavily embroidered cloth wrapped the lower portion of the man's face, leaving dark eyes and the hint of facial tattoos visible. A desert man of Midber in the mountains? What did they call themselves? Sandbloods. Yes, that was it. The Sandbloods were an ancient people. They alleged to have created the oldest civilization on Feldsvelt and were the most biased race.

Once, they dominated the southwestern part of the known world and pushed their borders into the far north. Whatever caused their downfall was lost in history. Now, they wandered far and wide to market the exotic wares of their vast kingdom, but they never ventured into the cold.

The leader scratched his nose, looking concerned. "Someone look around. See if they can find him."

"Serves him right if the fool wandered away and fell off the mountain," the man in the blanket said, hugging his covering tighter. "The man can't hold his water or his liquor."

"Tomorrow we head back for new orders," the leader said.

"About time," murmured the Sandblood, squatting across from him. "I will be pleased to get off this freezing dune of ice."

The bald-headed leader stood, then scowled. "Talk like that will get you killed," he threatened. "If you don't like this kind of business, get out. Meanwhile, shut up."

"There ain't much else to do up here, except speculate," came a voice from within the group.

Duran couldn't tell who spoke. He just hoped for more information.

The leader smiled, and it softened the hard line of his mouth. "Try sleeping. We'll be up at first light. I was summoned to lead this sorry group, and you're being well paid to find something to take back to our mistress. If anyone doubts me, take your complaints up with her. I'm sure she'll be attentive to your concerns."

"Let us not speak of her," advised the Sandblood. "I've no wish to bring attention to myself or borrow trouble from this sorceress."

Duran heard enough. He'd found the individual he sought. The bald-headed man was the leader. He inched backward. A quarter hour later, he reached the stunted scrub pines marking the tree line of the mountain. Moonlight glistened over the ground.

Duran wasn't taking any chances. He stared from behind snow-draped pines and listened for signs of any enemy. An odd scout could be returning to the encampment and stumble upon him by accident.

The soft crunch of snow caught his attention. He froze until he saw a small, white rabbit, its dark nose twitching, start and stop. Somewhere off in the distance an owl hooted. Duran searched the trees for the bird and in that instant of distraction; the rabbit vanished into the blue-white snow.

As if an all-clear signal sounded, Duran began snapping off long, thin branches. He had no idea how many to gather, but he'd promised Stav.

While he worked, he had plenty on his mind to keep his thoughts occupied, the most important being how to break Calandra's spell.

He needed to get off the mountain.

Sharing existence with a dragon gave him knowledge few men had ever gained. Treasure increased a dragon's power. Which meant he needed to deal with Narud's growing hoard.

What he planned to do required waiting until Stav fell asleep. He didn't like deceiving her, but he had no other alternative. If she knew, the woman might tell Narud. She was fast becoming the dragon's champion.

The thought left the taste of ashes in his mouth.

****

Twilight embraced the land. Rummaging through Duran's utensils tugged at Marina's senses and caused her heart to skip a beat. The man was such an enigma. She knew nothing about him, which made her attraction all the more baffling.

Thinking of him made her cheeks burn and caused her blood to speed through her veins. How could she finish the task that she'd set for herself if silly thoughts of Duran tormented her?

It took an enormous effort, but she shook off the potency of his appeal and found a knife. She used it to start a tear in the hide and tore a narrow strip. After accumulating enough strips, she started knotting them together. The fishermen of Eudes had taught her and her sisters the complex knots necessary to repair their nets. It was a fun task at the time, though she never anticipated putting the skill to practical use for herself.

She formed a square of strips, and then held an entwined piece of fabric about a foot and a half wide and two feet long. Looking at her achievement, she felt a delightful sense of accomplishment whorl through her and laughed with pleasure.

She continued working, waiting for Duran, working and waiting. Hours passed. Night lengthened and she dozed.

A noise pierced her sleep. Through blurry eyes, she saw Duran return. His expression appeared stern but she didn't care, growing warm beneath his heated gaze.

Marina smiled as genuine relief and joy filled her at having him near. Duran. She repeated his name to herself. It felt nice knowing his name. She hadn't realized how much the tiny bit of knowledge meant to her.

He sank down beside her and placed a muscular arm around her shoulder. The warm touch of his hand made her snuggle closer to his solid frame as he cradled her body against his. She inhaled deeply; the soft, spicy fragrance unique to him soothed her.

She awoke near dawn. A stir in the air, like a vibration made her skin tingle. Shafts of sunlight cascaded through the cave's entrance. She found herself curled within the loops of Narud's tail.

"Where is my treasure?"

"Your touch is warm," she said, ignoring his query. "I never realized it before. I thought reptiles were cold-blooded creatures."

His coils loosened slightly. *"Do not change the subject. It seems I have another misconception to correct about dragons. I'm warm-blooded, the same as you."*

Marina blinked at the word pictures appearing in her head. She started to rise, only to have Narud puff up his scales and trap her.

"What…What…" She swallowed hard, fighting alarm, and then tried to stand again. "What are you doing?"

"Answer my question." Smoke burst from his nostrils. *"Where is my treasure?"*

"How should I know?"

What game did he play? His anger sounded so genuine.

"Look at me!" Narud demanded. *"Answer my question. Did you steal it?"*

His accusation hurt, but she wasn't about to admit it to him. Gazing into Narud's glowing eyes, she found them both compelling and frightening. Her position made her vulnerable. He could squeeze the life out of her without exerting himself.

Well, Eudes raised no coward. "I am no thief!" she denied hotly.

"I want my treasure back. Return it."

She snorted. "If you lost it, go find it yourself."

"Where did you hide it?"

Her bravado could hide only so much. "I don't have your precious treasure. I swear."

"Find it! Someone has stolen what belongs to me."

"Narud, it wasn't me. I swear. I—" Marina flicked her gaze at the corner where the jewels and gold were stored. The spot was empty.

"No excuses. I want what is mine."

"Who would...?" Her voice trailed off.

"Who, indeed?"

She could not meet Narud's gaze. Duran had uttered the exact phrase. "Oh, no...You don't think it was Duran. I cannot believe he would commit such an atrocity."

"Luckily for you, my brave beauty, your thoughts are innocent. He does whatever pleases him, especially if it thwarts me. It makes perfect sense. His devious purpose is to weaken me by hiding my treasure. Foolish, foolish human! I will deal with him later."

Marina continued to stroke Narud's scales until they no longer puffed out. His low growl changed to a soft purr. The huge beast shared more traits with Sinner than she first realized.

"If you are so worried about someone stealing your treasure, fly us to Brenalin," she suggested as he watched her.

"Why should I?"

"Because you'll be rid of us much faster."

He stretched his crimson wings. The tips, slightly lighter with the hint of gold, spanned the width of the cave. Once again, the movement reminded her of her pet when the cat worked out the kinks of his body.

Or maybe the dragon was simply showing off, trying to impress her with his massive size.

"Dragons do not concern themselves with the hardship of others. If you journey from here, you do so without my help. Moreover, I'm not finished with you." Narud lowered his great head. Hot breath escaped his nostrils as he sniffed her, and then the strips of hide she finished the night before. *"What goes on here? What are you making?"*

She relaxed at change of subject. "Snowshoes," she answered. "To help us get down the mountain. Remember, I come from a fishing port."

"Explain."

"I'm knotting strips of leather like a fishing net. I'll attach them to branches, and they'll make it easier to walk in deep snow. It should please you that we'll be leaving you soon."

"We'll see, my brave beauty. We'll see."

****

Calandra whirled around, her thick braid slapping against her back. She threw the ceramic bowl against the far wall of her sleeping quarters. The pottery shattered with a pop, and the contents flew in every direction. Its destruction should have given her relief, but frustration curdled in her stomach. She'd felt the desire to break something since rising this morning. Things weren't going her way, and hurling the bowl hadn't provided the satisfaction she hoped it would.

Shocking the mousy serving woman, Hannah, had provided her with a smidgen of pleasure, though it vanished like a wisp of smoke. Hannah had been tardy by seconds, and now tears welled in her eyes and her bottom lip quivered. The sight pleased Calandra.

"What are you sniveling about? You don't expect me to apologize for your slow behavior, do you? The meal was cold."

"Beggin' your pardon, Mistress." She whimpered, curtseying and stooping to pick up the remnants of food and crockery.

Calandra studied her reflection in the mirror. Black hair, reminiscent of obsidian, shone. Her green eyes were wide-set, her features even, a small mouth her only defect. Her lips should have been fuller.

Beauty I want.

Beauty I shall have.

Beauty I am.

She chanted the spell under her breath. The same one every day. It should have worked on Duran and made her irresistible to him, but nothing had gone according to plan. After years of scheming, she should have achieved her goal without a hitch.

How could he claim an obligation to the bridal contract with the Eudes princess? A princess he didn't love. He loved her. Her.

What was the matter with him? Was she not beautiful? A lord's daughter? She would have brought knowledge and magic to their union. She could have made him rich, powerful.

Why hadn't the fool agreed to wed her? Yet he had rejected her.

And he paid the consequence.

The thought brought a smile to her lips. She glanced at her hands, her ring-covered fingers in particular, and then she wiggled them. Rich jewels sparkled.

Her goal was within her grasp. Duran would return. Magic tied him and her together. She would force him to his knees and make him beg her to reverse the spell. How she looked forward to Duran Abbas groveling at her feet. Her mouth watered as she savored the thought of revenge. Triumph could not come soon enough.

Movement reflected in the mirror. The cowering servant stared at her. She drilled Hannah with a look that sent armed warriors scurrying away in fright.

"What are you looking at? Are you spying on me? You think I don't know what the servants of Brenalin say," she shouted. "Get out. The sight of you sickens me."

All the servants in the castle disliked her. She'd seen the sly glances they exchanged whenever she crossed their paths. She'd heard them whisper behind her back.

Hannah's footsteps receded across the flagstone floor, and then the door's iron hinges squeaked. A click sounded as the latch fell back into place.

Sighing, Calandra finished her morning preparations. All the while, she longed for time alone in her workroom. Ages had passed since she'd had the leisure of preparing potions and reviewing her spell books.

Studying sorcery required voracious reading and long hours of practice. Soon, she decided. Soon, she would be able to spend all her time doing as she wished.

Today, Zell Abbas, the king of Brenalin, awaited her in the great hall.

She went down the stairs, calmed by the steady rhythm of her boots gliding over stone steps. Even so, her footsteps slowed as she went lower.

She shuddered and recalled the old king's voice, *"My son...where is my precious son?"*

Stopping at the bottom of the landing, she inhaled and gathered her courage. She flattened her palms on the thick, wooden door and pushed. The great audience hall spread out before her. Head held high, she entered where she felt unwanted by the majority.

The room stretched twice the length of her father's, Lord Pallon Genoy. He had anointed himself the title of lord when he laid claim to a minor territory in Demicland. Since then, of course, he'd added more land and had become one of the most powerful lords of her country.

Three score of horses would fit side by side inside the audience hall, and the wooden floor gleamed from the passage of thousands of footsteps. Rich tapestries depicting feasts, maidens, and mystical creatures covered stone blocks.

At the far end, a raised dais held two ornate chairs wrought of exotic wood. The king's chair, the larger of the two, was the Ruby Throne. A gleaming gemstone the size of a man's open hand held the place of honor in the center of its back. The lesser chair belonged to the queen and contained smaller rubies in its polished back.

It took an army to maintain this stronghold. Someday, Calandra promised herself she would banish anyone who gave her insult and have them replaced with men and women loyal to her and her father.

Servants and petitioners alike went dashing in and out of the great hall. Along the sides favor seekers stood in groups, whispering to each other. As usual, no one paid her any heed.

The king sat in his high seat, looking wan and worried. The last two months had taken their toll, ageing him faster than a virulent disease. His hair had turned white, his cheeks sunken. The man was a mere shadow of his former self. He'd grown old and wrinkled.

She felt her heart lurch as she gazed at him, recalling their first meeting. She had been an angry and frightened seven-year-old when her fostering began, shaking before the man with the booming voice. Then, he'd had height and strength.

"Your Majesty," she announced in a voice intended to reach the far end of the room.

The king's expression brightened. "Calandra, my dear, what has happened? Any word of Duran?"

She forced a smile, standing where the light outlined her from behind. She spared a glance at the group of men closest to her who turned in her direction. "Alas, no, Majesty."

His shoulders slumped. "I see," he replied, disappointed.

Calandra bowed her head, keeping her gaze downward. "I wish I was the bearer of better news."

"Bah!" he bellowed back like his former self. "No recriminations. You bring light into a room where only darkness exists. Step forward, child."

"Yes, Your Majesty." She rushed toward the dais, giving him a peck on the check.

A deep sigh rattled his chest. "I miss you when

you're not by my side, my dear. My day has started badly, and I so hoped you would bring me good news about Duran. I fear my son is lost to me forever."

"Let me make you a sleeping potion," she murmured low.

"No! I want to feel this pain. The ache of his loss reminds me how much I care."

She patted his hand. A web of bright blue veins crisscrossed his pale skin. "You must rest, Your Majesty. You are exhausted."

"Lost sleep means nothing. I require a clear head in case word arrives about Duran and quick action is necessary. Furthermore, squabbles arise daily I must handle."

"Who would dare bother you in this dire time?"

The king gave her a patronizing smile. "Today, I have settled an argument over cows in farmers' fields, soothed worries over brigands laying siege to the countryside, and that preposterous tale of a dragon flying over Brenalin is making people anxious. Pure nonsense, but they refuse to heed me. I am more concerned there has been no word about Duran. The men I sent out have found nothing."

She didn't care about peasants and farmers' cows. They were all idiots, minuscule pieces in a much bigger game. The brigands were her men. Brenalin's populace consisted of law-abiding citizens whose thoughts dwelled on tilling their small plots of land and managing the great forest rather than causing trouble or stealing from their neighbor.

She'd sent the main troupe after the missing servant, and the remainder stayed to harry travelers, keeping the country folk in an uproar so they would pester the king with their fears and complaints.

The dragon—only one dragon existed in the entire world, and she'd created him.

She pulled the king's kerchief from his pocket and dabbed at her eyes. She must appear sincere and genuinely concerned.

"It's unfair," she whimpered. "You work so hard. Your subjects don't appreciate how kind you are, how good you are to them. My father rules with a stiffer hand. He would never allow his subjects to burden him with their petty problems. You should do the same."

"Demic lords rule differently than other kingdoms," Zell responded.

She despised the way he spoke to her as a child. "Just as well! None would tolerate these bothersome peasants."

"Peasants, yes, but not bothersome. It is my responsibility to oversee the citizens of Brenalin. Demic lords fight amongst themselves for supremacy like dogs over a bone. It would be wise if they settled on one lord as have other kingdoms. Hostilities tear your land apart every year. Peace would bring prosperity to everyone."

Calandra stared at him. So the rest of the world viewed the lords of her country as animals. Let them. The idiots were insane to deem them nothing but fighting warlords, and then she thought, so what. Their opinions meant nothing to her.

Finding a particular spell book referencing the Ruby Throne had infatuated her. From it, she'd learned gemstones held powers they whispered only to dragons. Dragons conferred that magic upon a family or individual.

Brenalin's ruby bequeathed *immortality*. Sweet,

wonderful immortality. The thought of never facing death intoxicated her. She wanted it more than she wanted Duran.

Her joy was quickly crushed when she discovered eternal life could belong only to the rightful heirs of Brenalin. The entitlement belonged only to someone wedded to a royal Abbas.

What good was possessing knowledge if one was unable to own it? It frustrated her to no end. Becoming an Abbas consumed her.

Her reflection lasted so long, she missed the king's next words. A rise in voices alerted her. Her gaze shifted to the individuals, and they stopped their murmurings.

Frowning, she answered the king, "Forgive me, Majesty. I fear I was distracted. You were saying…"

"I was inquiring about your morning," he said in a fatherly way. "A strange look passed over your face. Are you unhappy? Tell me, and I shall make it right."

"It's nothing, my lord," she murmured, disgusted with how easily she fooled him. At least Duran offered a challenge. "A simple misunderstanding with someone. I must protect the innocent. They should not be punished for a silly mistake."

"I will not order you to reveal the culprit, but know this, my dear, you have the kindest heart. I couldn't have survived these weeks without you."

"You honor me." Her gaze fell demurely.

"I speak the truth," he said with his old vigor. "Duran's disappearance is a mystery we must solve. Every day I ask myself where he is. I might be able to understand if he has gone off on some clandestine quest, if he left to protect Brenalin, but why hasn't he sent word? I fear I may never see my son again."

How right you are, she thought, and then out loud, "Oh, my lord, we must keep up our hopes. I'm sure he'll return."

"Yes, yes," he answered in haste. "You miss him, too. I forget how close the two of you were."

She called forth a smile of assurance. "Of course, I miss him. Never think otherwise. Believe me, Majesty, I shall plan to give him a good tongue-lashing for not informing us. He'll not escape me without hearing how much he has upset us."

For the first time since Calandra entered the great hall, the king's rheumy eyes crinkled with merriment. "I await that day with glee."

As did she.

Chapter Five

Marina stood at the cave's entrance. The setting sun stained the sky with streaks of reds and pinks. In the distance, a spot of darker crimson rising and dipping in the sky grew smaller—Narud.

Earlier, he had spread his great leathery wings and launched himself into the air to hunt. Never had she met a dragon who loved to eat like him; then again, she'd never met a dragon.

Heaving a sigh, her breath fogged in the crisp mountain air. Dusk fell fast. All light disappeared. Duran would appear soon. His routine called for him to show up in the early evening and then vanish near morning.

She sighed again and returned to the warmth and safety of the deep cave. Sitting before the fire, her gaze slid toward the entrance with the sound of crunching snow. She released a breath when Duran rounded bare granite boulders, a brace of dead rabbits over his shoulder.

She smiled a welcome. "I see your traps were successful."

"There won't be much time to hunt on the trail. These will feed us for a few days. Are you ready?"

"Now? It'll be dark soon. Isn't it dangerous to travel at night?"

"Actually, it's safer. The colder air makes the ice

and snow more stable."

How long had he lived on the mountain to acquire his expert knowledge, she wondered? He laid down the rabbits, picked up his handmade pack, and shoved his belongings inside.

As she watched him work, uncertainty resounded in Marina's head. "Why did you remove Narud's treasure? He's very upset with you, you know. You need to return it or offer him an explanation."

He raked back his reddish-brown hair, glancing at the spot where Narud normally sat. "No."

"You've no right to abuse his hospitality," she argued back. "He's been kind to both of us."

Duran's mouth twisted down. "He doesn't give a damn about me. You, maybe. If losing his precious treasure causes him grief, all the better."

The bitterness between Narud and him was not lost on Marina. What ill will lay between them? The missing pieces were important, and puzzling things out, not a favorite pastime for her.

She felt if she could patch the hostility between them, it would go toward repaying the debt she owed them both for helping her survive.

Marina abandoned caution. "I'm not sure where you were raised, but in Eudes stealing is illegal. You must return his treasure."

"Stav," he began, impatience clear in his tone, "it wasn't all his treasure. Some came from the princess's caravan."

That gave her pause. "I'm sure she would not begrudge him a share. Tell me where you put it. I'll retrieve it for him."

This time his breath hissed between clenched teeth.

"I buried it."

Thief. Outlaw. Whatever Duran's identity, he was a formidable man, but seething with restrained hostility made him terrifying.

"Where?" she demanded.

Duran glowered at her. "Stop worrying about it, Stav. He doesn't need those jewels. He's not a real dragon."

Marina leapt to her feet. "Narud's real to me, and he's my friend. I won't forsake him."

"You think I like hearing you defend him?"

A reconciliation must be reached between these two. "There's more here than you're telling, isn't there?"

"Oh yes, and it's best if you are left in ignorance."

"Kubala's breath," she murmured. "You're really obnoxious. I swear sometimes you are more dragon than human."

Duran's breath hitched loudly. He stared wide-eyed at her. "I am nothing like him. He's gluttonous, selfish, and lazy. I'm just sorry you're caught in the middle."

Rapt silence hung between them.

"You're sorry," she repeated his words. "Then give back his treasure."

Duran shook his head. "No."

A sudden emptiness filled Marina. Arguing wasn't going to solve a thing. "What about those men we saw? What if they come after us?"

He glanced over his shoulder, bent, and then stuffed the cooking pot into his pack. "We'll be following them. I overheard them say they were leaving this morning. They'll be hours ahead of us."

Marina winced at his confidence. "And if you're

wrong?"

"Why all these questions? I thought you were eager to reach home."

"I am," she said, indignantly, "but I have no wish to die in the attempt."

"Afraid, are you?"

The challenge in his voice made her blood boil. "I know my safety weighs heavily on you, and I am very appreciative. But you need not concern yourself. I can take care of myself. Haven't I proven that? I mean, a real live dragon didn't scare me. Why should this? All I'm trying to do is be prudent about the dangers we'll face."

"If you're concerned, stay behind." Duran hefted his pack. "It'll take a week to reach Brenalin. You could survive here until I send someone to fetch you."

Marina became vaguely aware of Duran's height and how small he made her feel. She ignored the disparity. "You would desert me?"

A snort of derision came from Duran. "I'm getting off this mountain. You've convinced me I'm of no use up here."

Marina stepped forward. "I'm coming, too. If you insist upon leaving now, here." She shoved snowshoes at his chest. "I made these in case we ran into deep snow."

He stared at her, silent. His mouth lifted into a crooked smile, and then he ran his hand over the debarked frame. He plucked at the intricate knots of webbing and nodded. "Good job. Thank you, Stav. I like them. And you," he whispered, stepping closer.

She watched his blue eyes darken. So close. The heat of his body seemed to reach out and caress her. He bent his head, and she hoped he would kiss her. She'd never been kissed by a man like him—kissed, yes, but they had been mere boys.

"You constantly amaze me," he spoke again. "For someone who lived in a palace much of her life, how did you acquire the skill to make snowshoes?"

A swell of pride filled her and she wanted to please him. "I've seen drawings, but I can't guarantee these'll work."

Deep laughter filled the cave. The pleasant sound allowed her to relax.

"Accept the compliment, Stav. You are very clever and deserving of many more."

Marina felt her cheeks burn. They must have colored bright red. She'd never been called clever. Pretty, yes, which she hated, but clever! This man treated her differently, and she liked it. Their social positions were so far apart. They would never have met, or been allowed to carry on a meaningful conversation.

No matter how good it made her feel, her friendship with Duran carried a terrible price. All who traveled in her caravan were dead. Saddened by the reflection, she promised never to forget them.

Still, this period on the mountain would remain a precious memory to Marina for the rest of her life.

****

Duran drew a deep breath and expelled it. He dangled his pack from one hand and held a long, coiled rope in the other. He looked down at Stav and saw her staring at him.

"Tie this around your waist," he instructed.

"Why?" She frowned.

"Call it a safety precaution. I am accustomed to

walking the mountain in the dark. You're not."

Her hazel eyes darted to the rope several times. He slowly shook his head to stop thinking about how bright her eyes were.

"I've trusted you thus far." She accepted the rope and knotted it around her narrow waist. "It's best to do so a little longer."

If only trusting another being were easy for him, he thought. Curse Calandra! He would have sacrificed his life to defend her, but she changed all that when she used evil magic to turn him into a dragon.

Peering at the serving woman, he knew that same traitorous bent didn't exist in a single drop of her blood. Not her. Stav remained loyal, standing by her princess, defending her against overwhelming odds.

He vowed to return Stav to her family; that way at least one of them would have a chance at a normal life.

Unless…

The thought struck him with the force of a thunderbolt. What if Stav were to stay in Brenalin? Whatever her life before they met, she'd been forged and tempered into a wonderful woman deserving a better life than her old one. His father could grant her asylum and reward her for her bravery. One kindness begot another. She'd tried to save the princess and deserved to put servitude behind her.

"All right, let's go," Stav said, looping her snowshoes onto her back.

Duran's gaze locked with hers once again. Grinning, he draped his snowshoes over his shoulder.

"You take the lead," he said.

"Shouldn't you? You've lived on the mountain and know the trails."

A swirl of heat erupted within him. She need not know the perils of their trek. No need to frighten her. His strength would serve them far better in the rear.

"Don't worry. I'll guide you. We'll be fine."

She nodded, accepting his assurance.

A silvery moon cast shimmery light upon the ground. Duran kept an eye on the terrain ahead of Stav as they went. The trail dipped sharply in places, but they traversed the grade without encountering a problem.

Walking in single file, Duran smiled at Stav's pace and the gentle sway of her hips. He let his thoughts drift to the memory of her body—narrow waist, long legs, and pert breasts.

He'd touched her body, felt her velvet skin. She'd been warm and soft. To never touch her again developed into an unbearable torture. He found himself holding his breath.

Thankfully, the constant pace of the journey produced exactly what he needed. It yanked his thoughts from Stav for she was proving a far greater distraction than he ever imagined possible.

Hours ticked by. They wove around game trails.

Meanwhile, Duran worried about his other, more pressing dilemma. He needed to tell Stav about Narud. Maybe not tonight. But soon.

He planned to walk until first light. Exhaustion should make her sleep through the day. Her safety was assured. Narud would protect her.

"It'll take at least two or three days to descend the mountain," he told her after trekking half the night. "Crossing the glacier will be the most dangerous portion of our journey. The first place we'll encounter people is in Sparkler Valley. There are a couple settlements, but I think it's best if we avoid those areas."

She halted in her tracks and frowned over her shoulder at him. "I thought we wanted to find people to help us."

"And if they're in league with those brigands? What then?" He felt guilty watching disappointment wash over Stav's face. "We have to reach Demit Woods. The main road cuts through it."

Her entire body shuddered, but he doubted it stemmed from the cold. Draconic senses he had tried to deny caught sudden apprehension. She feared entering the forest.

Frowning, Duran continued, hoping to soothe her fears. "The road is well traveled. Brenalin derives much of its wealth from the forest. We sell our raw timber to every other kingdom."

A half laugh bubbled between her lips. "You sound like a good-will ambassador. I've overheard them singing the praises of their homelands in Eudes' court."

He realized watching the enchanting sway of Stav's backside let him imagine holding her in his arms, his body naked against hers. "Tell me about Eudes and your life there."

"I lived in the castle with my fam—the princess and her family," she began in a hesitant voice. "It is a wonderful place. The king's castle sits high on a cliff, overlooking the great ocean. I love climbing up in the turrets during the day. It has a fantastic view. The sound of breaking waves reaches up to the highest point. The ocean is marvelous to behold. Always constant, ever changing.

"Eudes is the largest port on the western side, bustling with people and activity. At night, hundreds of harbor torches sparkle like stars fallen to earth."

Duran found he enjoyed the sound of her voice. "You miss being there, don't you?"

"Very much," she answered with a ghost of a sigh. "No disrespect to your great land, but I had no wish to come. I wasn't given a choice. Duty compelled me to obey."

The tiniest ache squeezed his heart at the sadness he heard. He desperately wanted to pull her into his arms. The strength and strangeness of his emotions staggered him.

He had no business thinking like that.

Sighing deeply, he vowed to never order Stav, to always let her decide her own fate.

A full moon hung high in the star-lit sky. Half the night was already gone, and every night he lost precious minutes as spring drew closer and closer to the long days of summer.

Longer days for Narud.

Duran's only consolation was that traveling exhausted Stav and she slept through most of the day, much to Narud's irritation. He smiled to himself, recalling their lengthy argument throughout the day.

The next night, they stepped onto the precarious slope of the glacier. An omnipresent wind whistled. Only a mile wide, the length of the glacier stretched for miles and was the only way down the mountain. The vast expanse of snow and ice was lit with an eerie luminescence. The darker pockets he saw were blue ice in the day. Thunder rumbled in the distance. Somewhere within the massive accumulation of ice and land, pieces splintered and rock fell. The glacier spoke in a creaky, groaning voice. The noise provided a reminder of danger lurking beneath the beauty.

Less ominous, the sound of water trickled underneath. The spring run-off had begun early.

The glacier reminded him of an enormous white animal lying dormant on the mountainside. Long ago, he'd learned to respect it enough to know they must tread lightly for fear of waking the beast.

In spite of the danger, he loved the mountain and the glacier for its incredible beauty. He felt the same about it as Stav did about her ocean.

Fresh snow hid the brigands' tracks and made travel dangerous. It covered crevasses, and the unwary could easily blunder into one. Even so, he continued to let Stav lead, knowing it gave them a better chance at survival.

Thinking about the danger seemed to trigger disaster.

Stav vanished out of sight with a little yelp, followed by an ear-shattering scream lancing the night air.

He grabbed the rope, feeling rough hemp slice through his hands. The friction heated his gloves until they burned. The rope reached the end and his arms were nearly torn out of their sockets by the jolt. He clenched his jaw and dug his heels into the crunchy ice beneath the soft, new snow.

"Stav!" Her name was ripped out of his throat. "Can you hear me?"

No answer.

A chill froze his blood. He closed his eyes to the sensation. Terrible scenarios flashed in his head—the rope fracturing Stav's spine, her head striking the crevasse's wall.

Stav dead. The possibility left him empty and colder than the air around him, yet he refused to accept the prospect.

He edged to the icy rift, the rope dragging him forward.

"Stop!" Stav's voice echoed from below. "Duran, don't come any closer. The rope has slipped under my arms and is tilting me into the crevasse's side."

"I'll get you out." He relished the hot relief streaming through him. "Just hold on."

"To what?"

He almost laughed. Belligerence wasn't what he expected. His feet found little purchase in the slippery surface, but then quitting wasn't an option. His heart pounded, and he edged back from the dark hole that had swallowed Stav.

His gaze focused on the opening in the dim moonlight. "Maybe you shouldn't talk so much. Use your feet to keep away from the sides."

"If I get out of this alive, I'll have plenty to say."

He opened his mouth to protest, then just as quickly smiled. "I welcome the moment."

Her querulous tone told him she fought her fear with the same determination she'd used against the brigands all those weeks ago.

Suddenly, he couldn't go any further. Duran felt his biceps bulge with the strain. His hands were on fire, but he shoved the pain aside.

He drew in deep gulps of air—in through the nose, out through the mouth, expelling angry puffs of breath. Sweat dribbled down his back. His arms trembled from pulling, but the rope refused to budge. He rebuffed abandoning Stav.

"What's going on down there?" he called out.

"My snowshoes are stuck on something."

This couldn't be happening, he thought. Not now. He squeezed his eyes closed and knew he must remain strong if Stav had any hope.

"Can you reach them?" he asked.

The rope bounced in his hands, cutting deeper across his gloved palms. He pictured Stav trying to free the snowshoes.

"No."

"Try harder."

"You pull harder, human." Narud's growl rumbled in Duran's head. *"She cannot die. I will not allow it."*

He jerked, then froze. *"You will not allow it?"* he snapped back to his dragon self. *"If you haven't noticed I am the one trying to save her."*

"Do more. Stav cannot die."

"At least we agree on something." Straining with all his might, he dragged the rope up and looped it around his waist. *"Give me some of your dragon strength."*

"Why should I?" Narud demanded contemptuously.

"I don't have time to argue. You want her to live as much as I do."

"What will you trade?"

Duran swore Narud had balked before he uttered his ridiculous question. *"Your life, you arrogant fool. I won't stop trying to save Stav, but sooner or later my strength will fade."* He released a sigh as though to prove his point. *"If the change comes over me, in those precious seconds between man and dragon, I'll be pulled over the edge with her. It'll be too late for you, too. You won't be able to open your wings. Nor will dragonfire save you."*

"You lie! You think to trick me."

Under different circumstance, the uneasy edge in Narud's voice would have pleased him immensely. The dragon didn't want to die. Then again, neither did he.

"You're wasting time," Duran warned. *"Are you going to help or are you going to test me?"*

"This is extortion," Narud mindspoke irritably.

Duran tamped down his own anger. *"You don't have to like it. Just do as I say."*

"Indeed?"

Frantic anxiety had led him to use the bullying tactic. Honor remained Duran's only principle. No way would he allow Narud to live if he didn't aid in Stav's rescue.

"You shall pay for this," the dragon hissed. *"It is done."*

Duran's skin grew warm with a strange tingle, his shoulders rose, and his lungs filled with a deep breath of clear, cold air. The murk of impending doom lifted from his spirit. He felt stronger, alive. Invincible. Yelling with determination, he summoned strength from his core.

I am Narud. Narud is me.

Duran shook off the weird thought and began hauling up the rope. Wood snapping resounded from the crevasse. The snowshoes were breaking apart. He didn't stop. Inch by inch, he pulled Stav higher, letting the rope puddle at his feet.

One slim, gloved hand emerged, then another. His

relief soared. He grabbed her hand. The touch sent a curious emotion through him.

"You're almost there," he encouraged, thrilled to see the top of her gold bright head in the faint light. "Just a few more inches."

****

Marina latched onto Duran's proffered hand and scrambled out of the crevasse, thankful to be alive. She flung herself into her rescuer's arms.

Tall, strong, and handsome, he represented safety, security, and refuge. She clung to him for dear life, trembling, feeling the cold inside and out. She pressed her face against his solid chest and listened to his heart pound as hard and fast as hers.

Ages had passed since she awoke in Narud's cave. She had survived so much and then in a blink of an eye almost lost everything. The wistful yearnings swelling in her breast could not be denied. What she wouldn't give to marvel at the aqua walls of the great court again.

She shuddered, remembering the wide-open expanse of the ocean, the salt spray in the air, even the squabbling of gulls flying over her city. The instant her caravan entered Demit Woods, oppression had weighed down on her. The tall, grim-looking trees lining the narrow road allowed no shaft of sunlight to penetrate. Now, she added glaciers to the list of places she never wanted to visit again.

"Are you all right?" Duran asked, his voice a whisper. "How do you feel?"

The low rumble in his chest soothed her. She felt herself flush and then feared he would see the odd attraction expanding inside her. For some obscure reason, she knew if he saw, it would embarrass both of them.

"Extremely well," she said, wishing for a steaming cup of mulled wine to settle her nerves. "Considering I was just pulled out of a hole."

Duran's mouth twisted into a wry grin. "Lucky for us, it was a small one and you're safe. Narud helped."

"Did he? How?"

Duran stared at her, his expression neutral. "Remember when he lent you some of his strength. He gave me some, too." He glanced at the moon, which appeared angled much farther in the western sky. "Can you continue? I'll take the lead."

Her jaw dropped. "Not on your life! There's no way I could lift you out of one of those icy hells."

He shrugged his broad shoulders. "Just don't step on white snow. It hides deep crevasses."

"Everything is white!" she grumbled with a scowl, moving off.

Chuckles rippled behind her. "Just watch your step until we're off the glacier. We're nearly across. At the tree line, we can take a break."

The boom of ice and rock rumbled farther up the mountain. Marina shuddered and shot a glance at the steep incline. The glacier bid them a parting warning.

"Something to look forward to," she said. "After such a trying night."

"I know I'm pushing you hard, but I want to reach a tumble of boulders where a small cave exists before we stop for the night."

Marina swallowed back a groan. She trudged forward, studying the ground and burying her fear of plunging into another deep rift.

They hiked to the tree line without speaking. In a

small pocket of open ground, the smell of growing things, vegetation in wet earth, rot, and trees hit her quivering nostrils with the strength of a punch.

The promised break lasted far too short when Duran insisted they push onward. Too tired to waste breath protesting, she stood.

This time Duran took point, using his snowshoes to compress a path. Marina shadowed his every step. Fat, wet snowflakes began to fall. They caught on her lashes, and she blinked them away. She stifled a yawn with iron discipline. Great Kubala, she fought against being cold and tired and refused to show weakness.

"It won't be much longer, Stav. I know you must be exhausted."

Tears welled in her eyes. It was unsettling how he could read her mind like Narud. "Don't stop on my account."

"I'm tired, too."

They reached the boulders and scree, loose gravel sloughed off from decomposing granite a grueling hour later. Duran led her to a den the size of a wagon mottled with green lichen. Tucked against gray and white rocks embedded with flecks of shiny pyrite, it was large enough to offer them protection from the inclement weather.

Marina's muscles ached with the piercing cold of mountain air. Never in her life had she traveled so far on foot, for so long. Even blinking made her toes hurt. An exaggeration, yes, but it was close to the truth.

Duran took out his flint and steel to start a fire.

"Is it safe to cook?" she asked. "Those brigands might see or smell it."

He looked up at her and smiled. "The smoke will

dissipate as it leaves the cave, and the wind is blowing up the mountain."

Sharing a meal of boiled rabbit and hot tea from herbs Duran had foraged and then sitting before the cozy fire alleviated the worst of her aches and pains. Friction burns on Duran's hands looked red and hot, but he never complained so she would not either.

"Still worried?" he asked, cleaning the pot and plates.

She spotted a touch of red in his chin stubble. "Just a little."

Both man and dragon had saved her life. Protected her. Sometimes she found herself wanting to remain with both.

She owed them so much. Looking at the man, his brownish hair gleaming almost red in the firelight, she watched him unfasten the top of his heavy fleece coat. He revealed his tunic and a few curling hairs on his chest. As though he sensed her scrutiny, he turned his head to avoid her eyes.

She stared into the fire then, pieces of a strange puzzle falling into place—the cryptic hints Narud enjoyed dropping, the way Duran's eyes turned into slits, and the odd tingles she experienced as day turned into night and repeated again when night changed into day. The clues had been right under her nose all along, but she had failed to connect them.

"By Kubala, Glasto, Basilolis, and Yanna!" She invoked every deity known to Eudes in one sentence.

Duran and Narud.

Narud and Duran.

They were one and the same. Her heart pounded. Her pulse raced. Marina sat up straighter. How could she have been so blind?

It explained why Duran hid on the mountain and why her loyalty felt divided between the pair. In her heart, she thought of each as a friend.

"I know the truth!" she blurted out.

Duran spun toward her, his face dark. "Truth about what? I don't know what you are talking about."

She touched his arm. "You are Narud."

He jerked away and drew his heavy fleece coat tightly around his chest. "Me? A dragon? Don't be ridiculous."

"I just figured it out." No amount of denial would put her off. "Narud is Duran spelled backward. You can't deny it."

"So."

She saw his gaze study her face. "So, I can tell you're lying. The name is too much of a coincidence."

"It's none of your business."

Marina let his denial roll off her back. "I suppose never seeing the two of you together is another fluke. Ha! What I want to know is who came first? You or Narud? Rumor of a real, live dragon would have spread far and wide over the countryside, so it must be the man. Is that why you live on the mountain? You're afraid of being found out. I don't suppose you'd care to enlighten me." She threw the last bit in half-heartedly, hoping for, but never expecting him to agree.

A flicker of a smile came and went on his face. "All right, Stav, you deserve to know the truth." He acquiesced a great deal faster than she would have, and then he added a caveat that made her shiver. "Let me warn you, though, it's not a pretty tale."

Chapter Six

Duran stared off into the distance, letting the past scroll across his mind. A sense of relief filled him. The decision to tell Stav felt right.

"You've heard part of the tale already," he said, straightening. "From Narud, who told you true. An evil sorceress did create him. She…I…"

He stopped himself. How much to reveal? His gaze swept over Stav. "She created Narud by turning me into a dragon."

Stav's eyes widened in the firelight. "How monstrous! Who would do such a thing? And why? What crime merited such an unjust punishment?"

Duran clenched his teeth. "Crime? Dragon's Teeth, Stav! All I did was refuse to break my word and wed her." He picked up a pebble and tossed it outside where it skittered across the snow. "The spell happened so fast I couldn't stop her."

Stav patted him on the arm. "It's said when a man loves a woman, he is blind to the attributes of others."

He felt his heart rate increase. "Who said anything about love? I was promised to another, that's all. Duty compelled me to honor the commitment. I would have lost respect if I did not refuse Calandra. I can't change who and what kind of man I am."

"You didn't know what she would do." Stav's voice sounded dejected. "You couldn't read her thoughts."

It made sense. "I should have guessed. Calandra is spoiled. No is a word she does not enjoy hearing. She is accustomed to getting her way."

Stav didn't speak. He wondered if she believed his farfetched tale or thought him touched in the head.

"Not at the expense of others." Indignation burned in her voice. "That's wrong."

Exhaustion seeped into his bones. Duran was tired of living his dual existence. "Right or wrong, the deed was done. I can see her workroom and smell the dankness as though I'm standing right there."

Sighing, he continued. "That day, I remember seeing cobwebs glistening and shimmering high in the corners ready to entice and catch the unwary. I should have taken it as a warning and left without a backward glance."

"But you didn't." Her voice dropped to a whisper.

"No, I didn't. I thought my imagination was getting the better of me. I didn't want to hurt Calandra's feelings."

"Perfectly understandable."

He snorted. "She was fostered at the castle. I considered her a long-time friend."

Stav's hand touched his arm again. "Fostering occurs in Eudes, too. A rival lord gives up a middle child to prove loyalty. The ties are meant to last a lifetime."

Deep emotion tightened inside him. The heat of Stav's hand on his arm melted his objections.

"We forget sometimes an enemy stays an enemy," he ground out. "I looked Calandra in the eyes, full of hope, saw her flushed face. I thought if I let her down without crushing her tender feelings, it would be much better."

Stav's gaze locked with his. "Rejection is never easy, especially if a bond of affection existed between you."

She continually amazed him, remembering her defense of Narud. This time she offered an insight he never considered. He'd been focused on vengeance and hadn't given thought to anything else.

"A bond? No. Calandra professed her love, but I didn't love her. She was the sister my parents never gave me, and I told her so. That made her angrier. She went off on a tantrum, yelling, screaming, and telling me my bride would die. Her henchmen were on their way to kill her."

Stav gasped, fear flashing in her hazel eyes. "I lost my people the same way."

"At first I thought she jested." He hurried on with his explanation. "But she was serious. When I told her I would ride out to stop the destruction, she threatened me. That wasn't how she normally carried on. Wheedling was more her style. I should have been more perceptive or realized she would be upset and strike out in retaliation."

"It wasn't your fault, Duran." Stav's voice, soft with comfort and sympathy, pleased him. "You shouldn't blame yourself."

Stav had more compassion than the average person.

"I was headed for the door when she chanted her spell. I remember my body twisting and curling into a ball. I was trapped within the confines of a magical knot of energy. The pain made me dizzy. I couldn't think, much less fight back. I lost consciousness and woke in the mountain cave."

"Why would this…this Calandra be so cruel? She loved you. A person doesn't act like that if they love someone."

"Love had nothing to do with Calandra's conduct. She is evil. My refusal hindered her from attaining her goal."

Stav had no idea how lovely she looked with outrage turning her cheeks pinks. She looked beautiful. She made him feel emotions that he had no right.

"I'm not sure I agree with you." She smiled slightly. "If this sorceress is as powerful as you claim, she could have killed you outright. Yet, she didn't."

"That doesn't negate her betrayal," he growled. "She abused my family's hospitality, and no one has the right to murder or curse others."

"Did she give you no chance to break the spell?"

The prompting allowed a buried memory to inch forward. With the clarity, he cursed Narud! He wondered if the dragon kept it hidden from him on purpose. Calandra's full incantation began clear.

"After a year and a day," Duran said as if by rote, "your inner self will forever be. Fire and water will make the present become the past. Water spilled for love shall break the spell, or your inner self will remain free forevermore." He repeated the addendum to the curse without realizing it.

"Then there's hope." Stav smiled at him.

"Hope for what?"

"To solve the riddle. We can do it together."

Taken aback by her offer, his breath froze in his chest. "Does it make sense to you?"

"I am not very good at puzzles, but it's obvious fire and water are key."

Duran felt his lip curl into a sneer. "I cannot wait around and simply do nothing. I have to face Calandra."

Stav squared her shoulders. "If you were unable to stop her from changing you into a dragon, what can you do now?"

"Avenge myself is a start."

"What good will that do?"

Dragon's teeth! Stav came right to the point. He'd yet to figure out how to break Calandra's spell, but giving up was out of the question. He'd watched her practice long enough to know magic did not always behave in a straightforward manner. Sometimes it took a circuitous route. This might be one of those occasions.

He glanced up to see concern reflected on Stav's lovely face. "What choice do I have?" He drew in a slow breath and caught the faint scent of roses. "Calandra must pay. I cannot live like this any longer. Confronting her is the only answer."

****

Narud tucked his leathery wings against his side. He sniffed at Stav nestled in her bedroll, sound asleep. He'd been trapped within the shell of Duran's paltry human body until the sun chased away the night. He'd had to wait to personally make sure she was well.

Thick, long golden lashes fanned her cheeks above feathery scratches. Smoke curled from his nostrils at the sight. His tongue scraped over her bruised and cut knuckles.

Her eyes flew open, and she wiggled to a sitting position. "What are you doing?"

His tail twitched at her response. "*I do as I please. You nearly died last night. The world of humans is unsafe. Give the word, and I will fly you back to my cave.*"

Her slender body visibly relaxed, and the softening on her face made it clear that she would consider his offer. If not now, maybe later.

"I mean no offense, Narud, but I want to go home…to my own home."

He did not want to live a solitary life. Not being a natural-born dragon had drawbacks. Yet, never would he admit to fear or loneliness. Especially loneliness.

A part of him relished Stav's presence. There were moments he saw fragments of her life in Eudes. Stav with the royal family, an honored individual. Her laughing with two younger women who bore a slight resemblance to her, an older man and woman smiling at her.

Another part understood when he became whole and his human parasite was gone, Stav would become a shining reminder of his success. Especially when she accepted his offer of greatness.

"*I am patient.*" He spoke slowly, anticipating the day Stav comprehended how much she meant to him. "*It is a long way to Brenalin and even longer to Eudes. You may change your mind.*"

"I'll never stop missing my home, Narud." She dragged the top of her bedroll under her chin. "If you had family, you would understand the sadness and loneliness I feel. Do dragons even care about each other?"

"*I don't know.*"

Stav pointed an accusing finger at him. "You lied

to me."

Leaning forward, his shadow fell over her. *"I never spoke false to you."*

"You told me a sorceress turned you into a dragon, but you forgot to mention Duran and you are one and the same?"

His scales puffed out. This was his human side's fault. *"Omission is not a lie. It is practical necessity."*

"Omission is betrayal," she snapped back.

"He is human. I am dragon. We are not the same."

She rolled over to face the cave wall. "Maybe you're right," she said, her voice muffled. "You are not the same. Duran is an honorable man, and his life was stolen from him. He has been honest with me."

How dare she turn her back to him! He didn't need to see the smoke curling out of his nostrils; he felt it burn. The urge to spew dragonfire built, but then he controlled himself. It wouldn't do if he frightened Stav.

"You live under a false impression," he said coolly.

Slowly, she turned back to face him. "What?"

"Do not tempt me. The man omitted things from his tale of last night, too."

"How do you know?" she snapped. "Speak, so I can make up my own mind."

"How indeed."

A faint memory existed at the very edge of Narud's senses. Duran's family reached far back into the realm of history and once a male of that line found favor in the eyes of a dragoness. The child born of that union carried dragon blood. Which explained why the sorceress's spell worked as it had on Duran. His inner self was part dragon.

A breeze whistled up the side of the mountain. Narud craned his long neck to look outside at the blue-gray haze of sky. The sun crept over the far horizon. Each day lengthened to give him more time and less for Duran. He flicked out his tongue, tasting the warmth in the air. Today would be glorious.

He leaned over Stav, his hot breath caressing her face. Pleasure rippled through him when she reached up and began scratching behind his scales.

"Honesty cannot keep harm at bay," he said with forced neutrality. Her touch caught his breath. *"You nearly died in the crevasse. If not for me, you would have."*

"I know," she whispered back. "Duran told me you lent him the strength to pull me free."

Had he been human, he would have strained to catch her words. *"How do you expect to endure the perils of crossing the river, the wild beasts of Demit Woods, or evade the marauders hunting you?"* He sent her visual images of frothing rapids tumbling on and on, a skulking wolf whose long canines drooled at some unseen prey, and burly men coming at a run wielding swords and axes. *"You follow a treacherous path. The possibility for disaster is high. I would grieve if you were hurt or injured."*

She dropped her hand. "Why are you trying to scare me, Narud? I thought you were my friend."

The withdrawal of her touch left him at a loss. He would never let her go. *"I don't mean to frighten you."* The false statement meant nothing. He would never allow any harm to befall her. He needed to guide her to make the right decision. *"I would not take it kindly if you were hurt. Understand?"*

"Reminding me of the hazards is cruel. You are stressing the dangers of the trip, not life. I want to be with my people, live among them, share ideas with them."

"Humans lie, cheat, and steal. They war against each other. Most cannot be trusted. Why would you want to stay with them when you can remain with me?"

"Why do you want me as a companion if I belong to the same vile group?"

He flicked out his tongue. *"You please me."*

A crease formed on her brow. "How?"

"I find your company entertaining."

She wiped a strand of golden hair from her face. "Despite the pitfalls and heartaches of being human, the joys offset the risks. Duran and I wish to live among other people."

Narud doubted rebellion lay at the bottom of her persistence. The ring of melancholy sounded too sincere. *"We can share my gold and treasure,"* he offered. *"With me, you can wear rubies or diamonds or pearls any time you wish."*

She stared at him in astonishment. "Your treasure means too much to you. I could never accept your offer."

He stared at her, her gold-bright hair flowing about her shoulders. His admiration grew. *"You are a serving girl. I will treat you like a princess. I can find a wench to be your servant. Wouldn't you like that?"*

She shook her head. He grew tired of her obstinacy, and her stubbornness forced him to take action he would later regret. He recognized, amazed, that what he really desired was her willing cooperation.

"What if I promise to fly you home whenever you

wish?"

A gleam of interest widened her eyes. "You would do that?"

"Yes," he answered, savoring her expression, *"if you agree to stay with me."*

"Why make the offer now?"

"Because I can," he said softly.

Silence dragged. Icy cold filled his insides. He resisted the impulse to add more. He'd miscalculated her loyalty to other humans. He whipped his tail back and forth, making the ground shudder beneath its weight.

"That's no answer." Stav stared at him, her lips pinched together. "Since you cannot give me a satisfactory reason, I must decline your offer and continue my journey."

"Duran seeks the death of the sorceress. True?"

She watched his tail twitch. "I suspect so."

Narud let his massive muscles relax. *"The sorceress is my creator. If she dies before the spell reaches its conclusion, I could cease to exist. My dragon magic cannot protect me from such a fate. A life, no matter how it started, deserves a chance to continue its existence. I wish to live, too."*

"I'm sorry." The faint voice added to her sincerity. "I care for you, Narud, but I must help Duran. He has lost half his life and is in danger of losing everything. Please understand."

"This is not over. Where you go, I go, my brave beauty." He plucked off a ruby the size of a tomato from his decorated chest. *"Meanwhile, I must feed. You are safe here. A dragon need only rest in a place for it to be protected. Remain here. If you need me, hold the*

ruby and think of me. I shall hear your thoughts and come. Rest now."

He might have failed at convincing Stav to return with him, but a throaty laugh reverberated from Narud. He had given her something to ponder. Possibly doubt. And he dared to hope. It was all he could do.

Narud crouched, and then leapt, sweeping his wings down and fast, and launching his massive haunches into the air.

****

Marina napped during the day, too sore and tired to move. Never had she been pushed so hard. Lassitude invaded her body.

She had lived her whole life in luxury. No responsibilities. Little physical labor. Oh, she'd led an active life, interested in gaining knowledge many different ways. One of her fondest memories involved sailing with a fishing boat on the choppy waters beyond Eudes. She loved hearing the slap of waves against the hull.

Her twin sisters had showed a similar thirst for adventure. What fun they shared—Olla always eager and Woola half-hearted. They learned how to create the intricate knots fishermen used and even assisted in raking the great salt beds east of the city.

The memory of their adventures brought an intense case of homesickness. Marina nearly burst into tears. How she missed them and her parents. Would she ever see her family again?

Marina squeezed her eyes shut. *Was Narud right? Was omission not a lie?*

A sense of hypocritical guilt settled on her shoulders. She couldn't bring herself to confess her identity as Princess Marina Hersher.

The dragon's fractious temperament kept her silent. His actions were unpredictable and being apprehensive about his temper dictated she use caution.

Then there was Duran.

No question existed in her mind. He would look at her differently when he learned the truth. Regard her differently. She liked being treated as an equal. It hadn't happened often in her life. Her identity was clear to anyone with eyes, with guards or servants always accompanying her when she went out.

Her pathetic rationalizing didn't change her dishonesty with the dragon and the man. Remorse wrestled with her conscience while she clutched the ruby in her palm.

Eventually, she would have to reveal her identity. And then, she hoped her actions would be understood. And forgiven. They had to forgive her. They had to.

The sound of flapping wings drew her gaze upward. A vibration rumbled through the ground roused her to full alertness. She wiped a hand across her eyes and dragged herself to a sitting position when Narud ducked inside the cave.

This left Marina in a quandary. Duran and Narud's tale of metamorphism divided her loyalties. The attachment she felt for both went deep and was heartfelt.

Narud touched her arm with a claw, light and gentle as a feather. *"Glad to see you are fully awake."*

"I couldn't sleep anymore." She greeted him. "I'm pleased you're back."

"As am I."

A cloud of golden dragonflies hovered near the

cave's entrance. She watched the luminescent specks dart back and forth, but never venture inside. She shifted her gaze from them to the glowing coals in the fire so like the red slits of the dragon's eyes.

"I'm sorry this happened to you," she said in a hushed tone. "I wish there was something I could do to help."

"You know what I want."

She offered up the gemstone. "Here, this is yours."

He bent his long neck to lower his huge wedge-shaped head before her. *"Keep the ruby. Consider it a token of my promise of riches to you."*

Marina's heart broke. Narud harbored longings and desires the same as any human being. "I'll keep it safe for you," she promised. "Whenever you wish it back, merely ask."

Narud's vertical eyes brightened and he fluffed his scales. *"It belongs to you. Now and forever."*

If only she had something valuable to offer. "Thank you."

"You are a day's journey from a large settlement," Narud went on. *"It looks deserted. The chimneys go smokeless. No humans tramp the street. A mill stands still and quiet."*

A short hush followed during which Marina became extremely aware of the dragon's deep breathing and felt his warm breath fan her skin. "Maybe you frightened the people off."

"I flew high in the sky. No one saw me because they were gone. Stealth is advised when you to cross the bridge."

"A bridge!" Excitement seared through her.

"There's no call to shout."

"I'm not shouting. I'm surprised."

Flicking his tongue over the colorful gemstones on his chest, Narud groomed himself. *"A sturdy bridge crosses the river. The mill is on one side and buildings on the other."*

Marina gave him a sideways glance. "No one saw you?"

"Positive."

"Good. We can save much time crossing it."

"Fine, but not now. You are still tired from your ordeal. Rest now. I demand it. Sleep."

The mental command turned out to be impossible for her to disobey. She leaned against Narud's leathery side and into his warmth and protection. Her eyes grew heavy with sleep. She felt his tail curl around her tighter.

A chill woke Marina. How much time passed, she knew not. A bedroll covered her on the cave's floor. She had been dreaming of being ensconced within the cozy confines of the large feather bed in her old quarters at home.

Beyond the cave, a clear starry sky appeared. Footfalls alerted her to someone's approach. Worry never entered her mind. She had a pretty good idea who came.

A moment later Duran walked through the entrance. More of the strange, glimmering dragonflies joined those first ones she saw. They reminded her of huge, glowing mosquitoes, but their shape was impossible to see clearly. They appeared quite interested in Duran and Narud as though they possessed sentient reasoning. A most unusual behavior. In some ways they reminded her of the tale of Guardians of

Secrets, but she dismissed the thought as ridiculous.

"Narud spotted a settlement not far from here," she said, eager to pass along her good news. "Do you know of it?"

"Of course."

"Narud says there's a bridge we can cross."

"There are three settlements along the river." Duran shifted the way a man does when he has more to say, but seemed unsure how to begin. "They're lumber sites. None are permanent. People travel between them depending on which part of the woods is being harvested."

"You mean people just up and move away from their homes and businesses?" She shook her head in disbelief. "They leave everything? Do not the people of Brenalin have permanent settlements?"

"We are talking about the foresters." His gaze stayed level on hers, serious, sincere. "They have no other life. Demit Woods surrounds our land on three sides. The only place the forest does not grow is on the mountains. There are areas within the great woods where no living person has ventured. The areas we cultivate allow us to trade for goods Brenalin lacks. No other land provides wood in such vast quantities. Nor has any country, except Brenalin, done so for centuries. In turn, we value our trees and take care of them. Properly tended, the great forest will renew itself for eons."

Marina listened, trying not to feel the pull of his voice. "How do you know these things?"

He responded with a chuckle. "Brenalin is my home."

Marina tried to imagine living in a land with trees

so thick and dense the horizon became obscured. "Why didn't you mention this sooner?"

Duran raked his hair out of his eyes. "Look, I'm sorry. I forgot. I've had other things on my mind lately."

She spent a second wrestling with shame when a new wave of culpability washed over her. What business did she have putting this wonderful man on the spot?

None, when she kept secrets of her own.

"Forgive me," she said, adding a conciliatory edge to her tone. "It makes sense to have different customs than Eudes. We harvest a renewable product—salt from the great ocean."

Duran smiled at her. "You see, we are not so different after all. Are you ready to start again, Stav? We can munch on yesterday's rabbit on the trail. It's wide enough to walk side by side, and we can talk."

They stared at each other in the twilight. Her false name on his lips sliced right into her heart, a sharp reminder of her lie. All her guilt rushed forward and made her stumble, but Duran caught her, and his gentle hold kept her from falling.

Chapter Seven

Calandra bumped her hip against the sharp corner of the table in the center of her small workroom, the impact clinking containers and vials together. Her clumsiness stemmed from what she sensed about Duran.

On the move, he headed toward Brenalin with a will of a dozen men.

Her skin tingled. She felt him in her bones, almost smelled his scent when she took a deep breath. As creator of the spell, a one-way link existed between them that would continue until it ended.

Curse him! She wasn't ready. The man continued to surprise her in the most unpleasant ways. She had underestimated him.

A destructive hate boiled and swirled within him. The strong emotion overshadowed everything else. It obscured Duran's other emotions. He'd turned into a man on a mission. When he reappeared, she hoped to talk some sense into him.

And if she couldn't? Failure was not an option.

Squinting in the candlelight, she saw straw littering the floor, a place for vermin and insects to hide. Her slippered feet felt every jab from the sharp stalks. Shelves containing jars of herbs, powders, and noxious concoctions lined the walls.

She would not keep her workroom in this place.

When crowned queen, she would have free rein to do as she pleased, and she would require chambers befitting her new station.

Duran wasn't the only means of gaining the Ruby Throne's power. His father would do just as well. With trembling fingers, she reached for the container of black sage oil, which worked the opposite of curative green sage oil and destroyed memory and cognitive thinking, then powdered aluminum and dried cola leaves. The combination would put the king under her spell.

She had to be careful. Tricky potions required a deft hand to go unnoticed.

She had decided against magic, for the results were always immediate. She plucked a hair from her head and added it to the ingredients in the mortar and crushed everything into a fine powder.

As she worked, she murmured to herself.
Think not of Duran.
Think not of your son.
Think only of Calandra.
Think only of me.
For I am the one.

Realizing she chanted an incantation out of habit, she frowned, and then shrugged. A little magic couldn't hurt.

She licked the powder off her fingers, laughing with sudden joy. It tasted perfect.

She took heated water for the tea, poured it into a cup and stirred in the grayish powder until it dissolved. She trekked up the stairs from the castle's belly with the steaming drink as she reviewed the unfolding events in her mind with each step.

Her potion to unsettle Zell's stomach and make

food unappealing had worked to perfection. Maybe too perfectly. People noticed how much the king had shrunk in stature. They were beginning to gossip. They worried. Not even the oversized tunic he wore camouflaged his bony arms and chest.

Calandra slowed at the entrance of the great audience hall. She had no need to rush. This potion would work hot or cold.

She glanced around. Petitioners milled about wanting to air their requests before being sent away for the night. People turned in her direction. Several sycophants made no attempt to spare her from seeing their none-too-happy expressions. Others pretended to mold smiles on their faces. None meant anything to her. They were weak and wanting.

She started forward, and then the shock of seeing who conversed with the king slammed through her—Master Wizard Einer himself. She wondered what fabrications the inept fool put into Zell's head. He thought himself clever, creating that multi-colored cape that seemed to have a life of its own. Any novice could perform the trick. She vowed to eliminate him someday.

The king looked up and spying her, waved. Too late for retreat.

"Calandra, come closer," Zell said in his booming voice of old, his smile revealing affection she did not return.

She balanced the cup and saucer and took her time to walk to the raised dais. "You're looking better, Majesty," she lied.

Einer raised a bushy brow. "What have you got there?"

"A tea to relax our king." She would have sworn Zell's ashen complexion paled ever so slightly.

"Oh, my dear, you didn't have to do that," the king said in a gentle tone. "Your other worked wonders."

Einer smiled, then whispered in the king's ear before slipping out of the hall behind the Ruby Throne.

Relief swept over Calandra at the king's praise. She had worried for no reason.

She gave him her sweetest smile. "I care what happens to you, Your Majesty. Please, drink this while still warm. It's much more agreeable. I added a pinch of peppermint and brown cane bits. I know how you prefer your drinks sweetened."

He took a sip. "Hmmm, very good. Very good, indeed. You have my utmost gratitude."

"I try my best to please you." She turned to leave.

The king erupted into a fit of coughing. Attendants behind the throne rushed forward, but he waved them back.

"Calandra, please stay." He grabbed her by the arm. "Come, sit beside me while I enjoy your thoughtfulness and listen to these petitions. I have only a few more to hear."

She could have broken his hold but let him believe his grasp was stronger. "I would only be in the way, Majesty. I have no wish to intrude on you."

The massive ruby signet ring he wore on his index finger rolled on its side when he patted her hand. "Don't be silly. Having you near is pure joy."

She bowed her head and sat on a stool. She knew better than to claim the queen's chair.

The king motioned with two fingers at a nearby merchant by the cut of clothes. "Step forward, Jollo.

You've waited the longest. You wish to speak with me?"

Jollo eyed Calandra. "I seek no compensation for my loss," he began, apologetically, "but I hoped for a private audience, Your Majes—"

"Nonsense," the king interrupted. "Speak freely in front of Calandra. She and Dur..." Zell's voice trailed off.

"Be strong, Your Majesty," she said under her breath.

"Wise advice," he whispered back before returning his attention to Jollo. "Duran and Calandra were privy to all matters concerning Brenalin. I see no reason to change the practice now."

She patted his arm, keeping a proprietary hand on the king's arm. The simple potion worked better than any powerful spell could. Already the king was under her control.

Calandra sat impatiently, more bored than she'd ever been in her life. What did she care about a merchant's boon? Bitterness stung when she recalled the king's dismissal of her earlier advice regarding the populace of Brenalin. He had dared to preach the faults of the Demic lords.

Hearing the king's wavering voice, but not catching his words, she planted a false smile on her lips and nodded to the merchant as the man bowed and left after Zell announced his judgment on the case.

She knew Duran and his father believed Demic lords were squeezing them at the border, but they were wrong.

Only one lord did—her father.

Lord Genoy subjugated nearly all to his will in his

craving of additional land. Only a few Demic lords withstood him. Even those would surrender eventually. Her father's thirst for power drove him, and she totally supported his aim.

She'd told him of her plans to ask Duran to wed her. "It depends," was his response. "If uncooperative, magic would serve as a means to achieve your goal."

A clarion of horns blasted the air and shredded her reverie. Calandra shook her head when the last tinny note faded away and silence ruled. The occupants of the great hall rushed to the window to peer out in curiosity.

She glanced at the king. "Are you expecting visitors, Your Majesty?"

"None." He stood, wobbling on his feet. "Maybe they bring news of Duran."

She dredged up another smile. "Then let us see who comes."

She let him lead her toward the window. The crowd opened before them to give them an unobstructed view.

A procession moved like a colorful caterpillar of black and tan—Genoy colors. Great dun horses pulled shiny black wagons. The soldiers' horses were dun as well. Their uniforms were tan leggings, black tunics, and swords sheathed in tan leather scabbards.

A single pennant, inky black with a tan griffon, flapped in the breeze.

Calandra couldn't breathe. She shuddered and wrapped her arms about herself. Pallon Genoy had arrived, and he was early.

****

Calandra watched her father stride into the enormous audience hall as if he owned the room and all it sat upon. Confidence oozed from him, and it seemed as though he had stepped out of one of the enormous tapestries hanging on the walls.

In his mid-forties, younger than King Abbas by two full decades, his tall body was fit. He showed off his muscular arms by wearing a vest instead of a shirt. A wide leather overbelt was cinched tight at his waist, and he wore a plain, well-used sword on his left hip. A carved dagger with a jet handle rested on his right. His guards trailed behind him. No one would mistake him for an ambassador, and she knew that suited him just fine. He considered himself a warlord and liked to look every inch the part.

She met his gaze briefly, questioning.

"Your Highness," Pallon Genoy said with a slight bow of his head when he stopped before the Ruby Throne.

"Lord Genoy," King Abbas replied, a diplomatic smile on his lips. "How nice to see you. We were not expecting the pleasure of your company."

"Call me Pallon. After all, we've known each other for many years. I owe you much for fostering my beloved daughter over half the time."

Fighting a sickening roll in her stomach, Calandra nodded in slow motion. "Father."

"Calandra, my girl, is that any way to greet me?" His voice bore an undertone of criticism only a daughter would recognize. "We've been apart these many months. A loving daughter is missed most, you know."

She forced a smile and rose. Her slippers scuffed across the dais when she stepped down. She put her hands on her father's shoulders and leaned forward to give him a peck on his cheek.

"So nice to see you, Father," she murmured.

"What's this? I've ridden weeks to surprise you and you treat me like a stranger?" He grabbed her into a bear hug.

Calandra didn't have a chance to catch her breath. Her feet cleared the floor, and her eyes watered in pain. Her father squeezed hard. Fleeting displeasure showed on his face. He punished her in front of everyone and humiliated her on purpose.

"Don't be impertinent," he whispered in her ear. "I received no message from you about the prince. Why is that?"

She clenched her teeth together. "Complications arose, and I wanted to repair the damage before…"

"Spare me your excuses," he hissed. "I want results."

Air returned to her lungs when he released her. "I've missed you, Father. I have much to tell you."

"Good." He beamed at her. "I am eager to hear all after I speak with Zell."

In every respect, she acted the obedient daughter. She sat on the stool, waiting for her father to launch into a lengthy speech. She'd heard him work his oratory skills on people. This time, though, Calandra felt an oppressiveness press down on her shoulders. Frowning, she looked around for the cause of her troubling thoughts.

All she saw was her father and the king talking.

She dropped her gaze and let her thoughts turn back to Duran. What form would he use to make himself known to her? Dragon or man? Either way, the encounter should prove interesting.

****

Marina glanced at the nearby woods. She could already tell the difference in the climate. For the first time in ages, the night air smelled warm. The icy bite nipping at her nose and ears had disappeared. Runoff from melted snow gushed down the mountain while occasional snow circled the bases of a few wayward trees.

Favoring temperate weather, she was grateful not to have to endure the bitter cold. She came off the mountain and spotted the verdant new growth of ferns. She inhaled and smelled lush pines, definitive signs that spring was more than seasonal hope.

She and Duran walked side by side. An occasional stone from loose scree shifted underfoot. They'd seen no signs of men on the mountain. Not so much as a broken twig or overturned rock had been spotted. To her way of thinking, their absence was a good thing.

"What will you do when you find the sorceress?" The sharpness of her question startled her, but she trusted her instincts and Narud had aroused her curiosity.

"Kill her, of course," Duran replied. "I want blood. I want to kill her several times over."

She shuddered at the harshness of his response. "No, Duran." She touched his sleeve. "You can't. Think. How can you succeed against a powerful sorceress? She has her henchmen. Surely, they'll protect her."

He exhaled. "Calandra is overly confident. Her men won't be near. My father would question their presence."

Marina put her hands on his chest and felt the

beating of his heart. "You can't face her without being prepared."

"I will be ready by the time I arrive. I know the location of her quarters within the castle. She'll never expect me to return, and I can take care of her."

Marina swallowed a scream of frustration. Thank Kubala, he couldn't read her mind like Narud. "Duran, please, let me come with you when you face her."

Duran scanned the terrain. "No. It's too dangerous."

She rubbed her chin as she struggled to find the words that would make sense to him. "Listen to me. You have to use logic."

"I haven't felt very logical since this happened to me. Right now, my life isn't worth living."

Without taking her eyes from his, she took a deep breath. "You must remember this sorceress cast one spell with disastrous results. What if she casts another one?"

"She won't," he was quick to answer.

Too quickly, Marina thought. "Be rational, Duran. You can't just march up to her and kill her."

"Yes, I can."

What an impossible man. Why wouldn't he listen?

"Is that wise?" she demanded anew, hoping he would listen. "Do not let revenge consume you."

He eyed her, and his gaze held her prisoner. "If the situation were reversed, wouldn't you?"

Empathy resonated through her, then she shook off the emotion. "Logic is enhanced with a calmer mind. We should concentrate on unraveling the spell's riddle."

"Right now, I am too angry for logic."

"I've given it some thought, and fire is obviously you and Narud," she said, making sure she had his attention. "What I haven't figured out is the water. Mixing fire and water creates steam. Perhaps the spell is weakest at transformation. We could immerse you in steam, and then maybe you can choose your shape and make it permanent."

He dismissed her suggestion with a flick of his wrist. "The closest hot springs are northwest of us. It'd take weeks to reach them. I can't waste the time. My method is quicker. Once Calandra is dead, the spell will break. I have to believe that. It's my only hope."

"What wizard or sorceress would risk endangering themselves?" she asked, feeling unsure. "They would be vulnerable to all their victims."

"I don't agree."

Marina suddenly realized her fear went deeper than mere friendship. "Please, Duran, listen to me. Sometimes subterfuge works better than a frontal attack and is a lot less dangerous."

"I can't go on like this. I won't." His voice rose. "Every day that slips between my fingers is another day she wins."

A downed tree blocked the trail before them.

Marina spotted twinkling dragonflies high in the swaying evergreen boughs. Were they the same insects at the cave? It almost seemed as though they were sentient creatures. A ridiculous notion, yet she couldn't rid her mind of the suspicion.

Duran's gaze went where she looked, then glanced left and right as though weighing the merits of going around the deadfall. He took a step forward, and without so much as a by your leave, hoisted her over the downed giant.

"Thanks." She savored the heat that remained from his hands on her waist. "How many times have you been under a spell to know the sorceress's death will free you?"

He grunted. "I know what I'm doing."

"I wonder." From the corner of her eye, she saw him stiffen and frown, but she wasn't giving up. "Does Brenalin have a wizard? We could enlist him to fight magic with magic. A wizard's duty is to serve the kingdom. In Eudes, ours protects and serves the king."

"I doubt if he'd be of much aid."

"Why?"

"Wizard Einer is too old."

"Magical ability doesn't vanish with age. Maybe he just fell out of the habit of using his magic."

Duran smiled. "He did extinguish a forest fire with the snap of his fingers. They say the flames flickered and were snuffed as if air was suddenly denied them. Just like that, he saved Demit Woods."

"Maybe the wizard doesn't practice his art because people expect so little from him."

He stopped. "It can't be that simple."

With a burst of optimism, she pressed for an advantage. "Duran, hear me out. Your wizard obviously knows how to solve problems. He might be more skilled in breaking spells than creating them."

Duran's posture relaxed. "I appreciate your concern, Stav, but this is the path I've chosen."

"And if you're wrong?" She frowned. "Can you take the chance? At least consider what I've said."

The night waned, and they made good time for the balance of the trek. Marina didn't know how magic worked, but something told her killing Calandra would not free Duran. The realization sank her hopes. How could she make Duran realize the foolishness of his proposal?

He had saved her life, she told herself. He deserved her support, not disapproval.

An hour or so before dawn, they stopped to make camp near a grove of giant cedars. The aromatic trees had shed their needles for years, turning the ground into a spongy carpet. Wind swooshed across the treetops, not unlike the way wind lashed whitecaps on oceans waves. Marina dreaded being surrounded by the trees. The imposing woods frightened her, so she held the illusion of ocean and sky close to her heart to boost her courage.

Dragonflies danced and sparkled between the trees. They reminded her of silver fish skipping over the waves to avoid predators below.

Her spirits lifted thinking of the great ocean and its inhabitants. She put her fears aside, then gathered twigs while Duran dug a fire pit. She fetched fresh water from a creek glistening silver beneath the moon. Duran squatted before the fire. He sliced a piece of rabbit roasted the night before and handed it to her. She smiled with appreciation. They were both tired and hungry.

The flames crackled, popped, and provided warmth and light. She thought to study Duran while he wolfed down his food but found him watching her.

"What?" She saw something new in his eyes—desire. "What are you staring at?"

"You," he murmured. "You're very pretty."

A secret wish grew in Marina. Had Duran finally

noticed her as a woman? She had wondered if he ever would. The faint memory of his hands gliding over her injured body after the attack lingered in her mind.

Strong hands…gentle…

"Thank you." She offered up a smile. She'd dreamed of him looking at her. Dreamed of him touching her. Sweet dreams. "I think you're handsome, too; but I wager you've heard it many times."

"Not from you."

Her heart fluttered hard. "I could say it again."

Suddenly a twig snapped in the woods. Silence fell as if wild animals and human alike recognized the danger.

"Did you hear that?" She leapt to her feet and then peered into the darkness.

Another twig snapped, and a shadow moved among the trees.

****

"Quiet," Duran mouthed as he put his finger to his lips.

"But…"

His hand went for his sword. How he missed his weapon. "Ease away from the fire. We make easy targets in this light."

Duran didn't bother to check if Stav obeyed. She would. He cast around for a weapon of some kind. Bending, he snatched up a stout piece of firewood and hefted it like a club in his left hand. In his other hand, he grabbed a large stone. Stepping out of the circle of light, he aimed where he'd last heard the noise and threw the stone with all his might.

A cry of surprise erupted from the woods.

Duran's heart pounded in his chest. Animal?

Human? Male? Female? A wild animal, if attacked, ran away. No sound of twigs breaking or branches snapping in hasty retreat were heard.

That identified the unknown as human. Calandra's henchmen? He doubted that! They would have rushed forward in hopes of overpowering two lonely travelers. Who else could it be?

"Fear not, human," came a collection of voices in Duran's mind. *"We are with you."*

What magic was this? The voices sounded similar to Narud's, yet older and more powerful than the dragon's. Oddly, the image of diamonds, burning in a multitude of colors, materialized in his mind.

He dismissed his thoughts to bellow at the unseen foe. "If you don't want me to come in after you and beat you senseless, I suggest you step forward and show yourself."

The distinctive twang of an arrow hissed through the air and bit into the ground with a solid thwack at his feet.

He'd seen nothing.

"That could have been your heart, male," came a woman's voice from the woods. "Put your club down, and I'll come out."

The calmness of the speaker amazed him. "Step into the open first."

"She is not from around here. Make her come out of hiding." The strange voices in his head produced more pictures than words.

Duran felt Stav's rapid breath on his back. Glancing over his shoulder, he saw she gripped a short log. He couldn't help smiling, for she stood with him, ready to fight, a steadfast friend—someone he could trust to remain loyal. The realization brought the rise of a longing ache for her.

Whoever hid out there wasn't Duran's only problem. The changing time fast approached, and every fiber of his being screamed at an unimaginable pressure. His heart thudded. His mouth dried. The sensation of dragon talons clawing for release shredded his insides.

Little time existed for him to contemplate who—or what—belonged to the voices speaking with pictures.

He shoved this newest development aside when a ruggedly attractive woman stepped into the light with the careful grace of a woodsman. Before he could ponder the strangeness of seeing such movement in a woman, he took in the quiver full of arrows on her back, a sharp looking hatchet and water skins tucked into her waistband, and a knife strapped to her leg. Bulging travel pouches were slung over a shoulder.

"Who are you?" he demanded, noticing her long braid was out of the way, much as a man flips his cape over his shoulder to draw his sword in a hurry.

The woman eyed his weapon. "Luna's greeting. I am a fellow traveler. My name is Becca d'Firn of Froy."

"You journey in these woods without an escort?" Stav asked.

The newcomer swept her gaze over Stav with a curious glance. "I am a hunter and have been on a quest for nearly three turns of the moon."

Duran caught the fear in Stav's eyes, and empathy rose within him. She was having difficulty imagining someone impervious to the woods. The night was slipping away. He rubbed an itch on his nose, then grabbed his pack to forage among its contents.

"Where are you from?" he asked the newcomer.

"You call it the Wilds."

He halted, his gaze narrowing upon the woman. Could this Becca be one of the legendary warrior women who lived in the far Wilds? The arsenal she wore on her body certainly bespoke such a thing.

"I've heard about the Wilds," he said. "It's a place filled with strange creatures."

The warrior woman strutted closer to him. "Do I not look normal to you?"

A chuckle rumbled up his throat. "No one has come from there in living memory."

"Why is that?" Stav asked, staring wide-eyed at the woman.

The warrior woman unnocked her arrow to release the tension on her bowstring. Moving flipped her long braid over her shoulder to reveal yellow beads of various sizes and tattered feathers woven into the thick hair. Her lips pursed, a faint smile curling her mouth upward.

Duran looked between the two women and grunted as he continued to dig through his belongings. Dozens of tiny, glowing dragonflies appeared out of the darkness and hovered around his head, pestering him. What was the matter with these insects?

"Because the place is cursed," he said.

"Only for people who don't live there." The woman's voice sounded firm with determination. "I seek a powerful wizard. It's extremely important I find him."

"Who?" Duran could not prevent himself from asking.

Becca stood straighter. "Wizard Cress. He lives within a dragon circle in the great forest. These are the woods."

Duran glared at her. Narud rose, prickling his skin. A flash of red appeared, then disappeared. "I'm sorry, Becca. You've traveled a hazardous journey based on a falsehood."

"Why is that?"

He didn't bother to explain he believed her kind a myth until meeting her. "The wizard doesn't exist."

Becca shook her head and her braid swayed. "Your answer is unacceptable. He exists."

A twinge of empathy rose in him for her dedication. "The only dragon circle I know of is deep within the haunted region of Demit Woods. And even then, I cannot swear it is real. No one ventures inside that part of the great forest. No harvesting is done there; the area is left untouched, and for good reason…People who wander inside never return. I'm afraid someone has played a cruel trick on you." He went back to his pack and tossed out his extra tunic. He had to leave, fast.

"Rumors will not deter me. I must see for myself."

Stav leaned closer to him. "If you don't mind my asking, what are you looking for?"

"My hooks. They were in here last time I look—"

"You mean these?" Stav answered.

Duran glanced at the small box she held. "Yes." He snatched the box away and picked up the fishing pole he'd created from a long branch, then whispered to Stav, "I can't stay. The changing time is near. Get rid of her."

"Is she dangerous?"

"The women of the Wilds are a nation of female warriors, organized and governed entirely by women. They are trained in all weapons but are not considered cruel or cowardly. It is said, in battle, they carry their injured comrades away at the risk of their own lives. At worst, she may try to convince you to join her village. Keep alert, and you'll be fine."

"You're sure?"

"Nothing is guaranteed, Stav," he whispered when her mouth made a perfect O, a mouth he wished he could kiss.

Stav's gaze whirled from him to Becca and back to him. "Company would be nice."

"Promise me, Stav. I mean it." His whole body itched. A restless pulsing power radiated within him. "Narud is coming. I can't stop him. I don't know what he'll do."

Stav nodded, and relief flooded Duran. He could trust Stav. He stormed off toward the creek tumbling on its way to join Sparkler River. The sky turned pink. A misty red curtain fell around him.

He disappeared into the crack of dawn, but his hearing, half dragon, half man, caught Becca asking, "Where's he going?"

"Fishing," Stav was quick to say. "He likes to fish in the morning. Claims they bite better at that time."

Duran flinched. His thoughts were a jumble of confusion, worry, and fear. He hated leaving Stav to fend for herself.

He felt his lips curl back as Narud raged. The dragon in him was furious, demanding his freedom. His body burned. It felt as though the dragon tried to burn his way out. Duran fought a losing battle. Each day the creature gained more and more power. Sweat formed on his brow, and he started to tremble. His control slipped like water through fingers.

Just a little longer.

Chapter Eight

Marina watched Duran hurry away. The highlights in his hair had turned coppery bright, reminding her of Narud. When light hit his eyes just right, she swore his pupils took on a vertical slit like the dragon's, and the fine hair on her arms always tingled near dawn and dusk.

The sensation foretold the magical change.

Duran disappeared, and she cast her gaze about the campsite. He had spread out her bedroll near the fire. All seemed normal, and she hoped she wasn't deluding herself.

Something landed on the ground behind her with a thud.

Marina whirled around to see the warrior woman drop her pouches in a heap.

"Wait!" She held out her hands. "What are you doing?"

Becca sank down and spread her fingers before the fire to warm them. "Making myself comfortable. You have a ready fire. I plan to share it tonight."

"But…I mean…"

The warrior woman clutched at a moonstone amulet as though seeking comfort from the opalescent gemstone. "Do not people of your land share their fire with fellow travelers?"

A stab of guilt knifed through Marina. She felt the

wrongness of turning a person away from the warmth and protection of the fire, especially a woman. Not in these the forbidding woods.

"Hospitality is always offered to those deserving," she answered.

"Good! Then I'll stay. I ran into a band of men who thought to have sport with me."

Marina gasped.

The warrior woman laughed. "Their mistake," she said, her tone boastful. "I gave them a demonstration of a hunter's skills. They will think twice before they bother a lone woman again."

Silence fell between the women.

"My caravan was attacked, too," Marina said. "Can you describe your attackers?"

"They had the look of the homeless ones in my land."

Marina took a deep breath. "You are safe here."

"I am untroubled." Becca yawned, then raised her arms and stretched her tall, sinewy body. "Only tired. After I rest, I will continue my search for Wizard Cress. He's here somewhere."

Marina handed the remaining rabbit to her guest.

"My thanks," Becca said. "I haven't eaten much of late, good miss. Your generosity is valued, and I don't even know your name."

"I'm sorry. I forgot to introduce myself. I'm Stav from Eudes."

"Nice to meet you." The warrior woman grinned.

Marina liked the woman's open smile. It softened her sharp angles. "Three months is a long time to search for someone. How long do you intend to seek this wizard?"

"Until I find him."

The woman's words sank in. "Where will you look? You don't know where to start."

Becca chewed off a hunk of meat. Juices dribbled down her chin. "Yes, I do. Your husband said my search will take me to the haunted part of Demit Woods."

Hot embarrassment breezed like wind over Marina's skin. She felt her skin color. "What? Oh, Duran...he's not my husband. We met on the mountain."

A brow, slightly darker blonde than her hair, rose on the warrior woman's forehead. "I should have realized the fact since you wear no beads. Do you plan to take him as your mate?"

Marina's cheeks burned hotter. "Of course not!"

Slowly, cleverly, Becca began to smile. "May I?"

"You want to...to mate with Duran?" Marina stuttered, aghast.

Becca's laughter skipped through the trees. "He's handsome enough and has the proud bearing of a warrior. In my homeland, I am leader of the hunters and can have my pick of any man I wish. I've had this itch since stepping into your camp. It would be a great honor to return home with Wizard Cress and your companion's seed growing in my belly. We are a small village, and fresh bloodlines are always welcome."

Discussion of sexual partners was too much for Marina. The image of Duran, his arms and legs tangled with another woman, flashed through her mind. The idea of him making love to another woman sickened her. She prayed he wouldn't accept Becca's offer if or when the time came.

A sharp shake of her head got rid of the heart-breaking picture. "You'll have to ask him, not me."

"I will," Becca said in a matter-of-fact tone, and then she lazily stretched. "I could even become fond of him."

"Supposing you do find this wizard," Marina said, eager to get off the uncomfortable subject. "What do you need him for?"

"My people are dying." Becca's voice became flat, a thing filled with steel. "A plague is sweeping through Froy. It has come twice now, and each time kills the children and elderly. It must be stopped. Wizard Cress is renowned as a powerful wizard. He will destroy the plague. Or he can find a way to save my people."

The night sky faded fast, chased away by fuzzy, gray light from the east. A pale moon hung low in the changing sky. Marina's skin began to tingle. She assumed the mighty crimson dragon had risen from Duran's body.

Tendrils of mist rose from the river in the valley, giving life to abundant moss. It grew on rocks and trees alike, favoring neither one over the other.

Marina sensed more than heard something crush the underbrush not far away. A slight vibration rumbled through the ground. She closed her eyes and concentrated.

"Narud, stop! You cannot enter the camp."

****

"Narud, do you hear me?" came Stav's call. *"Answer, please."*

He heard the female human and paused. *"Elucidate."*

"Thank Kubala. A woman came to camp last night.

She's with me. She mustn't see you."

Stav's request didn't dampen Narud's good mood. He loved the sunrise. It gave him his freedom.

Huge muscles unused for hours stretched and became limber. His iridescent scales dried and shimmered with the flash of mica in the morning light. The gemstones on his chest glowed.

"What am I supposed to do?" he demanded in a rough voice.

"You'll think of something. Duran wants her to leave."

Interesting. Anything his human side wanted, he felt inclined to oppose. *"Does he now?"*

"Yes, but I wish for her to stay. I haven't spoken with another woman in ages. Please, give me some time to visit with her."

Narud felt his eyes smolder. He couldn't miss the opportunity to show Stav how magnanimous he was and antagonize Duran at the same time. Dwelling on how angry his human side would become, Narud exposed a toothy grin to no one. How could he refuse? Stav made the request.

A hawk soared, then dove on his prey. The sight reminded Narud he hadn't eaten in a while, two days at least. Hunger slowed his thought process, but he would rectify the situation shortly.

"Enjoy yourself, my pet. I will remain out of sight, but not out of your mind. You hold the ruby. Contact me through mindspeech if you need me."

"I will. I promise."

A sigh of relief laced Stav's words. Narud knew his yielding to her wishes had garnered him favor. Once he satisfied his stirring hunger, he would spend the day lazing around and guarding Stav, content to be near and make her happy.

He flapped his great wings and hurtled himself into the clear blue sky, careful to fly in the opposite direction of Stav's campsite. Miles swept away. In the valley below, leafy trees budded, their verdant limbs adding a rich color to the landscape.

He caught sight of a deer with a short white tail that flicked side to side grazing near the river, and to his delight, the animal froze in terror when his shadow passed over it.

Instantly, he tucked his wings to his sides and plummeted downward. His talons slammed through hide, tearing muscle and tendon, and entered the base of the deer's skull. Quick and painless, death came before the deer realized it. A good kill.

He consumed the raw venison in three bites.

A pool fed by snow runoff beckoned. He stepped into the frigid water and lifted his scales. Pure joy reverberated through him. Letting his scales stand on end allowed his sensitive skin underneath to release heat and cool him off.

Frogs chorused on the bank. Songbirds warbled in the trees. The sound was music to his ears. Bathing could become a favorite pastime. Only one thing could make the experience better—for Stav to join him.

"Ancient one, why do you bother with these humans?"

Narud jerked his head up. The voice, a multitude of pitches, had caught him unaware. His nostrils flared to catch the intruder's scent. He detected nothing unusual on the shifting currents.

"Who speaks?"

"You know us. Search your memories and remember. You spoke of us to the human female. We are the Guardians of Secrets."

"Impossible," he answered, irritated with the gleeful tone. *"Those noble creatures are long ago dead."*

"Then our ploy worked. Our intent was for humans to think they had destroyed all the dragons in the Great Dying."

"Show yourself."

"At the proper time, ancient one. We hide in plain sight. Only those we wish to see us, can. Meanwhile, be delighted to know that you are not alone. We remain close."

Narud swung his mighty head around. Why couldn't he see the Guardians? If memory served him correctly, they were the tiniest dragons with the ability to camouflage themselves, but still he should be able to sense them.

"Small is smart."

The whisper came with the haughty amusement only a dragon could issue, and Narud recognized their withdrawal. Then a familiar voice trespassed upon his bath.

"Fish."

This time he recognized his human half.

In no mood for pranks, he demanded, *"What trick is this? How did you create the other voice?"*

"What are you talking about? This is my first time contacting you today, and it is only to tell you to bring back fish for Stav and Becca. Stav told her I went fishing. If there are none, the warrior woman will become suspicious."

A fierce and reckless fury seized Narud. He was being tricked. No dragons survived the Great Dying. It had to be the cursed human. Somehow Duran found it amusing he would have to do his bidding to maintain the illusion.

For Stav's sake.

For his own.

Suddenly frustrated, Narud slapped his huge spade-shaped tail on the river's surface. The percussion rippled through the water. Stunned fish floated to the surface. He scooped a dozen or so between his teeth and carried them close to Stav's camp.

"Stav," he called through mindspeech, *"open your mind."*

Several heartbeats passed in silence. If any harm came to her…He dropped his burden and shambled forward, his talons crushing the pile of fish.

"I'm here, Narud. All is well."

Relief flooded his body, and a sound similar to a purr vibrated in his larynx. *"It is wrong for us to be parted. I miss your company."*

"Please, be patient."

The sincerity in her voice sounded legitimate, and he was strangely touched by it. *"What are you doing?"*

"Watching our guest. She sleeps soundly now. Though for a while, she tossed and turned with restlessness."

He visualized his lovely female human. Her smiling face, her delicate golden blonde brows arching. A servant with a will of her own, but he didn't mind the trait in Stav. No other human could compare to her beauty, inside or out.

"When will this other woman depart?"

"I have no idea."

"For once I agree with Duran. The woman must leave. I left you fish beyond the camp. They will give credence to the human's lie."

"Thank you, Narud. I knew I could count on you." She paused, and he sensed a struggle within her before she said, *"I feel obligated to tell you about Duran's intentions. He plans to kill the sorceress."*

Pleasure flowed through his veins. His good deed had paid off. For the first time, Stav placed his welfare before the human's. He was winning her over to his side.

"I suspected as much. Else why insist upon heading for Brenalin instead of your homeland?"

"You must aid him."

He didn't rise to her bait. *"Doubtful."*

"The sorceress is a danger to you, too!"

"How?" he asked, curious.

"She turned Duran into a dragon. The next spell could be against you."

"Magic doesn't work on dragons. We have our own, and are immune to puny, mortal magic. Calandra's spell awoke Duran's dragon blood when she cursed him to reveal his inner self."

"I can't let him face that vile woman alone. You have to help us. Is that too much to ask, to aid someone else for a change?"

Disappointment sank his hopes. He thought Stav had come to care more for him than Duran, but it seemed the attraction between his human half and Stav grew stronger, not weaker as he wished.

"Yes," he answered, and felt his fangs grate.

"Don't you care the tiniest bit?"

Her accusation appalled him. *"I care a great deal. One detail you seem to have overlooked is the sorceress gave me life. I am indebted to her."*

"At Duran's expense!"

Narud started hunting for a place to nest in the soft, fragrant woodlands. For the third time in as many minutes, he circled the same spot.

"Enough," he ordered, settling down. *"You want me to end my existence. You are the one being unreasonable. Now, enough of this subject. Find the fish. We do not want to arouse your companion's suspicion."*

"This discussion isn't over."

He hadn't meant to sound harsh, but she was such a willful human. Why couldn't she see his side? Narud fought to keep his fiery breath from frying the nearby woods to cinder. As the first dragon in thousands of years, he should be a creature to be revered, admired, even loved.

Somehow he wasn't impressing Stav.

He laid his head on the ground and closed his eyelids. He sensed the new human female tossing and turning as though besieged with nightmares. Pride swelled in him at recognizing her behavior. He had Stav to thank for enlightening him about this human weakness.

Hours slipped away. His gaze turned upward. The sun hung low in the sky. He hated the sunset. It meant the loss of awareness, a partial death, and put an end to his time with Stav.

Narud never once considered changing his mind. Duran did not deserve her as he did.

"Yes, I do," his human half answered as the day

came to a close and shadows fell over the land. *"I'll claim her as mine before I let the likes of you have her."*

****

Beams of moonlight pierced the clouds with dappled light. In spite of the nighttime beauty surrounding him, Duran shook off the effect of the changing time and brushed rust pine needles off his clothes. Hope faded fast that he would ever feel the sun's warmth on his body again.

Three and a half months had passed since Calandra cursed him, and he was no closer to finding a solution. He discovered beyond his frustration, beyond his fear, defeat loomed ever closer. Precious minutes of being alive were lost each day as spring lengthened.

Another thing bothered him. He walked through the woods, his brow puckering, feeling worry replaced by curiosity. He wasn't alone in hearing the strange voice. Narud had, too. They called themselves Guardians of Secrets. Duran had heard tales of them. Could the myths be true? They were the creatures of the past who kept the dragons' records. Why wouldn't they reveal themselves? What were they afraid of?

Stav sat before a small fire. Stepping quietly into the campsite, he dropped the string of fish and rabbits he'd caught and gave her a smile. He hated every moment away from her.

"I see you've been hunting." She grinned back. "I wondered what became of you."

"I thought it wise to replenish our supplies before we started out again. I'm proud of you, Stav."

"Why is that?"

"Your loyalty." He squatted beside her, then added

evergreen boughs to the flames to create thick smoke. "You came to Brenalin in service of your princess. You remained loyal, a characteristic I highly admire."

"You may wish to retract your praise."

His chest tightened. "Explain."

"I couldn't send Becca away." She turned her face away. "I wanted to speak with another woman."

"I know." His mouth curled into a smile. "Narud told me. You made a mistake is all."

She raised her chin, picking up two fish and laying them on the stones around the fire. "I asked Narud to stay away."

Duran froze in shock. That he didn't know. "He agreed?"

"Begrudgingly."

The tug of war between human and dragon was being won by Narud more often than not.

"It must have been an interesting conversation. Too bad I couldn't hear it."

Stav's gaze remained fixed on him. "I used reverse tactics on him. I told him you insisted she leave. I was pretty confident he'd do the opposite, and I was right. He even provided fish to support my fib."

Duran grinned, thrilled that Stav had beaten the creature at a game of wits. He busied himself cleaning and gutting the trout. As he worked, Stav informed him of Becca's encounter with the brigands. Listening, he clutched the knife so tight, his knuckles turned white. Calandra's henchmen! They didn't care who they hurt. He could hardly wait to put an end to her evil.

"Where is she now?" he asked as casually as possible.

"Scouting the area. She slept until noon but was

eager to break camp upon waking. I told her you were hunting, and we'd have to wait for your return." She eyed his stash. "It's a good thing you didn't make me out as a liar."

"Why didn't she leave? She's looking for a wizard. Why remain with us?"

"You should ask her," Stav said, her tone slightly odd. "Maybe she wants direction to this dragon circle."

Duran saw an odd flicker in her eyes as he stripped bark from narrow spruce branches he'd found. He felt his brows draw together in puzzlement, then pierced a cleaned trout with the branch and set it next to the fire.

He'd accompanied Stav too long not to recognize the subtleties of her lovely face, especially when she withheld something. It pained him to think she concealed another secret.

"I've told her all I know," he said. "What else does she want from me?"

Stav poked at the fire with a twig. "I suppose you'll have to ask her, if you're really curious."

"No need. We'll go our separate ways soon enough."

"Not quite true," came a voice from the wood's edge.

Startled, Duran pivoted, ready to fight. The warrior woman stood before him. Her ability to move through the woods without making a sound was downright disconcerting.

Becca stepped up to him and placed her fingers on his arm. "We think alike, we two," she said, brightening, holding up a brace of cleaned and gutted fish. "I searched but missed you. I did find where a large beast had bedded down. His tracks were of a size and kind never seen before. I followed them until they just disappeared."

The air crackled. By the look in her eyes, Duran suspected more than fishing drifted through her mind. What? He didn't have time to waste deciphering a woman's thoughts.

Instead, he raked his fingers through his hair and stepped away. "I went to check my traps. After Stav and I eat, we'll be on our way."

"You travel at night?" She twisted the beads in her solitary braid. "The Goddess Luna must guide you."

"I know nothing about that. We avoid many dangers of the road under the cover of darkness."

Becca cast a glance at Stav, then laid her fish next to his. "Grant me the privilege of traveling with you."

"We owe her our protection." Stav grasped his arm. "I'm sure the same brigands who attacked me threatened her."

For the briefest of seconds, he paused, but in that moment, her touch made the muscles between his shoulders contract with searing desire. How could he refuse her a single thing? He glanced around the waiting women, his gaze stopping on Becca. "I thought you were looking for Wizard Cress."

"I am. We are approaching the great forest. There are many miles before we go our separate ways."

He turned to face Stav and thought curiosity and despair mixed in her expression. Stay? Or go? He would gladly do whatever it took to make her happy.

"Stay with us then." He relented. "I know the best route. We leave in less than an hour."

He didn't get his wish. Late evening arrived when the trio finally set off. Woody ferns replaced young saplings as they entered the western side of the immense woods through a thicket. Rotting leaves and pinecones littered the ground, giving off the moldy scent of decay.

They stepped carefully for fear of twisting an ankle—or worse, breaking a leg—among the thickening maple, cottonwood, and poplar trees that fought for space among the conifers and evergreens. Squirrels and raccoons as well as dangerous wolves and bears filled the forest.

"Look!" Stav exclaimed, pointing to luminous flickers between the trees.

Becca glanced where Stav pointed. "Dragon lights."

"You mean dragonflies?" he corrected the warrior woman.

Her smile contradicted him. "We call them dragon lights in the Wilds. Ours are much smaller though."

"They aren't normally seen along well traveled paths," he said. "Many people believe them spirits and think they bring good luck."

Stav cast an admiring glance at the phosphorescent sparks. "We've seen them since we drew close to the woods."

"They are delightful," Becca added, giving Duran a smile.

"You've nothing to fear, Stav," he tried to comfort. "They're harmless insects."

"The dragonflies don't bother me. I was just hoping another route was available for us to take."

He heaved a sigh. Stav gave him the biggest, most delightful smile. He couldn't imagine life without her. "Are we having our first argument?"

"I wouldn't call it that, but I certainly could oblige you if we continue on this path."

Becca drew near. Duran chuckled under his breath. He loved Stav's difference from other women. Brave beyond comprehension in dangerous situations, she fretted over a simple thing like being in the woods.

They came across a narrow trail slowly widening into a road scored with deep wagon-wheel ruts.

"This is an old logging road," Duran explained. "It's not used much when the area is left to replenish itself. The great woods are divided into three parts. Slower growing hardwoods are planted in the north and south, and in the center, softer, faster-growing broadleaf trees."

In four strides, Becca stood in the middle of the road. "Let's use this. It'll make travel easier and faster."

Duran shook his head. "We'd be better off paralleling it. Safer, too. We risk exposure out in the open."

"A good point," she said.

His breath caught in his chest, and he scrunched his brows together when the warrior woman roughly elbowed Stav aside. No one mistreated Stav.

"No one," repeated Narud in his head. *"Let me destroy her."*

His muscles clenched to control his anger. "Rudeness does not become you," he said. "We are equal here."

A contrite look flashed on Becca's face. "No harm done. I wished to talk with you alone and merely took the opportunity."

For her part, Stav pretended as though she heard nothing. He watched her dig the toe of her boot into the soft loam. Duran suspected she knew what the warrior woman wanted.

"Talk about what?"

"You interest me," she said, her tone teasing. "Relax, Duran. You are from this land. I am a stranger. There is much you can teach me."

A dozen dragonflies hovered close, almost as though curious about their conversation. Duran noted their odd behavior, almost wishing he could study them, but the notion was out of the question.

He ran his hand through his hair. "Ask me anything, and I will try to answer honestly."

The warrior woman stepped closer. She fingered the yellow beads in her hair. "In my homeland, men give women beads to show their interest, but here I must make the first move. I don't want to talk. I would prefer a demonstration."

The hairs on his neck rose. "Of what?"

"Your love-making," she said matter-of-factly. "I am attracted to you and wish to bear your child."

Air rushed out of his nostrils in surprise. "Excuse me?"

"Mate with me." Becca's voice, while low, sounded sincere. "I wish you to father my child."

"Why me?"

Her smile warmed. "Do you see another male hereabouts?"

An air of intimacy floated around him. He squeezed his eyes shut tight in denial, unable to find a suitable reply.

"Is it so hard to imagine?" the warrior woman asked after a moment. "You are strong, a hunter, a warrior, a man whose courage will not fail, if tested. I would be proud to lie with you. A child of yours will have traits benefiting my village."

He couldn't believe it. Her words were laced with seriousness.

"You honor me."

A gleam lit her bright eyes when she edged closer to him. "I am the one pleased. Or rather, I will be if my assumption about you is correct."

His mind raced. He had to control his pulse.

At that moment, he saw Stav's expression crumble. She started to turn away as if to give him and Becca privacy. The sight broke his heart. It was too terrible, too painful. He could never hurt her intentionally.

"You misunderstand me, Becca. This isn't a good idea."

The woman's blue eyes widened. "Fret not over the child. Women of Froy can carry the seed in a dormant state. Our babe will be safe in my womb while I hunt for the wizard."

Gods help him! He groped for the right words. "What I am saying is that I can't accept."

A frown pulled down the corners of her mouth. "Should I bare my breasts to you? Some males set great value on seeing a woman's breasts before agreeing to mate with a hunter."

Dragons' teeth! "Do not take my refusal personally."

"The deed requires little time…" She paused, her expression brightening. "Unless you and I find favor with one another, then we can take as much time as we desire."

The conversation disintegrated, fast. "Surely, there is another man with the qualities you seek. I do not mean to wound you, but I am pledged to another, and until the matter is resolved, it would dishonor my betrothed's memory to bed you."

"Perhaps I could change your mind."

"I think not," he said with false calm. "We'd better keep moving."

They traveled in silence, their footfalls on the spongy forest reaching their ears alone. He feigned ignorance of how each woman watched him as the miles were devoured.

Rounding a bend, they skirted a ghostly tree stump split by lightning. Duran knew this part of the woods almost as well as the hairs on the back of his hand. He'd traveled over it numerous times to climb the mountain, though never at night.

Near dawn he called a halt. The sound of the Sparkler River rushing down the mountain roared just out of sight. He lowered himself to his belly and crawled to the edge of the overhang.

"We're here," he said softly.

Chapter Nine

Marina lay on her stomach, fascinated at the settlement slowly emerging from the darkness below. Never had she seen an eerier place in all her life—a village totally devoid of life, abandoned by the people who once lived and laughed in the buildings and huts. A white-water river thundered and divided a lumber mill from the town. The mill's enormous water wheel revolved from the power of the river.

A dust devil whirled and twisted across a wooden bridge connecting the mill to the village. Amazingly, nothing had fallen into disrepair.

"It's like the people just left," she whispered in awe.

"About a decade ago is more accurate," Duran told her. "Three wardens live here and make repairs as necessary."

"How do you know this?" she blurted, hoping he knew.

"Brenalins are a practical bunch in disposition. We accept the expediency of maintaining these places rather than letting them fall into disrepair and rebuilding every time the forest is ready for harvesting. It also gives travelers a comfortable place to spend the night in relative safety." His gaze searched the village. "You two remain here. I'll see if I can find one of the wardens."

Marina frowned. Duran seemed to possess a vast amount of knowledge concerning the activities of Brenalin. She'd dismissed her initial assumption of him being an outlaw, hermit, or shepherd long ago. So, who was he?

"I'll accompany you!" Becca announced, rising to her feet.

"No, stay with Stav."

Duran put his hand on Marina's arm. A rush of warmth swept over her skin, and she tried not to grin. He simply didn't know how his touch affected her.

"She's unaccustomed to being on her own," he continued. "Something's not right. Though it's early, smoke should be coming from at least one chimney and is not."

His calming touch made Marina want him to stay with her forever. The selfish thought made her heart skip a beat. A future together didn't exist, but that didn't stop her from enjoying the moment. His turning down Becca's unusual offer might have bearing on her feelings of delight.

"I'm afraid Duran has it right about me." She inclined her head and played along. "These woods are very frightening. I would be deeply indebted if you remained with me."

The warrior woman huffed and nodded at Duran. "Keep alert then and return safe."

His features softened with a quick grin. "The two of you should try and rest. If I am not back, cross under the cover of darkness. It's nearly dawn, and I'm going to check farther afield."

Becca wrinkled her nose in disgust. "And lose a whole day?"

"Better vigilant than sorry. I'll have your promise to remain here until the day passes."

From the corner of her eye, Marina saw Becca weigh his words before nodding in agreement.

"One person can move about unseen better than three," the warrior woman answered with an enticing smile. "I say go—leave before I change my mind and accompany you."

Brenalins might be practical, Marina thought, but the woman from the Wilds was persistent. More than caution prompted Duran's need to leave. In less than an hour, dawn would make an appearance in all its glory and Duran would turn into Narud. The last thing in the world she wanted was for the dragon to appear and cause an altercation with Becca.

"Be careful." Marina's fingers brushed Duran's arm. She thought he shuddered. "We've shared too much for me to retrain another traveling companion." Though she spoke in jest, in truth, she ached to feel his touch again.

Duran set off. Marina's heart pounded when his long strides carried him through ferns with the new growth of green fronds and into the wall of trees standing as stern sentinels guarding the road. She couldn't believe anyone would willingly enter such a place. An ocean of trepidation swelled up within her, and she gasped in wonder at its intensity. Could it be because she was surrounded by the trees? Or something else?

Becca pushed her long braid back from her shoulder, then scooped dry twigs off the ground. "We might as well make ourselves comfortable during our wait. Let's have a fire to heat water for tea. I brought some borage leaves from home. Nothing will lift our spirits more after a hard journey."

"I'll fetch water," Marina offered.

She returned to kindling crackling and popping from a small fire burning bright and hot. She handed the partially filled bucket to Becca, who poured the contents into a cooking pot.

"What makes this Wizard Cress so special?" Marina asked without trying to appear overly curious. "Does your village not have its own magician? And why send you in search of him?"

Becca watched the pot. "So many questions, but I will try to answer them. Though not in the same order asked. First off, I am the Chosen One of my village." The water boiled. She crumbled dried leaves into it, stirring. "It was my duty."

"Chosen One? I don't understand."

"Our village is ruled by a council of thirteen wise women. Whenever a task arises, we pray to the Goddess Luna for guidance on who is best suited to fulfill the task, but I volunteered and the Council agreed."

The sincerity in the warrior woman's voice prickled the backs of Marina's eyes. She had faced more dangers in the last few weeks in her life to understand one didn't go against destiny. "You did a brave thing."

"I did what I must."

Marina fingered the ruby in her pocket. She felt the gemstone warm beneath her touch, and she gave it a little squeeze. More than a precious jewel, the gift represented friendship, which she would treasure forever.

Narud came into existence at Duran's expense.

If only both man and dragon could exist…

Water splashing pulled Marina from her thoughts. A cup pressed into her hand.

"Becca." Marina spoke the warrior woman's name. "In your travels, have you ever heard of fire and water mixing?"

"How they could?" She blew on her tea. "Why do you ask?"

Marina decided truth was best. "I'm trying to help a friend solve a riddle."

"Duran?"

She nodded.

Becca's lips pursed. "I passed a place where it seemed fire and water mixed together and the underworld bubbled up." She spoke as though reviewing the scene in her head. "Cauldrons of mud gurgled, and roaring geysers sent steaming plumes skyward. It was like the two elements waged a war with one another."

Marina listened intently while steam, smelling slightly of cucumber, wafted from her cup. "They are opposite elements. Enough water will quench fire."

"An inferno will evaporate water." The warrior woman added the other half to the enigma. "Mixing them will cause the destruction of the other. Your riddle sounds unsolvable."

Marina took a deep swallow of tea. It tasted delicious and very uplifting, but Becca's response left a bitter residual in her mouth. "I fear you may be right, but I can't accept your answer. I won't."

"I assume you have a reason for asking."

Marina squinted in the glare of morning sunshine.

She didn't care what Becca thought of her. "Secrecy is necessary. I hope you understand."

One of Becca's shoulders rose and fell. "In the wrong hands, magic can be ill-used."

"A truer statement has never been spoken."

****

A dead pig alongside the road was a sure sign of trouble.

Dragon's teeth, Duran cursed. He discarded stealth and barreled over the bridge. His footfalls clattered on the wooden boards. He hoped no unwanted people were about to hear his thunderous approach.

Only a pig, but he feared far worse lay ahead. The wardens would never stand a chance against the armed band that attacked Stav's caravan and Becca.

Running from building to building, he charged through smashed doors. Interiors lay in shambles. Overturned furniture and broken pottery shards littered the floors. His thoughts turned to Calandra. He would strangle each and every one of her men with his bare hands.

He searched all the buildings, his curses growing louder.

With full daylight nearly upon him, Duran found no sign of the wardens. Could they have run away? He almost hoped they had fled. Yet, deep inside, he knew Brenalin character and doubted any would act the coward.

"Surrender, human, your time is up," Narud ordered in his mind. *"My ability grows daily. Give in now. Save yourself the grief. You can never win."*

Duran, as much as he hated to admit it, was tempted to agree. Some of what the dragon spoke was factual. Only, he wasn't ready to quit! Not yet. Not until he sucked the last breath from of his lungs.

"You don't know much about humans, do you?" He cocked his head. *"I will never stop trying to beat you."*

"You lack the strength to break the sorceress's spell. Weeks have passed, and you are no closer to solving the riddle. Once you are gone, Stav will teach me what I require in knowledge of your worthless kind."

"She won't stay with you," Duran shot back, determined to undermine the arrogant beast's self-confidence.

"Really? Are you so sure?"

He wasn't, but he refused to give Narud the satisfaction of an answer. He squared his shoulders. Even trapped, he vowed Stav would have her freedom.

Dragon laughter broke the silence. It echoed through his mind even as the change forced conscious thought into its dark prison and his vision turned red. The mist of change surrounded him, and he crumpled to the ground.

"Noooo!" He cursed with all his might, his effort useless.

Control slipped from his grasp, and Narud took over.

****

Marina sat cross-legged on the ground and sipped the dregs of her tea. She mulled over Becca's remark. The woman distrusted magic, yet searched for a powerful wizard.

Maybe she had misunderstood the warrior woman. The last few days had been exhausting. Dare she press for clarification?

"I want the warrior woman gone." Narud intruded into her mind. *"Make her leave."*

"Please, leave me alone. I'm tired. I need to sleep."

A growl preceded the dragon's answer. *"What about me?"*

Marina freed a heartfelt sigh. *"What about you? You are perfectly capable of taking care of yourself."*

"I wish to see you."

She crossed her arms and then peered into the woods, half-expecting the scarlet-colored dragon to waddle into view, knocking trees over in his haste. *"You can't! Not now. Your appearance would create a very big problem."*

"What am I to do with myself, then?"

"Go hunting. You are fond of doing that a lot."

"I am not hungry. Suggest something else."

Marina wondered if he tested her. He liked to play games for the sport of it. *"Tell me what you are capable of doing. As you are so fond of reminding me, I know very little about dragons, and most of my knowledge is flawed."*

"True. How about if I enlighten you with more dragon history?"

"What about Becca?"

"Look at the female. I sent her a command to sleep."

A quick check of the warrior woman showed her curled on her side, fast asleep.

Marina grinned. *"Very well. At least pick an interesting tale."*

"An easy task. Dragons are the ancient symbol of

knowledge and power in your human mythology. Once we existed all over this world. In swamps and bogs, mountains and deserts, oceans and seas, each area had its own dragon, for that was the way of things in those ago times.

"Listen to my voice and I promise you will not be disappointed. I will tell you of our first queen, a great white dragon who lived in the far north. Her power stone was clear selenite, a crystal sometimes called satin spar, that brought light into her thoughts and guided her in passing down fair judgments. Selena took her name from her gemstone. She ruled over snow and ice in perfect solitude."

Marina yawned though not from boredom. Narud's voice enfolded her. The deep, rich sound went through every fiber of her being, drawing her in, intoxicating her with his words.

"If she lived alone, who did she rule?"

"All dragons. We created a great society that endured in peace and harmony for thousands of years. Some of your kind were highly trainable and lived among us to learn our ways."

Her jaw dropped, then she laughed. *"Oh, Narud, in Eudes fishermen are renowned for inventing wild yarns, but I think you top the best of them."*

"You demean all of dragonkind."

Marina wished she could see him. *"Forgive me. My intent was not to insult or wound you. I hold you in the highest regard."*

"Apology accepted." He continued, seemingly content.

"What happened to her?"

"Who?"

149

"Queen Selena.

"She lived hundreds of years and birthed many wyrmlings. When her time on this world came to an end, she ascended to the heavens and now resides among the stars with others of our kind. Look to the north. You'll see a blue-white light. That is her inner fire shining down on the land."

Marina felt so strange. They were linked. Narud's words stroked her insides. Delicate strings touched her heart, limbs, and soul in a way she couldn't explain. She felt him draw a breath into his huge lungs and adjust his massive bulk into a comfortable position.

She started to climb into her bedroll.

"Stop, my brave beauty!" Narud ordered. *"A cold bed is never conducive to a good rest. Let me warm it for you."*

"You can't approach the camp. Becca might waken."

"She won't, but I don't need to be near to perform this service. Stand back a bit."

Marina tucked her hair behind her ears and stepped aside. A narrow stream of ultra-heated air flowed out of the forest to chase away the early morning chill.

"Done," said Narud. *"Retire now and sleep."*

She slid inside the toasty warm bedroll. Her eyelids grew heavy. *"This feels wonderful, Narud. You have my gratitude. Maybe I was hasty to criticize you."*

"Naturally." His tone rippled in jest. *"I could have told you that."*

She stifled a yawn. *"Tell me more about dragons."*

"With pleasure." Once again, the velvet essence of his voice caressed her mind. *"Did you know dragons returned to the great ocean? You call them*

merpeople…"

Her gaze lost focus, her eyelids grew heavy, and sleep took her. When she woke, the fire had turned to gray ash and night was about to fall.

The warrior woman tossed and turned. She moaned, obviously caught in nightmare. The sound had woken Marina.

"Becca," she half called, half whispered.

The dark blonde leapt up, fully alert, her bow nocked with an arrow ready to fire.

"Sorry," Marina said. "I didn't mean to startle you. You were having a bad dream."

The warrior woman's stance relaxed. "It is nothing to concern yourself about. I am accustomed to them." She looked around. "Duran has not returned. We will cross now."

Marina rolled her bedding. Becca passed her a chunk of dried trout wrapped in moss.

Her stomach grumbled as she took the food. "Thanks."

"His trail leads this way." The warrior woman studied the terrain. "We'll follow his tracks."

A narrow game trail, littered with a mix of long pine needles and fallen leaves, led through the shadowy woods. The last rays of the sun penetrated to the forest's floor. The wavering light reminded Marina of the dance of kelp, though not half as beautiful.

A slight breeze made young saplings sway and creak. Within minutes, they made their way onto the road. Becca held her bow level, an arrow nocked into place while Marina carried the travel pouches.

They scuttled across the bridge, keeping close to the railing. The smells of the village were thin and impossible to identify. Gone were acrid smoke and sweat and manure, as well as the musky drift of people crowded together conspicuously absent. They passed abandoned buildings, small huts, and a stable.

Becca lost Duran's tracks part way through the village.

Marina strained her ears, listening for any sound.

They eyed the structures as if expecting someone, anyone to step out. Not even Duran appeared.

Near the edge of the village, Marina spotted the corpse of an elderly man face down and half covered with boards as though someone hid his body in haste. Sadness stabbed at her, and the loss brought a moan to her lips. Duran spoke of three wardens. If the body she saw proved to be one, she hoped the other two were safe.

Becca pressed her finger to her mouth as they made their way forward.

They found two more bodies.

"The wardens," Marina said. "Why didn't Duran find them? We'd better bury them."

A frown darkened the warrior woman's lean face. "No time. Let's find Duran first. The men who did this could be near. They could have him. He could need our help."

Marina didn't know how, but she knew Duran was safe. Somehow a bond connected them. "He doesn't. Whoever committed this atrocity is long gone. Look at these bodies. They've been dead for days. We should bury them."

Becca glared at her. "Sweet Luna, if we find him hurt…or worse, you'll answer to me."

"I'll bury them myself, if you won't help."

Becca seemed to think for a moment, then nodded. "Shovels should in the stable. Stay out of sight while I fetch them. I'll be right back."

Marina pursed her lips. She'd endured much since leaving home and had become stronger in mind and body. No longer an adventurous child, she was a woman.

To prove her ability to contribute, she slipped her arms under the smallest man and tugged. Determined, she pulled with the same concentration fishermen used hauling in their nets full of a day's catch. The body moved an inch, then another and another.

"What are you doing?"

Marina jerked upright to see Becca. "I'm moving them into the forest. The ground is softer to dig if we don't run into many roots."

Her heart pounded in her ears as she realized what she had just said. Go into the forest? Had she volunteered the outrageous suggestion? Could she really have overcome her fear of the huge trees that crowded out the light? Had she changed so much?

Her family would have laughed if they knew. Not out of maliciousness, but because they would have thought it humorous. Everyone knew she abhorred confined spaces.

As a child she'd accidentally been locked in a wardrobe. Servants and family searched the castle for hours, only to find her curled into a ball, fat tears streaking her face.

"Becca." She shook herself out of the memory. "We can't leave them for wild animals to devour."

The woman stood, glowering at her. A gust ruffled the hem of her woolen cape. "I will do as you bid, but know this, good miss. I see much. You do not fool me. Neither you nor the male."

Chapter Ten

"I've been honest with you, Becca," Marina said, determined to brazen it out with the warrior woman. "Nor do you know me well enough to accuse me of being false."

"I'll not quibble. It saddens me to speak so, for I consider you someone worthy of being a friend; but you are not what you seem. I speak true. Then again, neither of you are what you seem."

For precious seconds, butterflies fluttered in Marina's stomach. Real guilt lay its heavy weight on her. "What if I say you're wrong?"

"You claim to be a servant, yet your palms are as soft as a newborn's downy bottom. You have the bearing of someone accustomed to others doing for you. Take whenever we stop—you never build a fire or make any attempt to cook."

The vise of a trap squeezed Marina. "You don't know what you are saying. I help."

"I do not say you don't pull your share." A wide grin brightened Becca's face. "You fetch water and firewood without complaint. But you possess no skills a maid would learn at her mother's knee."

"I was companion to Princess Hersher. Others performed those chores. I was never trained to do them."

"You lie poorly, too."

Marina clamped her mouth shut and clasped her hands behind her back. What other slips had she made?

What of Duran?

He had traveled with her far longer than Becca and noticed none of the things the warrior woman mentioned. If she owed anyone the truth, she did him.

Then she remembered Becca had said "neither of you." What did the warrior woman mean?

"What of Duran? Why is he not what he seems?"

For a scant second, Becca's blue eyes darkened. "He doesn't possess the reticent nature of a shepherd or a lone traveler. That first night, he went for a sword. Only one trained in weapons does so out of habit."

"Many men wear swords for protection."

The warrior woman fingered the chipped yellow beads woven into her long braid. "Where is his?"

Marina shrugged, mystified. "I suppose he has lost it."

Becca fixed Marina with an intent look. "There's his habit of appearing only at night. The great goddess Luna gifted females with night-sight, which is why we hunt at night. Our males do not enjoy the same gift. Where does he go? What does he fear us seeing in the light of day?"

Loyalty swelled within Marina. She pressed her lips together. Duran's secret would be safe with her. Her eyes held Becca's, proud, stubborn.

"I can't say, Becca. I honestly can't."

"Enough said. Allegiance should be respected. I suspect Duran would remain tight-lipped about you as well." Becca looked around. "I wonder what's keeping him."

Marina's mouth lifted in a smile, belying the worry

rattling her insides. Becca had one thing right. Duran was late. He should have returned by now.

****

Calandra knew perception ran the world. The gullible always believed it reality. Take when she joined the king in his audience hall. Most Brenalins disliked her, but they perceived her as a grateful foster daughter, waiting upon their sickly king, wishing him only well.

Their view couldn't be further from the truth.

Today she intended to spend time with her father. Pallon Genoy sat in the only padded chair in her chamber. He watched her from under furrowed brows, one leg crossed over the other, his freckled fingers steepled together. Not a good sign.

"Come closer, my girl," he said in a tone that made the softly uttered request an order.

Her feet moved by themselves. His perverse nature delighted in punishing for the slightest infraction. Let him believe he held power over her. He did in some small measure, but not for long. She kept her gaze aimed at the floor.

Taking hold and lifting her hand, he gently squeezed. "What news do you have for me, daughter?"

"None I can speak of freely."

He barked out a hoarse laugh, his grip tighter. "Oh, really? What have you done?"

Her heart beat faster. "Nothing, Father, I swear."

He squeezed harder. "You forget, Calandra, I know you. Lies drip from your lips as sweetly as honey."

"Do you really doubt my word?" Worry sharpened her tone. "Shall I fabricate something senseless just to please you?"

His lips thinned. "You are my only child, my heir. I am displeased that you hid something from me."

"Father," she pleaded, when the bones in her hand felt like they were being crushed. "Please, let me explain."

In a flash, a toothy grin gleamed on his mouth. "I do not mean to be cross with you. It's just that I depend upon you, and to learn you failed greatly disappoints me."

Calandra could well imagine her punishment. "I meant to protect Duran."

He released her hand with a shove. "You should worry about your own neck."

Fear shot through her as she absorbed her father's words. He didn't speak lightly. "Oh, believe me, I am."

"Then tell me all."

She inhaled a deep, ragged breath, letting words spill out of her mouth. She told him of the attack ordered on the princess's caravan, how Duran rejected her, the humiliation burning inside her and how in anger she'd struck back at the prince, and her surprise when Duran took the form of a dragon.

She revealed everything except the Ruby Throne's secret.

She watched her father under lowered lashes for signs of displeasure. The muscles in his arms flexed when he tightened his fist. His agitation grew. He could be volatile. It wasn't easy to stand and watch while he judged how her actions might ruin his plans, but she remained still.

At long last he looked at her, his moss green eyes cold. "Choose your next words with care," he warned. "Can you control the dragon through your magic, my dear child?"

She wasn't fooled by his endearment. "I am unsure. There is always a chance I might not be—"

"Might not!" His voice exploded. "Surely you can concoct a guess. What good is creating a dragon if you cannot control it? What possible use is he to me?"

"I—" She wrinkled her brow with effort of thought.

A sudden, sharp pain broke her concentration.

Her father had grabbed the tender skin on the inside of her arm and twisted it in a hard pinch. "At least tell me you can destroy him."

Her eyes watered from the stinging pain. Occasionally, she hated her father; yet at the same time, envied his focus.

"I doubt a dragon can stand against my all-powerful magic." She whimpered. "He will serve us for the rest of his days."

Her father arched a brow. "Be sure, daughter. I don't need to tell you failure will displease me. More to the point, your position depends upon my approval. I want no mistakes."

"I live to serve, Father."

He paused to consider her words. "Very good." His voice was softer. "Make sure matters go according to my plan. You know what I want."

She forced a smile, facing him, maintaining eye contact. "As you wish, Father. I shall not disappoint you."

"You better hope not!"

The threat wasn't lost on Calandra. Tiny beads of moisture popped out on her brow. "I should have sought your counsel, but it happened so fast. I—I never thought he would refuse me."

"I have always had concerns about your interest in Duran. The infatuation surprised me." He spoke in a neutral tone. "Remember, Abbas is the enemy, mine as well as yours."

Calandra squeezed her eyes closed. "I had hoped to gain control of Brenalin by winning Duran's heart. I never meant for it to be permanent, even though…"

Her father swiveled toward her, his eyes flashing. "Even though what?"

"No spell can be cast open-ended." She debated how much to reveal. How long would her father listen? "It is a three-pronged riddle. It must have a beginning, middle, and an end to work. I was upset when I cast it; therefore, the atmosphere was off—a mistake on my part."

Her father steepled his fingers again. Thank the gods enough distance separated them for him to grab her.

"How will you make it right?"

"I must wait for Duran to return. He will once he realizes the futility of his situation. Complex spells require proximity to reverse them."

Determination and icy resolve lit her father's gaze. "Fret not, Calandra. We shall triumph. Your magic has opened up a realm of possibilities. Use it carefully." He stood and walked to her to cup her face in his strong hands. "Focus on making sure future spells work to our benefit."

"That has always been my intent, Father."

He did not move. "As you've said, magic is unpredictable. Duran is proving uncooperative. Yet, I cannot blame him. No man would feel gratitude toward the practitioner who used magic against him. I certainly would not."

She caught his gaze, knowing she trod a dangerous path. "I know Duran. Magic has always fascinated him. I'm sure once he overcomes the shock of becoming a creature of myth, he'll be delighted in the experience and forgive me."

Her father stood abruptly. "Actually, Calandra, I doubt that. If Duran is enjoying being a dragon, why did he attack your men waylaying the princess's caravan?"

"I don't know. He disapproved of certain parts of my plan. He spouted on and on about honor and integrity, shouting at me he would protect the princess."

"Many men were lost. My men."

"Men's lives are the necessary cost for success."

Disapproval flashed in her father's eyes at having his own words thrown back at him. "No more mistakes." He glared at her. "I'll leave another squad to add to those you lost. Trust Commander Marrow. He knows his job. Tell him to instill fear, mistrust, even panic among the people of Brenalin. When the king calls for calm, his voice will be drowned out."

His gaze went around her bedchamber. He missed nothing—from the feather bed decorated with silken coverings to the tallow candles made from a dozen renderings of pig fat throughout the room. She watched his fingers stroke the smooth wood on the arm of the chair where he'd sat. She knew, and so did he. This room was filled with furnishings far richer than those gracing her bedchamber at Kale Castle. A far bleaker existence awaited her if he forced her to return.

"If you fail, your fostering ends."

"Yes, Father. I understand." *I won't go back. Never.*

Unless her traitorous actions against Brenalin were discovered. Then the choice would be ripped from her hands. She faced imprisonment. Torture. Death. Whatever punishment King Abbas fancied.

Her father tapped a finger to his mouth. "Your cunning plan will be for naught if Abbas's wizard figures out your involvement. What then, my girl?"

The change in subject suited her just fine. "The old fool knows nothing."

"Are you sure?" he asked, coldness in his tone. "Age can make a man cunning."

Calandra let the tension flow out of her shoulder blades. She trusted her knowledge of sorcery and judgment. "Magic requires intent, focus, and the ability to channel energy. Wizard Einer requests my assistance performing the simplest spells. His powers are fading."

"Is that a fact?" His tone held a tinge of disbelief. "He could be testing your level of expertise."

Cold dread shot through Calandra. The possibility never entered her mind. "I swear no one is aware of my participation in the prince's absence, least of all Einer or the king." She spoke with confidence. "You saw the king. His condition deteriorates daily. He depends on me. I remind him of happier times when his son was home."

"You make a fine distraction." His dark brows pulled together, his gaze piercing her. "But I urge you to use caution and remember those in power want to keep us downtrodden. Years of plotting and planning, years of living off someone else's gratitude will be worthless if you do not remain at Abbas's side."

"Yes, Father. I understand."

He smiled, his expression softening. "Calandra, I may not have sanctioned your actions, but we can make the best of them."

She couldn't believe her ears. He gave his blessings. Next time she might not be so fortunate. She tapped down the compulsion to shout with joy.

"We will succeed, Father. I know we will." She smiled. "How goes it with you? The invasion preparations?"

"My army waits at the border. They'll move as soon as I give the word. War will come."

"How much time before Brenalin is ours?"

He took her hands within his and squeezed gently. "Soon. First, though, I wish for you to try another tack. Since Duran is gone, wed the king."

A smile formed on her lips. "Oh, Father, how clever."

She'd had the same thought, but let him believe he spawned the idea. Perception made all the difference.

****

Narud moved into Stav's mind, soft and easy. The warrior woman remained with her. They were burying dead humans. He could rip the ground for her with his powerful claws to make the task easier. All she need do was make the request. But she would not, if only to keep his presence a secret.

For a human female, she demonstrated an unusually stubborn streak. While he admired that streak, he tried to deny how many times it interfered with his wishes.

Fortunately, time sided with him. The lengthening season had added two hours of daylight to his existence.

He loved everything about being a dragon—the freedom, the superiority, his treasure. Soon Duran would be gone. He would not have to share his life with his human side.

If only Stav would focus her attention solely on him.

Why did she constantly assist the weak human? Dwelling upon the thought made his scales lift, bristling. Narud wanted to roar his irritation to the world.

What else could he do to change her attitude? He'd given her space, taught her about dragons, and restrained belittling Duran, all with little effect on her opinion of him.

Then again, she was human herself. A beautiful, intriguing, human female. Her appeal stroked him on a level he didn't understand.

If only she were like him—draconic.

A blinding idea hit him.

What if he turned Stav?

The memory of a dragoness who fell in love with a mortal man—an Abbas, of all people—nagged him. She transformed her lover into a dragon and they lived happily ever after.

Narud's expression froze for a moment with his long, sharp fangs exposed. It wasn't fair! He was alone in the world, the last of his kind—feared, despised, and loved by no one.

Stav could join him as a dragoness. He imagined her as an extravagantly beautiful one, shimmering golden, with a tuft of spiky scales from nose to tail. They could soar the skies together, terrorize humans, and search for treasure.

His fantasy over, he touched her mind a second time. Exhaustion trickled from her. He dribbled a pinch of his strength into her. It was too little for her to sense, but enough to ease the tiredness consuming her.

Sighing, he heaved his huge body into the air with the flap of his wings. He glided on warm updrafts hitting the mountain side. Far off, along Brenalin's border, vast plumes of wood smoke curled into the air. Intuitively, he knew no town or village existed near the great forest in that location. It wasn't a forest fire. He tilted a wing toward the smoke.

Then a strange, more powerful inclination called to his heart—a ruby gemstone. The great jewel in the Ruby Throne. He owed allegiance to it. Pulled by an ancient summons and guided by ley-lines, he dismissed his original course.

The rubies set in his chest responded to the summons as well, pulsing in a rich, bright scarlet.

Within a short time, he dipped his head and gazed downward, attempting to see the town he knew existed below. He tucked his wings against his body and swooped lower. The clouds obscured him as he looked upon the rooftops of Brenalin.

Gold and jewels were hidden in cubbyholes, under straw mattresses, and buried near buildings by the humans. There never was too much treasure, he thought, when longings rushed over him like heat, the desire overwhelming his mind. Each sweet, glittering coin and gemstone sang to him to come and collect them.

Lower still, he followed temptation until a voice halted him.

"Narud," Stav called to him in mindspeech,

"where are you?"

"Here, my brave beauty," he answered, and with a strength of will he never knew he possessed, turned away from the hunger within him. He forfeited the pleasure of gathering prizes. Not all treasure was found in gold or gemstones. A far richer one with a soft rose scent called to him. *"What can I do for you?"*

****

Marina felt bone-weary. She used her last ounce of strength to dig a hole large enough and deep enough to bury the three wardens' bodies. She tossed the last shovel full of dirt onto the grave mounds. Fatigue washed over her. Her hands were no longer soft. Tender blisters dotted both palms like stepping-stones across a creek.

So tired, she thought, trudging back to the lumber village.

"You called me."

Marina blinked at the word pictures from Narud appearing in her mind. *"I did? I'm sorry to have disturbed you."*

"Liar."

A sudden flood of warmth welled up inside her. A thing so tangible, it felt as though Narud wrapped her in the coils of his tail. She vowed his tongue caressed her arm, leaving a moist trace tingling her skin. Oh, yes. This was far more than granting her a modicum of his strength.

It felt…carnal.

The wonderful feeling so astonished Marina, she realized it would be easy to remain with Narud.

"Then do," he said, reading her mind.

His words struck her with the force of a rogue

wave, sweeping her out to sea. She must have mulled the idea over in her head on some subliminal level.

"You shouldn't have done that." She tried to decide which bothered her more—the sexual intrusion or the mind reading.

"All I did was bring comfort to a friend," Narud clarified. *"There was a need, and I took action. You would prefer to suffer when it's within my power to soothe you?"*

"You should have asked first. You had no right."

"Why call me, then?"

She kept walking. *"Because I wondered where you were."*

"A lie." The dragon's voice sounded amused.

Her experience with men was minimal. She had been courted and kissed sufficiently to recognize the strange new emotions and sensations surging within her. *"I demand you stop whatever you are doing at once."*

"Or what?"

"You will be found out. Becca has eyes like a hawk. She will notice the difference and investigate. What then?"

"Does your concern mean you care about me...just a little?"

Marina would have sworn satisfaction emanated from him in volumes. The old tomes certainly had one thing correct! Nothing worse than an arrogant dragon.

She sank to the ground at the first building and stretched out her aching legs. She'd walked for miles, then dug for hours. She'd been so positive she would toughen up after a few days, but sadly her expectations fell short.

Lifting her gaze up to the clear sky, she saw it turn the gray of dusk. A pale moon hung low in the horizon, a poignant reminder of Duran. Night would be here soon and with it—Duran.

"Forget about him," Narud demanded, suddenly. *"Why dwell on him? What can he do for you? Nothing. Only I—"*

"Stav!"

It took a moment for her to recognize her name. Becca's worried voice sliced through Narud's tirade.

"Stav, are you all right?" She stared quizzically at Marina.

"I'm fine. Why do—"

"You wouldn't respond."

For a moment, Marina stared at the warrior woman. "Guess I fell asleep."

"No sleep like I've ever seen." Becca spoke mildly. "Your eyes were open, yet blank."

Marina shifted uneasily. "Sorry if I frightened you."

"Amusing, but not the point." Becca propped the shovel against the nearest hut. She adjusted her bow and quiver of arrows on her shoulder. The weapons were always close at hand. Pulling out two small parcels of fish wrapped in brown leaves, she handed one to Marina. "I was worried about you."

Marina accepted the food with a nod of thanks.

"Hey there!" Duran called out a greeting, appearing between buildings. "When did you cross the bridge?"

Marina looked up, realizing the ache in her heart disappeared. She had missed him. "At dusk. We grew worried when you didn't return."

He revealed a dry smile and proceeded toward them. "Let's go inside and use the accommodations."

"We can't break in," she said.

Duran walked over and then leaned on a door. The hinges creaked open. "Don't be silly. I'm a Brenalin, which gives me the right to use the facilities, and you're with me. Come on. We can cook a decent meal in a real hearth and sit at a table."

A hot meal instead of cold fish. Marina tucked her food parcel into a pocket and hurried after him. She noted his hair appeared dark red over his heavy cloak. He grabbed a skillet with one hand and nudged her toward an overturned trestle table and chairs with the other.

"Becca," he said, "would you mind fetching some water?"

"With pleasure."

"I'll do it, if you prefer," Marina offered, belatedly recognizing she'd done exactly as Becca had pointed out.

Laughter erupted from the warrior woman. "No, thanks, I'm glad to oblige. I spotted a winter garden near the stables. Maybe there'll be some vegetables left."

Duran knocked flint and steel together to ignite tinder he'd placed in a pyramid of kindling. "You'd better hurry. I'm starving."

Marina collected a broom and began sweeping. Dust motes clogged the air. Coughing, she performed her tasks as quickly as possible, then sank onto a chair to pull off her boots. She washed her feet, remembering her mother once told her webs should grow between her toes for the numbers of times she got them wet. Those were the days of innocence.

Her whole body ached, yet childish delight tickled her and she couldn't stop—she giggled.

Duran glanced over his shoulder. "What brought that about?"

"I'm so happy." Her answer came low, wistful. "It feels good to be warm, dry, and have my shoes off. I love going barefoot. I never thought to feel this carefree again."

Her happiness became infectious, and he smiled.

"I know what you mean. Sometimes little things make all the difference."

"Do you really plan to refuse Becca's offer?"

Duran added a stout piece of wood to the fire. "You're changing the subject, Stav. Moreover, that's between her and me."

"You're not intrigued?"

He frowned and gestured with a stick. "Call me cautious, but women who freely offer their favors make me leery."

A breath froze in her throat. "You're thinking of Calandra, aren't you?"

"Let's say I prefer my women to let me do the asking."

Marina broke his gaze to scoop trenchers off the floor. She wiped them clean and set them on the table along with the cups she'd found earlier.

"I'll see if I can find some bread," she volunteered.

Two solid cakes of unleavened bread were in a box perforated with holes on its sides in the first cupboard.

Becca returned with vegetables foraged from the garden. The fire heated the room toasty warm, a treat for the weary travelers. They sat around a table instead of squatting on the ground. All three acted like they supped at a palace with royalty.

Dinner over, the warrior woman stood and stretched. "Nothing is better than a fine meal with good friends. A fitting conclusion, I'd say."

Marina watched the muscles in Duran's arm tighten. In slow motion, his jaw twitched with a tic she'd never seen before.

"Conclusion to what?" he asked.

Marina munched on a raw carrot, showing none of the curiosity consuming her. For a man who professed no interest in Becca, his reaction seemed far stronger than it should be. Could his earlier protest have been feigned?

Becca stared into the flames. "I must bid you farewell. The Wizard Cress awaits. If you ever venture into the Wilds, seek me out in the village of Froy."

"Must you leave?" Marina asked.

The warrior woman nodded. "I scouted ahead, and the road diverges away from the forest beyond this settlement. Your path follows the road. Mine goes inward. It has been a privilege to travel with you, and I wish you luck in your quest."

"If you do not find your wizard," Duran said, "you will always be welcome in Brenalin."

"And in Eudes," Marina added.

Becca gazed at them with her bright blue eyes, a sly smile on her mouth. "My thanks. And now, unless Duran has changed his mind, I take my leave and do what must be done."

He shook his head.

"Goodbye, Becca," Marina said. "Kubala protect you and good luck."

The warrior woman leaned over and gave her a rib-cracking hug. "Luna protect you, Stav. A braver woman I have not met."

Duran stood and clasped Becca's forearm. She held his in the same manner. They gave each other several hard shakes.

"Stay alert," he said. "Tracks lead from the village for a ways. One set went off alone. The rest head for Brenalin, but with brigands, one never knows. They could backtrack."

"Fear naught. I'll be vigilant."

Dappled moonlight cast an eerie glow over the landscape. Marina and Duran stood together in the doorway and watched Becca disappear into the woods.

"Duran," Marina asked once they returned inside, "do you think…Well, do you think she'll be all right? Maybe she should have waited until morning."

"She's been traveling many weeks on her own. I'm sure she'll be fine."

With a sigh, Marina sat on the cot Duran righted earlier.

He settled himself down beside her and swept her feet into his lap. Her protest died on her lips. His hands were warm, and he started massaging the bottom of her feet. As a commoner, he committed a total breach of etiquette to touch a noblewoman, yet the caress of his fingers felt amazingly good.

"What are you doing? You can't do…" Her body throbbed at his touch. "I thought you wanted to keep going."

He placed a finger on her lips. "I've driven you hard the last few days. A night of rest will do us good."

His breath caressed her skin, sweet and warm.

"I've been catching sleep during the day."

"As have I while trapped within the cursed dragon's body," he murmured against her soles.

His fingers stroked the base of each toe. Heat bubbled up inside her. Her heart pumped wildly. The sensation was like no other. She lost herself in it.

"Is it truly so hard to share your existence with Narud?" Both dragon and man had become terribly important to her. "I wish the two of you could reach an agreement with each other."

Duran's head snapped up. His blue eyes glared at her with fire in them. "You don't know him. The concept of honor is meaningless to him. A time will come when you must choose one and forsake the other."

"I can't do that. I'll help you as much as I can, but I could never do anything to hurt Narud. Please. I can't choose between the two of you."

"Sooner or later you will have to."

"If you'd only show a little tolerance toward each other." She felt her heart break. "You will be together for the rest of your lives."

"Wrong deduction. Only one of us will survive." He kissed the tip of each of her toes, making them warm and tingly.

"Maybe you should explain," she said, torn about what she might hear, about what she felt.

"What is there to say? I want my life back." His strong hands intermittently massaged the soles of her feet.

"That will never happen." Narud's mindspeech came through loud and clear. *"In less than three seasons, I will no longer suffer the human. I will be free*

of him."

"What do you mean?" Marina sent the message to both.

"Get out of our heads, Narud," Duran hissed.

The look on Duran's face cut through her with a sharpness that matched the bitter lines set around his mouth. "Let him answer. We might learn something."

"He can't infringe on my time."

"Can't I? Who will stop me?" Narud tossed out the questions contemptuously. *"Certainly not you, human. The months are passing rapidly. You will not solve the riddle."*

Marina blinked hard and fast. No wonder despair consumed Duran. He was constantly reminded of his dilemma. The rift between man and dragon grew wider with each passing day.

She sat up and put her hand on Duran's arm to comfort him. His muscles tightened beneath the contact, but she kept her hand where she placed it. A sudden wave of compassion overtook her. She doubted the dichotomy within him could ever be conquered.

Narud's wants and desires were the same as hers, the same as Duran's. Marina wanted to cry at the hopeless of the situation. Both deserved to live their lives and be happy. The situation seemed impossible.

How could a man fight an enemy who lurked within him?

Chapter Eleven

Marina listened to the bilious hiss, so reminiscent of Narud, when Duran inhaled through his teeth. Could he read her mind like the dragon?

No, even if he could, Duran wouldn't. He was the noblest man she'd ever known. If only she could offer him comfort and erase the misery contorting his handsome face. It wasn't fair. He looked utterly defeated; no one deserved to suffer as he did.

Empathy swelled, misting her emotions. She leaned forward to kiss him. The instant their mouths touched, the kiss changed from one of comfort to something totally unexpected. His warm mouth burned against hers. Warm rivulets of sensations deepened inside her.

He twined his arms around her waist and drew her onto his lap. She felt him harden beneath her.

A hot rush tore across her lips from the wispy brush of his mouth. She'd never known a kiss could make her feel safe and passionate. He traced a seductive path down her neck and arm. His touch was suggestive and delicately vexing.

She couldn't have been more shocked. Or more thrilled.

Duran's hold tightened when she shifted her position. Her body pulsed with a primeval need. To find a man like him, so kind, so willing to listen to her advice, and treat her as an equal with respect wrought changes in her that she never anticipated. Was it wrong not to give herself to him?

Shaking, she almost believed they could share a future.

Then common sense won out.

Even if Duran defeated the sorceress, she was a princess. This moment of intimacy was an illusion. A fantasy. A terrible lapse in judgment.

"For—forgive me." Marina spoke from her heart, her voice choking. "This isn't the time or place. We…I shouldn't have kissed you."

His brow arched dramatically. "I thoroughly enjoyed it."

She turned away, tears filling her eyes and her heart shattering in a thousand pieces. "You don't really know me. You don't understand. I—I…"

He wiped the moisture off with the wide pad of his thumb. "Hush there, Stav," he said with tenderness. "We've only known each other a short time, but I know you are my friend, and I'm glad you kissed me. It was the nicest, sweetest one I've ever received. I know you did it to make me see reason."

She caught his wrist, eager to touch him as much as latch onto his rationale. "Yes. Yes. You do understand."

"Narud infuriates me most of the time. He makes me see red until I can't think straight, much less anything else."

She edged off his lap. "Then you see what he's doing?"

"Maybe. Why don't you tell me?"

"Actually, Duran, you should have figured this out long ago." She stared at him to assure herself he intended to listen. "Narud intentionally keeps you off balance. He wants you to focus on the wrong thing. And he's succeeding. You direct your anger at him or the sorceress. You are not focusing on the most important thing—solving the curse."

The fire sputtered, casting shadows against the walls. A piece of wood popped. Marina glanced at the sound, then back to Duran.

"You have a wild imagination," he said. "But, one thing is right—I've been a fool. I should have seen it myself. Thank you, Stav. He'll not trick me again."

"I merely pointed out the obvious."

Duran grimaced. "You did more than that. My insight would have come too late. Sleep now. It's best if we're not exhausted when we reach Brenalin. A day of rest will be good for both of us. Success is near. I can feel it."

Her heart pounded. "Here I thought you'd forgotten how to hope." She smiled.

"It's a recent development." He bowed his head, clearly amused. "A welcome change."

Marina took several breaths. She liked this change. "Well, I, for one, am glad to see it."

Should she confess her duplicity? Beg his forgiveness for her lie? Then she visualized his reaction, his anger, and his hurt to her confession. No, she had turned into a coward.

An undeniable one.

If he turned away from her in disgust, the loss would be unbearable. His friendship meant too much. He was the first, and only person to accept her as an individual, as a woman. His kiss proved that.

For some reason, she thought of her family, but

who did Duran have? Who cared for him? She knew of no one except her. He would be alone in the world. Alone with Narud. The dragon would consume him and delight in doing so.

Floorboards creaked when Duran walked to a cupboard. She watched him pick up the blankets she'd folded. He took two, passing her the majority. Sinking into a chair, he hunched over the table, tightening the blankets around his shoulders.

"Good night, princess."

Marina bolted upright. He had her full attention. "Why'd you call me that?"

"It's an expression." He peered at her. "I was bidding you good night."

"Good night to you, too, Duran. Sleep well."

Sleep didn't find Marina immediately. She couldn't stop thinking about their kiss. His lips. She'd never forget that!

The following day, Duran had left when she woke in late morning. What did she expect? He couldn't very well remain in the hut and let Narud come into existence inside the structure.

"Come outside, pet," the dragon called through mindspeech.

Through chinks in the door she saw the huge, crimson dragon pacing. Her delay postponed the inevitable. *"You are wrong to torment Duran,"* she responded. *"I care about you, but—"*

"No buts."

Her hand rested on the rope loop serving as the door's handle. *"If you continue to harass Duran, I can no longer be your friend. Stop interfering. As you are always so eager to point out, you are superior to puny humans. Give the man a measure of peace. I know you have it within yourself to be fair. Surely, you can show a little compassion."*

Silence followed her request. She wondered if the dragon even paid attention. Duran would not have made her wait.

"Possibly," Narud said moments later.

Marina stepped outdoors, a tight rein on her emotions. "Promise me. Or, we have nothing more to say. Ever."

"You demand?"

She folded her arms over chest. "So it would seem."

"What will I receive in exchange?"

The dragon's scales bristled along his spine. She'd upset him. Too bad. Still, the urge to back up made the bottom of her feet tingle, but she held her ground. He wasn't going to intimidate her. Not now. Not ever.

"My continued friendship. Isn't that enough?"

****

Duran called out when he approached the small hut. "Stav, come quickly! I need your help."

"What the…" She stumbled outside. "Who is he?"

Duran balanced an unconscious Sandblood over his shoulder. He'd debated leaving the man where he found him—in the ditch—then images of Calandra's cynical face flashed through his mind, and Duran knew he couldn't be as cold-hearted.

"A half-dead Sandblood. See his face scarf. I saw one with Calandra's henchmen. The possibility of two being on the mountain is slim. Desert men don't usually like our forests."

Stav took a nervous step backward, then froze, one

hand covering her mouth, one holding her stomach. "Why aid him?"

"Should I have left him to die?"

Her gaze flew to the man and, then back to him. "Of course not! I just thought…"

Her apprehension was perfectly understandable. The man might have killed her friends. "You told me to use reason," he said. "He might provide a clue how to break Calandra's curse."

The man moaned when Duran laid him on the cot Stav had used. Blood seeped from a ragged gash on his head.

Tilting her head, Stav's expression softened and the gold bright sheen of her hair caught the firelight. "You are right, of course. I let my fear get the better of me."

"You have never lacked courage." He stripped off his heavy fleece coat in the warm room. "You don't mind that I helped him, do you?"

"Mighty Kubala, no. He's a human being. I wish no one's death on my conscience, even an enemy's." A flush blossomed on her cheeks, and she turned and waved toward the hearth. "See, I managed to make a fire."

Most novices couldn't strike a spark without practicing long and hard. "I noticed."

Her lush mouth spread into a heart-stopping smile. "I watched you enough times and just gave the smooth side of the steel a glancing blow with the sharp side of the flint. The sparks only burned me a couple times." She held out her hand to show red marks, then shrugged as though unconcerned. "I'll put water on to boil and make bandages while you clean him up."

Pride lit Stav's huge hazel eyes. He felt a smile tugging at the corners of his mouth when he turned back to his patient. An embroidered scarf with symbols that were a form of desert writing he couldn't interpret covered the lower half of the Sandblood's face. Duran knew each symbol represented an event of some import in the man's life.

Duran unwrapped the cloth, careful not to damage it. A three-day stubble sprouted on the Sandblood's jaw. Candlelight revealed slashed and bruised skin beneath a tattoo of red, blue and purple whorls. The graceful design reminded Duran of birds in flight. They curled around and above the Sandblood's dark brows and disappeared into the thick hairline at his temples.

Holes riddled the desert man's clothing, and his leggings were smeared with dirt and mud as if he'd rolled down the mountain. Or been pushed, Duran thought.

The man did not stir when his garments were removed. A tangle of emotions—anger, frustration, and fear—sparked to life inside Duran. Obligation and responsibility were drilled into him through long years of training. He was an Abbas. Being dragon half the time had not eroded his sense of duty as prince.

At least, not yet.

This Sandblood was a visitor to his country, the same as Stav. Duran tried to hate him because he worked for Calandra but found he couldn't. The lure of information about the sorceress and her plans pulled at him.

"How is he?" Stav asked, returning with a pan of heated water.

Duran raised a shoulder and shrugged. "I'm not

sure. After I've cleaned him up, we'll decide what to do next."

"I know it's important to reach Brenalin, but you did the right thing bringing him here."

"Calandra's not going anywhere."

His jaw clenched speaking of the sorceress. His body grew hot, and the hairs on his skin prickled—the same as the dragon's scales when the beast grew upset. This wasn't the first time his anger caused him to think of Narud. Ofttimes, Duran felt they merged, leaving him unsure of his true identity.

Stav handed him the bandages, her fingers brushing his. Dragon's teeth, his body leapt with a life of its own at her touch. Something about her. Something compelling.

She looked at him. "Focus on her motive for wanting to wed you. Think, Duran. Does anything come to mind?"

He dipped bandages in and out of the hot water as he cleaned the cuts crisscrossing the desert man's arms and face. His patient moaned but remained comatose. A lump near his temple was probably the cause.

"You know as much as I," he said, finished.

"Surely there's more, something useful." Her hazel eyes flashed like green and gold jewels. "What would she benefit from such a union? I mean, besides the obvious and someday becoming the queen."

Something in her tone and the way her eyes beseeched him stopped Duran from snapping off a flippant reply. "Neither riches nor higher station were the impetus. Calandra has received offers from other lords governing larger kingdoms and rejected all of them."

"Maybe she truly loves you."

Duran jerked, splashing droplets on the floor. "Stop making excuses for her, Stav. She's not worth the effort."

"How can you believe I'm on her side?"

"You think you've figured out my problem," he barked, "but you haven't."

Anxiety increased on Stav's face. "You are forgetting the spell. Are you not?"

****

"Duran is deliberately keeping us apart. Let me kill this new human. You forced a promise out of me not to torment Duran, but it did not include others."

Narud's voice snaked through Marina's mind with a menace she'd never heard before. *"Killing someone is a bit more than tormenting them,"* she fired back, appalled.

"A minor difference to a dragon."

She yanked open the door and stepped outside to face the surly beast. Narud's red vertical eyes were hot slits, and angry bursts of smoke spewed from his nostrils, coinciding with each stomp of his massive legs. The ground vibrated. She'd never seen him so livid and dangerous—spiteful, pompous, bellicose. All of those. He acted different, frightening.

"For shame, Narud." Her heartbeat quickened with determination. "The desert man is not at fault."

"Duran is," Narud said, his speech sibilant. *"He let the woman remain. Now he brings another human."*

"You agreed Becca could stay. Duran wanted her to leave."

"Then why didn't she?"

Marina had heard of a petulant child. But a petulant

dragon? "You know why," she reminded him. "I desired her company. Why are you so uncaring?"

Narud lowered his long, sinuous neck. *"Are you blind to my side because I am a dragon?"*

"That's a ridiculous notion."

"I wish to be near you. When others are around, it is complicated. And...and I worry. I was confident you could defend yourself against a mere human female until I could save you—but a human male is faster and stronger."

Narud's logic made it impossible for Marina to stay upset. He cared. When he swung his wedge-shaped head down, she stroked him as he pushed it into her hand. Sinner demanded attention in the exact way. The reminder brought forth a smile and deepened her ache for home at the same time.

"I'm sorry, Narud. I didn't mean to cause you concern. There's nothing for you to fret about. Look at me. I'm fine."

"What if I could do more for you, Stav, much more? What if I bestowed dragon powers upon you? Just give the word and you can become a dragoness."

His suggestion staggered her. The notion came out of the blue. "A female dragon?"

"Interested?"

"Why would I want to become a dragoness?"

Narud raised his massive head as though surprised. *"Why not? I am offering you endless power, the ability to fly, fabulous treasure, and a long life."*

"You forget, Narud, I studied the missives written about dragons. There's never been mention of a human being turned into a dragon."

"For shame, my brave Stav, for believing your

precious human books would reveal the whole story. History is written by the winners, is it not?"

A good point. "If our most sacred tomes cannot be believed, what can?"

"Me."

"But…"

"Who would you rather believe?" A puff of smoke punctuated his outburst.

She knew the answer, but rather than argue let Narud continue his discourse.

"Has your kind forgotten the most basic of all truths? Every legend is based on truth, sometimes easy to see, other times hard to decipher."

"I doubted dragonkind's existence until meeting you," she admitted. "If such creatures existed, then I must also accept the fact some basic truth exists in those tales. According to them, your brethren were untrustworthy."

Narud lowered his long neck until his scaly snout stopped directly before her face. *"Some dragons were tricksters, but they are long gone. I am not. I will never be false with you. You have my word. Believe me, while not easy, it is possible to turn you into a dragoness."*

What a tempting offer. She wondered if he used dragon magic on her, then she blinked and stiffened her spine. She closed her eyes a moment, determined, and felt something else, willpower, stirring in her.

"What is the cost for this gift you offer? You always extract a price."

Narud grinned to reveal sharp teeth glinting in the sunlight. *"For you—naught. Even a powerful dragon such as I yearns for company of his own kind. It is not a weakness."*

"I never implied it otherwise. I was simply curious, however, how you will accomplish such a feat."

"Most magic is elemental, but this requires working with great visualization and self-discipline. It is imagination at its most powerful. You can have no lingering doubts. Believe in me, and a whole new world will open for you."

She watched crows fly away, a dark wedge against the blue sky before speaking, "I haven't agreed to anything."

"Yet…" Narud mused. *"Meanwhile, all this discussion has made me hungry. I need to feed."*

With that, he rose into the air and flew away, leaving Marina standing alone, perplexed.

****

Calandra overfilled the small vial, and it splashed onto the tabletop. A thin line of milky white streaked toward the edge and dripped to the floor. She cursed and set the vial into a holder, but the movement only made matters worse. Placing down the jug she poured from, she blotted up the mess.

How could she make a potion with her hands shaking?

She needed to test her father's theory about Einer. The thought of being fooled by the aged wizard infuriated her, and she refused to rest until the truth became exposed.

The spillage cleaned up, she hurried along the wide corridor of Abbas castle until she came upon a mirror. Stopping, she admired her reflection. In her mind, appearance went along with perception. Best to look attractive when tricking a man, for then image became a tool.

She wore her hair, glossy as a raven's, woven into a thick braid which swayed with each cant of her head. Numerous times Duran and Zell claimed the long locks her best feature. She needed a trim.

Her lips, too thin for her taste, narrowed at the thought. The fat barber with his soiled apron never performed the task to her satisfaction. Someday proper training would be mandatory for any servant privileged to tend her needs.

She turned at the jingle of tiny bells. Einer's long, white hair and beard hung straight as he approached. His clothes were an unbelievable mix of bold colors— prized cerulean leggings, pink undershirt, green tunic, and atop it all, a multi-colored woolen cloak that covered him from shoulder to floor and rippled with a soft rainbow glow. The elderly wizard needed no lantern to light his way. Seeing her, he flipped the glowing cape over his scrawny shoulders. His staff, which he always carried, was decorated with white tassels, silver bells, and glass beads.

"Oh, Venerable Master Wizard, I am so happy to find you," she greeted. "Your assistance is desperately required."

Einer's gaze flitted down the hall. "Did I hear correctly, my dear?" He wheezed softly. "You need my assistance?"

Calandra took a step forward. She heard an appalling raspy sound filter through his nose, a sure sign of the elderly. She never wanted to grow old or become wrinkled. Even his hands were disgusting with brown age spots.

She smiled to herself. If her plan succeeded, growing old would never be a concern of hers.

"Yes, Master Wizard. I am having difficulty with a summoning spell and wondered if you would assist me."

"By all means. I'm at your disposal."

She led him to the lower reaches of the castle where water dripped from the walls to puddle in small pools here and there. At present, she preferred the isolation and lifted the hem of her gown to avoid getting them wet.

What did irritate her was the constant jingle of bells on Einer's staff. He must be deaf not to be affected the noise.

Arriving at her workroom, Einer hobbled through the rushes and sagged onto the nearest stool. "Oh, my," he huffed. "What an exceedingly long way down. I never imagined so many steps. Now this dampness. My bones will complain for weeks. Why, my dear, did you pick such a location to practice your art?"

A flicker of annoyance undulated through her body. "I like my privacy."

That, and when her father's army reached the castle and began their assault, she would be safest in the dungeon. The siege would not take long. Abbas castle would fall with ease.

"Then let's get on with it. How may I help you?"

"I can't understand what I am doing wrong."

She indicated her worktable draped with a scarlet cloth. The brightly colored fabric corresponded to the shimmering red dragon that she wished to contact, but Einer didn't need to know that. Today, she planned to learn if the wizard was incompetent or pretending.

Einer shuffled to her workbench. He stared at the makeshift altar, fingering the red cloth. His eyes narrowed when his gaze swept over the candles, an incense burner scenting the air with sandalwood, a long sword with scrollwork decorating the blade, a container of salt, and a chalice.

Finished with his examination, he smiled approvingly. "I see nothing amiss with your preparations. You have no need for my humble self."

"I beg to differ, Master Wizard. My skills are nothing compared to yours. Watch, and I'll show you." She struck a match to a candlewick, and it promptly winked out.

Einer leaned closer. "Concentrate, Calandra. Keep your thoughts clear. Try again."

She failed to light the candle again and again.

"Here, let me try." Einer took the long wooden match from her hand and reached toward the white candle. The wick caught and filled the room with a burst of bright light.

Her gaze lingered on the candle before returning to Einer and giving him a bright smile. "I can't believe it. You succeeded on your first attempt."

"It was nothing." He nodded at the second candle. "You try the black one."

She struck a new match. The tiny yellow flame touched the wick, sputtered, and disappeared. After several attempts, she stomped her foot in annoyance.

"This is hopeless. There must be a draft or my spell is ill concocted. More research is necessary. I regret troubling you, Master Wizard."

A gurgle sounded when he cleared his throat. "You will solve the problem." He took a second look around her workroom, his open hand passing over the worktable. "Sometimes the simplest spells are the most difficult to perform."

Calandra seethed with dark rage. Her father had been correct. The old wizard played a dangerous game of deceit with her.

Her spell appeared simple enough, although it was far from it. A powerful blocking enchantment had been cast against igniting the candles. Only an exceptionally powerful wizard could have countered her spell. The fact Einer succeeded without even realizing it proved his talent far greater than he led people to believe.

She thought his hand paused over the sword. Did it? Had he guessed the owner's identity?

The blade belonged to Duran.

Einer gave no indication of his awareness, but she'd erred once in her judgment about him. She planned to be far more wary around him from now on. He would not fool her twice.

The climb up the stairs to the audience hall dragged on forever. They arrived to find the great room crowded with townsfolk, farmers, and merchants. They grumbled amongst themselves, their voices resembling a swarm of angry bees. Malcontents, the whole lot of them.

Moving away from the wizard's side toward King Zell, she kept a sharp eye on the scowling faces.

"What are you going to do about these attacks?" demanded an overweight merchant in a silken robe who stood before the dais. "The violence has intensified. Houses and businesses are being looted outside of Brenalin. Property is being destroyed. People fear for their lives. You must protect us. When will these cowards be caught and punished?"

Zell leaned forward, the winter-white fox trim on

his mantle draining what color remained in his complexion. "Resist them, Minorah. Fight back."

The man's fat lips quivered. "It will only anger the brigands. They will kill me and my men if we resist!"

A sigh lifted Zell's bony chest. "I'll increase patrols."

Calandra claimed the stool next to the king's throne and acknowledged the merchant with a perfunctory nod. "Have patience, good sir, and heed His Highness. Put your faith in him during his time of loss."

"Your confidence is most welcome, my sweet." Zell patted her hand. "It goes to reason Duran's disappearance and these brigands are related. Someone is orchestrating the events. I'm positive it is no coincidence. Don't you agree?"

"You know best, Your Majesty."

She would not fail to achieve her goal. She couldn't. Success lay within her reach.

Beginning with Brenalin.

The world next…

Chapter Twelve

Shadows flickered across the olive complexion of Marina's patient. She'd held vigil over the Sandblood the first night and through the next day, leaving his side only to speak with Narud and cook a potage from rabbit leftovers in case the man woke and found himself hungry. She'd sipped the broth several times. It was her first attempt to prepare a complete meal by herself, and her success tickled her delight. Each time she sipped, she sighed happily and wished Becca were here to taste her soup.

Through the window, dusk colored the sky with shades of oranges, yellows, and reds. Her skin tingled. She sensed Narud's departure as the moon peeked between tree trunks in the east. Duran would arrive any moment.

Leather supports creaked on the cot. She turned to look at her patient. He grimaced as he tried to sit up, only to sag down. She stood still, afraid to startle him. When he spotted her, though, his hands fumbled for his missing scarf. Her gaze slid to the covering on the table, where Duran had dropped it.

"Nice to see you awake," she said in a pleasant tone.

His cuts stopped oozing the instant his eyes opened. She'd never seen anything like it before.

"What's your name, good sir? Do you know where

you are?" She had hoped the questions helped him focus, for all he did was stare at her.

Ebony eyes sparkled. "Fahid, Sand born and bred, and where I am, I was hoping perchance you could tell me, sweet miss."

"How is he?" she heard from behind her.

Duran's voice. An unexpected thrill swept through her insides.

"Ask him yourself." She smiled. "He's awake."

Duran retrieved the face scarf on his way across the room and handed it to the man. "What happened to you?"

She absorbed every detail about Duran. Undeniably handsome, strong, quick-witted, compassionate, he would make some woman a loving husband—even though he could be intractable, hardnosed, and seldom changed his mind once set.

She had missed him. Had a single day really passed since last seeing him? It seemed forever. Could it be because the deeper into summer, the shorter the nights?

Fahid accepted the covering, reaching behind his head to secure the ends into place. "Nothing to tell, good sir." The decorative covering fluttered with his breath.

"Left for dead is nothing? I would have plenty to say about that."

"I am indebted to you." The Sandblood struggled to his feet, holding onto the cot for balance. "My experience will allow me to add another symbol to my *sharf*."

Duran frowned. "*Sharf*? That's what your face cloth is called? I hear you record significant events on it."

"We do."

Silence stretched in the room.

"An interesting way to chronicle history," Duran finally said.

"It is." Another bland answer.

Marina went to the river rock fireplace to stir the ingredients in the suspended kettle with a big wooden spoon. She scooped potage broth into cups. Duran could use nourishment after his transformation, and she suspected their guest needed to recuperate from his ordeal as well.

She nearly dropped Fahid's plate when she turned and saw the lump on his temple and every cut and bruise upon his head and hands had disappeared.

Laugh lines crinkled around Fahid's dark, mysterious eyes, changing the tattoo pattern from birds to lightning bolts when he accepted her food offering. He walked slowly to the fireplace, each step seemingly firmer than the last.

"Your wounds are all gone," she said in awe. "Are you all right?"

Fahid leaned against the hearth. "We heal fast."

"Almost magically." Duran voice was shaded with suspicion.

If the Sandblood noticed, he gave no indication. "Nothing almost about it. I belong to the Heyln tribe. We are charmed among the Sandbloods. We never sicken. If injury or accident befalls us, the damage begins to reverse immediately."

"Is that why I found you in a ditch, discarded like yesterday's rubbish?"

"We must be awake for the magic to work," Fahid said, unruffled. "Rare cases have occurred where one has died while unconscious. We do die of old age, and sometimes from a broken heart…" His twinkling gaze sought Marina. "One must have a reason for living, you understand. Moving me roused me and saved my life."

Duran grunted and wolfed down his broth in a single gulp. "You wouldn't want to unburden yourself with a bit of information, would you?"

Fahid performed a small bow when his tanned fingers touched his face cloth where his mouth was, between his eyes, and his brow. "Praise to the gods," he began, "if a lowly person such as myself can provide answers to you. Your kindness guarantees a debt of gratitude. Ask and I will tell all I am able."

"What were you doing in Brenalin?" Duran asked. "Nomads do not normally travel this far north."

"Rumblings in Midber of a great war were heard. The Heyln leader sent me to gather information."

"You heard of a war from thousands of miles?" Duran asked.

The Sandblood offered up an enigmatic smile.

Scowling, Duran looked none too pleased. "What did you learn?"

Fahid rolled his shoulders in a shrug. "That is for my leader's ears alone."

Duran shot to his feet. His chair crashed to the floor. "What do you mean? You owe me. I saved your life."

"For which I am truly grateful, *beser ser*, or good sir in your tongue. However, loyalty forbids me to speak."

Marina sat listening, rapt.

"What you were doing on the mountain?" Duran asked hotly.

"That I will gladly answer. First, though, let me sample this lovely lady's dish." He put the cup of broth under his scarf and slurped noisily.

Marina stared, astonished at how loud he ate.

"Simply delicious." A twinkle glistened in his dark eyes when he sipped again, equally deafening. "In my country, we acknowledge good food with noises of appreciation. How else will the cook or our hostess know we enjoy the fare served?"

She had never supped with a Sandblood when they visited Eudes, and her father had failed to mention the odd and noisy habit. She bowed her head in acknowledgement of his compliment.

"Can we get back to why you were on the mountain?" Duran demanded.

"Forgive me. I was told we were on a mission of mercy to locate a serving girl. I learned the real purpose was to kill her."

Marina flinched. So, a sorceress sought her death. What had she done to this woman? It had to be the same evil one who destroyed Duran's life. Two such evil people could not exist in Brenalin at the same time. What did she and Duran have in common to share such a powerful enemy?

Duran glanced at her. "Do you know why they seek her death?"

"No reason is needed if they are *gvald*. Men in my country call them fanatics." Fahid spat on the floor. "This band works for the sorceress in league with whoever plans to start the great war. Why do you ask?"

"Information mostly. If war comes, innocent people are in jeopardy. The king of Brenalin would pay for accurate information. He must be warned. I need details."

"What importance is it to you personally?"

Marina watched Duran stiffen.

"You insult me, Sandblood. I am a Brenalin. What happens to my country is important to me. If you refuse to speak of this war, explain how you ended up in the ditch."

Fahid's gaze studied Duran, as if considering his request. "I had a difference of opinion with my traveling companions. They decided to end our association in a rather lethal and painful manner. They pushed me off a cliff."

Marina gasped. She couldn't believe men could discuss murder as easily as the weather.

Fahid turned toward her. "Never fear, sweet miss. I am hard to kill, though I admit, your concern pleases me greatly."

Marina dismissed his flirtatious manner with a wave. "I'm sure someone waits for you at home. If you'd died, they would have been heartbroken."

"No wife or love, if that is what you mean."

Duran went to his pack and began stuffing items into it. "Since you've recovered, Fahid, we'll bid you farewell."

Fahid's eyebrows raised. "You leave now? In the dark?"

"There are advantages to traveling at night," Marina explained.

The desert man nodded. "I understand. In these uncertain days, stealth is always wise."

Marina gathered her gear. "Take care, Fahid. Finish the soup. A pleasure meeting you."

"Surely you'll never forget me?"

She laughed, positive the man had been a born tease. "I don't think that's possible."

"My heart would break if you had said otherwise. I wish you the best on your journey, sweet miss. Perhaps, someday I can properly thank you for all your kindness." He pushed aside his face scarf and flashed his white teeth in a wide grin. "Until we meet again."

"Good luck to you and a safe journey home," she answered, heading outdoors.

A gibbous moon brought dim light to the cool night. Duran shifted impatiently. Those odd dragonflies circled his head. His expression looked black and grim. What bothered him? she wondered.

"You'll never see him again," he told her when she stood at his side.

"What's wrong, Duran? Do you doubt Fahid's word?"

"His glib Sandblood manner is difficult to swallow."

She locked her gaze on him. "In Eudes, King Hersher welcomes Sandbloods at his court."

"He does?"

"For trading purposes." She stretched out a hand to touch his arm, but he moved away at the precise moment. Was it intentional?

"Is that what upsets you?" she asked to cover her hurt of his rejection.

He snorted, his expression pained. "I'm not upset. Not with you."

"You sound as though you are."

"Well, I'm not. If I overreacted, forgive me. Fahid thinks too highly of himself. Leave it at that."

Marina dragged her toe in the ground and gazed at

the giant evergreens. A breeze swayed their tops. Frogs chirped in the woodland's depths. A creature scampered up a tree, its tiny claws clicking on the bark. The forest was never silent.

Duran hefted his pack. A flush of anger simmered just below the surface of his handsome features.

"Is it safe to leave Fahid to his own devices?" she asked. "Did you really believe his tale?"

"He's not the enemy. We both know who is at fault."

Marina glanced over her shoulder at the hut. "What if he's concealing something?"

"Let him."

Sometimes Duran was as surly as his dragon half, Marina thought. She remembered when Becca asked to mate with him. Jealousy had reared its ugly head within her. Did Duran experience the same disturbing emotion? He certainly behaved sullen enough.

When he turned and started walking away without a backward glance to check whether or not she followed, her feet scurried after him. She tried to convince herself the brusque attitude was his male ego, not the real Duran.

They plodded up the road cut into the hillside for long, tiring hours. At the top, Marina stopped to catch her breath. She looked around in the dark. Glowing dragonflies flitted high overhead and in the thick underbrush. Never in her life had seen so many of the creatures. It was as though an infestation filled the great woods. They varied in size from microscopic to nearly hummingbird size. Some didn't even appear solid.

She refocused her attention on the road and noticed it straightened, carving a wide swath between trees towering hundreds of feet overhead.

They continued to make steady progress toward Brenalin. Day after day, Marina walked. When they rounded a stand of trees, she spied open fields. She'd never been so happy to see signs of civilization. A half-dozen thatch-roofed cottages squatted next to the forest in the vein of a narrow belt, and before them cultivated fields of winter wheat sprouted. Against the cottages, muted red, yellow, and white flowering plants grew. Someone loved tending a garden as much as she, yet she smelled no smoke escaping from the chimneys and saw no flicker of candlelight in the windows. The huts were deserted, the same as the lumber settlement.

In the distance, a huge walled city rose.

She sighed and relaxed enough to breathe. "We made it," she said in a low voice.

****

"Home," Duran whispered under his breath. "At long last."

It took single-minded determination to reach Brenalin. He'd been anticipating this moment for months with a feeling of expectation and dread until he'd nearly made himself sick. Learning someone threatened Brenalin with war ignited his urge to hurry to save his people.

He took Stav's hands into his, locking their fingers together. "We'll enter Brenalin tonight. It'll be dangerous, and I want your utmost trust."

She flashed a smile so fleet he hardly saw it. "You have that. You always have."

A warm glow heated his insides at her sweet words. "I know a way most do not. In the meantime, it's time to be accountable." Something akin to desperate need filled him to be honest with her. At night few people would be about, but he couldn't chance someone recognizing him and shocking Stav at the wrong moment. He sensed her go very still, yet her expression urged him to continue. He swallowed the lump in his throat. "My name is Duran," he said, never taking his eyes off her. "I am…I was Duran Abbas."

"It cannot be. You're Prince Duran Ab—Abbas?"

"I am he." It occurred to Duran her voice sounded more than confused.

"All these weeks," she said, her tone cold with shock. "You remained silent about your identity. Why tell me now?"

He wasn't wrong—irritation, anger, and something else—hurt. "I feared your reaction."

Stav drew herself up, bristling. "You heard Fahid say a sorceress sought my death."

"It changed nothing."

"It changes everything. You could have told me we shared a mutual enemy."

Her bluntness was one of the things that made Stav precious to him. "So much was at stake. I swear. I did it to protect you."

He ached to hold her close, to breathe in the scent of roses and assure her she would be safe and loved. The last thought brought Duran's head up. Love? Had his feelings grown so strong to give it a name? How did one fall in love? Could it be the willingness to do whatever it took to see a smile brighten the other person's face? To know they were happy? Safe?

Stav could never love him. It seemed ridiculous for him to consider the idea. She deserved better than him. He had turned into a monster, neither man nor beast.

Bile curdled his stomach. A pox on Calandra! She'd ruined his life. He had to destroy her in order to free himself.

"Why not stay a dragon?" Strange voices acted as one to ask. *"Most would deem it a great honor."*

"Who are you?" he demanded, his gaze searching for the cause of the voices and seeing nothing.

"You would not believe us if we told you."

"Try me." He waited for an answer, but none came. *"What do you want from me?"*

"Naught from you, human. The dragon interests us. He is the first of his kind in over a thousand years. Your curse has set him free. Be not afraid. Let us assure you your sacrifice will not go unappreciated."

"Sacrifice? You make it sound as though I will die."

High in tree branches those strange dragonflies hovered, and Duran couldn't help wondering if they were connected to the voices. He wouldn't have believed it possible weeks ago, but now…he wasn't so sure.

"The sorceress's curse will succeed. Your existence will cease once the dragon takes over."

"No! Find another victim," he spat back, surrender out of the question. *"I might have little chance to end the curse, but I won't stop trying until I draw my final breath."*

Stav touched his arm. The simple act let the tension flow out of his body.

He wasn't afraid of battling Narud, but facing Stav with the simple truth proved far harder. "It has not been easy keeping this secret to myself. I'll speak with my father. He'll make you welcome. You don't have to be a servant any more. You can fall in love, wed, and raise a passel of children."

A distant expression veiled Stav's eyes. "Oh, Duran, I don't know what to say."

"Say nothing now." He took hold of her hand and raised it to his mouth, brushing a kiss over her warm fingers. "If you choose to accept my offer, your life will be better off. I have a small holding that earns enough for you to live on for the rest of your life. I give it to you."

The smile she gave him was one he planned to hold close for the rest of his life.

"I'm honored by your offer, but I had hoped you would accompany me to Eudes."

He gathered her into a hug. Wisps of fragrant roses emerged from her hair to tantalize his nose. Warmth infused him in a wave of happiness, enhancing his passion when she sank into his embrace. When she looked up at him, his breath quickened. His gaze slid over her face, delighted in the shape of her nose, the tilt of her eyes, the lushness of her mouth. He'd given up trying to understand why Stav affected him the way she did.

"If you want," he began, "after I eliminate Calandra, I'll take you to Eudes. Or you may stay here. Whatever you wish. Your happiness is all that matters."

"You make me happy," she said in a low voice that went straight to his heart.

"Promise me you won't do anything drastic."

Her smile blinded him. "Like what?"

"If I knew, I wouldn't elicit your promise beforehand."

"I don't know what's got into you tonight," she

whispered. "Are we doing the right thing? It's unwise to underestimate this sorceress."

"I know. I know. I did that once." He glanced over his shoulder at Brenalin's thick walls. "We've endured hardships together, Stav; but I need to face Calandra. My biggest concern is you. You can't just wander around by yourself."

"Probably not a good idea. Take me with you. Whatever happens, we'll face it together."

****

Marina glanced at the solid wall hewn from blocks of speckled granite. It gave the impression of imprisoning the city within its hold. She touched the wall. Hard. Cold. Dead. Nothing like her beloved ocean with its constant movement, always full of life.

Duran tripped the latch of a metal door hidden in a stony niche. She found herself in a narrow corridor.

"What is this place?" she asked.

"We use it to move troops and isolate invaders if they manage to breach the outer wall." Duran led her through another door and down a short flight of steps.

The clink of metal and creak of leather alerted her to sentries patrolling on the ramparts. Overhead pennants flapped in the breeze. Silvery moonlight allowed her to spy the Abbas crest of a dragon with a giant ruby clutched in its claws.

Not a soul was about. The open-air stalls were closed for the night, but she knew when the city awoke, people would shuffle to the marketplace to make their daily purchases. Their voices would rise and fall as they haggled over goods and prices.

A pile of dull red rags near a deserted stall stirred. An Untouchable, one of the unfortunates who contracted the deadly, disfiguring disease that ate away the flesh, was recognizable by the color of his tattered coloring.

Marina shuddered, compassion instantly rising. An Untouchable lost everything. Their lives were wiped clean. Tradespeople hated them at their place of business, but the law required no one harm a victim of the disease. Untouchables went from town to town, begging handouts, an awful way to eke out a living.

Duran skirted the Untouchable.

She followed, afraid to lose sight of him in the maze of streets. He hastened through the town, taking a path only someone familiar with the twisting lanes could.

Following him, she reflected on what he said. The prince! Duran would have been her husband. Her conscience—tiny, cajoling, and ashamed—had remained silent about her identity. She told herself he needed to keep his mind completely clear. His mission came first, and he needed every ounce of concentration for it to succeed.

It wasn't right to permit Duran to believe…

What?

The truth.

Confession would come later. He deserved to know the truth. Maybe after…after the sorceress had been dealt with. Maybe then.

Deep in her heart, she feared confessing. Ashamed. And a tad selfish. She didn't know how Duran or Narud would react once they discovered the truth. And she didn't want to lose either one.

Duran was…

What?

A man?

A dragon?

Both were proud beings. Would they forgive her dishonesty? She understood Duran's reasoning. Would he accept hers? Deep down she held onto the hope he would forgive her lie, though once the truth came out in the open, she worried a gulf wider than the great ocean would separate them.

They clung to the shadows and wound their way down another crooked street. Marina could only imagine how angry Duran must feel being forced to slink through his own city like a common thief. They stopped at an intersection.

"It's good to see you going on with…" she began to say.

He turned to look at her, his countenance bleak.

She was going to say life, and they both knew it. They were close, and though she could not read his thoughts, she felt drawn to him in some inexplicable way.

Duran canted his head. She'd seen him do it before when he and Narud quarreled.

"No matter what happens tonight I want you to know how much you…er…your company means to me. I'm sorry you were caught in the middle of this lunacy. Very, very sorry. I haven't behaved well either. Intolerably, really."

"You had good reason."

"It doesn't excuse my behavior." He took her hand. "One never knows how they will react until a catastrophe happens."

She held onto his hand, gathering strength and courage from the touch. They neared a small door along the castle wall. She wanted to plead with Duran not to seek out the sorceress, but her own stubbornness, a trait her father always pointed out as a fault, stopped her.

A click sounded unduly loud when Duran's hand scraped the wall, then a door opened. She caught the flash of his teeth an instant before they slid through the opening into the castle.

She steeled herself. Committed. No matter what happened, she would see this ordeal through to the end. All she could do was hope things would end happily.

****

High ceilings, supported by arches and spiraling columns greeted Duran in the light provided by wall sconces. A sense of peace settled over him. He never expected to be within his home again. Inhaling deeply, he savored the aromas that were both familiar and reassuring—wood smoke, beeswax, several foods, and the hint of various perfumes.

A draft guttered out a torch stuck in the iron wall bracket nearest to them. An ill omen for what lay ahead? he wondered. The feeble glow of the moon seeping through elongated loopholes seemed a poor substitute.

As the heir apparent of Brenalin, he'd been taught to bring balance into his life. Training in military tactics and statesmanship were an integral part of his upbringing. Balance seemed nonexistent tonight. His emotions ran high. Eagerness filled him to use the brawn of his sword arm to dispense Calandra's false-hearted life.

Stav had one thing right, he thought. Revenge controlled him far too much. He needed to rule his emotions.

Tired of not seeing her in daylight, he vowed to stare into the depths of her gold-green eyes, to touch her smooth skin after the sun heated her cheeks. He didn't want to miss any of the little, important details about her.

First, he needed to make sure all was well with the great ruby in the Ruby Throne. The idea of paying homage to the enormous gemstone embedded in the wooden chair had lingered in the back of his mind throughout the journey. He turned and put a finger to his lips, then motioned Marina to follow him. The influence grew stronger and stronger as he had neared the castle.

He suspected Narud manipulated him. The dragon would want to possess the gemstone. Would the beast try to steal it? He shook with anger at the thought. The creature would not get it. The precious gemstone had belonged to the Abbases for generations.

"Come on, follow me." He led Stav up another passageway.

Carpeted floors muted their footfalls. He let himself be drawn down the passageway until they reached the great hall. His father never bothered with guards on the inside, saying if an enemy brooked Brenalin's massive stone walls, it would be a waste of good sword arms to station men before an empty room.

Duran stopped in his tracks and pushed open the door. The flicker from a half-burned candle made the great jewel appear a giant red glowing eye.

"About time you came back, Duran," said a voice from the shadows. "I've been waiting for days. What took you so long?"

"Who is it?" he demanded, whirling and tucking

Stav safely behind him. "Reveal yourself."

"As you wish, boy."

Tiny bells chimed and a soft shimmer illuminated a man when he emerged from the dark.

Duran grinned and hurried over to the elderly wizard to wrap him in a bear hug. "Einer, am I ever glad to see you!"

"And I you. I knew you weren't dead."

"Dead? Who would proclaim me so?"

The aged wizard knocked his shoulder with the long staff he held. A chorus of silver bells jingled with the motion.

"No one is sure, but I have my suspicions."

"Calandra." Duran spat, then noticed the direction of the wizard's gaze. "Einer, I'd like you to meet Stav. She's a traveling friend." He pulled back to watch the two nod at each other. "What gave you the idea I'd return?"

"I'm a wizard. I know things. Now, release me. You are crushing my bones."

"Worse has happened to me."

Einer frowned. "Tell me what occurred."

"I don't have time to explain. You'll have to trust me."

"I'm sure this involves Calandra," Einer said. "She has been a great disappointment. I failed with her."

"What do you mean failed?" Fear bit at him.

"I should have insisted she be forbidden to learn magic. She practices dark sorcery."

Duran listened, elated to have found an ally. "Indeed, she does. You always were quick for an old man," he said in a light voice. Stav leaned toward him, and he welcomed her close proximity. "War is coming to Brenalin."

"Genoy," the wizard uttered with contempt. "He was here a few days ago."

Duran's gut clenched. "It makes sense. Genoy doesn't travel anywhere without his army. The main bulk of his troops are probably hidden nearby. He plays a deadly game with Brenalin as the prize. You must warn Father of the danger."

"Why not you?"

Duran put his hand on Einer's shoulder. A faint glow rose from between his fingers. "Because I need to kill Calandra. She cast a spell on me, and her death will break it. Afterward, I'll explain everything."

Einer didn't bat a lash. "I'll hear your tale now."

"I don't—"

The ancient wizard thumped his staff on the floor. Crystal beads and bells collided together. "You are too late, boy. Your father is already ensorcelled by her. If I am to aid you, I must know everything. Let's have your story. My patience has reached its end in this game of wits and magic."

This wasn't the time to start arguing with his old friend or doubting his loyalty. It took less than ten heartbeats to relay details of the events.

When finished, Einer's expression turned dour. "You have forgotten one important detail."

"What?"

"Calandra is a sorceress of some merit."

That roll in his stomach worsened, but thoughts of the wretched woman winning grated on him. "So?"

Einer shook his head. "Do you know anything about fighting her and her magic?"

"Only that I must."

Duran contemplated the great hall. Torches cast shadows dancing on the walls. The shape of one shadow reminded him of a dragon. He watched the silhouette toss back its neck, smoke ballooning out of the huge head. The shadow's huge body seemed to vibrate with laughter. Then, the image vanished.

Einer's rheumy gaze brightened. "You seek revenge?"

"I seek justice."

The wizard's gaze never wavered. "You have good reason for being upset."

Duran bent his head. His time was short, and growing shorter every day. "As my friend, Einer, you would be a little biased, but I appreciate the concern."

"You'll be hard pressed to kill Calandra."

Duran squeezed his hands together, disliking Einer's words. He had survived his ordeal solely on the notion of destroying of Calandra and was horrified that he faced defeat. "Explain?"

"A mere mortal cannot kill a skillful sorceress. Even if you could, doing so will not break the spell. Magic doesn't work that way."

Chapter Thirteen

Magic doesn't work that way.

The wizard's words resonated in Marina's head and fueled her despair. *Why not?* she screamed to herself. Duran had placed so much faith in his revenge. To have those dreams and hopes shattered in a blink of an eye tore at her insides.

"She will not escape me!" Duran stood straighter than a blade. "She's betrayed Brenalin. Her malevolence tried to destroy me. She cannot…"

Marina's heart constricted hearing the pain lacing his voice. She slipped her arm around his waist and yearned for her closeness to offer him comfort.

The wizard raised a gnarled hand. "Listen to me. I know you're angry and hurt, but you have to trust me."

"It's not fair!" Duran's gaze searched the audience hall as though an answer could be found within the four walls. "You could be wrong. I'll not be swayed to give up my—"

"Silence!" Einer's voice rose into the rafters. "I didn't say you couldn't seek revenge. You'll listen to me first, unless you want your zeal to get you killed."

Duran offered up a cold, calculating smile. "If I am not careful, indeed, it will."

The old wizard slipped onto the stool next to the Ruby Throne. "Save me from the fallibility of youth."

"This nightmare ends tonight, Einer," Duran

asserted. "Nothing you say can stop me. I have to try. You know I do."

"I would expect nothing less, boy."

"I'll take that as approval." Duran grinned.

"You may take it any way you wish," Einer counseled in an undertone. "But trust me, you must."

Marina stood between the two men, twisting her head from one to the other. The aged wizard's voice had contained the steel edge of a warrior. Magic, power, and confidence oozed from his thin frame. It would be foolish to disregard him.

"Normally I wouldn't contradict you." Duran's tone turned apologetic as though taking a cue from her thoughts. "I know how you despise being nay-sayed. I've been so single-minded, I didn't expect resistance from you."

"You mistake concern for common sense. No wizard can reverse the spell of another. Believe me, I would if I could. So, I will do something else."

A flash of red hardened Duran's blue eyes. "What?"

Einer's mouth lifted with a ghost of a smile. "Both of you step forward and close your eyes."

Duran scooped up her hand and moved forward as requested. At his touch, a tingle raced through her body. Being near him always provided her with a source of strength and comfort. They shut their eyes and waited in silence. She knew Duran trusted this wizard with his life. Which meant she would, too.

Einer began chanting in a low voice. Marina had the distinct impression the words were deliberately slurred to keep them unidentifiable. The room grew warm, then warmer still. She thought the wizard drew power from the very air. The fine hairs on her arms rose when something thinner than a moist membrane settled on her skin and slowly dried.

Peeking through her long lashes, Marina saw Einer wink at her. She almost giggled.

"That should do the trick," Einer proclaimed. "Open your eyes."

"My thanks for whatever you've done," Duran said.

Gratitude was waved away. "It is a simple blocking spell. No magic can reach you. It's only temporary. I may want to contact you. How else may I help?"

"Protect my father," Duran said, as if he needed to.

"To the death. I pledge my life on it."

Beside her, Duran further relaxed. "I knew I could depend upon you. Inform him of the danger. Genoy has an army waiting to attack Brenalin."

Einer lifted a speculative brow. "You should be warned that Genoy left men in the garrison, supposedly as protection for his daughter."

"Have those men arrested," Duran ordered. "Calandra has others masquerading as brigands. I assume bandit raids have gotten worse lately."

"Indeed, they have." Einer pulled an object out from beneath his glowing cape that reflected candlelight with the sheen of honed metal. "Here. You might appreciate wearing this on your hip again. If not tonight, maybe later."

"My sword." The redness increased in Duran's eyes. "Where'd you find it?"

"Calandra had it secreted in her workroom. A little sleight of hand and magic, and I removed it right from under her nose."

He strapped on the weapon. "My heartfelt thanks."

Einer put his hand on Duran's shoulder. "I expect it would be a waste of breath to urge caution."

Duran shook his head. "You know the answer already."

The old wizard nodded. "Never fear. You will be her ruin."

"I don't need a wizard to tell me that, old friend." Duran glanced at her. "Stay with Einer, Stav. You'll be safe with him."

Marina studied Duran through narrowed eyes. "I'm coming with you."

"You are not accompanying me."

"Ordering me to stay behind doesn't work. Remember?"

He glanced at the wizard, who shook his head. Duran's gaze darkened, then he sighed and marched away. Marina hurried after him, determined to aid Duran. They wended their way through the castle, some passageways similar to those in Eudes, others far different. They climbed two flights of a circular stone stairwell used by servants during the day.

At the beginning of a long gallery, Marina slowed. "Wait! I'm frightened, Duran."

He slowed and took her hand. "Me, too," Duran said gently. "Fear is natural. I am always afraid before a battle, and this is no different. I wish half the soldiers of Brenalin had the strength and rare courage you possess."

Marina looked up at him through lowered lashes. His lips summoned up the memory of their first kiss. Her body trembled at the remembered passion. They deserved a future together.

215

Then why am I so scared? she wanted to ask. She didn't feel brave. Just the opposite.

****

The scent of perfume seeped out from under Calandra's door. Heavy musk. Jasmine. And some cloying fragrance Duran could never identify. The combination brought back vivid memories of his childhood—some good, some bad.

He'd walked past this exact spot a thousand times. Wiping sweat from his forehead, he focused his thoughts on the task ahead. It all seemed so simple— kill Calandra and break the spell.

Duran's gut knotted with despair. Why wouldn't Calandra's death end the curse? Though there was something to be said for the satisfaction of watching her life's blood flow out. If he didn't solve the riddle, he would cease to exist. Narud would triumph.

His muscles tensed with expectation when he thought of her face filling with terror.

"Would you rather see your blood, human?" Narud intruded into his thoughts. *"Or are you considering clemency?"*

Startled, Duran jerked upright, his face heating with anger. *"Leave me alone, dragon. Stay out of my head."*

Draconic laughter filled his mind. *"How can I do that? It is my head, too. We are one."*

Queasiness filled him. It had been so long since Narud interfered, Duran assumed their struggle for dominance had ended. At best, they had reached a stalemate. The falseness of his hope left a sour bile taste in his mouth. He'd only been fooling himself.

He put his hands on Stav's shoulders. "Stay here.

This won't take long."

"You can't approach that sorceress alone. We've come this far together. I won't interfere."

Duran rolled his eyes. She constantly resisted his efforts to protect her. "All right. Against my better judgment, you can come. Just stay behind me and keep quiet."

He opened the door, the well-oiled hinges silent.

Calandra sat at her vanity. Two decades had passed since her arrival at his father's doorstep with baggage in hand. She'd been a vision with raven hair and vivid green eyes, a contradictory mix of frightened, shy, demanding, intelligent, and charming.

She'd matured into a breathtakingly beautiful woman—beautiful and deadly. The evil filling her proved the stronger. Now the sight of his one-time childhood friend revolted to him.

He glanced at Stav and knew immediately which woman he preferred. Stav might be a servant, but her innocence appealed far more than anything he had ever seen. Her beauty lay within as well as outside.

The braid Calandra favored came undone, and her ebony tresses fanned down her back. His reflection moved across the mirror when he and Stav slipped into the room. One of the sorceress's inky brows arched. So much for catching her unaware.

"I hope we're not intruding," he quipped. "You don't seem surprised to see me."

The sorceress smiled in the mirror, but it wasn't admiring her own reflection. "I'm delighted actually," she said in a pleasant tone. "To what do I owe this unexpected pleasure?"

Duran rested his palm on the hilt of his sword. The

cold touch of metal was a reassuring feel. "As if you didn't know."

Calandra put down the brush and languidly turned to face him. "I counted on your return. You should have come to me sooner. I was expecting you long before now."

"I can't imagine why."

Calandra stood. "Why so unfriendly, Duran? Surely, you hold no grudge against me. What other person has had the opportunity to share his existence with a creature such as a dragon? No one. You should thank me."

A sudden rush of anger heated Duran's face. "Return me to my rightful place. I want that creature out of my life." He flashed a look at Stav, who moved up beside him.

Calandra pursed her lips. "I see you brought a little friend. By her gown, a commoner no less. The princess's missing servant, I assume? Why is she here? Her presence is most unwelcome."

To her credit, Stav gave no outward sign, other than flashing him a small smile. He strode over to Calandra. Her green eyes, cool with confidence, met his. "She is none of your concern."

Calandra's gown skimmed the floor as she inched back. "Send her away. You and I need to speak privately."

Duran glanced at Stav to reassure himself of her safety. "She stays. I have no secrets from her."

A black eyebrow rose. "None whatever?"

He looked at Calandra, narrowing his gaze once again. "You sicken me. For your information, I would take this woman over you any day." And he meant it.

Calandra's face reddened. "You prefer a servant over me? Over your precious princess?"

"I'll never know the princess, thanks to you. And, yes, I prefer her over you any day. There is a significant difference between you and this woman. Loyal. Brave. She has a heart where yours is a lump of ice. I trust her with my life."

Calandra assessed him coldly. "You'll regret setting me aside, I swear."

He snorted with disgust. How could he force Calandra to undo the spell? She would probably take great delight laughing at him. Short of beating her within an inch of her life, he would not receive a grain of satisfaction from her.

"How dare you look at me with repugnance," the sorceress rattled off in a sharp tone. "Wait until people view you as a dragon. The sight of a living, breathing monster will strike terror into them. They'll hunt you down. Their fear will turn them into a mob filled with bloodlust. Be careful, Duran. All they need is a direction in which to be pointed."

Her contempt infuriated him. The rasp of steel being drawn filled the chamber.

Resolve inside him hardened. "You threaten me?"

"No." She snorted with laughter. "I'm giving you a promise."

"Don't worry, human, your piddling life is safe. She won't harm you. She created me. She wants me."

Duran gritted his teeth. *"Begone, Narud!"* He could feel his breath growing hotter. Soon, his breath would be as hot as the dragon's. "Why, Calandra? I defy you to tell me. You did me a terrible wrong. Why hurt me like this? You knew I was committed to wed another. Our families would never have countenanced a marriage between us."

She waved her arm in the air. "You chastise me? You should hear yourself, Duran."

His thoughts flew. "Are you upset I find fault with your actions?"

"It's always been about you, yet you dare criticize me."

Frowning, he lowered his blade. "What the perdition do you mean? Why is it my fault?"

Calandra's eyes turned an icy green. "You are the high prince. Everyone looks up to you. You were always honored, admired. Your father never said a harsh word to you."

Duran shook his head. "Before you spout any more sanctimonious dribble, remember you brought this atrocity upon me because of jealousy."

"You think me jealous?" Her mouth snapped closed, and she plucked at the sleeve of her gown as if suddenly discovering lint defacing the delicate fabric. "Well, maybe a little. So what? I had a legitimate reason."

"Legitimate? Don't make me laugh."

Narud chuckled. *"That's right, human, accept no excuse for her appalling behavior."*

"Silence!" He ignored the dragon's mounting amusement. *"I will not allow you to deceive me."*

Calandra raised her brows. "You belittle me?"

Blood for revenge pounded in his temples. Dragon's teeth! He never thought killing her would be this hard. "I don't need to ridicule you. Nor can I ever reconcile the extreme thing you did to me. You destroyed whatever respect I once possessed for you, and soon my father will learn of your duplicity."

"Will he now?"

"You can still redeem yourself." His tone held an iciness. "Tell me why rumors of a war are starting?"

Calandra glanced at him cynically. "Why not? There is nothing you can do. My father plans to invade Brenalin. The fact I have no qualms about telling you should be warning enough that this information will never leave this room."

He glared at her. "You're too late. Einer is already aware of your and your father's treachery. He will notify my father, and my companion here will back up whatever he says."

"Really?" Calandra glanced at Stav. "I doubt anyone will believe a servant over me. Let her go. Kill her. You and I can still form an alliance. We will both benefit."

It wasn't normal for Duran to feel dread. Caution, yes. Every military commander experienced prudence before a confrontation. But this time! *Kill Stav.* His very bones ached as Calandra's honeyed words faded away.

"I daresay she might object. I know I would if my life were threatened."

The sorceress gave Stav a second look. "I can be generous. Instead of killing her, I'll turn her into a frog or a crow. Yes, I think a crow. I'll keep her in a little cage. You could visit her whenever you wish."

Duran inched closer to Stav. The scent of roses greeted him. He raised his sword again and pointed the deadly tip at Calandra.

"Your time for casting spells against innocent people is over. All you need do is remove my curse."

Calandra laughed, the sound cold and calculating. "Even if I wanted to, I cannot. Magic takes time, preparation."

"You will do as I order. Now." He glowered at her. Smoldering resentment built with each passing second. "Or you will die at my hands."

"You would kill me?" she asked innocently.

"Precisely." Narud's voice purred in Duran's head. *"Kill her. Do it now. Do it. She deserves to die."*

"Be silent!" Duran ordered back. *"I need no prompting from you. You say nothing I haven't considered."*

"What's the matter, Duran?" The sorceress's voice softened. "You keep frowning. Surely not at me. The dragon maybe? Nearly four months have passed. You and he should have become well acquainted by now. I imagine he is growing stronger and is a constant nuisance to your peace of mind."

Something pathetic hovered around Calandra. The sudden insight allowed Duran to relax slightly. "I did come to kill you, Calandra, but I have reconsidered. For the moment, I'll let you live."

"Such good tidings are pleasing to hear," she cooed. "I may not be able to reverse my curse immediately, but who's to say I won't try at some future date. You need me."

"Talk no more!" Narud intruded, his tone insistent, no longer coaxing. *"Kill her! She must die. That's what she has planned for you."*

Lies. Dragons lie. Do not listen to him, Duran ordered himself. There had to be a reason the dragon wanted the sorceress dead. Before Narud could say more, blinding hatred erupted in him. His body shook, his mind recoiling from dragon poison curling through his veins. A hot, burning loathing ate away at every bit of humanity inside him.

He gritted his teeth. He barely had time to think, barely had time to fight the sensation spreading through him before his control broke.

He glared at Calandra. "You have no idea about the monster you unleashed. He wants you dead by any means." He tossed his sword away and leapt at Calandra with arms outstretched, his hands reaching for her lily-white throat. They fell to the floor with a grunt.

Dragon laughter echoed through his head.

"Duran, no!" Stav screamed.

"Get away from me," he grunted, his hands clutching Calandra's throat and squeezing.

"She's baiting you," Stav yelled. "Don't do anything you might regret later."

Duran rolled when he heard Calandra mumble under her breath. Somehow he found his sword, fingertips locking on the hilt. He swung and heard Calandra suck in a gasp. A bright red line the width of a piece of thread dotted her fair face. He adjusted his hold on the sword's handle and jabbed at her body. His blade couldn't touch her. Whatever spell she'd created protected her.

Stav grabbed his arm and tried to drag him back. His fear of injuring her by mistake proved stronger than his desire for revenge, and he followed. The red haze of insanity faded.

"Mind your friend." Calandra scrambled to her feet. "Despite her common appearance, she is proving wise. You dishonor yourself by behaving like a madman. No one has done what I did," she said, her tone boastful. "I have made you more than a mere mortal. I, Calandra Genoy, created a living, breathing legend. You should feel honored."

"You can still kill her," Narud's voice whispered coldly. *"Catch her unaware. Her life means nothing."*

Duran snorted in loathing and fear, though not at Calandra. Somehow Narud had managed to control his body. A sickening realization formed in Duran. The beast was his nemesis as much as the sorceress.

"Go away," he mindspoke vehemently. *"You deliberately attempt to distract me."*

"I am the stronger. Did I not just prove it? You are failing, human. Soon you will be gone forevermore."

"My spirit will haunt you till the end of your days. Now begone." Duran looked around the room. He hoped the sorceress didn't notice the delay in his answer. "Honor has nothing to do with it, Calandra. You wanted something from me. When I refused to grant your request, you struck out at me."

"Oh, Duran." Her voice turned velvet soft once again. "I never meant to hurt you. You must believe me. I did it for you. For us. I wanted us to be together for now and forever."

"Calandra—"

"Listen to me, Duran," she interrupted him, her green eyes bright. "I beg you. Together no one can stop us. I know secrets, things that can make you unbeatable. We—"

"Liar!" he snapped, sharply. "The sight of you sickens me. You betrayed me! You betrayed Brenalin."

"I betrayed you? Come now, Duran. You knew of my affections. Yet you did nothing to dissuade me. Don't deny it. You think I enjoy hurting you as you did me?"

"You should have thought of that before you cursed me," he answered, much calmer with the murderous rage gone. "Why would I follow a woman who only thinks of herself? The path you follow is disgusting to me."

Anger flashed in Calandra's eyes. "There's no need for us to quarrel."

"Leave him alone," Stav said, bluntly. "Haven't you hurt him enough?"

A long time passed before Calandra replied. "And how will you stop me?"

Stav sighed. "All I know is you committed a terrible wrong."

"How can it be wrong?" Calandra chuckled. "From one woman to another, I can tell you he's a foolish man. I offered him the world, and he was too ignorant to comprehend it. Such a pity."

"You're the one to be pitied," Stav countered, "not Duran."

The sorceress only smiled. "I should have realized he would inspire loyalty in the lower classes. You are a fitting companion in his final days."

Duran heard enough. Stav collected too much attention from the sorceress. "Insults again, Calandra?" He stepped forward.

Calandra arched a dramatic brow. "Do not trifle with me. Perhaps you would prefer another demonstration of my power." Her fingers fluttered as if she were weaving a piece of cloth and she chanted, her words easy to hear.

Begone this night.
Begone from here.

Begone from my sight.

The air glimmered softly in front of Stav and Duran. He stared wide-eyed when a mist formed. An odd tingle touched his skin, darker in feeling than Einer's magic. It itched as though poison oak had been rubbed against his flesh.

The tips of Calandra's bejeweled fingers brightened. She pointed at them and shafts of white light surged out to merge into one thick mass.

Suddenly, Stav threw herself in front of him, her arms thrust toward the ceiling. A loud bang exploded in the room. Perfume bottles shattered on the vanity. Their heady contents spilled on the tabletop and dribbled to the floor.

Duran's ears rang. He wanted to retch.

The shimmering veil fizzled and disappeared before his very eyes.

Calandra rubbed her fingers as though they hurt. Her eyes turned deep green and angry. "You are protected by magic. Who? Why?"

Duran ignored the sorceress. "Stav," he murmured. "Why'd you do that?"

She brightened and smiled. "To save you."

"You could have been hurt. Are you all right?"

"No harm done."

The sorceress shook her head. "Of course. Einer. I should have eliminated the old fool long ago."

"Once again, Calandra, you issue threats when your will is thwarted." Bitterness oozed from his tone. "We have reached an impasse. Unless you want to waste time attacking us with magic again. You can't hurt us, and we cannot touch you. We're deadlocked."

The sorceress froze. "Begone from my sight. I care

not for you. I will win in the end."

Duran scowled. "You may be right, but my quest is to break your curse." He looked at Stav, their gazes concurring silently, then they hurried from Calandra's chamber. They didn't stop until they stood outside the same castle door they had entered a lifetime before. Cold night air greeted them.

"What now?" Stav asked, bent over with her hands on her knees and panting.

A brittle gray light spread across the star-filled sky. He counted to ten before answering. "We've got to get out of here." Brimstone tasted in his mouth, a reminder of the dragon's presence. "Narud…used…me. He attacked Calandra. Not me. Somehow he took over my body."

"Oh, Duran."

To him, it sounded like her heart broke. "I'll have to put my faith in Einer to inform my father and protect him from Calandra's evil." He laid a finger on her face. Her skin felt soft and smooth as silk. He wished with all his heart he could stay with her. "Nor can you remain in the castle while Calandra is alive. You wouldn't be safe."

Stav started to say something, and then stopped at the sound of a wagon creaking and groaning past them. Duran saw candlelight flare to life and flicker in several buildings.

Morning showed in the twilight of a grey dawn. The city stirred.

He looked up at the castle, his home. So close. So close, yet so far. Longing and disappointment welled up inside him. Nothing had been resolved. He hadn't broken the spell. Calandra still lived. A curse still ruled his life.

Worse, Narud had somehow managed to gain power over his body.

The evening had become a disaster.

Duran cast a sidelong glance in Stav's direction. "Forgive me, Stav," he said, dejected. "This isn't how I envisioned the night turning out. We need to leave."

Her expression turned firm. "Then let's go to Eudes. You can't defeat Calandra alone. They'll help with their army. We can return and defeat the sorceress and her father."

Her positive attitude made him smile. That gave him all the hope he needed.

They raced the rest of the way out of Brenalin.

Nighttime disappeared. Narud awoke.

Chapter Fourteen

Several hours past dawn, a second man entered Calandra's quarters. Unlike Duran, this one came in answer to her summons. He stood respectfully, but from the way his gaze swept her room and his nose twitched at the cloying fragrance of spilled perfume, he disapproved of being there.

An untidy beard had sprouted on his face since she'd last seen him, and he smelled of sweat and dirt. He might disapprove of her perfume, but his stench offended her. She wondered if Commander Marrow would be amused to discover she considered his presence a violation, a debasement of her environment.

She set her boar-hair brush down on the vanity and turned to face him. "A couple is fleeing Brenalin," she opened without preamble. "Find them."

If her directive surprised him, he concealed it well. "Where do they go?"

She eyed the bald-headed man with all the warmth she'd expend watching a beetle scurry across the floor of her workroom. "My guess is Eudes. That's where the woman is originally from. Take your men and find them."

"Aye, Mistress."

"You do not ask who these people are, Commander?"

A frown of displeasure passed over his face. "No,

Mistress. I trust you would tell me if necessary."

"A very good answer, Commander."

Marrow gaped, uncomprehending, for several seconds. "Do you wish them returned to you for punishment?"

She laughed, displeased.

Marrow tensed; veins in his thickly muscled neck throbbed.

"Certainly not. I never want to lay eyes on them again."

His brow wrinkled in consternation. "What are your orders, then?"

"Kill them, of course. How the deed is done is of no consequence to me. Do with them as you please."

Marrow inclined his head, this time a feral expression flashing across his face. The man's reputation preceded him. He didn't just like killing. He enjoyed torturing his victims.

Duran had disappointed her. Rejected her. Angered her. His dismissal of her affection tore at her heart. The prince might as well have sentenced her to die. Whatever punishment Marrow meted out, Duran deserved. And his little servant, too.

The Abbas secret was not the only thing of importance she'd found in Einer's dusty tomes. An ancient prophecy sent shivers of fear through her. She'd committed the script to memory.

Foster child, foster thyself. Filled with twisted love, this child seeks to share Brenalin's royal throne. If successful, eternity awaits. If failure arises, death prevails.

She was the foster child named in the prophecy. Who else could it be? More than merely wanting to wed

Duran, she needed to become Brenalin's queen or she would die.

"The woman is no one," she added, smiling at the waiting soldier she had yet to dismiss, "a servant. I'm sure you'll appreciate the irony. She is the very one you searched for in the mountains. It seems she slipped through your clutches and came here." The man flinched. "I'm sure you'll redeem yourself, Commander, and will not fail this time."

"Aye, Mistress," he said in a clipped tone.

She accepted his deference as her due. "The man might prove more difficult. He has a soldier's training and is quite skilled at fighting. Consider him dangerous."

Marrow's eyes glittered. "It doesn't matter how good a fighter he is with odds of one against a dozen."

"Even if you spot the woman alone," she warned anyway, "do not apprehend her during the day. Wait until after dark."

If possible, Marrow's expression turned dourer. "Is there something I should know about her?"

Annoyance flared in Calandra. He dare question her? It proved the man was her father's minion, not hers. "Just follow my instructions, Commander, and you will be safe enough."

He bowed his bald-head. "I meant no offense, Mistress. My men and I can handle a man and woman without any trouble."

The fool! Did he think she couldn't tell he would disobey her orders the first chance he got? His arrogance would get him killed. "Under ordinary circumstances, I would yield to your military expertise, but in this case, you must trust my judgment. She has a protector you would not wish to face, no matter how many men you command."

He straightened to his full height, an impressive sight. "I fear no man."

"The crux of the situation, Commander, is her protector may not be human."

"The dragon," Marrow uttered softly.

His insight impressed Calandra. Perhaps she judged him too quickly. She felt begrudged to compliment him. "Another good answer, sir; and more important, accurate."

"The creature killed several of my men at the caravan."

"Nighttime is safest for you and your men. Unless you wish to face the dragon."

"It will be as you wish," he said, tight-lipped.

For an instant Calandra let herself be comforted by his words, then pulled herself upright. "Be sure you do."

"Consider them dead." He glanced at the window.

She smiled. "Do not disappoint me, Commander."

"I have no intention of doing so. I follow your orders."

"Good."

Marrow withdrew, and she went back to brushing her hair, a task she performed every day with pleasure.

****

Marina leaned against a tree in the great forest where they'd run after leaving the sorceress's sleeping chamber. Tall evergreens, heavily laden with pinecones, loomed over their heads and scented the air with clean pine.

"The princess isn't dead." She uttered her

statement without considering the consequences.

Duran gave her a derisive look. "Do not jest, Stav! Of course she is. I saw her body through Narud's eyes."

Duran's tone filled with such scathing that it nearly unnerved Marina. She had anticipated her words would bring him a measure of hope, not hostility.

"You saw a body—Stav's," Marina said, determined to tell all. "My father ordered us to change clothes before entering Brenalin. I am Princess Marina Hersher."

Red flashed in Duran's eyes. The look of exhaustion scoring his handsome features vanished with a flash of betrayal. "Why tell me now?"

"It was time." *Maybe past time.* A bleak vision of the future without Duran leapt into her mind. She put her hand on his arm, reluctant to meet his eyes, but knowing she had no other choice. "Oh, Duran, let me explain so you'll understand why I waited. My caravan had been destroyed, the people murdered. I was afraid. I didn't know who you were, then time passed and…"

"No quarter exists for me to complain." He sounded wretched, but forgiving. "I am guilty of the same offense, Stav…or I should say, Marina. I guess I'll just have to accustom myself to thinking of you as Marina."

"I should have done the right thing and told you immediately," she uttered quickly, still stunned at his quick acceptance.

He pushed a hand through his thick, dark hair. "Why didn't you tell me when I told you?"

"You were about to confront Calandra," she said, feeling obligated to explain. "I feared distracting you."

He edged closer to her and took her hand. "A

logical reason."

His strong fingers wrapped around her much slender ones. Her belly clenched with sudden longing. Dare she show her yearning with so much at stake?

"I wanted to tell you. I really did, but my deception had gone on too long. I was afraid of the outcome."

"You did right."

The man couldn't be fairer, she thought. "After learning who you were, I was more afraid. We were to have wed, and I deceived you. You told me how much honor meant to you. I wasn't proud of my dishonesty. I—I—I was being selfish, too. I didn't want you to hate me. I was afraid you'd be so angry you would leave me. I—I—"

"Hush, my sweet." The bump in Duran's throat bobbed when he swallowed. "Forgiveness starts now. We kept our secrets and have made amends now. I don't regret a moment of time we have spent together. Not a single wonderful minute."

The glow on the horizon turned fiery gold. Sufficient light allowed her to see tiny blue and green flecks in his striking eyes. No red gleam whatsoever. She leaned forward and flattened her palms on his chest.

"Kiss me."

"With pleasure." He lowered his mouth to hers.

She felt like she floated through the air. His kiss fueled an inner passion until she surrendered to the throbbing rhythm in her body and wrapped her arms around his neck. Nothing else mattered. She let the world spin around her.

Sensing subtleness in the air, Marina opened her eyes and gasped with dismay. The sun climbed higher on the horizon. A tear rolled down her cheek. It wasn't fair. She wanted the night to stay forever.

Duran followed her gaze. *"No!"* He scrambled away from her. "Unfair. Not now!"

Marina watched a red mist form out of the air and spread over Duran's body. The transformation from man to dragon began. Nothing would tear her away from his side.

The strange haze increased into the size of Narud. It pulsed, thickened, and solidified. Duran's moans were laced with anguish within the dense center. His cries tore at her heart. The pain must be terrible. She cringed in sympathy for him, willing to absorb it for him.

Suddenly, the mist burst into flames. Marina rolled back from the spurt of heat. No mortal could withstand such a fire. Then, the flames winked out. The ground wasn't scorched. No odor of burning flesh or vegetation tainted the air.

Where Duran once twisted in agony, Narud stretched his powerful limbs. He opened his jaws, his black tongue slithering out for the first taste of cool morning air. Narud's tail whipped out and coiled around her possessively.

"Sleep, my brave beauty. You endured much during this night."

Choice was stolen away from her. She obeyed the draconic order. Her eyes drifted closed.

An undetermined time later, she awoke to scant illumination of a fire burning itself down to a pile of red embers and gray ash. It cast enough light for her to see the dragon's iridescent scales and be reminded of coral growing in the deep waters along the southern reefs.

Marina scooted up and found herself in a cave. The cavern smelled of earthy, dry soil, but she didn't care. The warm and cozy sensations made her feel renewed. She wondered how the dragon found this cave, and then remembered a dragon's nature could locate caves easily for their lairs. They were deep enough inside this one she couldn't see the entrance. She wasn't complaining, just curious.

Her thoughts turned to Calandra. No one had told her the sorceress would be tall and shapely with an elegance impossible to imitate. And evil. The foul stench of malevolence had permeated the air of her sleeping quarters. Marina had wanted to gag. Never had she been more afraid.

She freed herself from Narud's coils to stand. The air felt much cooler away from his warmth, and the temptation to snuggle back against him had her looking at him.

"Where are we?" she asked.

Narud peered at her calmly. *"A league from Brenalin. There's nothing to fear. I've protected the cave. No one will find it…or us."*

"Narud, do you care what's happening in Brenalin?"

"Speak your mind, pet. You will, even if I object."

"Very well, I will." She was positive it was vital Narud understood. As a dragon, he could help. "A dangerous army is on its way to conquer this land. They will destroy everything in its path. It's war!"

"Truly?"

He rose from his resting spot. Marina noticed he sat on a thin sheet of pearls and rubies. She spared a moment to wonder how he'd acquired the jewels so quickly. Dragons certainly had a knack for finding treasure wherever they went.

She felt, more than heard the gentle brush of Narud's chuckle fill her insides. The touch felt like a caress and her desire for his closeness shocked her, wanting more.

"Of course you do, my pet." Narud answered her thought.

"Don't be rude."

"So, you are the princess. I should have guessed. You and I are fated to be together. My instincts about you being the perfect mate for me were correct. I shall be the first dragon king in centuries. You will be my queen."

She ignored his proclamation to focus on the problem. "What about Genoy? He's going to destroy Brenalin."

Yawning, Narud clicked his sharp fangs together when he closed his long snout. *"What about him? Where is this dangerous army you spoke of?"*

"I—I do not know the exact location." Her admission did not make her feel any better.

"Well, what do you know?"

She folded her arms. "The Sandblood spoke of a coming war. The sorceress confirmed her father, Lord Genoy, has his army ready to attack Brenalin. I must reach Eudes. My father can send troops to stop the invasion. He'll understand one conquest will not satisfy Genoy. Eudes could be his next target. Do you think me wrong?"

"Exceedingly." The dragon smirked at her.

"Then do something."

Narud lowered his great head. They were nose to

snout. His red eyes peered directly into her hazel ones. Marina worried she'd gone too far and struggled to control her annoyance, to keep her voice calm.

"Do you provoke me intentionally? Squabbles between humans are of no concern to me."

"You should care."

A puff of acrid smoke burst from his nostrils. *"Why should I bother with them? Let humans kill each other."*

"Stop thinking of yourself."

"Was I?"

Who baited whom? she wondered. She drew in a deep, calming gulp of air and held it, then exhaled it. "Lives are at stake. People will be murdered or worse." She squeezed her eyes shut, despising the image her own words created. Her blood chilled. A moment later, she opened her eyes, saying, "Unless you can save them."

"Of course, I can. But why should I aid Duran's kingdom?"

Arguing with a dragon made her want to pull her hair out in chunks. "Narud, if I could get my hands around your throat, I would strangle you. Can you not see the obvious? This is your land. Your home. Do you wish to see it laid to waste? You should be outraged someone plans to attack it."

"It means naught to me."

"Think, you fool! Why do you think Genoy invades Brenalin? For the land? For Demit Woods? No! He seeks dominance over you. First, he'll seize the Ruby Throne. You are tied to it, are you not?" She caught her breath, slowing her words and pulse together. "Once he holds the throne, he'll control you."

The scales on Narud's back lifted. His sharp black claws dug deep gouges in the packed earth. *"No one rules me,"* the dragon hissed. *"I am a dragon."*

Thank the lesser sea gods! She'd hit a sensitive spot. "I never met a dragon who didn't have a high opinion of himself."

"I am the only dragon you know."

He had her there. "Maybe so, but everything I ever read claims all dragons share one trait in common."

"And that is?"

"An over-inflated ego."

His thick tail twitched, the spade shaped tip barely missing the dying fire with each pass. *"Haven't you learned by now when you speak of dragons, you know very little?"*

The gruff manner did not deter Marina. "And how many dragons have you met? Or does being a dragon impart special knowledge?"

A growl rumbled from the huge cavity of his chest. *"Dragons are not all alike. We are very different beings."*

She began stroking his scales, conscious how he liked her to touch him. "Please, Narud, how many innocents must die before you realize you are their only hope?"

"All right, to ease your fears, I admit this is my land." His gem-studded chest suddenly glistened when flames flared up. *"And I am loath to let a puny human destroy it. I will help...because you ask it of me."*

"That is most welcome, Narud."

"Do not be so quick with your gratitude," he said so quietly she barely heard. *"You may not like my tactics. If this army exists, I will kill many humans."*

"Genoy's army violates Brenalin by stepping a foot upon its soil." She dismissed his warning. "He must be stopped, and you are the only one capable of doing so. The innocent must be saved." She paused, catching her breath. "Just be careful. Great danger is involved, even for one such as you."

"You worry overmuch. No harm will come to me."

Stories of the dragons' annihilation surged forward in Marina's mind. "A certain amount of confidence is good, but reckless bravery is pure idiocy. Remember dragons aren't infallible. If they were, your brethren would still be alive."

Narud harrumphed. *"Who's to say they aren't?"*

"What do you mean?" His comeback piqued her, despite her knowledge to the contrary. "Other dragons? They've been dead for thousands of years. You are the only dragon on Feldsvelt."

"The Guardians spoke to me."

"The Guardians of Secrets?" She remembered their full name. "I want to know everything, but we have no time to discuss this marvel. You need to go. Take care of yourself, Narud. I wish I was going with you."

"Be glad you're not," he said firmly.

"How will you approach Genoy's encampment unseen?"

"Simple. I'll fly high above them. I do not fear them or their feeble weapons."

Marina released her breath in a long sigh. "Someone's bound to notice a real, live dragon. You'll strike terror into their hearts, but once they're over the shock, you'll be vulnerable to Genoy's archers."

"I won't be seen. Leave the details to me."

"I hope you're right. I have no desire to see you

hurt." She put her hand on his jewel-encrusted chest. "Return before sundown."

Narud's tongue flicked out, and skimmed the surface of her arm. His tongue was another reminder of Sinner, because their tongues were much alike in texture.

"Never fear, my brave beauty, I shall return victorious." He waddled awkwardly toward the entrance, sending tremors through the ground as his clawed toes clicked sharply on the rocks. *"Come, see me off."*

Outside, thick, dark gray clouds, the color of mackerels, shrouded the sky. Drizzle soaked the ground, trees, and shrubs.

Narud spread his wings and heaved himself up. He circled their campsite before heading north, dipping once in farewell.

Marina disregarded the rain to watch his antics, a smile forming. She cried out, hoping he heard, "Come back to me."

****

The hunt was on.

A quarter hour passed with Narud following the ley-lines toward Brenalin's border. He snorted as he flew on, shooting puffs of smoke from both nostrils, his powerful wings beating in unison.

Come back to me, he had heard her shout.

Oh, the joy of those words.

The foul weather lessened. Bright golden sunbeams pierced the clouds. He twisted his neck around to catch a flash where sun blazed on Stav's gold-bright hair. Her tresses shined with the same metallic glimmer of his scale tips.

He knew of her ignorance that dragons were fierce protectors of their individual lands. They fought each other, males for breeding rights and females for territory. Centuries of bloodshed had passed before they established their orderly society.

Humans, on the other hand, never achieved a truly peaceful coexistence. Oh, they professed sophisticated cultures, boasted about the equity of their laws and the grandeur of structures they built. The history of humankind was pitted with growths and declines like the marks on men's faces who'd suffered from the pox.

He hoped Stav would recognize the evils of humanity and come to accept his offer to become a dragoness. Dragons mated for life. She would be his companion for centuries to come. He imagined them together, sharing their kills, hoarding their treasures, and raising their wyrmlings.

Thus far she had refused him.

He understood now. Stav, a princess. It was an immense decision for her and explained many things. He accepted that.

He would ask her again…and again.

Until she agreed.

He flew on for miles. Slewing his head around, he spotted sunlight dance off swords and spears. The enemy gathered below. A dozen companies of infantry sloshed in the lead through the mud. Archers followed them. After those came the cavalry, riding in formation. In the rear, cannon and supply wagons rolled slowly.

A sizable army crawled across Brenalin. His land.

Behind them, farms lay in smoldering ruins, their occupants dead or dying. Narud's gut twisted with anger. This army spared no one in their quest to conquer.

Genoy dared to think he could lead an invasion with impunity. Did the supercilious human mistakenly believe Narud would allow the contemptible human to control him? Hardly. Genoy was not the legitimate heir. He would never sit upon the Ruby Throne. Soon, he would learn the error of his arrogance.

This land belonged to the Abbas line.

To him.

No one attacked his domain. Duty required he give his protection. Narud vowed to slay every enemy soldier in the molten fire of his flames for the terror they brought to his land. They would feel his wrath by fire, talon, and teeth.

He circled overhead, his great jaws opened wide. He loosened a mighty roar in challenge. For a second, silence lay over the land as thick as any blanket. Frantic eyes turned skyward. Every living creature in the forest—birds, beasts, and humans—shivered in fear.

The battle started. Searing hot orange and yellow flames spewed from his mouth, acrid smoke from his nostrils. All who saw his magnificent display would believe he tried to burn the earth to ash.

"Die! You will all die," Narud sent his threat through mindspeech.

Dragonfear awoke in the people below. He had learned over the months that dragonfear made humans think only of their own deaths, made them fear life, made them weaker beings than they already were. Whether it was the sight of him, the dragonfear, his roar, or the flames, Narud didn't know or care.

Pandemonium broke out. Soldiers broke ranks, stumbling and colliding with each other. Officers yelled for order. No one listened. Everywhere people cried and screamed. Horses stampeded. Wagons overturned.

Diving with claws extended, he passed over them, letting flames scorch the air.

"Dragon!" he heard many cry in panic.

"Run."

"Hide."

"We are doomed!"

"Shut up, you fools," shouted an officer, "or, I'll split you open myself."

Narud roared again, just for the fun of it.

Voices screamed in terror. Booted feet ran, making sucking sounds as they slipped without traction on the muddy ground.

A lone rider, a high-ranking officer by his sleeveless vest decorated with silver and gold piping and a chest full of shiny medals and braid, galloped through the troops on a black stallion snorting with nervousness.

"Take heart, men," the newly arrived officer shouted. "We can beat one dragon—be he real or imagined."

Another officer gave his superior a baleful stare, then ordered, "Listen to Lord Genoy. He is correct. This creature could be an illusion, sent by Brenalin sorcerers. Do not be afraid. Show them the mettle of Demicland soldiers!"

Narud's heart rate increased. Foolish humans. He'd show them how real he was. He searched for the colorful little lordling a second time, but lost sight of him in the confusion.

The soldiers quieted, their panic ebbing.

A line of archers appeared out of the chaos and

formed ranks. They stood on the battlefield, weak and trembling.

Orders were shouted, "Take aim, you dolts. On the count of three."

"Fly away, Ancient One. Danger is present. You are the only one of your kind. Do not place yourself in jeopardy."

Narud spun around in the air, searching. *"Where are you, Guardians? I know you live. Why hide from me?"*

"You will see us when the time is right."

"What do you want?"

"To save you from utter folly."

He swooped lower as though fleeing from the Guardians' logic. *"I made a promise to rid Brenalin of Genoy's army. I mean to keep my word. Now go away. The matter is closed."*

His affection for Stav bound him to act. He did not want to live without her and was convinced this deed would elevate him in her estimation. Maybe high enough for her to give serious consideration about becoming a dragoness.

His dragoness.

A volley of arrows darkened the sky. The whirring sound reminded Narud of angry wasps. He breathed his own arrow of fire. Wooden shafts disintegrated into ash. Soot fell to the ground like black snow.

The moment he'd waited for came. Thus far, all he'd done was scare them. Not attack. Not harm.

The humans attacked first. It was not his fault the humans panicked at the sight of him. He had every right to defend himself. They'd tried to kill him.

Retaliation came swiftly.

Narud spewed balls of dragon fire that consumed men and woods without discrimination. The reek of sulfurous brimstone filled his nostrils along with the coppery scent of blood and burning flesh.

He made another pass, bombarding the supply trains. Chaos erupted again, with more men falling and dying, screaming. Hopelessness echoed in the cries of animals and men in pain.

A smidgen of benevolence tried to surface within him. He watched for signs of retreat and when he saw none, he unleashed more dragonfear, igniting soldiers' worst fears, making them believe their demise was near.

Then he spotted the Genoy lordling attempting to sneak away. Fiend! Narud sent a fireball into the coward's back. Fire engulfed him. The lordling ran screaming, his arms flailing, before collapsing and curling into a smoldering, charred mass.

The death of their leader broke the remaining soldiers. In a mad, disorganized rush, they retreated the way they originally marched. Narud knew the tale of his triumph would be carried throughout the lands. No sane leader would consider attacking Brenalin for many a time.

Elated, he folded his wings tight against his body to glide low over the land to view his victory. Bodies littered the blackened, ash-covered battlefield. He almost was loath to leave the beautiful site.

"A foolish act, Ancient One. Nonetheless, well done. Those below were greedy. Rapacious humans. Their destruction was necessary."

Narud gloried in the praise. *"It was nothing."*

"A word of caution," the Guardians mindspoke. *"Let us hope your action does not bring the wrath of*

other humans down upon you. This world is a dangerous place. Especially for dragons. Your survival is essential. We can teach you the tools you need to stay alive. Let us help you."

"Maybe another time. Show yourselves."

"It is still too soon."

Narud had already dug deep into his memories to pull forth a fact about the Guardians. They were known for their secretive nature. So be it. He would let them remain ambiguous.

Rolling over in an aerial dance, Narud concentrated on pleasanter matters. Marina would be proud of him. Destroying the great army had to impress her.

He was a hero today.

Chapter Fifteen

Marina shaded her eyes with her hand. Time moved at a crawl, measured by the slow movement of the sun across the cloud-dotted sky. Hours had passed since she last saw Narud.

Until now, she hadn't given much consideration to the lofty heights a dragon must fly. What if he became wounded and fell? The fall would kill him. She shuddered at the painful thought.

She dug into her pocket for the ruby gemstone. The instant she touched it, a rush of energy spread through her hand like the incoming tide and brought her strength and courage.

A flyspeck in the sky grew bigger. An eagle? No. Narud? Oh, yes!

Thrilled, she jumped for the pure joy. She clapped her hands and watched the dragon perform graceful loops in the air. Never had she seen anything like it. He looked beautiful.

"Narud, you silly creature. What are you doing?"

"Celebrating. Brenalin is saved."

"What of Genoy?"

"Dead."

The vile man deserved his fate. *"His army?"*

"They are no more. The lucky ones died quickly. Others crawled away. Few escaped unscathed."

"My heartfelt thanks. And welcome back. I wish I

could have seen your triumph."

His crimson scales dazzled like fine ruby gemstones in the bright daylight. *"It was magnificent. I was magnificent."*

"I'm sure you were brave and courageous." And thankfully, he looked hale and hearty.

She squashed whatever sympathy she might have felt for dutiful soldiers obeying orders by the memory of her caravan's attack and the grisly deaths of her companions. They were innocents. Nothing excused what happened to them.

Warm air swooshed over her skin when Narud landed on the ground in front of her. The foul odor of burning flesh clung to his scales.

"Your praise pleases me greatly. You see how strong and powerful I am. Could the puny human, Duran, do what I did? I think not. Only me." He took in a large gulp of air. *"Have you given more thought to becoming a dragoness?"*

"I already gave you my answer."

"It never hurts to ask a second time. You might change your mind."

"I can't accept your offer."

Thin bursts of smoke spurted from Narud's nostrils. *"Why not? With two dragons, the danger of invasion to my country or yours would become non-existent. Think about it, my sweet. Together we can protect both. Interlopers will never endanger either one. If they tried, they would face our combined wrath."*

Marina listened while Narud's unblinking red and slit-pupiled gaze captivated her. When he stopped, she walked up to his side, her feet cushioned in the soggy ground. "You are trying to tempt me into something we both would later regret."

"How could you regret being my companion or becoming a dragoness?"

His draconic arrogance appeared endless. "My apologies, Narud, if I seem ungrateful. Believe me, I'm not. No one could have done what you did, but being a dragoness is not the life for me."

"If you haven't tried, how can you reject my offer out of hand?"

A chill went through her. "Hold on there! I am not the only one to think about. My family believes me dead. I cannot let them grieve under false pretenses. I won't."

"Truly?"

"Truly," she repeated, wanting to put an end to their argument. "Now, before you say another word, I'm going to take a bath and wash my clothes." She gestured toward a small stream where faint gurgles and bubbling enticed. "I'd like to indulge myself before we start our journey again."

"Would you like me to heat the water?"

"No need. As a child, sometimes I was allowed out on the fishermen's boats. I rode the ocean as the waves rose and fell. Breezes nipped at my face and hands. To this day I find cold water invigorating. It fills me with a rare fervor."

Narud blocked her path. *"I will stand guard while you bathe."*

"I can take care of myself."

"Indulge me this time. I want nothing to happen to you."

"All right. Come along, if you must."

She stroked Narud's sinewy neck as if he were a great cat. The dragon began purring with satisfaction. From her touch or from the fact he believed he'd won the agreement? No easy way existed that allowed her to refuse him.

She thought of home. Her parents. Her family. They would be beyond themselves with happiness to find her returned to their bosom.

At the creek's edge, she stripped off her boots and leggings. She left on her gown, planning to wash it right on her body. She'd braced for cool, if not icy water; only to sink into toasty warmth that turned her stomach to mush.

"Narud!" The beast remained conveniently out of sight, but she still complained, "I told you not to heat the water."

"I did not want you to catch a chill."

"I like chilly water."

"So be it. It shall be as you wish."

Cold water rushed downstream to wash over her. It stole her very breath and made her shiver. Thank Kubala, timing was wrong for spawning laks, a migrating fish that spent its early life in fresh water and then swam to the ocean before returning to the stream or river that generated them. Those fish were important to the industry of Eudes. She could only imagine the catastrophe if they'd encountered heated water. A whole season would be destroyed for a few moments of her comfort.

The balance of her bath passed without incident, and she made her way back to their campsite beneath a darkening sky. Glittering dragonflies emerged from the woods. This time the radiant insects kept their distance.

The behavior was as odd as the times they converged *en mass* on Duran.

She entered the cave to find a small fire burning in the center of the floor. She smiled at Narud's thoughtfulness. The dragon had flown off to hunt for his evening meal. Doffing her gown amid a cloud of moisture, she laid it on a nearby rock to dry and wrapped herself in a blanket.

He really wasn't a bad sort…for a dragon.

What she felt for Narud wasn't the same as her feelings for Duran. She couldn't identify it. It stemmed from many different things. Flying popped into her head. Precious gemstones could be hers. Why did he want her to become a dragoness? Even though being one might prove interesting.

Her fantasy shattered when she thought of never seeing see her family again. Deep in her heart, though, she would miss Duran the most.

****

Three days after leaving Brenalin, Duran remained alert. A sense of urgency prompted him to travel fast. He had longed to stay in Brenalin, feeling guilty after leaving his father and Einer to face Calandra's malevolence without him.

When he thought of his confrontation with the sorceress, his gut tightened. The longer they had talked, the angrier he'd become. And then to have Narud taunt him at the same time. The dragon stole precious time away from him and his autonomy.

Fear left a sour taste in Duran's mouth. Losing a fair fight was bad enough—but the sorceress's confrontation had gone terribly awry.

Suddenly he didn't want to dwell on his

disappointment and cast about for a way to focus on something more pleasant. Stav…no, not Stav. Marina. Marina's safety came first.

"We'll rest here for a while." They had reached a small clearing which looked like a good place to stop. If trouble arose, the princess could escape into the trees while he guarded her rear. "We've been charging through these woods for days. I've been covering our tracks. We probably can light a fire. The wind's blowing enough, the smoke will not attract attention."

"You don't need to convince me."

Weariness laced her voice, and he regretted pushing her so hard. "We cannot tarry long, but a short rest will do us good."

"I'll gather wood and start a fire," she said. "You go catch us something to eat."

Duran swallowed a laugh. She treated him as though he had never told her of his position or that she had been raised a princess. Their bond of friendship had been forged through unimaginable hardships and made stronger. He rather liked the idea.

He glanced up at the stars winking in the black sky. Thin clouds floated over the moon. Besides the stars and moon, good fortune shined down on him. He made his first kill in seconds and returned to find Marina had dug a small pit, rimming it with rocks before making her fire. Smiling, he realized she'd acquired enough skills to make a good woodswoman.

After eating, Marina tossed the rabbit bones of her meal into the flames and licked the grease off her fingers. She lifted her head and studied him. "I've been thinking. You may not like what I'm going to say, but please hear me out before you object."

The lure of her voice captured his attention. "Sounds serious."

"I think it is. Here goes." She sighed. "Maybe your transformation into a dragon was fortuitous."

"What?" Anger and alarm raced through him. "How can you say that? You know how much I despise being Narud. How hard I am trying to break Calandra's cursed spell."

"Listen to me, Duran." Marina's hazel eyes pleaded with him. "Narud saved Brenalin. He destroyed Genoy's army. If you hadn't turned into a dragon, he wouldn't have been here to beat Genoy back."

He bit his lip until blood fouled his mouth. "We didn't need his help. Brenalin has its own powerful army. We can stand against any force."

A quiver shook her chin. "You wouldn't have known about them in time. Remember, we learned of the army from Fahid. You wouldn't have met him if we hadn't been coming from Narud's lair. The alarm wouldn't have been raised before Genoy attacked. It would have been too late."

"Hold on," he said, keeping a tight rein on his temper. "You don't know that!"

Narud wiggled below the surface of his mind. With his head awhirl with emotions, the dragon sought to steal another chance to take over his body. Except this time Duran was ready for him. He controlled his feelings and beat Narud back with the power of his will. Victory tasted sweet.

Marina smiled. "You're proud, Duran, but pride is a feeble weapon when pitted against steel. You must lay it aside."

"No!" He gritted his teeth against the rush of red-hot resentment. He couldn't let his resolve weaken for a single second. If he did, Narud would surface. "I won't," he said to both Marina and the dragon.

"Do you hear yourself? Each day you sound more like Narud. You're even given to uttering one-word responses just like him."

He stood and dumped a bucket of water onto the fire. Hissing and smoking, the flames fought a losing battle. The analogy was not lost on him. Did he face the same fate?

"Another inaccuracy. We have a long, tedious night of travel ahead of us." The wordiness sounded alien to his ears. "I want to deliver you to Eudes, so I can return to Brenalin. I need to face Calandra without interference from Narud or you. Are you ready to go?"

Marina nodded and stood. "Of course."

She'd never looked lovelier. Over the past weeks and months, his viewpoint toward her had evolved from wanting to be rid of her to enjoying her company, to friendship, to love. But what could he offer her? Precious little.

Being cursed had prevented them from wedding, possibly expecting their firstborn. On the other hand, if he hadn't been, this chance of becoming friends would have been lost. That would have been a greater loss.

He stared at her, her eyes wide and appealing. She looked so enticing. If only they could live together as husband and wife. In his heart, she belonged to him.

He drew her close, and a connection sparked between them. His fingers brushed silken curls from her face. It felt so right to hold her in his arms.

Bending his head, he kissed her, tasting honey. Nice. She moaned softly. Desire increased. He deepened his kiss.

"Indulge me, my sweet Marina."

He lifted his mouth from hers. A seductive smile touched her lips. The sight reminded him that he looked forward to it every night.

He kissed her again, his breath coming faster and faster. The passion of their embrace gave rise to another response between his legs. He couldn't stop himself. His body ached for hers until his hands covered her bottom, kneading the suppleness and heat of her body.

Marina glided her fingers over his jaw. He leaned into her palm, savoring the contact and smelling the faint aroma of roasted rabbit on her skin.

Warmth spread through his loins even as guilt flashed through his mind. "I'm sorry, Marina. I had no right." He ended the embrace. "I shouldn't—"

"Hush," she interrupted him. "Next, you'll tell me you shouldn't have kissed me."

His arms tightened around her again at her words. Their bodies flattened against each other.

"I'll never lie to you, Marina," he said with genuine affection, "but I won't make a promise I can't keep."

"Duran…"

He didn't let her finish, covering her mouth with his, unwilling to let her tell him something he didn't want to hear. She sighed and he smiled to himself. She held his heart and wasn't even aware of it.

The world faded away. Turning back was impossible. This was their night.

He sucked in a breath as his body hummed with arousal. His tongue swept into the moist cavern of her mouth. She melted against him. Her breasts, full and taut, pressed into his chest. The sensation sent his body soaring with an almost painful tightness.

With a cry, Marina yanked free.

Misery swelled at the separation, conscious of the loss of every delectable curve of Marina's body. "Marina…"

Her breathing came out rapid and heavy. "Duran, I—"

"Say nothing, my sweet. That went too far."

"But—"

"Say no more." He snatched up her bedroll and shoved it into her hands. "The fault is mine."

****

Days blurred one into another. Marina slept during the day and walked all night. Duran refused to speak, and she worried that it was because of their kiss. Kisses, she corrected. She had counted three and wished for dozens more.

With dawn tinting the eastern horizon, the promise of a warm afternoon seemed a sure thing. Spring fast rushed into summer. She lay on the ground, a bed of boughs cushioning her body and scenting the air with pine as she soaked up the sun and watched fluffy clouds scudding across the sky.

Narud had gone hunting. Why did he want her to become a dragoness so much? Why had he helped Duran? Saved Brenalin?

And why had Duran kissed her, not that she objected?

His kisses were wonderful, fabulous. And probably the last she would ever receive from him. The last thing she wanted was to embarrass him, so she consoled herself with the knowledge he had kissed her at all.

The sun warmed her body. Her eyelids grew heavy. The memory of Duran's kisses weighed on her mind, as they did every day. They really had been breath-stealing.

She tried humming to stay awake, but the rhythmic sound produced the opposite effect, lulling her to sleep and dream.

She is in Brenalin, secluded in a small chamber she'd never seen before but somehow knew was off Abbas's private chapel. A red dragon in a stained-glass window peers at her curiously. Today she will wed the high prince, Duran Abbas. She can hear voices coming from the chapel as members of his family and other nobles enter and take their seats on the benches within.

Stav is with her, smiling radiantly, happy because the serving girl knows how passionately Marina loves her future husband.

She enters the chapel and walks down the aisle, the hem of her silk gown rustling. People fall quiet as she passes. She has eyes only for Duran, who beams at her as she draws closer and closer. She holds his gaze, her heart brimming with love.

In a blink of an eye, the nuptials are over. Another whirr of events speeds her through the day and into the night. Duran and she are in his bedchamber. The wedding party that accompanies them, laughing and cheering along the way, is gone. They are alone.

"Do not be nervous, pet," he says, attempting to calm her.

"I'm unafraid," she answers. After all, Marina has come to know this man better than any bride deserves and has given him her heart. "Perchance you should be the one to worry, dear husband. I've waited many a

lonely hour for you to become my very own. I plan on ravishing you this night."

"Then I'd best remove my clothes," he teases back. "I wouldn't want to ruin such fine material."

Marina smiles. "No, let me. It will be much more enjoyable if I do it myself."

He smiles back. "Only if I am allowed to do the same to you."

She takes a deep breath and nods, relishing the lustful optimism filling her. Together they take turns removing each other's garments until they are standing atop a pile and naked as the day they came into the world.

Duran kisses her, a kiss that sears through her. She does not remember closing the distance from where they stood to the bed until she sinks down, engulfed within soft bedding scented with lavender.

When he pulls back, Marina feels deprived. "More," she complains. "I want more."

He laughs. "Oh my, you're a greedy little wife. I promise you, you shall have as much of me as you desire."

She loves the sound of his carefree laugh and feels a blush rush from the roots of her hair. "Laugh all you want, but I'll expect you to keep your word."

"Tonight, you will have all the pleasure you seek. What we both want. But first, close your eyes."

"My eyes?"

"What better way to learn about what transpires between a man and a woman than with your eyes closed? Trust me, pet, it will heighten your other senses."

Her eyelids close. "Then teach me all about being

a woman, about becoming your wife. I want to learn everything."

Duran runs his finger along her arm. "There. Can you feel the difference?" he whispers in her ear.

Fine hairs on her arm rise. Her eyelids flutter.

"No, no, my sweet. Keep your eyes closed."

She squeezes her eyes tight. His fingers run down her arm again.

He is right. Her sense of touch ignites. "Oh, yes."

"Good." His hand strokes her inner thigh. "How about this?"

Before Marina has a chance to answer, his tongue is on her skin. Warm. Wet. It drives her wild and she squirms with pleasure. He laughs.

Marina has heard serving maids talk and whisper among themselves about what happens between a man and a woman. Never was there any mention of this burning anticipation that steals away her willpower.

"Don't keep me waiting," she says.

He lowers his head, and the heat of his breath brushes over her lips. "Patience, my sweet. We have all night."

She opens her eyes to meet his gaze. For the briefest moment, his pupils glow red, then the strange color is gone. A smile tips the corners of his mouth. He is so sure of himself, and he has all the right to be content, for she is his.

His hand skims her body, touching all the places she imagined Duran would caress her. How she had waited for this moment. His thumb drags across her ribs, scarcely brushing the underside of one breast.

Marina moans with need and reaches to stroke his handsome face, only to let her curious hands slide down over the hard planes of his chest. It's such a nice chest, too, like heated silk over steel. Her hands drift lower.

"You feel so good," she says. "I never want this to end."

Duran rises up on his elbows, his gaze dark with passion. "It won't...if you're good."

A tingle ripples through her body. "And if I'm bad?"

"Lesson number two, my pet," he says between kisses. "It's all right for a good wife to be naughty in the bedchamber."

"It is?"

Duran laughs again. "Oh, yes."

Marina finds herself gasping, every nerve and muscle tingling with a need so new, so wonderful she wishes to cry. "Do not toy with me, my lord husband."

"The truth be told," he says, "I can hardly contain my desire for you."

She receives all his love during the night.

They fall asleep in each other's arms. Marina wakes the next morning and sleepily rolls toward Duran, seeking his lips for more of his delicious kisses.

She reaches to touch his mouth with hers and the flick of a scratchy tongue parts her lips.

Pulling back, Narud's red eyes regard her. She is entwined within the dragon's muscular coils. As she stares at him, confusion fills her. Though she loves both man and dragon, she cannot stop the tears from trickling down her cheeks.

Narud's long tongue snakes out and flicks away her tears as his hold tightens.

A startled cry awoke Marina from the amazing dream. A sense of loss pressed down on her as the dream faded from memory. She didn't know whether the sorrowful noise came from her losing the intimate contact with Duran and Narud or from guilt at her wanton imagination.

Completely roused from her sleep, she lifted her chin, inhaling more than pine in the air. A westerly breeze blew over the land. This time sea brine drifted in the currents of air, and the tang of salt coated her lips.

It made her realize her goal lay within reach.

Soon everything would be all right. She wanted to believe it more than anything in the world.

Then why did she feel like crying?

Chapter Sixteen

Near midnight, Duran squinted into the woods. His dragon senses tingled, itching uncomfortably. Admitting the existence of those senses proved to him how much Narud had become a part of him. He'd denied and hidden those abilities from himself and Marina from the very beginning.

A twig snapped.

He tensed uncomfortably under the full moon's eerie light. Every instinct screamed danger. In the woods. Up ahead. The peril was too real, too imminent for him to refute.

He flexed his sword hand. His fingers burned as he saw no escape from the clearing—only a tumble of large boulders to protect his back and a place to hide Marina.

"I'm so hungry I could eat a mule," she said beside him, unpacking their supplies. When he didn't respond, she looked up at him. "What's wrong?"

"Ambush," he whispered. "Men are waiting in a circle to attack."

To her credit, she didn't panic. "Are you sure?"

He inhaled deeply, his nose twitching. "I can smell them."

Her gaze flickered past him into the forest as if she could penetrate the darkness. "How many?"

"A dozen. Maybe more."

"What are we going to do?" Her response was a mere whisper.

"I'm going to fight them."

A frown pulled down the corners of her mouth. "Can we fend off that many?"

"Not we," he said. "Me."

She shot him a look of disbelief. "They outnumber you." She began picking up rocks and stuffing them into her pockets. "I guess it is a good thing I'm a fair shot."

"Stay out of this," he ordered. "I don't want you hurt."

A bald-headed man with a wild black beard emerged from the woods. Duran recognized him immediately—the brigand leader. Another man appeared at his elbow and all too soon, ten…no, eleven more came forward to ring them.

Duran noted the careful positioning. These were not normal brigands, but trained soldiers. Hadn't he noticed how they searched in a grid pattern on the mountain?

"There's too many of them for you alone," Marina whispered, still beside him.

He gave her a smile of encouragement. No need to cause her worry. He turned to face the newcomers, his gaze coming to rest upon the bald-headed man. "I expected you to turn up sooner than this," he said in way of a greeting.

The bald-headed man frowned, puzzled. "Me?"

"You or someone like you. You're here to do Calandra Genoy's bidding."

"I am in the service of Lord Genoy. He will be the new lord of Brenalin."

Duran's jaw clenched. "Genoy is dead, may he burn in the Land of the Dead. He was evil, nothing more. The dragon destroyed him and the bulk of his army."

Soldiers turned to look at each other. Uncertainty and fear reflected on their faces.

The leader's expression remained blank. "Then my allegiance passes to his daughter."

"Trust me," Duran said, "she will be next to die."

"Not by your hand," the bearded man said. "Your life ends here. Make it easy on yourself. Lower your sword, and I promise your death will be swift. And the woman will not be touched."

Duran's heart constricted. Knowing now she was the princess only added to his concerns. She must be protected at all costs. He glanced at the men surrounding Marina and him. Their initial shock had faded. They would follow whatever orders were given.

"You didn't bring enough men to do the Genoys' dirty work," he countered in deadly seriousness. "Calandra obviously considers you expendable. It's not too late, you know. Turn around and leave us in peace."

Moonlight glinted off sword blades when the soldiers shifted in preparation to rush them. Someone snickered.

The noise made the leader straighten. "I cannot leave. I have a duty to perform."

"Duty to the dead?" Duran questioned with a sneer.

"Fear not, human, I am with you. We will not fail. We must protect our female."

The soft whisper of Narud's voice in his head came as a welcome. *Our female.* He couldn't agree more. Marina belonged to both of them. For the love of

Marina and her safety, he would form allegiance with the dragon devil.

"For Marina's sake," he said through mindspeech, his teeth clenching, *"I'll do whatever is necessary. Use me."*

"I cannot," Narud said, sounding in conflict with himself.

"What do you mean? You made me attack Calandra."

"A fluke. Your heightened emotions weakened you. They allowed me to sneak inside and influence you."

Duran promptly set aside his rush of relief. The gods had finally granted him a boon. *"Give me your power, then. Marina's safety is paramount."*

"In this, we are of one mind. My power is yours."

Once before, the intoxicating potency of dragon strength flowed through his veins, but on that occasion he had wrested it with a demand. This was different.

Narud offered the power freely. Hot. Liquid. Unimaginable. The dragon's great life energy swelled and rippled through him. A part of himself became the dragon, as if he reacted to a darker side of himself. He felt invincible from the tips of his fingers to the end of his toes.

Dragon and human merged and blended into one to imbue Duran with a magical strength. His eyesight became clearer, his hearing sharper, and his sense of smell intensified. His other reflexes were keener, too. His body felt whole and ready, eager for the fight to begin, committed to winning.

"Lay down your weapons," he ordered the brigands. Was that a wisp of smoke he exhaled? "I give you one last chance."

The leader stood, assuming a relaxed, self-assured stance. "I appreciate your caution," he said, his voice confident. "You recognize your peril and wish to live."

A pebble overturned as Marina leapt forward, one fist clenched and one raised to loosen her arsenal of rocks. "May the gods of Eudes fall upon you," she shouted at the brigands. "All of you."

The soldiers laughed.

His heart slammed into his chest. "Hush, Marina," he whispered, gently pulling her back. "Climb onto the boulders."

She sucked in a loud breath. "No. I won't leave you alone to fight these men."

He loved her even more at that moment. "Staying will hamper my sword arm. You put us both in danger, if you don't obey me. Go on, get up there. Now."

Her fingers brushed his hand. The touch, so brief, so sweet, would stay with him forever.

A soldier reached for her when she turned to comply with his order.

Duran unleashed his sword and Narud's wrath in a single motion. The blade slashed through flesh, muscle, and bone, splattering a spray of blood over the clearing. The soldier dropped to his knees, dead, in mid stride.

Marina scrambled to safety.

Two more soldiers screamed a battle cry and rushed him. Duran let the dragon guide him. A red haze covered his vision for a split second. His gaze burned with raw rage.

Number eleven went down with a grunt.

Duran spun around at the whirr of air being cut by a blade. He sent the tenth man to his grave. On some visceral level, he recalled the younger soldier who had stepped out first to stand beside the leader.

Mistakenly, these men believed their greater numbers put the odds in their favor. Their cries of fury filled the woods when they charged, each one desperate to deal him a deathblow.

He met each opponent with a killing swing of his blade as they slashed and hacked at him. Swords clanged, the harsh, ear-piercing music of fighting. They performed the dance of death.

Another soldier dropped, then another. Seven remained.

Throughout the fighting, Marina lent her support by throwing rocks. The occasional yelp of pain from a soldier cut through the noise when she scored a hit. He allowed himself a smile. She'd always been a fighter and loyal in the face of adversity.

A quiet ensued when the brigands pulled back to regroup.

"You engage in battle well," the leader said, huffing from exertion. His smile had slipped long ago. "But I have no plans to let you pass this way. I will cleave your head from your shoulders and then the woman's. But, now, it will be after we have our fun with her—that is my vow to you."

"We shall see who prevails." Duran roared his rage like a wild animal…or more like a furious dragon. No one threatened the woman he loved.

The bald-headed man gestured toward his men. "You were lucky. No more dallying. I am the best swordsman in all of Demicland. It is your turn to die."

The soldiers rushed him. Steel clanged. Duran slipped under their guards, hacking and slashing. He had put his trust in Narud's innate abilities, and his faith proved valid.

Duran lusted for blood, smelling the sickly-sweet odor, tasting it in his mouth, and seeing it puddle on the ground. The dragon would not forgive those who trespassed. They dared to threaten his domain, and more importantly, Marina.

Death ruled the clearing. Four more blundered within reach of Duran's sword arm and paid with their lives. Those remaining weren't so confident in their numbers.

Despite his success, Duran tired. His muscles quivered from exertion.

Gods give me strength, he begged silently.

"Gods my eye. It will be strength from me or none at all," Narud answered his plea.

The exhaustion suddenly sloughed off. His muscles were renewed with fresh strength and power. Duran didn't hesitate, not for a heartbeat. He swung his blade and fought with Narud's fury and all of his expertise.

"What's the matter with you lackwits?" The leader shouted at his final two cohorts. "Show some courage. Kill him. He's only one man."

"You step within reach of his sword arm," said one with the battered look of a veteran. "He fights like the devil."

"More like a dragon," Duran answered with a smile. His eyes burned, and he saw them glow red in his reflection on one of the soldier's shields. "You don't really know who you are fighting. Your ignorance is going to get you killed."

****

The final brigand to raise his sword against Duran was the bald-headed leader. An ugly smile spread within the man's bearded face. He had bided his time until the battle consisted of one on one. Marina assumed he thought his men would wear Duran down.

Duran glanced up at where she waited. The tiredness reflecting off his features made her wish she had more rocks, but she'd thrown them all.

"Don't worry," he said as though he read her thoughts.

"That's right, don't worry," the brigand leader repeated, his voice harsh and cruel. "You die next. That is, after I have my sport."

Duran hefted his sword. "You mutter bold words for one with only moments left to live."

For a brief moment, neither man moved. Then the bald-headed brigand lunged and slashed his weapon in a smooth arc. Air swooshed. His polished blade glinted in the firelight.

Duran dodged his strike.

Marina held her breath. She knew nothing of fighting, nothing of swords. She watched, worried, and prayed to the gods. The ringing of metal sang through the night air as swords clanged together. Duran and the brigand charged each other, over and over, retreating and swinging their swords, throwing immense strength behind their blows.

Each time the blades crashed together, she flinched. She had an uneasy feeling the brigand played with Duran. Her heart pounded and she bit her lip, stifling her moans. What if her beloved died? Sometimes just looking at him made her want to throw herself into his arms. She wanted to tell him how she felt, how important he meant to her, but she dare not.

Abruptly, the brigand leader violently slashed at

Duran. When he skittered backward across the clearing, the bald headed man rushed forward, his mouth curling in an evil smile.

In a blink, blades hacked through the air. The brigand's came down. Duran ducked under the other man's arm with his blade slicing up.

A look of surprise came over the brigand's face. He glanced down, seeing Duran's sword buried into his stomach.

"I was wrong," he said, dropping his weapon. His hands covered his middle to stanch the flow of blood. It was too late. He collapsed, dead.

A bout of dizzying relief threatened to overtake Marina. Then she saw Duran's knees buckle as he gradually bowed to the ground. She scrambled from her perch and rushed to his side. Dead bodies of Calandra's henchmen surrounded him. Thankfully, the night wind carried away the worst stench of blood and gore.

She put a comforting hand on his shoulder. "Are you all right?"

His chest rose and fell with labored breaths. Blood oozed from dozens of small gashes on his arms. "Just exhausted."

"You saved us," she said still in awe of his victory. "You defeated them all."

"Narud helped."

In her mind's eyes, she visualized the ruby dragon gloating at the success of the battle and boasting of his participation. She would have wagered her dowry that Narud would demand payment.

"I'll wonder about his motives later. First, let me check your wounds. Take off your tunic."

He dropped his sword arm, his fingers uncurling

from the weapon clutched in his hand.

Marina worked quietly. Most of the wounds were superficial, and thank Kubala, none required stitches. The small cut on his cheek had stopped bleeding without any care from her. A deeper one sliced his upper arm. She applied pressure to halt the bleeding, cringing when he flinched, his lips tightening against the pain.

Finished, she turned to gaze at the bodies scattered on the ground. "What about them?"

Duran used the corner of a fallen man's tunic to wipe his blade clean before sheathing it. "They are carrion," he said, his voice cold and harsh as he put back on his tunic. "Let the beasts of the forest feast on them."

For once, she agreed with all the rage and hatred she sensed inside him. These men tried to kill them. They deserved the repercussions.

"You're right. We won't waste time on them."

"We need to keep moving." Duran gestured toward the east.

She gave him a soft laugh. "I cannot tell you how glad I am we are alive to do so."

Her words were meant to encourage, although she wasn't sure how far her legs could carry her. They plunged down the path with the pale light of the moon guiding them, too exhausted to think or make much progress, still numb with shock.

Before long, fatigue caught up to them.

Wordlessly, they stopped.

Marina gathered wood for a small fire—not for cooking, but for light and warmth. Duran struck his flint to the shavings, and sparks leapt to life, followed by the warm glow of crackling flames.

Pulling cold rabbit from her pack, Marina divided it into two pieces, offering Duran the larger half. His gaze fixed on her hand holding the meat before accepting his portion with a nod and biting off a chunk.

Sitting before the low fire, Duran ate his meal in silence. She watched weariness etch deep grooves on his handsome face. Awareness seeped into her bones of the impossibility of facing a dozen hardened fighters and winning. But he had.

She ignored her own tiredness, determined to watch over Duran. He needed rest and peace now. She forced herself to stay awake. Duran stretched, then settle into his bedroll. His eyes gradually closed and his breathing slowed almost immediately.

An owl hooted in a nearby tall pine. She turned toward the sound, but the bird remained hidden in the thick boughs. What she did spot, however, sent her heart racing—the sky turning light gray.

She flicked her gaze to where Duran slept fitfully, moaning as though fighting a nightmare. From the battle? Or Narud demanding his freedom?

The air around Duran began turning red. She saw him twist and turn. Even deep asleep, he fought the mist of change when it seized him in an unbreakable grip. The mist grew to Narud's size, thickened, and hardened. The silhouette of the dragon shimmered in the center.

Marina closed her eyes and sighed. When she opened them, the mist had vanished. Narud stretched his long, muscular neck toward her.

"We won. Why did you stop your journey?"

She glanced around, fighting a yawn. "Duran was

worn out and defenseless."

"No harm would have touched him."

"I didn't know that!"

"Would I lie to you?" Narud sounded wounded.

"If it suited your purposes. Yes. I believe you would," she told him, her voice raspy from tiredness. "Please, Narud, let me sleep for a while. Afterward, I would be grateful if you told me another tale of dragons."

"Then sleep."

Permission to close her eyes was all she needed. She lowered her head and let oblivion take her. She slept unashamedly, without dreams penetrating her deep slumber.

Hours later, Marina heard a voice.

"Wake, my pretty pet."

Marina stirred with a groan and blinked away her tiredness. A bright sun rode high in the middle of the sky.

"I've decided it is time to enlighten you about the ruby dragon. I have nearly all their memories now. Little about them is left unknown to me."

Marina flopped over and sat up with a sigh. "Why?"

"Why what?"

"Why tell me?"

"Because sometimes a speck of information makes all the difference in a person's opinion."

She knew the dragon well enough to wonder what tricks he planned. She understood he would not yield her any peace unless she listened. Wrapping her arms around her knees, she rested her chin on top.

"Go ahead," she said, yielding.

A rumble spewed from the depths of the dragon's huge chest. *"A biddable human. I am much pleased."*

Marina smiled. "Nothing I said would have stopped you."

Narud settled his massive bulk on the ground, his tail wrapping around her. *"In ancient times, the ruby dragon was often the most misunderstood dragon. He contained elements of fire, considered the hardest element to control."*

She patted his scales. "I would think all dragons did pretty much what they wanted."

"A falsehood perpetuated by our enemies. Many dragons loved music and worked in harmony with humans so they could listen to their music. Ruby dragons, obviously, were red, and all red dragons symbolize energy and courage. As the color of blood, we represent birth, death, and rebirth. Perhaps that is why I am the first of my kind to return."

The depth of his words reverberated through her. How could she make him understand? Marina looked up at him. She swore he cocked the ridges above his glowing eye like she would an eyebrow.

"Narud, you aren't a real dragon," she said softly. "You were created by a malicious sorceress."

"Of course, I am real. Touch me. Feel. I am flesh and blood, the same as you."

Flesh and blood. Visions of what occurred in the woodland clearing flashed through her mind. Calandra's henchmen were dead. The waste sickened her. If they hadn't attacked Duran, they might still be alive.

Narud seemed to understand her remorse. *"What is the gemstone in Eudes's Throne?"* he asked out-of-the-blue.

She blinked at the change in subject. "An aquamarine."

"Ah, yes, I know of it. A lovely jewel." He seemed eager. *"The most precious is a clear blue, the color of deep lake water. You have many of its characteristics."*

"I do?"

"Absolutely. It helps people have clearer vision. Since I brought you to my cave, you have tried to make Duran see me as an individual. True?"

He had her there. "Yes."

"So, you are like your beloved aquamarine. Did you know once every gemstone, whether precious or not, attached itself to a dragon."

"Really." She smiled.

"The harmonic call that brought dragons to this world was a strange and powerful one. Only dragons can hear the gemstones of Feldsvelt. No other creature is so blessed. They told us their most precious secrets."

Marina's sleepiness totally evaporated, replaced by keen interest. Talking with Narud always proved fascinating.

"You have intimated this before. How can gemstones speak?"

"Not in the way you think. Gemstones are of the earth. They were formed with the creation of this world. They wanted to share their secrets with the rulers of the land where they resided for millions of years. Unfortunately, no one could hear them until we dragons arrived." Narud settled his powerful body into a heap on the ground.

"Secrets?" Marina asked.

"That's the beauty of it." Enthusiasm built in his

voice. *"Each gemstone possessed a different secret."*

Marina narrowed her eyes, then her curiosity got the better of her. "Why is none of this in our history books?"

"I have no idea. Dragons didn't write your tomes. Humans did. I suspect the truth is draped in layers of superstitions."

Icy cold wormed its way up Marina's back. She opened her mouth to contradict the magnificent beast, and then seeing his crimson scales shimmer, changed her mind.

The tip of Narud's tongue peeked outside his mouth. *"Oh, pet, am I obliged to remind you of the atrocities your ancestors committed on mine? Humans annihilated dragons in the Great Dying. A sad time for all dragons, but I do not blame you. We are not responsible for the actions of those turned to dust."* He stretched his powerful body. *"Wouldn't you rather hear about something more interesting than ancient, dry history?"*

Marina laughed, the sound surprising her. How long had it been since she felt any joy worth expressing? Trust Narud to cheer her up.

"Such as what?"

Narud snorted. *"As much as I dislike repeating myself, I will. Besides having limitless power, treasure, and long life, your chosen gemstone's secret is another reason for you to accept my offer to become a dragoness. Eudes's gemstone would reveal its secret to you."* He fixed her with hot red eyes that seemed to burn inside her. *"Who better than a princess turned dragoness?"*

"Narud!" she retorted with conviction. "I have

277

already given you my answer."

"You play a dangerous game, my pet." Narud's tone grabbed her attention. *"The human does not approve of deceit. He may say he forgives you, but he will never forget. I, on the other hand, am a dragon, and deceit is something I can appreciate."*

Chills ran up her back. "Duran understood my reasons."

"You left him no choice."

All the mention of secrets made Marina wonder if Narud read her mind. Had he discovered her most private thoughts? Or had he known her real identity all along?

"I respected your privacy," the dragon answered her inner thoughts.

"You are reading them now," she said grimly.

"An easy task when you are yelling them in your mind."

Embarrassed, she glanced toward the west. Narud followed her gaze. The sky burned with color. Red. Orange. Yellow. Clouds looked like they were on fire with the falling sun. Even the long, thin cloud capping Brenalin's highest mountain glowed fiery red.

"By Mighty Kubala!" Marina said, clapping her hands. "I understand now. It makes perfect sense. I know why Calandra wanted to wed Duran."

"What? Why? Tell me."

"You gave me the answer, Narud. All this talk of secrets has opened my eyes and made everything clear." Insightful bliss filled her. "Thank you, thank you. I'm so happy I could kiss you."

"Tell me," Narud repeated, his tone holding a dual edge—one hinting of curiosity and the other of fear.

She grinned at him. "You aren't in any danger, my friend. Have faith in me in this. I know what I'm doing." She glanced at the setting sun now turning the sky cool shades of purple and lavender-gray. "It's nearly dusk. Let me tell Duran. He deserves to know first."

Chapter Seventeen

Narud gathered his rage close. He felt like a forest fire burning hotter on a drought-stricken summer. The destructive force swept through him, making his heart flip-flop. The worst thing he could think of had happened.

Duran had won.

Marina favored the puny human over him.

He hated Duran. He hated her.

No, he retracted his thoughts. Never her.

Not sweet, brave Marina. His princess.

Molten anger built thick and hot until cankers burned his lips and then dissipated as quickly as it came. Stomping his massive legs, the ground shook.

"Why do you always side with him? Always you give him the benefit of doubt. Never me."

"Narud." She said his name with a soft whisper. "Narud, I am sorry. You know I would never…You can't believe. If I discovered something that affected only you, I would share it with you first. I swear."

"Tell me what you discovered."

Her eyes brimmed with tears. "It involves Duran."

"We are one. I am he, and he is me."

Straightening, Marina sighed. "Very well, since you gave me the idea. But if you give me any reason to regret telling you first, I'll never forgive you. I suspect Calandra learned the secret of the gemstone in the Ruby

Throne. I can't swear this, but I'm positive it's why she used magic against Duran."

Narud remained still, his thoughts jumbled together. Dragon's teeth…the validity of what she said made sense. He stood glaring at her, unwilling to concede the argument or halt the bursts of smoke escaping his nostrils.

"The secret will not be granted to her. The sorceress gave me life, but I wager there is one thing she does not know."

Marina raised her gaze to face him. The dragon had done it again—aroused her curiosity. "What is it?"

"The gemstones left the bestowing of their secret to the dragons' discretion. We deem who is deserving and who is not."

"She could demand it."

"I have spoken."

Marina saw Narud's tail twitch in the air. He had a right to be upset. His very existence was threatened.

"Narud, listen to me," she said to alleviate the growing tension. "You did a wonderful thing last night."

He lowered his long neck. *"It was necessary."*

"You saved us from Calandra's henchmen." She stroked between the bony ridges on his head. "What if Calandra sends more men after us? More than Duran can handle alone."

The dragon shifted his position. *"He can beat anyone she sends against him. He has me."*

"And who do I have?"

"Explain?" he asked, his tone suspicious.

"You say you care." The image of the battle flared in her mind. "But a sword will kill me as quickly as anything."

His iridescent scales puffed up. *"No harm will befall you. I will not allow it."*

"I would be inclined to believe you if you flew me to Eudes. It's not far."

Narud raised his mighty head, his red eyes glistening like coals. *"Why would I want to do that? It shortens my time with you. Precious little remains, as it is."*

His logic gave Marina pause. "I have a reason for wanting to reach Eudes as soon as possible?"

"Clarify."

"I'm aware you think I favor Duran, but you are mistaken. Magic created you. Magic can save you. I believe with all my heart that you deserve a chance at life, too. I want to find a way to save both you and Duran."

Smoke blew out of his nostrils. The dragon swished his great, thick tail back and forth again. *"Truly?"*

"Yes," she said with sincerity. "I need to search the library at Eudes. The answer is there. I know what to hunt for now—myths about gemstones."

Marina loved learning. Once, she even considered entering the House of Women, where she could continue her pursuit of knowledge. In the end, she elected not to. Ironically, acceptance into the House meant severing ties to her family. Even her name would be lost, for every novitiate chose a different name as a sign of a new life.

Before Narud could answer, a red shimmer disturbed the air. A loud growl of protest emanated from deep within his mighty chest and smoke billowed out his mouth. He whipped his dangerous tail on the ground, battling the change. Marina could only imagine his frustration when the unstoppable metamorphism claimed him. He was as powerless as Duran.

She hurried over to Duran when he appeared lying on the ground. "Are you all right?"

He swayed to his feet, brushing bits of debris off his clothes with slow and stiff movements. "Fine. I wish I could say repetition made this easier, but the pain remains as intense as the first time."

Tears moistened her eyes. "Oh, Duran, if only I could do something for you."

"All I desire is to break Calandra's spell."

"I swear, together we will," she answered him, determined to help. "As a matter of fact, I've learned something that might make a difference. I was talking with Narud just before the change occurred and—"

"Stop! Anything that dragon agrees to, I'm against."

She gritted her teeth. She had to stay strong. "Hear me out...Please. Stop thinking of Narud as your nemesis. He told me that gemstones have certain powers."

"Gemstones?" His voice was tight. "I've warned you not to trust a word of what he says."

"Just listen."

He snatched his oilskin travel pack off the ground. "All right, speak. Convince me."

She watched Duran stuff his pack with gear. "The discord between Narud and you clouds your mind. You are being biased," she began, doing the same with hers. "Try being more open-minded. Narud says, in ancient times, gemstones relayed information to their chosen dragon, who shared it with humans they deemed worthy. It gave them certain powers. We can't dismiss the possibility some dragons did that."

"You believe this…this wild tale."

"Circumstances prove the accuracy of his words."

He paused in his packing. "What makes you so sure?"

She reached for a pot. Their hands touched when he stretched for the same one. The contact sent something intense and primeval through her, intriguingly erotic.

She thought of their kisses, but set the memory aside. "Becca and Fahid. Becca told us the women of her village can hold off pregnancy at will, and we both saw Fahid heal before our eyes. That's magic no wizard can execute! It has to be the gemstones. I wager those people have forgotten how they received their special gifts. What if this knowledge fell into Calandra's hands and she wants the power of the Ruby Throne?"

Duran flicked a suspicious glance at her, his jaw squared. "All right, Marina, you have my attention. Go on."

"It's possible she cast the spell on you to gain it," she said, daring to hope. "We have been focusing on breaking the spell, forgetting her motive for wanting to wed you."

"She loved me." He sounded bitter. "At least, that's what she claimed."

"I doubt many people would consider her method of demonstrating love normal."

With a smile, Duran set off in the direction of the great ocean. "I think my transformation into a dragon shocked her. After all, what wizard or sorceress would produce a creature capable of destroying them?"

Marina struggled to keep up with his long strides. "You have a good point, but surely somewhere in our history a wizard or sorceress was overzealous in their use of magic to gain what they desired."

"Greedy people always commit despicable crimes." He slowed his pace.

"Then you agree the gemstone tale has merit?"

He chuckled, but the sound lacked mirth. "While your story defies logic, it is better than what I've been thinking."

"Which is what?" she asked, aware a swarm of butterflies filled her stomach.

Silence fell. A red glare flickered in his gaze. "You may not like it."

"It doesn't matter," she said, beating down her trepidation. "Tell me. I want to know."

His jaw twitched. "Sometimes I wish I was dead."

Marina froze with misery. His pain must be unbearable to contemplate suicide. She'd been drawn to him from the very beginning—his exceptional courage, his kindness.

Her gaze rose to Duran's. "Maybe that's Calandra's plan. Incredible as it seems, if you can't break the spell, she figures you'll kill yourself before you'd let Narud free."

Duran jerked to a stop. "Are you saying she's manipulating me?"

"I wish I knew," she said, then returned to her original line of thought. "Maybe people needed to request the secret in order to receive it. Maybe that's what Calandra discovered. I'm hoping a book on gemstone lore will give me a better idea."

"It seems farfetched," Duran conceded and then resumed walking.

Man and beast were uncannily similar—gruff and loving at the same time. "Have you a better idea?"

"You believe Narud?" Duran asked, his tone neutral.

"Narud only told me about the gemstones. I reached this conclusion on my own."

He grunted as only a man unwilling to listen could. They stopped to glare at each other—two strong-willed people, both too stubborn to speak. They began walking again, the tension persisting.

This was their last evening in Demit Woods. The strange dragonflies appeared more agitated than usual, if persistent dragonflies could be considered usual. They hovered on the edge of the forest in a thick mass with each step Duran took.

She glanced over her shoulder at the strange insects, wondering and brooding. They walked for quite a while before Marina noticed the moon no longer slanted through thinning woods. Instead, twisted scrub pine and low brush grew in sandy soil.

They neared the ocean.

Time was running out. For her. For him. For all of them.

****

Duran cursed under his breath. He sensed Marina wasn't finished trying to convince him, and they were less than a night's journey from Eudes.

For an instant, he had touched her mind with his, a trick he'd recently picked up from Narud. He tried to soothe her worry, not wanting their last hours filled with tension or spent in argument.

They were close enough to her homeland for her to be more familiar with the terrain than he. He never anticipated the sway of Marina's hips to capture his full attention as it did. His body responded in a very keen way. If they stopped now, he'd gather her in his arms and possess her over and over.

Marina halted abruptly. "I know what I've been telling you stretches the imagination, Duran, but you must accept it."

Duran feared his attraction to Marina, his one-time bride, the true threat. "So, you've sided with Narud. I think I know why. He's offered to turn you into a dragoness."

"So?"

He clenched his fist. "Being a dragoness is a great temptation. When I thought you were a servant, I offered you a simple estate. As princess you had no need of my land. No wonder you rebuffed it. But becoming a dragoness? Dragon's teeth, Marina, nothing compares to that."

"You are being unfair, Duran. Just because I suggest something you don't want to grasp doesn't mean I'm wrong or being disloyal." She tossed long strands of hair out of her face and looked him square in the eye. "I turned Narud down not once, but twice."

He had no possession except anger and frustration. Marina offered hope, a plain, tempting thing. "I wish there was a simple answer. Are you willing to jeopardize my life or Narud's to prove your theory?"

She gave him a sharp look. "No, of course not. What other reason is there?"

"Consider the consequences." He resumed their brisk pace, despite the way his feet sank into sandy ground.

"What do you mean?"

Something shifted in his gut at her determination, the sheer sincerity of her expression. He slowed his steps. "I've listened to your theory, Marina, but people will be suspicious if you suddenly reappear after disappearing for months, and then immerse yourself in searching old texts on dragons and superstitions."

"I have pursued studies all my life. No one will think it strange." Her protesting voice sounded firm and strong.

Duran squared his shoulders and centered his traveling pouch on his shoulder. "Won't they? By now, even the people in Eudes have heard about a dragon flying in the skies of Feldzvelt. Your caravan was attacked. Not by a dragon. We know that. But people saw Narud's tracks at the site. Those in Eudes will pose many questions to you." He lifted a hand when she started to protest. "No, let me finish. As far as people are concerned, you and Genoy's soldiers have seen this dragon. Genoy's men have fled back to Demicland. That leaves you. They will demand answers. It's only natural. What will you tell them?"

"Trust me. I know how to hold my own counsel."

She sounded so sure. He almost believed her. "Refusal might make them more insistent, more curious."

"I can handle them," was all she said.

The battle for dominance with the beast was nearly a lost cause. So many times, Duran's hopes had sagged. Yet as long as a kernel of his humanity lingered, he would seek a means to end Calandra's spell.

The notion of Narud living on while he became

ensnared within the great beast for eternity brought a rush of agony Duran wasn't sure he could endure.

But he declined to surrender. Life meant too much to him.

Could the crazy tale of gemstones and secret powers really be his last chance to become whole again? He tried to assess the situation objectively. If he threw away the opportunity...who did he serve? Should he accept every word she uttered? How could he not? He was living proof dragons existed.

Salt-brined air gave him his first clue they neared the great ocean, and then a new sound curled around his ears.

Intrigued by the powerful, crashing sounds, his feet moved faster. A thin, rolling fog obscured the shoreline in ghostly shadows. Then the great ocean emerged as the fog thinned. Foamy white waves broke along the beach. The coastline appeared deserted except for them. When the sun rose, the flat expanse of beach and water would make it be nigh impossible to miss seeing a red dragon, yet Duran stood and listened to the undulating waves crash against the shoreline. He let the crisp breeze on his face wipe away his worries and leave him feeling as though he didn't have a care in the world.

If only that were true.

Marina came alongside him and slipped her hand into his. "Beautiful, isn't it?"

"I've never seen its like," he said, awed. "The scope and power are beyond imagination. I'm glad my first time seeing the ocean is with you."

"Truly?"

He laughed, wondering which statement amazed her more—that he'd never seen the ocean before or he how glad he was to share it with her. "Heaven forbid if I become too old or jaded not to continue experiencing firsts in my life."

"I agree." She gave his hand a gentle squeeze and looked around as though searching for something. "I've changed, you know. I used to fear Brenalin's great woods. They were so dark and threatening. I imagined all sorts of creatures hiding behind every tree, but after traveling with you, I'm no longer afraid."

Inches separated them. A warm rosy scent mingled with the salty air, and he found it an intoxicating combination. His heart pounded madly with longing.

"So I've noticed."

She turned toward him, her eyes wide and full of hope. "More importantly—do you approve of how I've changed?"

"I thought you pretty special from the very beginning."

To his surprise and pleasure, she dropped her hold on his hand and stepped into his arms to ask teasingly, "Which is it? Pretty? Or special?"

"Both, pet."

Stroking the gold-bright strands falling loose over her shoulders and down her back, he didn't want to let her go. Not now. Not ever. What he felt for Marina could only be called love—the easy, comfortable kind that was natural between the right man and woman. True love. Feelings he once doubted, but no longer.

She anchored her arms around his neck. "Oh, Duran," she whispered, her breath caressing his skin.

A quiver of excitement ran through him. He loved the way she had softly uttered his name with the hint of laughter and invitation; because they had been together for so long, the thought of never seeing her again left an emptiness inside him nothing could fill, or maybe it was the hum of excitement building within him. Whatever the cause, tonight would be their last time together. Afterward, Marina would be safe with her family.

He slid his hand through her hair to the nape of her neck. Her warm skin felt right to him. If she allowed, he would show her how deep his love ran.

****

Enfolded in Duran's warm embrace, everything else ceased to exist for Marina. This was their final evening together. The realization caused an ache of sorrow to arc through her chest. Her lips quivered when she looked up at the wonderful man who had suffered so much.

"Tomorrow we'll be in Eudes," she said. "Let's remain here for the night."

"Is that what you want? If we tried, we could be there tonight." Duran traced her eyebrow with the lightest touch. "We could push forward."

"Only if you are in a hurry to be rid of me."

"I thought you were anxious to reach home," he said softly. "Your family has mourned you these many months."

Longing shuddered through her. "I'm less inclined to leave you." She let a smile lift the corners of her mouth.

"I can make our last night together one neither of us will ever forget."

When Duran's strong arms drew her closer, her world shifted beneath her feet. His confidence and assurance were so much like Narud, Marina thought fondly. Then his lips came down on hers. She nearly burst with happiness. Elation shot through her with a rush of desire, need, and throbbing. Her dream came true. Clinging to him, she deepened their kiss, positive if Duran released her, she would crumble at his feet.

She opened her eyes to see affection reflected in the blueness of Duran's gaze. The emotions roaring through her body gave her no time to think, even if she dared. Her body felt on fire.

He drew back. Her breath caught at the loss of closeness. No! No! He couldn't leave her unfulfilled.

Duran should have been her husband. Her virginity, the only gift truly hers to give, was his for the taking. The possibility thrilled her.

Then he pulled back farther. "You're sure?"

She smiled. "Positive."

She seized his thick fleece coat and dragged it off his broad shoulders. Duran tossed the coat to the ground and eased her to the marsh grass, smelling slightly like hay and still holding a portion of the sun's warmth trapped within its long, flat blades.

The ocean serenaded them.

Sitting down beside her, he untied her bindings and lifted her gown off her body. A cool breeze kissed her skin. The burning inside her kept her warm.

She watched Duran remove his leggings and tunic to expose strong legs and a wide chest with dark hair that crossed the broad expanse before plummeting downward. Her eyes followed the narrow line of hair, and she promptly averted her gaze.

Duran chuckled softly. "What's the matter, princess? Don't I please you?"

"Oh, yes, you please me very much."

"Good. I plan to do much more."

He sank down beside her, then kissed her softly. She parted her lips to invite his tongue inside. Her fingers moved to his thick hair. When she felt his hands caress the flare of her hips and travel to cup her breasts, she moaned. He nuzzled and suckled until her breasts ached. Her heart drummed so loud, she could barely breathe. Somehow he knew just where to touch to turn her body into liquid desire. His fingers created shivery sensations in her.

Marina didn't know if Duran eased atop her or if she dragged him into position. It didn't matter. She lurched against him until he filled her.

They moved together, hot and pulsing, surfing on currents of yearning. She forgot everything. The world disappeared. Nothing mattered except for the two of them.

Duran's thrusts were like the tide, advancing and retreating. Release approached and receded. She wanted him more and more. Their movements matched the music of the waves. She arched to meet his firm drive and surrendered to the ripples of release flooding her body. Then she heard him groan, felt him tense…felt a rush of heat that nearly overwhelmed her.

For two heartbeats, she couldn't think or move. His essence filled her with sweet bliss. Loving him was the best thing to ever happen in her life. She would hold him and the memory of this night next to her heart until her dying day.

Chapter Eighteen

"Leave!" Narud ordered Duran through mindspeech. *"This is my time."*

The sun's rim broke the edge on the horizon. Narud wanted to spend the dawn with Marina, but the human fought to prolong holding her close.

"A little longer is all I desire," Duran answered. *"You cannot begrudge me precious moments."*

"Mind your mouth. I can and do. Leave now."

Narud forced the human to roll away from Marina. The mist of change formed, and moments later, he emerged from the flaming vapor. The soft hues of dawn were long past. Glaring sunlight brought every grain of sand into focus. He'd lost cherished moments. The human had stolen from him. A raging chaos filled him. He grappled for control. The frustration…the misery…the fear.

Somehow the puny human had staved off his rightful appearance through sheer will power. The transformation had been delayed by only a few minutes, but it seemed an eternity to him. Duran had slowed the magic.

Narud had never accomplished the feat. Was the human becoming stronger, not weaker? Something forbidding, dark, and cold touched his draconic mind. Had sharing Marina's love increased Duran's strength? How else could he have managed to hold back the mist of change?

Smoke burst from his nostrils. A faint memory of Duran in control, Marina's silken limbs, and both humans' shuddering sighs nagged at the corner of his mind. Human love freed a powerful magic all its own—the power to heal, to take away pain, and many other things. Love was a magic he knew little about. It belonged to humans. The foolish beings valued it too highly to discard easily.

He prompted himself that humans were complex creatures. Take the female, for instance.

Stav…or Marina, *a princess*. It explained the mystery he had sensed surrounding her and why she had refused his offer to become a dragoness.

Narud narrowed his eyes to give the slender female a grim look. Her skin glowed with the luster of a pearl. Her mouth, slightly swollen, reminded him of dark garnets. Her gold-bright hair curled in long strands. So beautiful…He'd known she was special from the very beginning, and he felt possessiveness swell in him. She belonged to him. He wanted her. A treasure worth keeping. She would make an extraordinary dragoness.

"Hunger gnaws at my belly," he announced. *"I must hunt. Proceed forward. You should reach your homeland by nightfall."*

She gulped. "You're going to leave?"

"Unless you wish me to stay," he said, almost hopeful.

She straightened her gown. "I—I thought we could—"

"Could what? Say what's on your mind. Otherwise, I see no reason to stay."

"It's nothing."

295

He watched her hand slip into her pocket. The instant her fingers coiled around the jewel, warmth infused him.

"So be it. You possess the ruby I gave you. If you need me, call through mindspeech. I will hear you, no matter how far the distance."

"But…" she said quietly.

"What?" His mindspeech sounded like an outcry. *"Did something happen last night?"*

"It was private. Nothing I need discuss with you." She backed up, raising her hands when he lumbered in her direction. "Leave me alone, Narud. I warn you. Stay away from me."

He stopped and stared at her in the bright light of day. He had the right to be angry. Duran stole time from him. He would never get it back. Did she not realize he held the key to her ultimate happiness? That he was the right choice for her.

"What is this? You fear me? Why?"

Marina looked at him. "Can you see what I'm thinking?"

"No. It is probably a good thing, too. If I did, I might not like what I find."

"Do you know what happened between Duran and me?" The woman watched him attentively.

Narud narrowed his slit-pupiled-eyes. A hiss escaped from his mouth. Ah, so they arrived at the root of the problem. *"You know the answer to that. I was there! The human tried to block me out but could not. You disappoint me, Marina."* He used her real name for the first time and liked the sound of it in his head. *"I cannot say I am pleased with what occurred last night on the beach. I expected better of you."*

Marina caught her breath. A shattered look reflected the pain of his hurtful accusations. She turned to him, her hazel eyes, which always reminded him of sultry smoky topaz, rare yellow citrine, and brilliant green grossular, filled with tears.

"I couldn't help myself." Tears tumbled down her cheeks. "I swear, I didn't mean for it to happen, but I love him."

Narud seethed in silence, wondering if she would cry in his defense. *"Is he worthy?"*

"You think I would do what I did without being sure?"

His claws dug great gouges in the sand. *"What of me?"*

She pointed at small ships bobbing on the waves, a bellyful of wind filling their sails. "This isn't the time or place to explain all. You need to get out of sight."

Narud perused the ocean-going vessels. *"You think I care about them?"*

Her expression softened. "People are on those vessels. They'll report seeing you. I don't want you in danger."

"Now you mock me. Nothing can harm me."

"Go! You invite disaster, if you stay."

Narud shook his massive neck. *"No! I am not fooled. You send me away because you are ashamed of your actions with that human last night."*

"What a thing to say! You seem to forget I am human, too."

"You need not be." He exhaled a little puff of smoke to calm himself. *"It is a good thing I have a well-developed sense of worth, my sweet. Else, your behavior would deflate me. Go now…before I change*

my mind and fly you back to my mountain cave!"

She stiffened. "You wouldn't dare."

Her attitude started to irritate him. *"Wouldn't I, my brave beauty? Little you know. Soon you will be back in the warm embrace of your family. Enjoy your time with them. I give you that much!"*

"You give me nothing!" She sounded pained. "Duran offered to return me to my family, and you promised to cooperate. You have a way of conveniently twisting things to fit your needs or forgetting about them all together."

"I have honored my word. Yes?"

"Yes, but—"

"Good." He cut her off, satisfied with the turn of events. *"We understand each other then. Go! Reunite with your family. When I am ready, I will come for you."*

****

Calandra Genoy had been summoned to the king's private chambers. Would he propose this night? She'd been dropping hints for days. Her potion worked better than she realized. She suppressed her glee with a hard, twisting pinch to her arm.

"Pour me a glass of mulled wine," she ordered Hannah, waiting to assist her. "And be sure you don't spill a drop."

She knew making the suggestion would cause the servant to become so nervous spillage was guaranteed. Calandra waited with her eyes narrowed, watching. Deep reddish-purple liquid splashed up the sides of the glass as the girl approached. Tears of strong wine rose within the glass, but not over the lip. The edge of a thick rug on the slate floor lay within inches of her feet.

One more step…

Hannah saw it, too, and her eyes widened in terror. If the tiniest drop spilled, Calandra would let her go. The girl's family was poor. The loss of her wages meant starvation.

Calandra's expectations were dashed when the girl handed the glass of wine with a bow of her head, not a drop lost.

Calandra clamped down her fury. She had yearned for the servant to fail. Sipping the wine, tasting a hint of vinegar, she spit the liquid from her mouth, and then threw the goblet to the floor. Glass shattered. Ruby red wine sprayed the wall and her gown alike.

"Help me remove this gown," she snapped. "It's been soiled."

Hannah rushed to her side. She struggled to unfasten the two-dozen garnet bead buttons at the back of the gown. Calandra hated the pale pink garment, but it fit well and accented her curves in a way to make men stare.

She fidgeted. "Hurry! The king awaits me. I cannot stand here all day for your convenience."

"I am sorry, my lady," Hannah replied in a weak voice. "I do not want to damage the buttons."

She stuck out her arm for the servant to undo the closures on the sleeves. Hannah fumbled with the tiny buttons. "This is ridiculous," Calandra barked and tore at the sleeves, hurling garnet fasteners in all directions.

The king had summoned her for a meeting in his royal apartments. The past week he informed her of her father's death. She pretended great sorrow, letting fake tears flow freely, but inside she thought good riddance.

Commander Marrow had disappeared as well. The

coward probably caught wind of the dragon decimating her father's army and had deserted her.

A quick change and she adorned herself in a fresh gown of dark green. She floated down the long corridor on the upper level. At a massive door, she knocked lightly. Anticipation made her mouth water with sweetness.

"Enter," came a muted response.

Calandra stepped into the room. Many years had passed since she'd last visited these apartments. As children, she and Duran often played ball and jacks before the fire while the king went over paperwork after the queen died.

The huge chamber appeared as she remembered, well furnished with a mix of dark cherry and light maple furniture beneath a vaulted ceiling. Rich tapestries, barely smaller than those hanging in the audience hall, decorated two walls. A large rug in blues and purples covered the floor. The enormous canopied bed included a headboard with a frieze of trees, symbolic of Brenalin. A well-stoked fire crackled in the hearth, even though the day provided plenty of warmth.

The last item of note in the chamber belonged to a portrait of a beautiful woman wearing an old-fashioned gown. Duran's mother, she recalled, admiring the depiction. He'd inherited more of her looks than his father's.

Her gaze continued around the room, coming to a halt at a glow near the window. Einer. No one else showed within the chamber.

"Master Wizard Einer, His Highness summoned me," she said in a biddable tone. "Are you finished with him? Or shall I return later?"

Bells jingled as the aged wizard seated himself in a chair facing her. The sound left Calandra cold.

"Do you know why you were summoned?" the wizard asked.

She forced a smile to her lips. "I assumed the king wished to discuss some matter of great import with me."

"He didn't summon you. I did."

Calandra froze, not quite able to believe what she heard. A palpable tension suddenly weighed her down. She forced her expression to remain impartial.

"You, Venerable Wizard?"

"Yes." A wheeze emanated from his chest as he spoke. "The king will not be joining us."

"Pray," she said, feeling trapped while trying to remain calm. "Enlighten me. Why not?"

Einer took a deep breath. "Do you recall my objections when you first begged permission to learn sorcery? You thought me jealous at the time. Do you remember?"

She winced a little. "That was many years ago."

The corner of Einer's mouth crooked in a small smile. His milky eyes stared at her, his smile not reaching them.

"I never feared your ability, child. I am one of the last wizards of true magic. So few of us are left we forget others will never achieve our level of skill. No one. Not even you…even if you live forever."

Fear snaked through her. Why use those words? He was about to expose her treachery. She should have confided in him upon first discovering the secret of the Ruby Throne. His assistance would have been invaluable. Unfortunately, that time had passed.

She chose her words with care. "The knowledge to learn magic can always be found by those willing to look."

Einer's white beard quivered with the shake of his head. "Foolish child, not if the teachers are gone. We grow tired. Die. Few have found assistants worthy of imparting their secrets. You…" His shoulders slumped as his long bony fingers rapped out a rhythmic pattern on the wooden arm of his chair. "You came close. I had high hopes."

Calandra's temper rose. "Death comes to all in the end. You will be missed, naturally; but I have read the old tomes. They will suffice."

He laughed at her boast, then hacked out a cough. "Your statement confirms my suspicions," he said between gasps.

A blush expanded on her cheeks in a wave of heat. "You never liked me."

"You speak in half-truths," he began slowly. "You first arrived at Brenalin as a small, frightened girl. You garnered my sympathy then. It was the woman that child grew into I find contemptible. Meanwhile, let's return to those tomes in which you place such faith. Sorcerers wrote them, you know. Do you think we'd part with vital information for the wrong eyes to peruse? Some skills must be learned at a master wizard's side." He tapped his right temple. "My secrets are kept safe in here. You will never learn them."

Intense fury boiled beneath the surface of Calandra's cool exterior. She stepped forward. The wizard's cape increased its glow and undulated ever so slightly. Did he maintain his power through his cape? An interesting notion.

She patted her mouth as if she did not give a whit. "A dull tale, Master Einer. Very boring."

"Really? I'd have thought you would enjoy the hearing."

He taunted her. He'd pay for his mistake of underestimating her. "Why are you telling me this? I made no such request. Nor have any interest."

Einer looked directly at her. "My life is sworn to serve the rulers of Brenalin. I take my oath very seriously."

"And your point is?"

"You always were clever, Calandra. Clever. Bold. Resourceful. I overlooked the extent of your malevolence. For that, I blame myself. But, now, you have struck at both Duran and the king. I cannot allow you to continue."

Denial was beyond question. "What do you want?"

He rolled a bony shoulder in a shrug. "You are evil wrapped in a striking package. I think that is why I never suspected any real harm would come from your dabblings. I was wrong, of course, and promise more diligence in the future."

Calandra wondered if she should make a break. She glanced at the door. "You are mistaken, Master Wizard." The lie came effortlessly. "I am exactly as you see…an orphaned female fostered among kind people who permitted me to learn a skill benefiting all of us."

He shook his head. "You misled us—Zell, Duran, and me. You have tricked, lied, and deceived us. Tell me why, Calandra."

"You've already made up your mind about me. What else would it be, but avarice?"

Einer sat straighter. "I doubt greed motivated you. Something more insidious, perhaps," he said in a quiet tone. "You acted with maliciousness when you cursed Duran because he chose to honor his commitment, but that isn't the reason you punished him."

"So," she taunted. "I am unafraid of you."

He shook his head. "You should be. Your time will come."

"You mock me. It only proves me right."

Their eyes locked. "Evil never triumphs," Einer said. "Some appear to win for a while, but eventually they are overturned."

"What proof do you have of these accusations?" she asked, certain he knew nothing of the Ruby Throne's secret.

Einer sighed. "Nothing tangible."

Pity pulled down his mouth, and that infuriated her. "I do not know what game you play, Einer." She deliberately dropped his title. He didn't deserve her respect. "Duran disappeared these many months past. King Zell mourns his son's loss. He has honored me by requesting I become his queen to ensure the Abbas line does not cease with him."

A teeny-tiny lie. Zell was too drugged to contradict her, and she would never tell.

Einer's gaunt body stiffened. "You will never be queen."

"Zell might have something to say about that. You need proof of your accusations, and you have none."

"Proof isn't necessary."

She recognized a bluff when she heard one. "What can you do? Tell the king? Whatever you say, it will be your word against mine."

Einer glanced briefly out the window. "My first thought as well. No, I will not burden him."

"Why not, if you are so sure of yourself?"

"You have drugged the king. In his present condition, he is unable to comprehend the situation. I may be old, Calandra, but am no fool."

She snorted a laugh. "On the contrary, you are both."

"Reserve your slander until I finish. I have more to say."

His conviction rang with strength. She considered him for a moment, then waved at him to continue. "By all means, proceed."

"You were not the only person Duran saw when he came here. He told me of your hideous misdeed. I had to dash his hopes and tell him no sorcerer can reverse the spell of another."

Pride straightened her spine. "Because I am more powerful than you, old man."

Einer gave her a look of pity. "You know very well magic has rules. The solution might be as simple as letting your spell run its course. Then I will cast one on the dragon and turn him back into a man."

The possibility sent a chill through her blood. "Do so, then. Don't talk about it. Prove it! Show me your power."

The wizard stood, the heavy folds of his multi-colored cape billowing around him. The shimmer definitely brightened this time. "You want a demonstration?" He sounded incredulous. "I should have known. As a child you always insisted on verification. This time, though, I'm happy to oblige you."

She stood and watched him utter a chant, but the words were muffled. Einer thought to trick her. The fool. She sensed no outlay of power, no expenditure of energy.

"You conjured something?"

"Tsk, tsk, Calandra. You know better. Magic doesn't have to be showy to be effective. King Zell is now warded against further attempts you make upon his person. In a few days, Zell will return to his former hearty self."

She gasped, suddenly afraid.

Einer smiled. "Yes, child, I know about the potion. I was too late to do anything about it. But, be warned, Calandra, your evil will no long work here. I've seen to that."

Red hot resentment burned through her. "You presume to warn me? I'll show you."

Calandra wiggled her fingers rapidly, snatching threads of magic from the air to create flames dancing mere inches above her palm. Compressing the flames into a white-hot ball with her thoughts, she felt the orb pulse, glow, and burn. She threw it with all her might at Einer.

In a flash, Einer flicked his fingers as he would a mote of dust. Her weapon disappeared with a puff of smoke.

His eyes shone with a sad, probing look. "A twisted foulness is within you, Calandra. It grieves me to breathe the same air as you."

He tried to incense her into demonstrating more of her power. It meant only one thing. He didn't know how powerful her strength. Comprehending his motives revived a measure of her confidence.

"I will not waste my energy to battle you with magic, old man." She sneered. "You are the past. I represent the future. You fear me, as you fear your own death."

"You are right about one thing, Calandra. Death comes to all," he told her with a trace of sadness. "We will see who will be next."

The old wizard didn't scare her. Success was hers for the taking.

Chapter Nineteen

Marina watched Narud crouch and then leap up to catch thermals of wind. His iridescent scarlet scales shimmered in the morning sunlight like flakes of red metal. Anyone looking at the sky would take note of the sight, and that worried her. As well did his parting words.

He would come for her.

What did he mean? Confusion seemed the last thing she needed in her life. The dragon always made her doubt. She remembered first seeing him. Both awe and fright had swelled within her. Yet, a mysterious force she didn't understand drew her to him.

He would come for her.

Narud's words echoed in her mind again. Were they a threat? A promise? She'd fretted how to tell him about her and Duran's tryst, only to learn he knew all along. Little slipped past the dragon. She'd allowed herself to be ensnared by him. The realization wiped away the joy of being close to home.

She trudged on the shoulder of the road, carrying both packs. Duran wouldn't want his personal property left behind, and the extra weight drew her closer to him.

Marina licked her lips. Sea brine tinged the air, the taste and scent familiar and pleasant.

The wind blew harder than she remembered. Clouds scudded across the sky like the ever-changing canvas of a disgruntled artist. In Brenalin, Demit Woods protected Duran and her against the unpredictable buffeting. She found herself missing the safeguard and the great forest she once feared.

Several times, she turned her gaze westward where she last saw Narud. He could be anywhere. The dragon could have flown hundreds of miles out of spite. It would be just like him to force Duran to walk the same trail over and over.

Deep down, she prayed it wouldn't be the case.

She had no reason for expectation. Just hope.

As the day came to a close, vessels sloughed low through ocean swells. Fishermen returned from long, laborious hours with their hulls full of fish.

At a gnarled pine near the road's edge, she settled down beneath wind-twisted boughs. Not far away, the city waited. Candles glowed from windows. The lamplighter executed his nightly duty, illuminating lanterns on posts before total darkness fell. No gates or walls encircled the city. The buildings were shadows of one, two, and three stories.

Within Eudes, one main street paralleled the docks where long piers jutted out into the water. Warehouses, taverns, and inns were thickest on the quayside. Narrower streets darted out in straight lines away from the ocean.

A huge square opened up in the heart of Eudes where a colossal statue of Mighty Kubala stood facing the great ocean. The god was adorned with a trident as a symbol of power in one hand and the other stretched out to gather his beloved seafarers near.

Many times, on special occasions, her family led processions to the site where her father would address the populace.

In her mind, she went left of the square, where an immense covered market spread out with stalls full of wares and produce. By day, traders and peasants thronged the market. She'd spent hours with her sisters fingering various merchandize—a bolt of woven cloth that felt like velvet but felt as light as silk here, a finely tooled leather belt there. They sampled soft cheeses from the great desert Midber, gobbled bites of berry melon from Tanz, admired tiny trees in pots that mimicked the shape of full-sized ones from Nihon, and munched on sweet-salty nuts from Valencia. So many delightful finds. And she would gladly give everything up for a life with Duran.

Her gaze shifted to an above-ground cemetery across the road. Eudes lay situated below sea level. The odd burial was mandatory because if tropical storms hit the city, they threatened to submerge it with massive surges of water. Flooding raised caskets and floated them down the streets, along with mud, heaps of debris, and rubble, disturbing locals and frightening visitors.

A driftwood twig snapped. Someone approached. She poked her head up from the base of the tree in an attempt to penetrate the gathering darkness.

"Marina?" A soft voice called her name. "Marina, where are you?"

The silhouette of a tall man came into view. Duran. Gazing into his eyes, her heart thrummed in her head. Her love for him welled up inside, rippling through every inch of her body. Reaching for his hand, her fingers interlaced with his. He drew her close, circling his arm around her waist. She leaned into his hard body, smelling the hint of brimstone clinging to his skin and clothing.

"I was afraid Narud would fly you far away," she whispered.

"Thankfully, he didn't."

"How did you find me?" She couldn't let go of him.

"I'm not sure." He started to nuzzle her neck with delicate kisses. "I just followed a hunch. It must be some form of dragon instinct. Sometimes, I don't know who or what I…" His voice faded.

An awkward silence followed.

Her heart squeezed along with his pain. She ached to feel the softness of his lips. "I know who you are, Duran. I'm just grateful you're back with me. You'll be with me when I reunite with my family."

He glanced at the blue-pitched rooftops of Eudes to the castle situated high on the bluff. "I'm happy we're so close. Should we go around? Through the town? Which way is faster?"

"The shortest route is through town."

Duran swept a hand out. "This is your homecoming. You must decide. Choose."

Marina strained to move, only to discover indecision rooted her feet to the spot. "I don't know." A tear rolled down her cheek. She didn't want to leave Duran.

"What's wrong, pet?" he asked, moving closer. "You want to go home, don't you?"

"I must look a fright."

"You look stunning to me, Marina. Your family won't care about your appearance. They'll be as proud of you as I am when they hear your tale of survival. You've surmounted unimaginable obstacles, faced dangers from all directions." He brushed a light kiss across her forehead. "You began this journey with one goal in mind—to return home. You never wavered or faltered. I can't tell the number of times your courage kept me going."

His declaration made her cheeks burn with humility. "Enough, Duran, I cannot let you do this."

A thoughtful look appeared in his blue eyes. "Do what?"

"Demean yourself. Regaining your humanity is a far graver hurdle."

He swept up own pack from the ground and took hold of her hand, inundating hers with his heat. He guided her toward the city. "We might as well keep moving."

Scrambling alongside him, she saw him frown at the city. Eudes utilized no city watch for her father decreed soldiers were unnecessary in the merchant city. All goods were sold and traded within its streets. A standing order existed if marauders overran the city, the docks were to be burned. What good was a port city without docks? It ruined the purpose of attacking the city. Where could their ill-gotten gains be sold? No other port existed like Eudes.

Dogs barked as they entered.

Marina squeezed Duran's hand. "You mustn't take any more chances on my account," she said. "Our adventure is over."

Maybe the timing remained off, for he came to an abrupt stop. He lifted her chin with his thumb and finger.

"It'll never be over until the sorceress is gone."

Stupid. Stupid. Stupid. She was such an idiot. How

could she have been so heartless? So forgetful of his plight?

"You told me yesterday that you loved me," she said. "I never responded, did I?"

Duran stared at her for a long moment, tall and broad-shouldered, visibly trying to determine the words before they tumbled off her tongue. Marina wondered what he thought she might say. It was wrong to keep him in suspense. She started to add more, but he held up his hand.

"You don't have to tell me anything."

She touched his lips—sweet, warm. She would much prefer to taste them, to feel his body pressed against hers. "Yes, I do. I want to. When informed of our match, I ranted against it. I had no wish to leave my home or wed you. My father sent me off to Brenalin the very night he told me of the arrangement. He feared I might run away."

"Would you have?"

Marina bit her lip. "I don't know. I—I was loathe to wed any man who was a stranger. Oh, I knew duty demanded I do so eventually. It wouldn't have mattered which prince was chosen as my husband. But—"

"Hush, my love. Say no more."

"Duran, I have to finish. Please, let me." She placed her hand on his arm. The muscles beneath his clothing tensed. "You need to know I love you with all my heart and soul. I would have been proud to call myself your wife."

Fine lines branched out around Duran's eyes. He gave her a bright smile. "Thank you for telling me. I know it wasn't easy. No one likes being subjected to the will of another, and you were being forced into a

313

loveless marriage."

He understood her so well. "It no longer seems so horrible."

Duran exhaled a sigh, and then clasped her hand, his fingers closing tenderly around hers. "I have to have you in my life. If I break the curse, will you marry me?"

A proposal! Her heart sped up. To say he stunned her was a gross understatement. "Oh, Duran," she said, hoping her voice didn't quake. "Do you mean it? Are you sure?"

"I do. I am. Absolutely."

"Then I accept with pleasure."

He drew her into his arms and held her tight against his body. Words weren't necessary. His lips met hers. She closed her eyes and gave herself over to the lush kiss. His tongue slid inside her mouth, exploring the recesses. Her heart raced faster. Memories of their night of naked love on the beach sprang to mind. Warmth spread all over her and made her shivery inside. Hot and cold. She felt absolutely wonderful.

This was definitely the wrong place and time.

She pulled back with a smile and took hold of Duran's hand, desperately needing to maintain physical contact with him. At the steep knoll leading to the castle, they paused. Before them were two hundred and twenty-three steps. One for each day of the year. Marina knew the number by heart because she'd counted them numerous times as a child.

Sleepy gate guards snapped to attention at their advance. Recognizing three, Marina called them by name. The few servants still up and working gasped at them, but none approached. The hum of their voices faded as Marina and Duran hurried across the bailey.

They pushed open doors the height of two men and adorned with brass tridents, Eudes' symbol.

Marina's feet moved faster. She led Duran to a small chamber off the great audience room where muted voices from inside drifted into the hallway. The well-oiled doors swung wide without a creak of hinges. Cool air seeped in from a bank of open windows on the far side of the room. Yards of blue hangings billowed on the windows, rendering the impression of being under the ocean.

No one inside noticed the door opening. A good thing, Marina thought. Everything seemed as it should be, exactly as she expected to find. Nothing changed.

Nothing…except her.

She had grown, matured. She wondered if the changes on the inside would be visible to her family. Were they the reason for her nervousness? The prospect of being reunited with them had sustained her for these many long weeks. She tried to swallow and found her throat constricted. Deep in her heart, she would never settle back into her old life.

And to her reckoning that was not a bad thing. Not at all.

The twins, Olla and Woola, sat at a gaming table, playing Pillows, a card game at which they were equally matched.

Her older sister, Tempa, regal in a pale sea-green gown, held a needle in hand and nimbly worked on a linen square. She had been pledged to the Prince of Koll, their nuptials set for next year. Marina suspected the piece would find a spot inside her wedding chest. The prince would live in Eudes after the marriage for he was a second son, and Tempa would inherit the crown upon their father's passing. The prince's family paid a fortune to garner the marriage for a favorite son. Of course, Tempa had seen the young man beforehand and encouraged her parents to accept the offer.

Her parents huddled over an ornate desk on the far side of the room. Each took the administration of the kingdom seriously. They prided themselves on providing a benevolent rule and making fair decisions for the citizens, and that increased Eudes' prosperity.

Suddenly, she ducked back along the hallway wall. "I can't do this," she said, her voice a shaky whisper. "What am I going to say? How should I act?"

Duran traced her face from temple to jaw with a feathery touch, then his fingers moved to her mouth. Her whole body tingled in anticipation. She stood and held her arms at her sides, hoping he would kiss her.

"You've nothing to fear, my sweet. Just be yourself." He whispered encouragement. "They'll be happy to see you. Everything will be fine. Go to them."

She stood frozen when Duran slid off the straps of her pack. The weight disappeared from her shoulders. Smiling warmly at her, he turned her around again and gave a nudge in the small of her back. She would do whatever he wanted.

Cowardice didn't exist in her. She was not one to feel sorry for herself. The desire to come home was what had given her the determination to survive.

Marina stepped into view. "Father. Mother," she called out in a soft voice.

Silence fell.

All the air was sucked from the room. A feeling of peace infused Marina. Tears welled in her eyes, blurring her vision.

****

Duran watched from the doorway. The tingling of Marina's skin, velvet soft, beneath his fingertips turned into a bittersweet sensation. He shivered, unable to imagine life without her. To reunite Marina with her family had become the hardest task he'd ever set for himself. The impulse to carry her far, far away was a constant battle. He loved her. Never so much as at this moment.

He consoled himself that he'd done the right thing. All that remained was to make sure Marina's reception was as it should be—warm and loving.

The people at the far end of the chamber sat frozen. They must think Marina a ghost. Duran held his breath. She deserved the best from these people. If they mistreated her or made her uncomfortable in any way, he would not hesitate to snatch her back and have Narud fly her far away.

No sooner did he think this than a tumult of joyful voices erupted. The demonstrative reaction, although slow in coming, elicited a smile of pleasure and pride from him. Bliss glowed on Marina's face, and that pleased him. She looked beautiful. Wonderful. Happy. That pleased him even more.

She twisted her head in his direction. His heart swelled, and he started to step forward. A whirlwind in the form of a tall, youthful woman raced for Marina and wrapped her in a breath-stealing hug.

"I can't believe it's really you," the girl squealed in a high-pitched voice full of delight.

Marina never received another chance to look at him again. A second teen, obviously the first's twin, ran up behind. She pulled her sister's arm away to hug

Marina, too.

"Rina!" she cried. "Is it you? Where have you been? How did you get home?"

Laughter bubbled from Marina. "Olla. Woola. How I've missed you. What trouble have you gotten into since I left?"

"None, we swear," they said in unison.

A man, the king by his well-cut leggings and sable-trimmed tunic, looked shocked enough for his hair to have turned from silver to snow-white. Moments before, a sad look had seemed permanently affixed to his countenance.

He escorted a woman, the queen by her regal bearing, by the elbow. She fared no better than he. Dark circles stained the skin beneath her eyes and her build appeared unhealthily thin.

Both beamed at Marina.

A young woman who looked about five years older than Marina approached last. She had fair hair, green eyes matching her gown, and a flashing smile that brightened a face Duran suspected usually showed a serious visage.

Marina hugged each person, smiling and crying at the same time. "Mother! Father! Tempa," she said.

"Is it really you?" her mother asked, catching Marina by the shoulders. Tears flowed down her cheeks and her nose turned red.

Joy swelled in his beloved's eyes. "Yes, it's really me."

"Rina," her father said, "we thought you lost to us forever, that you were dead."

Light, merry laughter bubbled from Marina. "My death was a gross exaggeration. Your ruse and insistence that I exchange clothes with Stav saved me." She stole a glance at the columns where Duran remained while the reunion took place. "There's someone I want you to meet. Someone special who aided in my return."

"Yes, yes," the king said, beaming. "We wish to meet the person who returned you to us. We owe him a huge debt of gratitude."

"Duran…Duran," she repeated.

"Duran?" the king inquired, his eyes narrowing. "As in your betrothed Duran Abbas? You have been traveling with the high prince unchaperoned?"

The edge in the king's voice did not bode well to Duran's way of thinking. Ofttimes, he'd heard a similar tone of disapproval spring from his father. His concern solidified and became a palpable, tangible thing. He did not like anyone, Marina's father or not, assuming she'd committed a wrong.

He moved out of the shadows.

****

Marina heard the twins ahhing the instant Duran stepped into view. Beneath their exclamation came the rustle of silk when they edged closer to her.

Woola yanked on Marina's arm. "You must tell us everything that's happened to you. First though, when was the last time you bathed? Both of you stink."

"They cannot bathe together, you fool," murmured Olla to her twin.

Marina flushed. The impetuous girls made her suddenly aware of her road weary condition. Sand dusted her skin and heavy snarls twisted the curls of her hair. Her gown fared no better. The once serviceable gown had seen better days, with travel stains and a hem frayed beyond repair.

"I don't remember you having such a sensitive nose, Woola," she bluffed, glad Duran stood next to her. "I do agree that the luxury of a bath and a set of clean clothes would be most appreciated."

"I don't mean to be presumptuous," Duran said, his tone cautious, "but if two baths could be prepared, I would be deeply indebted."

Her mother regarded him with cool reassurance. "The return of our beloved daughter means everything to us. A bath is the least we can provide. I'm sure someone in the household is of a size to match you, Prince Abbas."

"Among family and friends," he replied, "titles are unnecessary. Call me Duran."

The king summoned two servants with a loud clap of his hands. One took Duran, and the other escorted Marina.

Marina escaped into a rose-scented bath in her old quarters with the twins attempting to follow and continue their barrage of questions. Thankfully, her mother clucked her disapproval and forbade their wishes. She smiled at the memories she'd accumulated on her journey home. Duran and Narud stood in the forefront.

Duran was tall, handsome and very male.

Narud was a dragon, magnificent and dangerous.

She'd been frightened, confused, and angry in the beginning, and not in that order. She had changed, grown stronger, fallen in love.

Suddenly, the familiar clickity-clack of tiny claws on wooden floorboards yanked her attention to a streak of white fur darting toward the tub.

"Sinner!" she cried out in delight. "How I've missed you."

The cat rubbed alongside the tub as though overjoyed she'd returned. She scratched him behind his ears. Stepping out of the bath, she scooped up her pet and let him lick behind her ear. The scratchy tongue reminded her of Narud's, only much diminished in size.

After being fed, bathed, and dressed, impulse drew Marina to the window to gaze out at the ocean for a moment. She heard waves lap at the rocks far below and admired the way stars dotted the night sky like diamonds. Ages had passed since she felt carefree enough to run barefoot over the beach, her feet warmed by the sun.

She pushed the memory away to return to the family chamber with Sinner trailing behind. Duran had finished first and was being mobbed by her family with questions from the twins.

She smoothed down the folds of her gown, wanting to look her best for them, and for Duran who had never seen her in royal attire. She wore a lush gown with strings of aquamarines twined in her blonde hair. A large gemstone dangled from a pearl necklace. She'd never felt lovelier, especially after spotting the admiration gleaming in Duran's sea-blue eyes.

Nor had she seen him in anything besides his fleece coat and brown leggings. Olla and Woola flanked him on either side as he faced her mother, father, and older sister. The blazing fire in the hearth behind him set fiery sparks in his brown hair. Just last night she'd run her fingers through the thick cloud and now he'd cut it!

Someone had barbered his square jaw without a nick. His smile wooed the twins, for sure, and probably the rest of her family. Joy filled her. She wanted them to approve of Duran.

The fire popped, and she glanced toward it. Looking back, she found everyone staring at her. Duran winked at her, and she scooped up Sinner, who responded by purring loudly in her arms.

She smiled at Duran, then her parents and sisters. "I'm sure you have many questions," she said, "but where to start?"

Her mother chuckled. "The beginning is usually best."

"Oh, yes, we want to know everything that has happened to you," Olla said.

Marina started her tale with slow, halting words. She told them about the caravan attack. Of Narud and how the dragon was caught under an evil sorceress's curse. How he had shared a portion of his strength with her. The crossing the glacier and falling in the crevasse. Meeting Becca and Fahid. And confronting the sorceress. Then finally Duran destroying the brigands who murdered the loyal Eudians of her caravan.

She bent the truth only slightly, leaving out two vital details—Duran as Narud and the fact they were lovers.

The twins held hands, bowed forward, their gazes fixed on her as if trapped. Tempa stared off into the distance as though visualizing every incident in her mind's eye. Her mother sat silent, tears streaming down her face. Her father's gaze danced between Duran and her, his expression alternately frowning and smiling.

Finished, silence greeted her. Her audience stared at each other, appearing confused. Then, grinning at her, thunderous applause rent the air.

"What a wonderful tale, Rina," Tempa spoke first. "I never knew you had the makings of a great bard."

"Everything I said was true," she insisted.

The twins giggled as only young girls are wont to do. One glance at them told her they would not be influenced into believing anything else.

"Marina," Wolla said, "you left to wed the high prince and return with your betrothed and an amazing tale of a dragon. Is it the same creature who wiped out Genoy's army?"

Rumor always flew faster than the wind, she belatedly remembered. It only made sense for the surviving soldiers to spread word of Narud. "How many dragons do you think exist in this world?" she asked.

"We don't know," Wolla exclaimed. "Where is this dragon now?"

Before she could make up an excuse, her father stood.

"It's late, and we're all tired," he announced. "We do not mean to disregard the ordeal you experienced or dismiss your bravery, Rina." It was the second time he used her childhood nickname, a fact not lost on Marina. "What you have told us is much to grasp in one evening. Best we continue this discussion tomorrow."

"When will your red dragon return?" Olla asked, her eyes gleaming. "Can I meet him? Touch him?"

"Olla, he's not my dragon!" she corrected, saddened her younger sister missed the gravity of the situation. "He's a man unfairly cursed. It's tragic."

"Hardly tragic," Olla said. "Romantic."

****

Marina spent the next four days in the library.

Today the unexpected arrival of her sister Woola broke her isolation. Had she ever valued privacy before? Marina wondered. She could not recall.

"Father wishes to see you, Marina," she said, munching on a peppermint treat she had brought with her.

Thus far the dusty tomes refused to relinquish any of their precious secrets. Lack of discovery made her reluctant to leave. "I'll be with him shortly."

"I think he means now."

"I can't. The answer to the sorceress's spell could lie in the next page."

Her sister crunched on the candy. "Do not tarry, Rina. He seems anxious."

Mighty Kubala! He knows Duran's secret!

"What does he want?" Marina tried to keep her voice calm.

Of the twins, Woola might be less adventurous, but she could sniff out a mystery in an instant and had a long memory.

Her sister rolled a shoulder as only the young could. "He probably wants to discuss Narud. No one has been as close to a dragon as you in thousands of years."

"Don't be silly, Woola. He doesn't need me. Father has wizards at his disposal to learn about the creatures."

Woola peered over her shoulder to spy on the pages of the tome she studied. Her curiosity could easily turn into something else. The crunching of her sister eating the sweet recalled the noise Narud made when his strong jaws crushed bones.

"Maybe it's something altogether different," Woola said. "I'm positive Yanna, because she is the goddess of love, sent you to Brenalin to meet the prince."

"You are too young to be a romantic, sister." Marina marked the page in the old tome, closed the cover, and stood. She fought back a sneeze tickling her nose.

"How can you not believe she didn't manipulate the situation?" Woola licked the corners of her mouth. "And I'll have you know, many girls are wedded and bedded by the time they are ten and six. In two months, I'll be ten and seven."

"Oh my, so old."

Woola glared at her as she pulled another sweet from a pouch and jammed the treat into her mouth.

Marina took advantage of the silence to look around. The morning, awash with golden sunlight, did not cheer her. She had longed for a day when she might return home. Since returning, she thought—many times—maybe her wish had been hasty. She just wanted Duran.

He'd left her a note and her father a similar one. In hers, he expressed his love and devotion. In her father's, he vowed to return and fulfill the marriage contract.

But when?

And how?

His absence left a gaping hole in her heart.

Her inability to find a clue to break Calandra's curse had become an increasingly crushing burden. She'd learned one item of merit—a curse could have a literal or figurative translation. Most spells were intended to influence fate, and because magic existed alongside the forces of nature, the convoluted energy did not always perform as its maker expected. A great deal depended on the practitioner's intentions at the time of the enchantment. Which meant she needed to question Duran to gain a clearer picture of Calandra's objective.

To complicate matters, she'd not heard a single whisper of mindspeech from Narud. She missed him and worried the dragon remained upset with her. Her hand went to cup the ruby she kept safe in her pocket. Initially cool to the touch, the gemstone swamped her palm with heat. Did Narud feel her touch when she held the jewel? She hoped so.

Woola led her to the great Aquamarine Hall where the walls were awash with sun through windows of rippling bluish-green glass, giving off the illusions of being underwater. Travelers came from throughout the world to see and admire the beauty of the chamber.

Strangely, the room, normally packed with people, was devoid of petitioners and supplicants. Her father sat in the high seat of Eudes. The moment she entered, his gaze fell upon her, an odd look on his face.

"I hope my summons didn't interrupt something important." He waved her forward.

She smiled. Her father had always been considerate. It was one of the many traits she loved about him. "You know it did, but I needed a break."

He rose when she reached the dais. "Not having much luck?"

"No, and it's extremely discouraging."

His eyes narrowed with concern. "Nothing else?"

It would seem her father saw through to her very soul. "I wish you wouldn't look at me like that." She rubbed her hands over her face to hide the blush threatening to make a showy appearance. "It makes me nervous."

A knowing look glinted in his bright eyes. "I can't help myself, Rina. You've changed. Your ordeal has been good for you. Your cheeks have color and sunshine sparkles in your eyes."

Marina's chest rose with a sigh of relief. "Thank you."

He stepped down and ruffled her hair. "That doesn't mean I do not worry about you. You stay closeted in the library archives day after day."

It struck her as a fair concern. "I am trying to learn all I can about magic."

"Why is that? Magic was not a subject that interested you before. History, yes. Dragons, yes. But actual magic, no."

"It does now," she answered warily, trying to guess her father's thoughts.

His expression relaxed. "I thought as much. Have you discussed this with our wizards?"

"I consulted them first," she answered frankly. "They have tried to help, but sadly have no knowledge of use to me. Why do you ask?"

Her father's confident demeanor didn't diminish. "Because I wanted confirmation from your own lips. And I want to know the rest of the story. The part you omitted from your mother and sisters."

Her heart suddenly pounded in her chest. "I don't know what you mean. There is no more."

"Come, come, Rina, I haven't been king for all these years not to deduce when someone is hiding the truth from me."

A wise man, her father knew when to pick his

battles against the females of his family. This obviously was one of those times. "Why aren't you satisfied with my answer?"

He glanced around the room, only to smile and lead her toward the bank of windows. "No doubt you recall our conversation before you left. I told you then you were stronger than you imagined. Do you remember?"

She wondered at his meaning and worried why he wanted an answer. She couldn't fathom a guess. "Yes." Worry crept into her voice. "I was positive you were punishing me. On the journey to Brenalin, not a single day went by when I didn't search for a reason. Or fault you! It took me a long time to realize you believed you were doing the best for me…and you did."

"Nothing teaches a person about life like experience. I cannot believe your nosy sisters haven't figured out the man cursed as a dragon in your epic tale is Duran."

Shame flared inside her. "How…"

"Oh, Rina, parents know their children far better than they admit sometimes." Amusement laced his tone. "It's a failing of parents around the world. One you will experience, too, once you are blessed with your own."

"I miss him so much," she whispered, hoping her time with Duran would bring a child into her life.

"I understand," her father said, his own voice low. "It would please me, daughter, if you would tell me of your plans."

She took a deep breath. "I'm going to solve the riddle and save Duran. And Narud, too. They are so different, yet so much alike. Both deserve to live. I must do all I can for them."

He patted her hand with affection. "I can't blame you for loving the prince. It pleases me greatly to learn you have found what your mother and I cherish."

"I do love him, and he loves me," she said with assurance.

He drew her close. "Love is the most pernicious sorcery of all. It can bring happiness and joy, or grief and sorrow. Whichever it will be is the greatest anomaly. It makes one strong and weak at the same time. You can do anything if you set your mind to it. I'm confident the solution will come to you."

Tears welled in her eyes. It felt so good confiding in someone. "Oh, Father, help me. Help Duran and Nurad. The pledge between his family and ours is what triggered the sorceress to curse Duran. I cannot quit until he is free."

He gave her hand a squeeze. "Consider the resources of Eudes at your disposal."

She threw herself into her father's arms, sobbing with happiness.

A second later, her joy was shattered by a noise not heard in Eudes in thousands of years—the slow flapping of dragon wings.

Marina blinked, disbelieving. Narud? It couldn't be. He wouldn't appear before everyone. The sight of him would frighten the entire populace. Surely, he possessed more sense than that.

She ran to the window.

Narud's crimson scales flashed in the bright midday sun. He performed a slow loop over the ocean. Her initial shock dissipated. The beast was showing off. His nature wasn't mean, but he did delight in tormenting people. Something in her swelled within her. She would willingly submit to his arrogance and haughty demeanor. She didn't care.

All that mattered was in seconds she would see Narud once again.

Chapter Twenty

No matter how hard Narud concentrated, his efforts to put Marina from his mind proved useless. His memory of her held him prisoner, and he no longer wished to resist.

For four long, unbearable days, he'd heard nothing from her. While her stubbornness was impossible to understand, she should have contacted him through mindspeech. Fortuitously, each time she touched the ruby, his dragon instincts flared up at the contact, and his heart warmed with her appreciation of his gift.

Lack of communication meant he had vied for her affections with the male human and lost. It galled him to come in second. A dragon, obviously the better choice, should be her first choice. He would convince Marina. He would. But how?

He had stomped around his mountain cave each day, causing the ground to shake and boulders to tumble. Yesterday, in frustration, he'd spewed fiery brimstone and burned a hectare of trees to crisp sticks. What had taken Duran and Marina weeks to travel took him less than two hours to fly.

This morning, after shredding his kill and feasting on tasty, raw venison, he had settled upon a bed of pearls and rubies. His treasure. The one unfairly stolen by Duran. His only problem, the normal comfort he found in treasure, evaded him.

He'd dragged the jewels higher up on his body. They tumbled over his massive sides as if he bathed himself in them. His mood remained sour, a bitter taste in his mouth. He snorted brief plumes in the icy cold of his lair until he lumbered outside and launched himself into the thin air. No matter how high he flew, eddies carried the scent of ocean to him and with it, a reminder of Marina. Then he remembered several bluish green aquamarines glistening beneath the watery depths. Sailors used the gemstone as a charm against drowning. Though he entertained no fear of drowning, claiming one for himself and adding it to his hoard might alleviate his loneliness. He flew west.

The great ocean spread across the horizon for as far as the eye could see. Whitecaps broke atop crests of waves where the shore dropped off beneath the blue-gray water.

He soared high above his target. His quest for the gemstones was a lie, a falsehood to deceive his subconscious. He came to see Marina, his beloved.

Emotions spilled from his human core to color his own. While it helped explain his feelings, the ache inside him did not soften. He must see Marina. A need. A hunger. His life was meaningless without her. Even if she chose Duran over him, he couldn't deny himself the pleasure of her company.

In that instant, he forgave her weakness. She was human, after all, and therefore, prone to error.

He turned toward the coast.

Toward Eudes.

Toward Marina.

He dipped low over the city, curious. People screamed at the sight of him, their feeble cries ascending in the air. They mattered not. Marina did not stand among the frightened masses. He sensed her presence on the bluff.

"Foolish dragon. Leave the female human alone."

The Guardians! This time the number of voices was vastly smaller than in Demit Woods. *"Do not interfere with me, Guardians,"* he warned. *"I am the first dragon in over a thousand years, and you have yet to reveal yourself or your purpose. I do not have to follow your rules."*

"We are trying to help you. Guide you. How can we do so when you will not heed us?"

Flaring his nostrils, he sucked in great gulps of air to pinpoint their scent in the air. His tormentors were near and their frustration genuine. *"Show yourself, and I might listen to you."*

"We are in plain sight. Use your dragon instincts to see through our disguise."

"Instincts are hunches. I prefer concrete evidence."

"We will not beg. Go! Dally with the human. Learn for yourself that humans are distrustful. We will welcome you when you realize the truth."

The Guardians' tone possessed the same arrogance as his own. He glided on the currents, swinging his neck back and forth, but saw nothing. *"I do not believe you."*

"You are mistrusting the wrong beings. This infatuation with the human female will lead to disaster." A great sadness edged the words.

Narud expelled a puff of smoke. *"Begone. You mean to trick me."*

He thrust his powerful wings a half dozen times

with his powerful wings and climbed higher in the currents. He sought a place to land at the castle where Marina's presence was the strongest. He never promised to stay away from her. Rather, just the opposite. He vowed to come for her, and he was here.

His return to Eudes never encompassed aquamarines but a far more precious treasure. A prize worth any sacrifice.

"Marina, I am here. Where are you?"

****

The word pictures in her head were as clear as a bell. Grinning ear to ear, Marina nearly shouted out her joy; and then some instinct made her pause. *"Narud! As much as I've missed you, there is great danger here. You must leave."*

"I want to see you."

He wouldn't dare! He couldn't. But he was.

Narud revealed himself to the populace.

A huge shadow passed over the bailey. She heard a flapping sound much like canvas catching a breeze that made her look up. The noise faded when guards shouted warning cries at the top of their lungs. They ran along the castle battlements, panicked, bearing spears and bows when Narud orbited in the broken clouds. People ran for cover out of the bailey.

Since Narud's destruction of Genoy's army, rumors of the beast were aplenty, both good and bad. One had him carrying off a farmer's entire herd of livestock; in another he destroyed a field of corn with dragonfire; and one even claimed he plucked a young girl from a watery grave. The stories were slated to become legends. Even Marina hardly knew which ones to believe.

The guards assumed an attack loomed and went on the defensive. Officers shouted for calm. A skilled bowman could hit a moving target and Eudes's archers were among the best. The alarm gong in the tower pealed its eerie song over the castle and grounds.

Narud wheeled overhead. He hovered above the castle, drew his long wings close to his body, and dove toward the ground like a giant falcon. Soldiers scattered. Amid their screams of terror and amazement, he angled his head up and pulled out of the dive to loop in the air. Marina swore the dragon exposed a toothy grin as if he enjoyed the uproar his presence created.

"Narud," she screamed in mindspeech, anxious and furious. *"What are you doing here?"*

"I had to come. Four days and no word from you."

Her shoulders sagged. In all fairness, her trepidation didn't give her the right to criticize. If she had contacted him, she could have forestalled him.

"Is something the matter with you? With Duran?"

"Always it is the human you favor. Why could you not love me?" he shot back, swinging his great head sideways as though searching for her.

She saw no easy way out. *"You've put me in an impossible situation."*

"Explain."

"I do care about you."

"I sense you have chosen to live without me." Narud flew straight at the castle, pulling up at the last second. *"I had to see you one more time. Come outside, my love."*

What was he up to? *"So you can carry me off?"*

"Would that be so bad?" He sounded deflated.

She shook her head. *"Being here is dangerous for*

you. Don't you see the guards? The archers? This is no game, Narud. They will shoot you. You are in great peril."

"What does he want?" her father asked beside her, unable to hear the inner conversation.

She'd forgotten his presence. "I'm not sure. He misses me. I am trying to make him leave, but he refuses to heed me."

"Misses you?" her father repeated in amazement. "How do you know?"

"He told me. I hear his words in my head. Despite our differences, dragons are very complex creatures with as many feelings as we have."

"Look at me, my sweet," Narud said. *"Do you really think they can hurt me?"*

He performed another graceful loop in the air. The sight elicited animated cries. Several guards spit and raised two fingers, giving the Eudes sign against evil.

Marina's muscles clenched. She was in no mood to tolerate the dragon's antics or her peoples' superstition. Danger mounted with each passing second, and her frustration with the situation increased as well.

Narud's scales glistened and flashed scarlet and gold in the sunlight. Her gaze traced the slope of his vulnerable belly where dozens of colorful gemstones twinkled. Were they enough protection? She hoped so.

Then horror dawned on her. The spot where the precious gems winked and sparkled provided an ideal target for expert bowmen. Even as the thought materialized, archers nocked their arrows, the broad metal headed points aimed straight at Narud.

"Narud, look at the archers! They prepare to fire in defense of the castle. You must leave."

"Let the puny humans try to injure me," he answered back. *"I do not fear them or their weak weapons."*

She would have sworn his scales puffed up with importance. *"You can't kill them. They are my countrymen. They are only performing their duty."* She was filled with a sudden, unexpected fierceness.

"If you are worried, tell them I mean no harm."

She spun to face her face. "Father," she pleaded. "He's risked everything to see me."

"He cares deeply for you. And you for him?"

She latched onto his arm. "Yes, oh, yes. You've got to do something. Prevent them from harming him. I will die if he's hurt."

"I know. I know. I'll stop them. Keep talking to him."

He dashed from the room, heading for the battlements. She sighed with relief as her father grasped the need for speed.

"Do you see me, Narud? I'm here." She leaned out the window and waved her arm until Narud swung his mighty head in her direction.

"Come to the roof. I will land there."

"No! You've frightened these people enough. They'll attack if you get too close. You cannot prevail against these odds. You must leave this place. I fear for your safety."

"Do you, now?"

"You—"

A volley of shafts scored the air. Narud circled, heedless of the arrows and spears being hurled at him.

Marina shrieked, frightened to the soles of her feet. She couldn't tear her gaze away from the scene unfolding outside. The arrows rose to their zenith, seemed to pause and then plummeted downward. Men rushed over the battlement preparing a second barrage.

Narud roared. People shuddered in fear. A fireball the size of an egg shot from him. An archer's leather jerkin ignited where the missile hit. Screaming, the man flailed his arms in a panicky attempt to smother the flames.

Marina felt crestfallen. Her body froze in place. Narud was gorgeous and deadly, and she loved him.

Whatever happened with Duran and his curse, Narud was real to her. She feared to look away.

"No! They don't know what they're doing."

The dragon pulled up, smoke billowing from his nostrils. *"For you, anything."*

Warm relief flooded her veins. Marina started to thank him when another whirr erupted, louder this time. A second deadly hail of arrows turned the sky black.

Time slowed.

Her world shifted on its axis. A great roar split the sky. Dozens of dark shafts protruded between the flashing gemstones on Narud's soft underside.

Bellows of joy coursed through the soldiers and peasants.

Marina screamed. Too late. She clapped her hands over her mouth in a vain attempt to muffle another scream.

Narud began to fall, rolling in the air, his leathery wings flapping in vain.

In the bailey, people scattered in all different directions. Those fearing the great beast would crush them raced away. Others, braver or morbidly curious, huddled in groups. The ground shook when he crashed.

Dust shot up to the height of four tall men.

A cry of anguish clawed its way up Marina's throat. She clamped her hand over her mouth to stem her anguish and then almost doubled over with the intensity of her grief. Narud. No. Her vision blurred with hot tears.

"Fools!" she screamed at the people below. "You stupid, idiotic fools! You killed him!"

She hated them. All of them.

Marina wrenched up the hem of her gown and raced out of the great audience chamber, half-blind with tears. She stumbled down the hallway on numb feet, knocking against the wall, shoving people out of her way. Let them gape at her. She didn't care.

Only one thing mattered—reaching Narud. She ran in a daze. People gathered in a circle around him, cheering his death. *Curse them!* Desperation added strength to Marina's muscles. She poured her anger into her fists, beating upon the backs of those who dared block her path.

"Let me through!" she demanded. "Move! Get out of my way, do you hear?"

His great wedge-shaped head inched up when she knelt beside him. Blood fountained soundlessly from dozens of wounds, his great heart pumping out his life's blood. Already, a thick, dark stain expanded on the ground. She cradled his head in her lap.

Hot tears streaked down her cheeks. She tasted salt on her lips and saw the droplets sizzle upon his scales. He groaned and twisted as if her touch inflicted added blows to his already injured body.

"Narud," she whispered, gathering him closer. "Oh, Narud."

"Marina," he said in breathy gasp.

She gently stroked the sensitive ridges atop his head. "Yes, my love."

"Every breath hurts."

The realization of Narud dying appalled her. His death eviscerated her heart in ways she could never imagine. He was being cheated out of his life. "I'm so sorry."

"It's not your fault. You warned me. Desperate beings do not listen well, and I was desperate to see you once again."

"Why didn't you defend yourself?" she asked.

"You asked me not to hurt them. I honored your request."

Sickening guilt rolled her stomach. "Oh, Narud, I am sorry. Don't talk. Save your strength."

A deep shudder ran the length of his body from snout to tail. *"Feel my heart. Feel it. It beats with my love for you."*

"Narud, please don't die. Please."

"I'm not afraid of death. I would rather come to my end in your arms than live without you. Grieve not for me."

More tears welled in her eyes. "Tell me what to do. Don't leave me. You can't."

"There is nothing you can do, my love." His voice grew faint. *"You are my most prized possession. I am glad it is I and not the puny human who will see you last."*

"I care nothing for your battle with Duran. Save your strength. Don't talk."

He didn't listen. *"You are precious beyond all riches. Remember the dragon tales, my love. Remember them and think of me. Remember me."* His mindspeech dwindled.

He faded before her very eyes.

Duran, too.

Marina's skin tingled. A familiar red mist began to form out of the air. She spared a glance toward the sky, assuming dusk neared, only to spy the golden ball of the sun high overhead. A red mist formed.

"Stand back, my love. It is unsafe for you to be near."

She laid her head on his. "I don't care. I'll not leave you. Not ever."

"You must."

"No," she said firmly. "Oh, Narud, I love you."

He moaned thinly. *"I love…"*

The mist of change thickened. Burnt sulfur defiled the air as intense heat enveloped her. The fine hairs on her arms stood straight up. Life meant nothing to her without Narud or Duran. They were one and the same, and to love one was to love the other. Too late, she realized, their love was like an anchor to hold her heart steady in the worst storm. To find true love, only to have it snatched away made no sense. All the unhappiness, pain, and arcane suffering she'd experienced coalesced into a single anguishing moment.

She gasped a deep breath, felt her chin tremble. Hot, scorching air filled her lungs. People screamed around her.

The tale of the white dragon queen's ascension upon her death leapt into her mind. It was one of the first stories Narud had told her about dragons. Shamed, she recognized a selfishness in herself that she never knew she possessed. Was she holding Narud back? Her jaw trembled.

She tenderly kissed the bony ridge closest to his eyes. "Go to the stars, my love," she whispered softly. "I will look for you there each night."

His robust body shuddered. The death rattle rasped from his mouth and the once strong muscles went limp.

No, no, no, she raged.

In a span of a breath, Narud's large red eyes closed and he slipped away.

Dead…

Which meant Duran was gone as well.

Marina slumped. Sorrow wracked her in waves of nausea. The red mist thickened even more. She felt the weight of the dragon's head disappear from her lap. Her insides turned hot, cold, and then hollow. The emptiness magnified until she longed for death to take her as well.

****

Calandra winced and cried out in surprise. She staggered beside the king. Stinging pain sliced through her as if ugly welts suddenly erupted all over on her body. Her head throbbed with intense waves of pain.

It didn't take much imagination to figure out the last scrap of magic connecting her with Duran disengaged.

"What is it, my dear?" Zell asked, scrutinizing her.

A whimper of pain slipped from her mouth before she slowly straightened. "Nothing, my liege." The weight of his impenetrable scrutiny made her pause. "I—I merely misstepped."

The king's gaze flitted over her. A tremor caused his bony hand to flutter. After a moment, he patted her arm. "You must be careful. I wouldn't want any harm to befall you."

Her headache worsened. An ugly rash speckled her hands. She scratched at it vigorously. The malady had been Einer's doing. Who else would dare attack her with magic? More likely, he attempted to make her other spells fail as well. For days, she'd been unable to cast the simplest spell. Her lip curled into a sneer. How she hated him, his interference. The old wizard would pay dearly for his meddling.

"You are too kind, Your Highness," she replied. "I am forever grateful."

"All I ask is for you and Einer to make peace."

She batted her lashes. "I don't know what you mean."

"Never assume people around you don't see what is occurring. This rift between the two of you must be healed." Sadness laced his words.

Calandra fixed her gaze on the king's features, pretending a concern she did not feel. "I have no quarrel with the wizard. He is the one who finds fault with me. Though I know not the cause."

Zell drew in his white brows. "Then I'll ask him."

Her heart raced. "I pray, Your Highness, do nothing. Please. Let the matter lie."

"As you wish, my dear. I will speak no more of it."

She rubbed her arm, the itchiness almost unbearable. "I will try to make amends with Einer for your sake." It was a lie, but he need not know.

One good thing—Einer had been unable to alter her spell on the king. She assumed he tried, but found no proof of success. More curiously, he'd let her duplicity remain concealed. She'd waited, expecting ruin every day. She even feared it. Surprisingly, none came. That wasn't how she would have handled the situation, if it were reversed.

Mostly, Einer watched for her to make a slip in demeanor or behavior. Calandra harbored no doubts that if he suspected she coveted the crown, he would take immediate steps to thwart her efforts. He was too late!

Success was within her grasp. She let out a soft, satisfying breath.

Last night, Zell had proposed.

Her plans were moving forward. By the time the meddling wizard discovered she sought marriage in order to acquire the Ruby Throne's secret, the ceremony would be over, and that suited her just fine.

Since sighting the dragon, more and more people had sought the safe haven within Brenalin's thick granite walls. The meticulously fitted blocks were impenetrable against attack from men and dragon. Centuries of protecting the city from enemies verified their ability. While dragonfire could not harm stone, the gates imbedded in their triumphal arches were constructed of wood, and wood burned. Dragonfire would destroy them with a few blasts, or the creature could fly overhead and ignite rooftops.

The moment she and the king entered the great audience hall, people bowed and scraped. Sycophants, all of them. She glared at the people milling about the great room, her gaze flashing with fury.

Calandra took two steps when muscle-wrenching pain slammed into her, the final bond shredding between her and Duran. She froze in her tracks, alarm burning her insides. Her headache intensified. The magical tie with Duran had severed completely. Was the dragon gone? He was a creature of legend, a wielder of great power. At nearly midsummer, he should be at his strongest. Surely, he survived. He had to. He was the key to her desires. The great ruby in the throne would only share its secret with him. As queen, she could demand the ruby's immortality, and the dragon must grant her request.

What of Duran? She shoved aside a twinge of regret at his loss. He had only himself to blame. He should have agreed to wed her. She wasn't worried. Confidence gave her strength and poise few others possessed. Although, her curiosity was piqued.

Who survived? she wondered.

****

Duran lay flat on his back, his eyes squeezed tight against bright flashes searing through his body. Pain. He swam through a maelstrom of agony, through streaks of fire. His last conscious thought had been of magic pulsing through him, brushing his skin, tingling, burning, marking him.

The worst of the fiery sensations subsided. Malodorous fumes of sulfur and the reek of blood filled his nostrils. Groping for the tiniest hold on reality, he stirred. Sharp rocks bit into his back. His chest ached in a dozen spots. He heard someone crying.

So death felt like this. He never expected to possess senses in the afterlife. Or feel pain.

Wait! He recognized that voice—Marina. His heart thumped so hard he thought it would leap out of his chest. He fought back a scream of protest. His beloved couldn't have perished with him. He squeezed his eyes together against the agonizing thought. To cause her death would be the worst of all horrors.

He concentrated on finding a calm center. As he did, the sunset colors blocking his vision lessened. A brightness he had not seen for months formed before him. Shifting shapes became visible. People stood around him. Daylight warmed his skin. What a wonderful phenomenon. He never expected to enjoy the sensation again. Comprehension struck with a thunderous clap. Calandra's spell had been destroyed.

He hadn't died. He lived.

Narud died. The dragon was gone.

"Not gone. Merely asleep," said a dozen voices in his head. *"Within you, the Ancient One lives, as he always has and always will. He will rise from his sleep if the need is strong enough. We leave you now, human, to live your life."*

"Wait!" Duran mindspoke. *"Who are you?"*

"You know us in your heart as the Guardians of Secrets."

He frowned. *"What secrets?"*

"None that concern you, human. Our identity will remain undisclosed to your kind until the time of dragons returns. Farewell. You will not hear from us again."

Before he could ask anything else, cool, gentle fingers stroked his head. All thoughts of replying to the strange voices were shoved aside. He smelled roses. Marina. Sweet, marvelous Marina.

"Don't cry, my love." He winced when he reached up with muscles stiff and sore, attempting to touch her face, to feel her skin. "I'm here."

"Duran?" Her voice sounded incredulous. "You're alive!"

His insides warmed. "Thanks to you, my love."

She swept a worried look over him that went right through his entire body. "How do you feel?" She whispered, sounding unsure.

Her presence was palpable. "Like I'm human again."

"Narud?" she posed the dragon's name.

"Gone."

"I thought I'd lost you." Her fingers feathered over his face like a blind person seeking confirmation of an item.

The contact stole his breath away. "I plan to live a long time with you by my side."

He strained to move as he eyed the crowd consisting mostly of guards standing around, staring at him in awe and fear. He sat up. Many backed up. A few nervously fingered the pommels of their swords.

"What happened?" Marina asked.

He laughed, relishing his freedom. "Does it matter?"

"I want to know."

He glanced longingly at her. A gleam appeared in her hazel eyes that he'd imagined seeing numerous times in daylight. "You broke the curse."

"Me? How?"

"Fire and water," he answered. "The dragon represented fire in the curse, but we never deciphered water's meaning. Your tears, my sweet. Your tears and your love. Instead of struggling to maintain a hold on my humanity, we should have been teaching Narud how to become human. The gentle touch of your tears broke through the barrier. Narud sacrificed himself by giving the last of his life energy. His last words to me were, *Live. Live through me.*"

Marina leaned over him, her mouth touching his. Her warm breath flowed over his cheeks, and he tumbled headlong into the kiss. He thought he'd lost her, never imagined to experience the pleasure of her kisses again. He knew being with Marina had always been the way it should have been. Forever.

"Oh, Marina…"

She straightened. "Are you hurt?"

"I'm fine. A little sore is all."

"Let me help you."

She wrapped her arm around his waist, and he leaned into her nimble strength and warmth. Narud had one thing right when he couldn't conceive of life without Marina. Neither could he.

People edged backward. The king pushed his way through the crowd and rushed to his other side. Olla and Woola came forward as well. Duran waved away his helpers. On the ground, dozens of triangular scales glinted, the last remnants of Narud. As he stared at them, they seemed to harden into flattened red diamonds that captured dancing flames within their cores.

Marina followed his gaze, her eyes sad. "My heart tells me I'll miss him for the rest of my days. My mind says he did a selfless act and didn't deserve to die."

"For once I agree with you about Narud."

She lifted her chin and smiled. "What now?"

"Calandra." He uttered her name as if poisonous, and with the word came a burst of hate.

"I'm coming with you," Marina said. "She's dangerous. You don't stand a chance alone."

"I know that all too well."

"We'll come, too," the twins said in unison.

"I forbid you." The sharp voice belonged to the Eudes king. The twins' expressions wilted. "No one is going anywhere unless I decree it. This sorceress is a survivor. Whether it stems from magic or an innate ability is yet to be determined. Before anyone rushes off, we need to formulate a plan against her that will succeed."

Duran smiled. "I see where your daughter received her intelligence."

"Well spoken," the king said. "I'm glad to see you again, Prince Duran."

"What about those?" Marina asked, nodding to the ground.

Duran's boot tip scattered shiny scales with a clatter. "What about them? They fell off Narud. Why do you ask?"

The king sighed with a father's resignation. "She's got that look again. I've seen it often enough to recognize trouble when I see it. What scheme are you concocting, Rina?"

Marina's chin rose. "Father! Must you censure me?"

"Protesting will not alter the fact." He snorted.

Duran listened and smiled. "You can settle the matter by simply telling us what you have in mind."

She picked up one of the scales and then turned it over. "Dragons are creatures of great magic. We can make a shield out of these to protect us?"

"A shield?" Duran tried to picture Marina's suggestion. "What good will that do?"

She raised her chin higher. "We need something to protect us against Calandra's magic. Narud's scales may contain a residual amount of dragon magic. I think he would appreciate the irony of our using them against her."

Duran accepted the scale when Marina handed to him. "Has anyone told you lately that you have a brilliant mind?"

"You inspire me," she said. "You and Narud."

"We'll talk of this inside," the king said, the quiet power in his voice herding Marina, her younger sisters, and Duran out of the bailey.

Chapter Twenty-One

Marina and Duran were swept into the family quarters where her mother and older sister waited. The stunned look on their faces stilled Marina from speaking. Of course, they were shocked. A dragon had flown in the sky above Eudes, a feat not observed in thousands of years. Then, the creature turned into a man, something never seen before.

It was one thing to hear an epic tale, quite another to bear witness.

Duran turned and put his hand on her arm. The scarlet fire she first glimpsed in his eyes upon the spell breaking had slowly faded. A tiny twinge squeezed her heart. She couldn't help wondering if the flash of color was the last she would ever see of Narud.

Duran scraped his fingers through his hair. "I leave tomorrow for Brenalin, my love."

He'd called her his love. She slid the dragon scales atop a small table near the door and tried to calm the wild thudding of her heart, not that it did any good with his admiring gaze upon her. "I'm coming, too."

Duran growled in disapproval. "Not possible."

What if he didn't return? Her pulse raced. She would never know what happened to him. Worse, to never see him again tore her apart. "Who will watch your back?"

He tilted his head to one side. "Marina, listen to

me. I want you to stay here, out of harm's way. Your safety comes first. I must face Calandra alone. I know her better than anyone."

Marina remembered seeing Narud cock his head the very same way when she argued with him. The poignant reminder fortified her determination. "Somehow your attitude doesn't surprise me. But you overlooked one little fact."

"What?"

"Calandra tried to kill me, too. I deserve to see her fall."

Sadness filled Duran's blue eyes. "Even if I agreed, which I haven't, you would slow me down."

Her family gathered close together while they listened to Duran and her argue. Tempa smiled. The twins held hands. Her mother wore an expression of concern. Her father's complexion turned blotchy, a sure sign of concern.

Duran's lack of confidence in her ability wounded Marina's dignity. "Did I hamper your progress on the journey here?" she demanded. "No! And I won't—"

"Enough!" her father interrupted. "Neither one of you are leaving until I give permission. I am still king around here. My wishes will be obeyed."

"Yes, my dear husband," her mother added, her gaze aimed at Marina and Duran. "But it is customary in all discussions to let the parties speak before a decision is reached."

Laughter rippled from the king. "That may be the way for normal things, but this concerns my family. I have a fatherly duty. I want guarantees before I agree to let my second oldest child traipse across the land."

Marina doubted she had anything to fear from her

father. This was no consolation, though, when she looked at Duran and saw him stiffen, his expression guarded.

"What are we talking about, Your Majesty?" he asked.

Marina squeezed Duran's arm a fraction. Despite their earlier disagreement, an understanding passed between them. They stood united against anyone, her family included. "It's all right," she said.

The twins regarded them with sympathy. Marina hoped her younger sisters would speak in her defense. Then, watching their glowing faces, she decided it best if they didn't interfere.

Her father's eyes flashed with annoyance. "Before I agree to anything, I require a promise."

"Promise of what?" Duran asked.

"That you'll send word of your success."

Whatever tension existed in the room evaporated in a wink. The meaning was clear. They had the king's blessing.

The corners of Duran's mouth lifted in a wide smile. "A rider will be sent on the fastest horse to Eudes within an hour of vanquishing the sorceress."

"Excellent." Her father smiled.

"We'll die of impatience, if you don't," Olla said, her twin eagerly nodding in agreement.

"We will, I promise," he said.

Marina's ears perked up. Her heart soared. "We? Do I hear correctly? I can accompany you?"

Duran dropped a kiss on the top of her head. "What other choice do I have? If I disagree, you'll simply steal away and follow me. Correct?"

"I'm glad you understand me so well."

He brushed loose strands of her hair away from her face and looked lovingly into her eyes. "Understand and love."

She loved him in return.

She believed in him.

She always did. Always would.

Her father stepped in front of them. "Before anyone rushes off, both of you must soothe a parent's concerns."

Duran stiffened once again. "What do you mean?"

Marina blinked at her father, feeling her heart beat faster. He was an honorable man, like Duran. He'd given his word. She trusted him not to break it after granting them permission to take their leave.

With a stern look, the king sighed and clamped a hand on each of their shoulders. "I have a final condition."

Duran's eyebrows hooded his eyes. "Which is?"

"You will wed first. A simple ceremony will suffice for now." His stern expression faded when he beamed at them as only an affectionate father could. "A state wedding can be held once you have resolved the problem of this sorceress. It is the only way I will grant permission for either of you to leave Eudes."

"If you don't want him, Rina," Olla said, "I'll take him."

Woola removed the candy stick that kept her from talking most of the time from her mouth. "You can't have him. I want him."

Marina laughed at the absurdity of the idea, edging closer to Duran. "He's mine."

****

Duran watched the twins' mouths form perfect O's.

He'd seen Marina wear the very same expression a time or two. Warmth infused him as he recognized the mannerism as a family trait.

The turn of events couldn't have made him happier.

Evening lamps were lit and incense of sweet sandalwood ignited in golden bowls in the royal family's private chamber. A warm ocean breeze ruffled the gauzy curtains. The twins must have commandeered all the flowers in the kingdom for the room to brim with the season's first roses, lilies, and daisies, the heady aroma more potent than the strongest perfume.

Duran willed himself to stand and admire Marina when she glided into the chamber wearing a simple blue-green gown flowing over her slender curves. A huge aquamarine dangled between her breasts, although jewels were unnecessary. His bride-to-be outshone them all in his eyes.

Afterward, they headed for her old sleeping quarters to share their first night as husband and wife. The twins fell in step behind them, but Marina secured the latch before the girls could enter. They pounded on the door, demanding entrance.

He went to the door and jerked it open. "Go away!"

Olla and Woola jumped backward from his looming figure. They wrapped their arms around each other as though they needed protection, then quickly recovered.

Olla let go of her sister. "We want to come in."

The girl was going to be a real challenge for a man someday, Duran thought. "We are in the midst of our first night of marriage. It is customary to spend it alone."

Marina came up behind him and brought the scent of roses to tease his nose. She slipped her hands around his waist. His stomach muscles tightened involuntarily at her touch.

"You heard my husband. Do as he says."

Both girls' expressions crumpled.

"Someday you'll wed and have husbands of your own," Duran said, almost sorry for those unknown men. They would surely have their hands full.

Olla perked up. "When?"

Marina ducked her head under his arm. "How should we know? Go ask Father to find you someone."

Both girls' eyes widened, bright smiles on their youthful faces. "An excellent notion. We will," they chimed in unison as they flounced off, calling, "Father!"

Duran buried the instinct to laugh at the girls' antics. Discretion was a better path with his new in-laws. He became aware of Marina putting her mouth to his back and blowing. The heat burned through his clothing.

He turned around, and she gave him a dreamy smile. Her arms rose, lifting the swell of her breasts. He was quick to admire the view as she undid the clasp of her necklace. The gemstone worth a king's ransom swung slightly on the end of the golden chain.

"Hold out your hand," she requested.

"I don't understand." He did as she bid.

She lowered the jewel and chain into his open palm. "For you, with all my love. Aquamarines are said to bring a soothing influence to long married couples."

"Thank you, but I have nothing for you."

"I don't need a thing," she murmured. "I have you.

That's all I want. All I ever wanted."

Aware of the delightful curves of Marina's body, his own responded with a speed and red-hot heat that nearly sent him spiraling out of control. He swallowed as she worked the laces of her gown loose enough to step out of the pool of silk and reach for him. Her hand ran down his chest. He swallowed again, trying to maintain control over the rapid beating of his heart.

A coy smile tugged at Marina's mouth. Mischief filled her marvelous eyes. She was downright stunning, and he loved her.

Desire lit Duran's belly. He lowered his mouth to kiss her, tasting the honey sweetness he'd come to expect. She kissed him right back, pressing her body against his.

He released her to step back and strip off his clothes. Marina's eyes brightened, and her expression turned wanton. Duran fully intended to see her satisfied.

For hours, they shared their love on lavender-scented sheets where they yielded to each other in a blissful wedding night.

He awoke the next morning and glanced fondly at his wife nestled against him. Her gold-bright hair spread over the pillows like a sheet of gold. Narud had it right about her being a far more valuable treasure than any gemstone. Duran loved her so much. She owned his heart and soul.

The prospect of sharing the rest of his life with Marina conveyed a smile to his mouth. He shifted his position on the thick mattress. The movement woke her. Her eyelids fluttered open and she stretched, much like the big white cat that curled up at the bottom of their bed some time during the night.

"Do we leave, husband?" she asked, her voice husky with sleep.

Duran felt a small tingle. "Would you say that again?"

"What? Do we leave?"

"No." He smiled. "Husband."

Her cheeks flushed and she returned his smile. "Whatever you wish, my loving husband."

They passed a portion of the morning in bed reacquainting themselves with each other. The task was one which both proved eager and willing participants. Late afternoon passed before they left for Brenalin. They rode westward, the rhythm of their journey broke only to change mounts, eat, or steal a few hours of sleep.

By daylight, Marina was more beautiful than ever. Every time his gaze fell upon her, desire tugged at him, and he deemed himself the luckiest man alive. He would never tire of the sight of the golden sheen of her hair and the way her eyes lit up with openness and honesty. He thanked the gods for her indomitable courage. He learned to think of her as Marina, but deep down he would always cherish pleasant memories of Stav.

Moments before they left Eudes, she showed him her creation—a fiery colored shield constructed of Narud's scales. He knew she grieved over the fact that Narud forfeited his life, but Duran didn't pressure her to talk about it. Let her mourn in peace. She would speak of the dragon when ready.

Three days of hard riding brought them to less than a day from Brenalin. They reined to a stop and agreed to rest for the night. They wanted to be refreshed before facing Calandra and her sorcery.

Marina sat beside him, before the fire he built, her legs crossed. "Do you think she knows the curse is broken?"

He held his hands over the flames, deciding candor best. "I would bet on it."

He thought about Calandra's lively green eyes, her black hair woven into a thick braid. He could see her as a child sitting beside him at the hearth, spinning her charms, beaming at him when her efforts proved successful. She always sought praise and hated failure, venting her anger by destroying whatever displeased her. The recollection made him grimace at his own foolishness. He should never have trusted her.

Marina touched his arm.

The memory vanished instantly.

"We must be careful," she said.

"I'm not afraid. I have to face her." He looked up at the stars sparkling in the night sky. "Let's not dwell on Calandra."

Marina's expression twisted into a compassionate one. He's never seen her quite as serious. "I don't blame you for not wanting to talk about her."

Duran pivoted and grasped her hands, savoring the contact and her closeness. "You know there are some things I never thought to enjoy again. Oh, Marina... Look at the stars. They're beautiful—not as much as you—but without you I would never have appreciated the view again."

"Narud told me dragons turned into stars upon their death. Do you...do you think he is up there now?" A slight warble found its way into her voice.

"It's impossible to say," he said, keeping his voice

steady. "I know you cared for him, and he for you. I'm afraid I'm not much help in the matter. I wish the right words would come to me to bring you the comfort you seek."

"Having you here with me is all I want, and he was part of you. I'll have my memories."

The next morning, they reached Brenalin.

Duran reined in his mount at the yawning gate embedded in the thick granite walls. Guards peered down at them. Fear nibbled at him. Would they allow him passage? Then, recognizing their prince, they shouted and cheered him.

Duran waved in response.

He smiled at Marina, saying, "I feared never seeing my home in daylight again."

The cry of approval started by the guards rippled through the town faster than they rode. That sound grew louder and louder as they wove their way down the city streets. People leaned out of windows to wave at them. They chanted Duran's name from doors and on the corners of the streets.

Still, the exuberant, friendly welcome surprised him and tugged at his heart. He worried his prolonged absence would have allowed Calandra to turn the people's loyalty away from him. Maybe she hadn't taken the time. More likely, she never expected him to return on his own accord.

Word arrived at the castle before them. Einer awaited inside the main door. The aged wizard, wearing his flowing multi-colored cape, looked haggard. Half-moon circles stood out dark beneath his eyes.

"Welcome," he said, stepping out to greet Duran and Marina. The tiny bells and beads on his staff matched his footsteps with their own sweet chime. "Calandra's in her workshop. She fled there the moment word of your arrival reached the castle."

Duran raked his fingers through his hair. "Then that's where I'm heading."

"Take care. Haste increases errors." Einer shook a finger at him. "Caution is recommended when entering the viper's den."

Marina stepped up and put her hand on the older man's arm. "He won't be alone. I'll be with him. Whatever happens next, we face her together—Duran and I."

"Just return," Einer responded. "Alive and unspelled, if you please."

Marina stood beside him ready to defend someone she cared for, much like he saw her the very first time through Narud's eyes. A warrior. Ready to protect. His heart swelled with unconditional love for this wonderful woman. She'd become an intense part of his life. He knew without her, life held no meaning.

Duran cleared his throat and patted the wizard's shoulder. Light beamed between his fingers where his hand rested. "Go to my father. Stay with him. We'll meet you in his quarters after Calandra is vanquished."

Einer gave a final scowl. "He will grieve, but he will understand."

Duran and Marina left Einer outside where they found him. They stalked down the stairs into the belly of the castle with steady steps. Cool, damp air filled their nostrils. The musty odor of mold grew stronger the lower they went, and the stone floors became slippery underfoot.

Duran led the way to Calandra's workroom. He felt

exceedingly older than his actual years and prayed to all the gods of Feldsvelt for success. He braced himself and pushed the handle down. The door swung open. Duran scanned the cluttered interior. He noted dusty bottles on the shelves, and an unpleasant tang in the air offended his sense of smell. This workroom and its contents would be cleansed by fire when he finished.

The sorceress sat upon a tall stool in front of a bench.

"Hello, Calandra." He stood, ready to draw his sword.

Calandra spun at the sound of his voice. "Duran! I've been expecting you. I heard you had returned. What now?"

"Now you die."

The sorceress slid off her perch. "You are mistaken. Now I finish what I should have months ago." She stepped toward the entry. Her expression became a mixture of loathing and disgust. Nothing of his old friend remained.

He tensed at the whisper of fabric behind him.

A faint warmth. The scent of roses. Marina. She pressed her body against his back. Ignoring the distracting sensation, he kept his gaze fixed on his enemy.

"Halt!" he ordered, daring Calandra to disobey.

"Most clever of you," she said quietly from a few feet away. "I never expected you to solve the riddle."

His muscles tightened. He would defend Marina and himself with his life.

Straw rustled as Marina followed him inside.

"I trusted you, Calandra. Once you were near and dear to me," he said. "I was blinded by our childhood bond, but no longer. You betrayed me."

Calandra's breaths echoed hard and fast against the stone walls when she saw Marina. "Oh, my sweet Duran, how wrong you were. I was your friend. I am still." A smile lifted the corners of her mouth. "I probably even loved you. Who knows? I think that's why I didn't have the heart to kill you outright. I always hoped for a reconciliation."

Duran's gut roiled. "Don't delude yourself. You disgust me. You should not have wronged me."

An undignified grunt came from the sorceress. "Perchance I should have been more circumspect with you when I cast—"

"No excuses, Calandra. I only tell you what—"

She held up a hand. "Stop! Enough of your tale of woe. You could have saved yourself all this trouble, if not grief, if you'd consented to my original request."

He gestured with a wave to encompass the workroom. "I would think, Calandra, you would have figured out by now I have no wish to marry you."

The room turned icy cold. Icicles pricked the air with the sorceress's anger. She clutched her hands into fists. "Do not look upon me with pity."

He glared at her for a very long time. "What you see is loathing."

Her nostrils flared. "How dare you talk to me like that. I'll never forget…or forgive you for putting another woman before me."

"I didn't have a choice."

Cold laughter gushed from Calandra. "You could have said no. Your father would have voided the betrothal contract."

Duran drew himself to his full height. The cords on

his neck tightened with restrained fury. "You're wrong again. My honor would have forbidden me to allow him to act in such a disgraceful way."

She glanced at Marina, laughed again, still with no humor gracing the hollow cackling. "You didn't love her."

"Perhaps not then, but I do now."

Her chilly green gaze rose to defy him. "I don't believe you."

"Your days of trying to destroy people's lives are over." He stepped toward her.

Calandra dodged out of his reach. Her leather slippers scuffed along the rush-covered flagstone. With a contemptuous sneer, she pointed a finger at Marina. "If not for this slut of a servant, matters would have turned out differently. She is the cause of all this trouble."

"You're wrong, Calandra. Marina is no servant. She is my wife."

Gurgling noises poured out of the sorceress's mouth.

Duran put his hand on the pommel of his sword. "All I want to know is why."

"For good reason." Calandra spread her hands as if in defeat. "I needed to wed a legitimate heir to the Ruby Throne."

A lump rose in his throat and he didn't dare relax his stance. "Why?"

"I needed to be the queen. Behold Brenalin's future queen." Calandra's words boomed in the small room.

"Spare me your lies," he said, much calmer than he felt. "My father would never wed you."

The sorceress merely smirked. "He has proposed,

and I have accepted."

Let her step closer. Just an inch. He could grab her throat and squeeze the life out of her. "Einer knew of your evil and put a protective spell on my father. Your evil magic doesn't work on him. I'm sure he went along with you, but neither man is fooled by your treachery."

At length, Calandra drew a long, deep breath. When she spoke, her whispered words had a distant, almost trance-like quality. "Einer couldn't stop me. Oh, he might have told you he could, but your father proposed. The Abbas honor you hold in such high esteem works to my benefit now. He won't retract the offer. Nor do I mind telling you, because it's too late for you. I've seen the future. I know its secrets. I will have access to the Ruby Throne's immortality."

Duran froze, shocked. Marina learned of the special powers of gemstones from Narud. He never expected someone else to know of them as well.

"Dragon's teeth," he swore. "Are you referring to the Abbas legend?"

Calandra's face paled. His knowledge of her secret aspiration staggered her. "What do you know of it?"

"It isn't a secret, Calandra. We've known about the immortality for generations. It's a foolish notion. Who would want eternal life? Who would want to watch their friends and loved ones grow old and die? Not me. Not a single Abbas. We rejected the offer when it was made thousands of years ago."

Her complexion, always pale, went whiter. "No! I don't believe you. You're a fool. You're all fools. I want it."

A tumbling rush of cold washed over Duran. At his side, Marina shivered but held her ground. Bravery such as hers could not be feigned.

"I'm sorry for you, Calandra. My father's marriage offer was false, a means of stalling you. Think on it. Whose idea was it to keep it secret? Yours? His? Your expression says it all."

"No!" Calandra howled in fury. A line of perspiration popped out along her hairline. "You lie!"

****

Marina saw the instant the sorceress decided to act. Hatred twisted the other woman's face into an ugly countenance. She raised the shield in front of Duran and herself.

Calandra seemed lost in her own world, confident in her power. She sneered at them. "Listen and die.

Death to those who defy me.

Death to the high prince

Death I see.

Death to you, Duran Abbas."

She raised her arms and made huge circles in the air. Her hands began to glow as beams of magic shot from her fingertips. Magic whirled around the room in wisps of golden light.

A soft and inviting web spun around Duran and Marina that appeared not the least bit dangerous, but Marina suspected otherwise. The urge to bolt grew unbearable. Her feet itched to run, but something told her any movement ensured death.

"Protect us, Ruby Throne. Let not magic touch us," Duran said. A dragonish thunder in his voice startled Marina.

She glanced at him, half expecting to find his eyes glowing crimson the way they did on occasion while Narud was alive.

Then magic struck the dragon shield. The air exploded.

Marina's arm quivered as a powerful force bounced off the crimson shield. Her fingers tightened. The intensity of the blow nearly knocked her down, but the unshakeable strength in Duran's arm steadied her.

A terrible scream filled the workroom.

She peeked over the crimson edge to see a magical light fade, replaced by a black mist at Calandra's feet.

The mist did the unthinkable.

It moved.

The sorceress's eyes widened in fear. She raised the hem of her gown and began tramping her feet on the strange cloud surrounding her.

A look of shock, near panic, twisted her face. "How? How?" Her voice sounded harsh and dry as a crone's. "I am protected against magic."

Duran stepped closer, pity mirrored on his face. "Maybe from others, but this is your doing. The shield was constructed from Narud's scales. It reflected your own foulness back to you."

Mist crawled up Calandra's body. She beat at it with her hands. Wispy tendrils broke away and twirled in the air. Then they returned to reunite with the mist. She tried to move, but couldn't.

"Help me, please." She stretched out her arms. Tears that seemed genuine fell from her eyes. "I'm your childhood friend, the sister of your heart. Remember?"

Beside Marina, Duran opened his mouth, then clamped it closed. A storm filled his gorgeous blue eyes. He shook his head. She didn't blame him one iota for his refusal.

Marina watched magical bands crawl out of the

mist to snake around Calandra's legs, twining and writhing, slowly moving up her body. They looked moist, shiny.

With a shriek of terror, the sorceress pulled at the bands to no avail. Soon sweat drenched her face. Her fingers trembled. Calandra, her green eyes wild, looked around the room for a means of escape. Her fearful expression told them she did not believe the transformation happening to her.

Calandra twisted and beat against the undulating bands. She screamed out her frustration and lost her balance. On her knees, she swayed even more.

"All your fault. This is all your fault." Calandra hurled the accusation.

Marina watched the strange mist pour into the other woman's mouth, ears, and up her nose. The whites of her eyes turned black, her skin darkened. Horrible magic worked on the sorceress.

The bands hardened and began to contract.

Marina winced with regret. She could feel the sorceress's suffering. No one deserved to die in such a horrible manner.

Calandra's screams went on and on. Marina covered her ears, sure she couldn't endure listening to the agony a moment longer.

All of a sudden, an uncanny silence filled the workroom.

Calandra became cocooned in black bands. Then a small pop sounded.

All that remained of the sorceress was a handful of dust.

"The nightmare is over," Marina said, a small flutter of hope developing inside her.

Duran dropped his gaze to hers; his eyes warm with undisguised affection. "Yes, thank the gods. Let's get out of the evil place."

They raced up the stairs to reach the great audience hall in time to see a fiery sunset. Marina felt her skin tingle the same as it did when the transformation between dragon and man happened.

She looked up into her husband's eyes. Yes, her husband. She would have sworn his gaze flashed crimson for a split second.

Like Narud.

She prayed to Kubala that the mighty dragon knew they were safe and happy, all thanks to his sacrifice.

Pressing against Duran, she savored the wonderment of his touch and let his strength warm her. As she clung to his comforting body, her breathing found and matched the rhythm of his.

He wrapped his arms around her and rested his chin atop her head. "Our future is beginning. I adore you. Love you. I want to grow old with you loving me."

"I'm so happy," she replied against his chest. "I must be dreaming."

"If you are, so am I."

Laughing, she tilted up her head and demanded another kiss. Duran complied by feathering a delicate kiss over her mouth. "Then I hope this dream lasts for an eternity."

A word about the author...

Award-winning author Darcy Carson grew up reading everything her mother brought home from the library. Reading romances became her favorite topic. Eventually her love of those novels led her to start writing them. She resides in a Seattle suburb with her husband and a prince of a toy poodle.

Thank you for purchasing
this publication of The Wild Rose Press, Inc.

For questions or more information
contact us at
info@thewildrosepress.com.

The Wild Rose Press, Inc.
www.thewildrosepress.com

To visit with authors of
The Wild Rose Press, Inc.
join our yahoo loop at
http://groups.yahoo.com/group/thewildrosepress/